HONOR AMONG
CENTER

MW00619694

I wish to dedicate this book to Sha.___ ,...., Adonis Clayton who died before its publication. These words are the legacy he leaves behind.

We dedicate this book to:
You.
Sharieff Adonis Clayton, we honor you for the endless hours of writing and strategically planning your masterpiece. Demanding that every sentence combined to share the most precious jewels of knowledge.

To you, for our four babies who still look to you every day for guidance and direction because of the significant role you played in their lives.

To you, for the way you showed me what real love is every day.

To you, for our sunrise talks about how we can change the world, starting with our world, where we live every day.

To you, for helping us all realize exactly how important family is and how dire it is that we cherish each and every moment, because we don't know when the last will be.

To you, for all of those who have had life-altering experiences because of your presence and influence.

We all dedicate our blood, sweat and tears to you, because you did it for all of us.

We dedicate this book to our hero.

You.

Until the next lifetime,
Ajana Clayton

iii

A. C. Clayton

Foreword
"Watch for the peacocks."

That was A.C. Clayton's instruction to me upon our first real building session. We'd met in passing previously, but didn't get a chance to speak until our mutual friend, hip-hop journalist Jonathan "Gotti" Bonanno, made this meeting in my office happen.

It was around 2008 and I had just taken over as the editor in chief of the highly influential hip-hop publication *XXL*. With so much going on in my life at that time, (rigors of a new position, the first year with my third daughter, taking care of my ailing grandparents, learning more about myself, etc.) there was no way that I could concentrate on his pitch for me to read his debut book, *Honor Amongst Thieves*. I couldn't hone in on the wisdom he was imparting on me. My vision was foggy; I was so focused on getting mine by any means. Yet here was a mountain of a man in stature and status, seeing clearly. He saw my fogginess all on my face; he probably heard it in my voice, as well. "I sure will," was my response to his advice of "watch for the peacocks," not knowing exactly what he meant.

Was I supposed to watch for the peacocks that I read about in Neil Strauss' book, *The Game: Penetrating the Secret Society of Pickup Artists,* in which he explains peacocking as the flashy style a man can have in order to get women to fall desperately in love with him? Was I supposed to watch for the peacocks in my inner circle that fought for a spot in my spotlight? Was I supposed to watch for the peacocks that were doing anything to get my attention so I could get them ahead because of the platform I controlled with a few printed pieces of paper? I didn't want to act like I didn't know exactly what he meant, so I just kept it in the back of my mind. I respected our dialogue, which covered so many mind-elevating topics, and placed the manila envelope with the book on my crowded desk.

A few days later that same week, I was invited to a radio show. It was a low budget session, basically me looking out for some friends. I was honored to be there, but it was late at night and the neighborhood was extra hooded out. I was tired and wanted to get it over with. I walked into the foam-padded booth and my eyes landed on the only spot in the foam that had been carved out. In the foam-free space was a huge painting of a grand-sized blue, green and purple peacock. My jaw dropped. It was as if Clayton had placed it there for me to see. I was mystified by it my entire time speaking. I'd never seen a painting of a peacock this big...ever. Randomly seeing it in this place snapped me to attention. The message wasn't all the way clear just then, but I knew it meant something. The spiritual energy of the moment told me so. Clayton told me so.

But I still didn't read the book right away.

I'm ashamed to say that the envelope sat on my desk for weeks. Months even. Clayton and I stayed in touch over email and texts; he would just check in on me and I did the same with him. He didn't press me about the book. But I finally decided to check it out while on vacation. Clayton weaved words about New York street toughs so brilliantly, and I couldn't believe I'd waited so long to get into it. I so honestly recognized the world he'd crafted. I saw it in my real-life family and friends. Shit, Clayton reminded me of my own uncles. Strong-voiced and stone-willed men of respect. How they moved throughout the blocks of our concrete jungles and jails and commanded salutes from street soldiers. Their well-earned striped reputations preceding them. How they always had the words that kept you on point.

Reading about Kay-Kay and all of his drama, I only saw my cousin. He is so much like Kay. He has raw brute but will always enjoy a laugh. The pressure they both put on others in the battle of blocks and bonds made life so much harder for them. They both constantly play mental and physical chess with, at best, those who pray for them in family and friends, and at worst, those who plot and pray for their downfalls. They are smart beyond their environments, but somehow allow their spaces to keep them there, essentially locked up even while they are free.

This mentality was one Clayton once had. After doing more than a decade of incarceration, he returned home with a renewed mission of reforming himself and those like him. Especially focused on youth, Clayton attacked this group with vigor. He aligned with the youth organizations, CASES, Exalt, and A Community United to not only spread his wisdom to the wayward youngsters he was assigned and adopted, but he stood side by side with them so they could witness an honorable man in action, as most of them never had a positive male role model to emulate.

Transformation is a chemical change as much as visual. You can take on a renewed outlook on life, like Kay's brother JB, but others don't always know your change of status. They don't see the internal chemical change you've undergone to strive toward your ultimate potential. As fate would have it, the people responsible for Clayton's senseless killing this year didn't know about this chemical change. All they saw was the physical, which Clayton used in his mission to harness and harbor those attracted to strength and sway them to a better path. His killers only saw his strength as intimidation.

The tragedy of life lost always includes family and loved ones hurting. But the tragedy is also in all the conversations that were never finished or even had. Clayton and I had a great understanding. I loved *Honor Amongst Thieves* so much that I offered to write the foreword of the next installment in the book's series. The roles reversed this time, though. Now I was the one checking in here and there about the second book and its completion. He would let me know, "It's almost ready, comrade. Gonna need your words soon."

Well, here are my words, comrade: You did it again. Another reflection of the real. This book is a testament to your hard work, vision and passion. It will not compare, however, to how you guided so many troubled individuals to a new path on life. You saw the God light in them, as God did with you. I'm honored to have known you and I keep prayers going for your family and your soul. Your great, inspiring life lives on.

"Cultivate the genius. For there's nothing more beautiful or exquisite than seeing a mind blossom." – A.C. Clayton

- Datwon Thomas, July 2015

...Watching for the peacocks...

A. C. Clayton

Youngblood, I was in it

The dirt and grime

I was in it

The OG bible taught me how to swim it

So here I stand... Winning

Scarred but grinning

While gritting my teeth

Not a saint or a sinner but a thief

I'll steal what I feel is a need,

Or else... why breathe

CENTER OF GRAVITY

Chapter 1: loose ends

There are many roads to the edge

1991

Two friends, we'll call them Thing 1 and Thing 2, casually stepped into the elevator laughing in hysteria. Marveling at the irony of the hit-and-run sexcapade they had just pulled off on identical twin sisters who lived on the 11th floor. They were on familiar stomping grounds, the Van Dyke housing projects, one of the toughest in Brownsville. In the middle of smashing the twins in the same bedroom, the door flew open and a little boy about four years of age walked in—only to witness in horror, both women positioned like dogs, submitting on all fours.

"Mommy, are you okay?" The shock in his eyes could be felt in his words.

Without slowing down her own rhythm, she pushed her hair weave to the side before replying in assurance. "Yes, Pootah. Mommy and Auntie are just doing exercise, so go play. We'll be out soon."

The guy behind his mother began gyrating faster and faster, harder and harder, until his mother's words were no longer coherent. She was reaching an orgasm and sounded like she was speaking in tongues. The boy bolted from the room in bewilderment and fear.

Reflecting on their recent adventure as they rode the elevator down to the lobby, Thing 1 asked, "Why did you speed up on that bitch when she was talking to her shorty?"

"I was teaching the lil' nigga a lesson," Thing 2 responded.

"Hmm, what lesson?"

"How to exercise, my nigga. How to exercise." The two friends erupted into more uncontrollable laughter.

"Did you see the look on that little nigga's face? Yeah, he'll never look at his mommy and auntie the same," Thing 1 philosophized with pride.

"Fuck them stupid bitches. They always acting like they too good. Now, all of a sudden, they want to throw us the pussy. That's because they hear we're on the rise. Bitches always want to be with stars, feel me? Plus..." Thing 2 paused before sharing his final thought. "It's good shorty knows early in life that his moms is a whore."

They laughed as the door to the elevator opened revealing a disheveled and graffiti-tattooed lobby. A familiar and friendly face greeted them.

"Homie! What's goody?" Thing 2 asked, happily surprised. Both men stood directly in front of the elevator door, unintentionally blocking the entrance to the guy they referred to as Homie.

"Ain't nothin'. What's good with you two?" he responded in total comfort around the cobras.

"We just finished knocking down those twins on the 11th floor," Thing 2 shared conspiratorially.

"Who? Rakim's baby mom and her twin?"

"Yeah, those bitches. We figured while he's doing those 15 years, somebody gotta keep her lubed." The two friends, Thing 1 and Thing 2, once again found the humor undeniable.

Thing 2 finally asked with genuine curiosity, "What you doing on this side? Don't tell me you fucking Rakim's bitch as well!" His inquiry laced with a tinge of jealousy.

"Nah man, I only come over here these days if money is involved."

Thing 1 and Thing 2 immediately stopped laughing. *Now this nigga was talking their language.* Unintentionally out of reflex, like stagecoach robbers, they began circling the wagon.

"You got a lick, Homie?"

"Yeah man, a light 40 rack score. Pocket money, but easy shit," Homie replied remaining unfazed.

"Yeah that's no real bread to split," said Thing 1 disappointedly. Becoming their spokesman, Thing 1 began fishing for a way in on the score. "We thought maybe it was something we could get in on."

By this time, the guy they called Homie began walking towards the staircase at the far corner of the lobby. Suddenly, with a spin and pivot maneuver quicker than Mayweather's, Homie startled them both into paralysis. The 9-millimeter Beretta with the mini silencer was whispering a death chant before the two friends had any chance to register what was happening.

No sooner than the lifeless bodies hit the floor, Homie began looking around to make sure there were no witnesses. Satisfied, he quickly dragged both friends' bodies into the staircase area. He propped them up as best he could on the steps to make them look as if they were asleep. Homie knew that no one would find them until at least the morning. This was Van Dyke and the steps were off limits at night to anyone with common sense.

Homie took one last look at the two. "Like I said, easy money, dummies." He wished this would bring Ice and Innocence back, but at least it brought closure to that. The twins would get their 10 racks in a couple of days when everything quieted down. They played their role and the reward belonged to them.

Homie nonchalantly walked out the side door of the building and immediately made his way to a payphone. The voice on the other end answered after the fourth ring.

"Jo-Jo, talk to me."

"Piece of cake," Homie said with a cocksure boast.

"Good. I'll see you tomorrow." Then the line went dead.

A. C. Clayton

"I had become a local legend. In all humility, I was as local as local news could get. I was seated at the center with a small constellation of colorful planets orbiting my gravitational pull. With the wider universe welcoming my expansion, I grew to accept the fact that I had become the Center of Gravity..."

Kay-Kay

It took no time for me to gladly pay up on the $20,000-a-piece markers I placed on the heads of Ike and Miz. Both of them were found slumped in their project's hallway staircase. These were the two clowns who had sided with Papa Doc and tried to lure Ice into a set up. Before Doc's demise, he confessed to me with the whimpering bravado of the condemned that it was Ike, Miz, and one other, who were also responsible for the botched hit that killed Ice's niece, a little girl named Innocence.

Ike and Miz committed to a gamble that they hoped would pay off handsomely. What they failed to understand was the nature of high-stake gambles—the loser can, literally, lose it all. So their legacy in the hood would be erased before it could even be written. There were a few other loose ends that needed to be tied up, but for the most part, the ones that required immediate responses had been handled.

My thoughts were with a headless Dice. He was the leader, or in his own words the spokesperson, for the network, *Circle of Friends*. They were a group of kats who put me on to the game for real. They took me out of nickel-and-diming and made me a true player, before betraying me for someone they assumed had a stronger hand. Such was the nature of the game; only the ruthless win. So far, I was winning, but I understood all too well that the moment I cared more for luxury than arms, I was a dead man.

I recalled a conversation I had with Dice one day when I was second-guessing my involvement in the drug game. It was after my partner Champ was shot and I'd been living in a crack fiend's house for over a week. Witnessing firsthand the devastation left by the product I was pushing caused my second-guessing. I was wrestling with giving everything up and confided in Dice. He listened to my internal conflict before offering this analysis:

"Peep game, young lion, because you're not seeing the full picture. A guilty conscience can be reconciled; it can be cured. But what can't be healed is a broke and powerless spirit. We..."
Pointing his finger at him and I to emphasize the connection,

"Chase the bread cause the bread leads to power. Power is your ability to make shit happen regardless to opposition." Dice paused in contemplation, gathering his thoughts. *"Always study the history of the money, young lion. Don't just take it on face value that so and so has money, or even this family or that family comes from money. Ya dig? If you follow these money trails, you'll discover its history. You will often find that its origin, I'm talking about the very genesis of its foundation, was based on crime. The Kennedys were horse thieves and then bootleggers. Read about the robber Barons, the unfair practices and bribes they used to corner markets. Read about the Dole family, that propped up dictatorships in Latin America that oppressed its own people so that the Doles could exploit the land."*

"Dole family? Like the fruit company, pineapples and shit?" I asked sarcastically.

"Exactly! This country was built on the backs of free labor. Literally built on our fucking backs, for over 300 years with no compensation. Not even a thank you. Like a whore who makes her pimp rich and then when she is of no more use, all worn out and shit, he asks her 'what have you done for me lately?' Shit, let's not forget that the very origins of this beautiful land of the free started with not only the theft of this land from the indigenous, but their outright slaughter to ensure that the land they took could never be reclaimed.

It's not just here; it's the same truth all over the planet. History of humanity has been a history of crimes against humanity. It's a criminal's story, in which the greatest part of the crime is convincing people that the crimes never occurred. The fucking military is really nothing more than mercenaries and hitmen for big corporations. If that's not criminal, if sending people to their deaths under false pretenses is not criminal, then we should do away with dictionaries. The predators rule the world, young lion, not the prey. So you could have a guilty heart if you want. You could walk away from the game, live from check to check, benefit to benefit, scratch-off to scratch-off, wait for an inheritance. Or, you can get it like the rest of us, with dirty hands and a clean conscience. You get it first by any means, because once you're established, it's easy to buy respectability. Once you got that, historians will step in and erase all your crimes."

Even though, I agreed wholeheartedly with Dice, I never second-guessed my decision to abort the drug game. Cocaine was the truth. It was the Devil's essence in powdered form. And I watched that white Devil walk into Gail's home and tear that family apart; tore it to shreds. Even now I feel for her kids, who go to sleep and wake up to that nightmare every day and night. Knowing in their guts that their lives are in danger, but clueless as to whom the real enemy is—the drug dealer or the drug. And the saddest part of it all is I sat in their house for an entire week feeding their nightmare. So I washed my hands of my powder partnership, knowing that I would never be able to clean the residue that stained my heart. I couldn't promise myself with a certainty that my hands in the drug game would never get dirty again, but for now I walk away. Strangely, those dark shadows of guilt that seemed to always lurk nearby in my mind were lifted. Chased away by a conscience that refused to surrender itself. I felt invigorated.

Still with making money as my mission, a wider world with an abundance of possibilities opened its arms to me. The need to compensate for the financial loss of giving up my most lucrative operation compelled me to explore other options. Options that very few of my peers had ever considered.

I wanted to be able to play in the revenue circles of Donald Trump and refused to accept anything less. I began devoting hours each day to solitude and study, learning the stocks and real estate hustles. I sold my first investment, a small Radio Shack in Brooklyn, to my uncle who was already running the day-to-day operation. Then I invested a large chunk of my money into acquiring my first piece of property—a 17-unit, four-story tenement building in Crown Heights, Brooklyn. I hired the neighborhood Mr. Fix-it named Paul to be the super of the property. He was so efficient and skilled that it required very little attention. I was a few months shy of my 22nd birthday and my hands were still deep in the streets.

The peacocks had become my marks, my willing victims by virtue of their need to be seen. It only took me about a month, on average, to learn everything about their operation. From stash houses and suppliers, to where they lived and where they hid, from where they played to where they laid. It was only after I acquired every bit of this information that I approached them with a stern and direct proposition only fools chose to decline. And why should they? If they had worked legit jobs or ran legit businesses they would pay to play with Uncle Sam. In the streets, I was the equivalent of Uncle Sam and I claimed the territory that these peacocks grazed in. Since I didn't mind the grazing, they shouldn't mind the paying.

The pressure put on those who showed resistance was seriously intense—ferocious in demonstration, if you will. It was meant to shock and awe. It was public so that these examples would be avoided in the future. For the most part it worked.... At least in the very beginning.

Chapter 2: hibernation is over
I hide from no woman or man
I am

Peaches

Peaches watched from the back seat of her parked BMW. She was silently taking in the scenery, savoring its sights and sounds. Finally, she was back in Brooklyn—the place of her birth and her exodus. Parked across the street from the world famous Junior's Restaurant, Peaches felt invigorated. She was in the land of the gunners, back in her element, ready to take her place amongst the hood constellations.

Peaches knew that her best tactic was to remain unseen. She could live as a mystery and survive, or go to the light and die. But 'best tactics' were not what brought her home, and hiding in the shadows was a thing of the past—it was a reality for a moth, not a queen. To be a prisoner of fear felt akin to death. It was time for her to meet her nemesis, but it would be on her terms, not his. She had remained abreast of Kay-Kay's dealings for the past year. He had walked away from the drug game entirely. How long would such a foolish move last? Who knew? But so far, he had not missed a step.

After winning the war with Papa Doc in such a convincing fashion, the throne was his to do with as he pleased. He could've opened up crack spots on every other block in NYC unopposed, and yet he chose to train his eyes on the extortion game. Talk about a lack of ambition, of not reaching your potential. Kay-Kay was the poster child for the underachiever. Still she was impressed—to think how far they both grew in the game. Ironically, she was proud of him and knew that although Kay-Kay chose not to ascend to the throne, everyone in the kingdom (including whoever became the king) had to pay. Kay-Kay was squeezing every-damn-body from the Dominicans in Washington Heights to the Colombians in Jackson Heights; from the Haitians and Jamaicans to the Russians in Brighton Beach. The courage of this kid was admirable. If she could think of nothing else, she had to give him credit for his courage.

Chapter 3: the gambit

We call them snitches because we play games,
They call them spies and win the war.

Kay-Kay

1991

About a year in, I began running into a bit of an unintended snag. The police in one precinct began hounding my hounds by pulling them over for no obvious reasons, locking them up on minor offenses, and questioning them as to their reasons for driving around in the area (as if they were driving through Beverly Hills and not the hood). They were fucking with them and it was pissing me off. It was obvious that one or more peacocks in that hood were snitching. The greater possibility was that they might very well be working for the police directly. The amount of money made in the drug game was enough to tempt even the most sanctimonious of cops to try their hands in it. Whatever the case, I refused to back down from the challenge.

"We gotta smoke 'em out, Kay. That's the only way," my top lieutenant Jo-Jo chimed in.

Handbone continued to feed his white spotted bamboo sharks in silent contemplation. It was just the three of us sitting in Handbone's spacious, though Spartan, living room discussing our options.

"I agree, but how?" I asked.

"I don't know, man. I wanna say kill all them mothafuckas we suspect."

I knew that Jo-Jo was speaking out of emotion. He hated snitches with an unparalleled passion. James, his older brother, was serving an 18-year bid because his best friend took the stand against him in a crime they committed together. The friend ended up walking away scot-free, moved down south, and eventually became a preacher. Jo-Jo was devastated by the betrayal and hated the hypocrites we knew as snitches.

"We gotta make them reveal their hand," Handbone finally interjected. "We need to see how deep-rooted the problem is."

"Again, I agree, but how?" I asked.

The three of us grew silent. The buzz from the 200-gallon shark tank was the only sound present in this room of tranquility. I stretched back on his black leather couch and closed my eyes in contemplation. A chess move I learned in prison slowly floated to mind.

"A gambit," I declared aloud. "We're gonna bait 'em with a few pawns."

Handbone was nodding his head in agreement not sure of what I had in mind, but he understood the concept of a gambit. Jo-Jo, on the other hand, was still waiting for precise directions.

"We need at least three pawns without criminal records," was the only instruction given.

You see, in order for the police to be an occupying force within our hoods and stay one step ahead of us, they must employ and cultivate spies. Refusing to study the mechanics of the trap until it ensnares us is no one's fault but our own. The fact that we don't use their spies as double agents before the beheading, and that we don't infiltrate the police ranks the way they do ours, speaks to our own folly and foolishness. The thought of staying one step ahead of law enforcement never crosses the minds of the impulsive and so they crumble like sand castles when the tide rolls in. Structurally stronger than a sand castle, I was determined to withstand the currents in the seas of change.

Sure enough within two weeks we had our answers. All three of my pawns had been arrested for attempted robbery of two separate complaining witnesses. The witnesses weren't the peacocks themselves, but rather two people associated with them. In both instances, it was people we knew were connected to them. Immediately, I posted bail and sent all three and their families on vacation. Their sacrifice would not go unrewarded. Just as the devious peacocks would not go unpunished.

Throughout the years, this became our strategy. The front line of my racket, the day-to-day hounds, didn't have felonies. This ensured that, for the most part, their bail would be low and if the charges were too strong for my legal team to be sure of a certain victory, a skid-bid or probation was the most damning outcome.

This allowed us to spot the eyes and ears of the pigs early. I watched crews rise and fall in blinks of an eye because they lacked the discipline and structure to survive. They lived precariously and impulsively in the jungle, while failing to understand its terrain.

Chapter 4: at odds with a madman

Peaches
1991

Peaches waited patiently for Roc, her righthand man, to arrive. He was driving in from Jersey City with a trunk full of their remaining arsenal. The war had forced her to return to New York much sooner than she planned to. The Feds were combing through the streets of Newark, looking for whatever loose ends were left. They were looking for the Ice Queen—a name she still found funny.

She thought about Roc, how far they had come and how close they had grown in such a short time. His name fit him well. He was truly reliable and trustworthy. To think that the war and her meeting Roc all started practically at the same time.

She could not believe her luck; she was running late to her beauty appointment and ultimately, everything else afterwards. Jacqueline, her stylist, would be upset of course, but the tip Peaches left behind always seemed to cheer her up. Besides, this would be the last time she went to Jacqueline. Peaches had been going to her once a week for the past three months. And though Jacqueline was good at what she did, Peaches knew she had overstayed her welcome by at least two months. She knew better than to be predictable, it was the type of mistake that could claim her life. She prided herself on taking precautions, on overlooking nothing, believing that her sense of alertness made the difference. It was the reason she wasn't dead or locked up.

"Gurl, you late." Jacqueline's southern drawl echoed over the crooning baritone of Toni Braxton's "Love Should Have Brought You Home."

"I know, Jacqui. I'm so sorry," was the extent of Peaches' apology. Peaches removed her jacket and slid into the chair.

"Gurl, I was beginning to think you weren't coming. The least you could do is call and let me know you're running late."

Taken aback by Jacqueline's determined rant, Peaches hesitated before repeating herself.

"I said I was sorry. What more do you want?"

"Yeah but sorry don't c..." The shrill of the phone momentarily distracted them both. Jacqueline appeared confused as to the origin of the noise. Finally, after three rings, she reached for the phone and picked it up. "Yeah, hello?" Jacqueline answered.

Peaches looked on rather surprised. In the entire three months of knowing her, Peaches had never heard Jacqui answer the phone unprofessionally. Jacqui glanced briefly at Peaches before turning her back. Whoever it was on the other end, Peaches thought, must be someone important because every three seconds Jacqui would mumble in a low submissive voice, "Yes" or "No."

In the mirror, Peaches could see Jacqueline's darting eyes scanning her surroundings. That look made Peaches uncomfortable. She wasn't quite sure of the sudden uneasiness she felt, but it was too strong to ignore. Jacqueline hung up the phone, took a deep breath, gathered herself and asked, "Wash and set, right?"

The whole vibe had grown so weird to Peaches that she decided to cancel right there on the spot. "Baby, before you begin, let me run to my car and get my purse. I can't believe I left it behind." Jacqueline began to protest, but Peaches was already out the chair putting her jacket back on. Jacqueline must have sensed that she had lost a customer because she tried to smooth things out.

"Gurl, I'm just having a bad day. Come on, sit back down in this chair. Don't mind me."

"Jacqui, I'll be right back. I left my money in the car." As soon as Peaches walked out of the beauty salon, she began nonchalantly scanning the huge parking lot. Everything appeared normal, but she still couldn't shake the feeling that something just wasn't right. Her suspicion heightened when she looked back through the window of the salon and saw Jacqueline back on the phone. 'Was she calling the police?' Peaches began to wonder.

Quickly, she made her way to the car. As soon as she safely escaped the parking lot, she decided she needed to figure out what was going on. Peaches parked her BMW on a side block not too far from the salon and walked back. Carefully, she walked, playing Jacqueline's bizarre behavior back and forth in her mind. Five minutes later she found herself sitting in a cafe across the parking lot of the salon, her eyes glued to Jacqueline's every move. It didn't take long for her to realize her hunch was on point. A black van slowly pulled up in front of the salon. The passenger side door opened immediately and a giant hulk of a man emerged. Peaches knew who he was, but didn't know his name.

He was an enforcer for Abdul, her number one competitor. Up to this point, she did not see him as a rival, nor could she recall any harsh feelings towards her from him. But his soldier was clearly there for a reason and by the look of his frustration, he wasn't there to relay a message. Peaches watched as Jacqueline intercepted him at the door trying not to scare her customers.

Jacqueline spoke to the Hulk then pointed toward the exit and the direction Peaches took. The Hulk was visibly upset. As he spoke, Jacqueline kept shaking her head in apparent bewilderment. Peaches imagined that the Hulk was asking Jacqueline why Peaches left so suddenly. What did Jacqueline do or say that alarmed her? But Jacqueline pled innocent with that 'your guess is as good as mine' demeanor. The Hulk walked backed to the van, spoke to the driver, raised his hands helplessly in the air, and lit a cigarette. A minute later, a black Porsche pulled up next to the van.

Peaches knew the Porsche's owner all too well. He had promised to take her to get her own Carrera when she got her money right. He always acted like a mentor, but apparently it was nothing more than an act. She knew she had a lot to learn about this game and reading these actors was one lesson she had better learn fast.

Abdul's muscular and athletic frame ascended from the tiny car effortlessly. A politician's smile sat plastered on the canvas of his calm and well-groomed face as he greeted his soldiers. Abdul listened intently as the Hulk explained the problem to him. He patted the Hulk on the shoulder while speaking a few words of encouragement before walking toward the salon. The Hulk followed, no less than two steps behind.

Once again, Jacqueline intercepted her guest at the front door. Her demeanor was a lot more passive than Peaches had ever witnessed from her before this moment. Abdul, still jovial, gave Jacqueline a hug and kiss on both of her robust cheeks before breaching her mind with what appeared to be an avalanche of questions. The interrogation went on a lot longer than it had with the Hulk. It was obvious that Abdul was asking for a play-by-play of what went down. When he was finally satisfied with her ability to follow his instructions, like an animal trainer in a zoo or circus, he dug into his pocket and handed her a treat—a bankroll of money, her reward for compliance.

As he walked back to his car, Abdul was still all smiles. Seeing him like this made Peaches feel that she was, perhaps, overreacting. That with such a welcoming smile, there was no way he could mean her any harm. But his smile was the snare, like a cuttlefish hypnotic and disarming. Many men had been suckered by his charm. Abdul was an alien, the Men in Black *kind. Unzip his skin and a slug or worm would appear at the controls. She had heard about his ruthlessness and his exile from Philly by the police. He was a stone cold killer who could keep a smile on his face while dismembering a body. The Hulk was still talking as Abdul jumped back into his Porsche. The only sign of his frustration was when he abruptly sped off, leaving the Hulk in mid-sentence.*

Peaches knew she was at an advantage in knowing that they had her in their scope. They could not be sure if she knew, so they would not feel pressed to strike immediately. They would wait for another opportunity, but she was determined to strike first and make sure it was lethal.

That's when she began keeping Roc by her side at all times. His nickname fit his personality. Like a '75 Chevy, he was her "ole reliable." He was fiercely loyal to Peaches and took her and Kameek Jr.'s safety to the bone. A limited talker, Roc made no attempt at giving Peaches any advice. He simply rolled with the punches as long as Peaches was the one throwing them.

At first, she suspected Roc of wanting what all niggas wanted from her—either a quick come up financially or some pussy. But Roc proved her wrong on both occasions. He had girlfriends throughout the years that Peaches either knew about or met, and had never once pressed her romantically. Although she paid Roc well, she was willing to stake her life on the fact that he would roll just as hard for her for free.

It felt like just yesterday, she was sitting in a car similar to the one she presently found herself in, thinking that this was the first time since knowing Roc that he really needed her. She recalled the day vividly. He was upstairs in the ICU visiting his mother. As far as Peaches knew, Roc's mother had been sick for a very long time with a list of ailments ranging from heart disease to diabetes. Now his mother was dying, and Roc was visibly suffering in silence.

Peaches was horrible at consoling the hearts of those who lost loved ones, never learning the words of healing or even empathy. So she avoided the mourners as much as she could.

But now it hit home and whatever support Roc needed from her she would undoubtedly give. Just like he gave her from day one.

"Listen, I know you need a job and from what my good friend Shazz says, I could count on you. I trust Shazz's judgment, but let me tell you right off the bat, don't look at me like I'm some weak bitch you can get over on. I'm just as tough and less merciful than any nigga you ever dealt with. Crossing me is like signing your own death certificate." It was her standard speech to all her potential workers, but she meant every word of it. While the gravity of her threat sunk in, Roc stood unfazed at its possibilities. He prided himself on being as loyal as they came, so the penalty for disloyalty was worthless chatter.

"So what exactly you need me to do?" he asked.

"I need you to hold me down, roll with me while I handle my business, that's it."

"So you need a bodyguard?"

"Yea, I guess we can call it that."

"Hey, call it what you want. You're paying. When do you want to start?" Roc asked.

"How about right now? Ain't nothin' like on-the-job training. I got a little running around to do, don't mind the company."

From that day until the present, they evolved into an inseparable force. Roc became her shadow and more importantly, her shield. She filled him in on the potential problems with Abdul just to see what his heart was made of, but he remained stoic and unimpressed.

As the spring blossomed into summer, Abdul's psychopathic impulses defied all codes except that of a barbarian. Anything and everything counted in the pursuit of happiness. Even some of his own crewmembers began abandoning ship, relocating halfway across the country. They tried to dodge the tidal wave of destruction—a guarantee of karma they were afraid to claim. Clearly on a warpath, Abdul's march grew relentless. It was like he was on a suicide mission; his actions became increasingly irrational. The death toll rose and each time, his name was at its root. He had to know that the Feds and Newark Homicide would be on him before summer's end.

One dealer whom Peaches supplied had this take on Abdul's actions: "Look, his God Allah is turning him insane. He's punishing him for making a mockery of his religion. How you gonna call yourself a righteous man of God, yet sell every fucking drug under the sun? That's why I'm not going to find God until after I get my money right. 'Cause I refuse to play with God's word." Peaches wasn't sure about that take, but she was smart enough to lay low and avoid Abdul and his clan.

Shit really hit the fan in late July when a hustler named Chop apparently escaped Abdul's torture chamber. He had been beaten with a steel chain, tied to a table, stabbed in his hands and face with an ice pick, and made to watch another well-liked hustler named Cory succumb to his wounds and die. Chop swore his escape was a miracle and was looking for some financial help to leave town. They brought him to Peaches and she listened horrified by this broken man's story.

She had no doubt that had Abdul snatched her up that day at the salon, she would have been broken before she died as well. She couldn't ignore Chop's plea for escape, nor could she ignore the call for revenge. Revenge, not for Chop, but for the very code of the streets itself. Abdul had to be stopped, his rabid disregard for the law of the land had to be punished.

Roc emerged from the hospital a changed man. His mom laid on her deathbed and he was powerless to change what was to come. He slid into the passenger side door and exhaled deeply. He refused to look at Peaches for fear of exposing his vulnerability. With watery eyes he spoke. "The doctor is saying she may not make it through the night." He tried to continue, but only managed squeals and squeaks as his words choked in his throat.

Peaches affectionately laid her hand on his shoulder encouraging him in a soothing whisper, "It's okay to let it out." Like the hefty weight of snow on a compromised tree limb, Roc could not resist the calling for release. He looked directly at her for the first time, his face, a dam of bewilderment and pain, finally broke and the floodgate of hopeless tears rolled down his cheeks. He leaned into Peaches' embrace and allowed the grief to pour out. When he could cry no longer, he gathered himself, wiped the remaining tears from his face and said, "Thanks." There was no reply needed and none was given. They sat in silence for what could've been hours in the comfort of Peaches' car.

Throughout the months of Peaches' plan to lay low, she had not been idle. She had been gathering as much information on Abdul's operation and whereabouts as possible. Most of his goons were easily accessible; she could reach them anytime she so desired. But Abdul and his partner who had no name were elusive. All she knew was that Abdul lived somewhere between Newark and Philly, which narrowed her options down to about 300 miles. His nameless partner posed an even greater puzzle. From all she was able to gather, Abdul was the enforcer while 'nameless' was the brain. She figured she had to start somewhere, so she picked the Hulk.

The Hulk's baby's mother lived 40 minutes away from Newark in Patterson. Predictably, he made the drive most nights to see her and his kid. Peaches, Roc, and her 17-year-old shooter, Lil' Boo, sat quietly in a commercial plumbing van for seven hours straight. Finally, around 5 a.m., the Hulk's Pathfinder pulled into the driveway. Like a caged bull, Lil' Boo was ready to be released. But Peaches had, at the very last minute, decided to change the plan.

She took the .45 Bulldog from Lil' Boo's hand and crept out of the car. She met the Hulk as he stepped out of his jeep with the gun aimed directly at his head. Startled and visibly afraid, his hands involuntarily went to the sky.

"What did you want with me?" she asked.

"W-w-with you?" he managed to stutter out.

"Don't play stupid with me."

"I don't know what you talking about Peaches. Honestly, I don't. I'm here to see my wife and kid, that's all." She ignored his indirect plea for mercy.

"At the beauty salon, nigga. When y'all came for me in that black van."

The spark of recognition in his eyes confirmed his guilt. He must've known the jig was up because he attempted to make a run for it. A deafening bark followed by six others awoke the tree-

lined middle class block. Her first shot tore through the side of his face. She saw his flesh actually depart from his cheek. As he stumbled and attempted to get away, she unleashed a volley of shots into his back that left him sprawled face first on the floor. Instantly, she ran over to what appeared to be a lifeless body and fired two more rounds at point blank range into his back.

Peaches felt alive. Her adrenaline was in overdrive as she stood over him, her chest heaving, wishing he would just get up so she could do it all over again. The screeching tires of the plumbing van broke her trance. She jogged to the waiting van and hopped in. Both Lil' Boo and Roc sat in stunned silence. Peaches kept mumbling to herself, "It was too easy, he made this shit too easy. It was no challenge."

Crystal awoke to the foreboding succession of gunshots piercing the peace and tranquility of suburban life. Immediately, she knew that Reginald was in trouble. No other explanation even remotely crossed her mind. She had warned him that it was just a matter of time before his dirt followed him home. The screeching of tires told her that it was safe to look out her window. Six-year-old Reginald Jr. appeared out of nowhere to grab hold of her hand. She identified fear in his eyes. He, too, knew something had happened to his father.

No words were spoken as mother and child were being drawn inexplicably into an unforgettable tragedy. A force greater than them both guided the duo to the living room window. Crystal slowly parted the curtain and peered outside. What she saw made her spring into action; Reginald was bleeding profusely, yet he was attempting to stand. Quickly, she ran out the door, but just before she reached him he collapsed thunderously to the pavement.

"Crystal, are you okay?" A neighbor's shout could be heard, but all she could yell back was "Please call 911!"

Reginald was lying face down on the ground, struggling to mumble something to the best of his ability. With all of her strength, she heaved him onto his back and was met with a spray of blood across her face from one of the bullet holes lodged in his neck or chest. She wasn't sure which. She'd never seen this kind of carnage. Her panic almost sent her into a state of shock before she looked up and saw Reginald Jr. standing over both her and his father in a mortified daze.

She reached for her son with the intent of scurrying him back into the safety zone of their house. After uttering one final and coherent word to Crystal, Reginald Sr. took his last breath.

Only hours after the paramedics, police, news reporters, and coroner left did she repeat Reginald's last word to his uncle Abdul. His stunned response, "You sure he said Peaches?" told Crystal all she needed to know. She had warned Reginald that Abdul would be the death of him. Now here she was, left to pick up the fragments of an unthinkable trauma—a ghost refusing exile from the mind of her now fatherless child. It took a couple of hours for word to reach Peaches and ultimately Newark. The Hulk was dead.

"Peaches, I'ma have to pass on the move tonight. I wanna be by mother's side when she makes the transition."

Compassionately, Peaches replied, "I understand wholeheartedly. I already cancelled the meet indefinitely. Hopefully your mom pulls through and we're back to business as usual. But either way, my priority is with you." Peaches was usually cold and at times completely absent of emotions. Her words in this moment touched Roc profoundly. For her to put business on hold indefinitely meant she must have really grown to care for Roc.

"Thanks," was all Roc said.

Fucking bitch had the nerve to think she could get away with murdering Reginald, *Abdul thought. He knew Peaches was a potential problem long before she struck. That's why he attempted to scoop her lil' ass at the beauty salon before she decided to get in his way. But something went wrong. The bitch Jacqui tipped her off somehow. He knew it, but couldn't prove it until now.*

Peaches' strike proved his suspicion. How else would she know? Nonetheless, it was meaningless now. Peaches would suffer dearly before she died. He would personally enjoy her torture. Abdul chalked it up as one more piece to clear off the board.

He had known that he was being watched by the Feds since winter. He knew that they were building a case against him that would put him away forever. It's why he started crushing all the sucker niggas, refusing to leave anyone he didn't like or trust behind. When the Feds finally came for him, and they would, it wouldn't be the words of the suckers he had to worry about disputing. Not that the possibility of a trial was even an option. When the Feds finally came, he would crush a couple of them, too. He refused to be taken alive, to be humiliated and degraded. He was born free and he would die the same, even if it were in infamy. Abdul was about to leave his house when he realized he was forgetting his insurance card. He reached in his closet, pulled out his trusty grenade and placed it in his jacket pocket.

It was his surprise gift for the Feds. "Game over, mothafuckas. You're colliding with a real killer."

Peaches figured she had no choice but to shake. Abdul would be out looking for her and she was not going into hiding. In fact, she was determined to show her face more than ever to let the hood know that she was standing up for them.

"Look, it's not too late for ya' to step. This shit is about to get ugly and you guys can still blend back into the hood if ya' want. I'm not running. I did that once in Brooklyn. I'm not running anymore."

Roc just looked at her like she was crazy. Lil' Boo was the one who spoke for the both of them. "X that Peaches. We're in this together. If it's our time to go, then so be it." Peaches loved Lil' Boo's heart. He was down for whatever, young and naïve, but reliable.

Like Peaches, Abdul was a supplier. He strictly supplied the east side of Newark initially and Peaches sold a little in the west and a little in the north. But since Abdul's warpath, he had become the chief supplier of the entire city. Every other supplier ate after he was done with his product. Peaches immediately began approaching Abdul's dealers attempting to cut into his market. Most dealers would've preferred to deal with Peaches, but Abdul was still alive and no hustler wanted to risk facing Abdul's wrath. They weren't sure how this war would play out, who would win or lose, but the safe bet was on Abdul. Peaches understood their hesitancy and had expected no other response. Her purpose was only to show them that she had the heart to challenge Abdul. The word spread like wildfire: Abdul and Peaches were at war and the city of Newark was bracing for yet another all too common bloodbath.

Parents kept their kids inside out of fear for their safety. Days went by without a single confrontation, but everyone knew it was nothing more than the calm before the storm.

Chapter 5: abandoned nations' return

Kay-Kay

1992

It was 8:37 a.m. when I parked my Benz behind a green minivan. Alicia and my mother were my distinguished passengers. I immediately reclined my seat and closed my eyes. Alicia sat in the passenger seat fumbling with the radio dial. A nervous chatter went back and forth between her and my mother. I had a long night in the streets and was functioning on fumes. Their conversation seemed frivolous and, therefore, annoying. I tuned them out as best as I could, trying to steal a few precious moments of rest.

A black sports car pulled up behind me and a 4-Runner Jeep double parked next to me, boxing me in. I had no worry. The drivers and their passengers were here for the same reason—a celebration.

We were parked in front of the Queensboro Correctional Facility waiting for them to release prisoners whose time was up. Every single morning, except Saturday and Sunday, looked like this. Today was the release of my big brother. My mother's "Praise God" was timed to precision—every twentieth breath she uttered it. Her nervous anticipation was infectious and the butterflies in my stomach kept sleep from taking over. Alicia was all smiles, happy that this day had finally arrived. Over the years, Alicia and JB had become penpals and she considered him her big brother, as well. She caressed my face, sending an early morning shiver down my spine. I kissed her hand and gave her a wink. She blushed knowing all too well what was on my mind.

At precisely 9 a.m., the gray steel door opened and men with shiny faces carrying netted bags with their belongings in them began emerging. Car doors flew open, and women and children began to pour out. Alicia and my mother were amongst them. I thought about a movie I once saw where the men were returning from war and were greeted by bands, balloons, and loved ones. Somehow this similar scene seemed more intimate, almost primitive and sacred. The lost sons, brothers, and fathers returned.

Then I spotted JB's glowing face; he was smiling from ear to ear. My mother flung her arms around his neck, pulling him down to her level. Alicia was jumping up and down like a schoolgirl clapping her hands as if she was at a carnival. I got out of the car and walked toward my hero—the first person I ever recalled imitating. We embraced the way brothers do.

"Finally free," he triumphantly exclaimed.

"Man, parole is a mothafucka," I responded matter-of-factly.

We were sitting at a diner waiting on our order when JB began revealing his game plan. Our mother had increased her "Praise God" by 17 breaths and Alicia was still clapping every chance she got. If it weren't my family, I would've probably considered them members of a circus.

"Our community needs a strong voice, new perspective on old problems. I plan on rolling up my sleeves and being that voice."

"JB that's wonderful," Alicia exclaimed. "I'm so excited for you."

"Baby, just be careful. There are a lot more nuts walking these streets nowadays," my mother chimed in after stealing a glance my way, as if I was one of these nuts she was referring to.

"Yea bro, shit ain't the same as when you left—this crack is making people go insane," I attempted to engage in the small talk.

"Do you have to curse in every sentence?" my mother challenged.

"Curse? I didn't curse one time! What are you talking about?" I inquired, truly perplexed.

JB jumped in, "Yeah, I know it's crazy out here. I watched the news and read the papers every chance I got. That's why I feel it's my mission to become a part of the solution."

"Uh oh, Nelson Mandela returns," I jokingly chirped. No one found the humor in it.

"That's wonderful, baby. Just remember, before you can help others, you must first help yourself." JB simply nodded his head in agreement at my mother's wisdom. Then almost as an afterthought, JB reached across and put his hand on my arm and said, "Yeah well, the first person I gotta save is my little bro."

Thus, the tone and temperature were set for my brother's first week home. I chauffeured him around from appointment to appointment. I took him shopping to get his wardrobe together and dropped him off at a few homes of his friends who were still locked up, so he could pass on messages and check on their kids. We even took one of his friends' elderly mother grocery shopping.

Like me, JB valued his word and was determined to live up to his promises. These excursions gave us ample time to catch up. Like sitting in a confession booth, I told my brother everything except the things that were truly beyond the borders of his self-righteousness. Our discussion always turned into a relaxed debate.

"So how long do you think this lifestyle will last before you are called to the carpet?"

"Ah man, this is prolly gonna be a lifestyle that is passed on from generation to generation. I'm trying to build generational wealth with this."

"You sound dead serious when you say that." JB seemed genuinely stunned.

"Serious as cancer, big bro. You sound dead serious when you talk about resurrecting the community and that back to Africa mumbo jumbo," I countered.

"At least my mission is to help."

"Mine, too."

"Yeah, help yourself."

"Yours, too."

"How is my mission to help selfish?" he asked.

"Because you want to do it in public, in the spotlight. You want people to say, 'Oh, JB is for the people. He represents us.' It's the ultimate ego trip. It's a peacock with different feathers, that's all."

"I'm sad you see it that way."

"I'm sad you can't," I countered.

By the end of the first week, JB had gotten his business in order and was ready to start exploring on his own. I was tired of chauffeuring the holy man around and he, I'm sure, was tired of waiting on a sinner to get him from point A to point B.

We parted ways in relief. I was glad my brother was finally home, but disappointed that he lived in a bubble of make-believe. He was glad that I was still alive and free, but sad that I had been in his own words, "co-opted to the dark side: living blissfully in a nightmare." I dropped him off at the train station. He was on his way to start a revolution. I went on my merry way to oppress some peacocks.

Chapter 6: the drought

Kay-Kay

1993

The cocaine drought of '93 became something for the record books. The peacocks were frenzied, trying to figure out their next move. The U.S. Coast Guard had seized two huge shipments with a combined weight of 21 tons of cocaine off the coast of Miami. The media described it as the *'biggest cocaine seizure in U.S. history'* and *'the war on drugs finally takes a turn for the good guys.'*

The peacocks were clueless as to their next move. Just like the average working Joe, the peacock has bills to pay at the beginning of every month. It amazed me how these morons could hustle so hard and never put money away for a potential rainy day. Some of them didn't even put aside money for a lawyer or bail. It was almost as if they truly believed that they alone had the Midas touch and that no matter what, the dough would always flow. Well, reality was smacking them hard in the face and I would too, if they thought for a second that their hardship meant anything to me.

Our agreement was non-negotiable. They would continue to pay their monthly tribute or else. Of course, I began preparing my team for the 'or else' part; anticipating a few of the colorful would expect me to ease up on the sanctions. While I felt for them, I knew that at the end of the day, their hardship was a direct result of their own naïvety. Shit, even squirrels store nuts for the barren days. If a fucking rodent could do it, why couldn't a peacock?

Peaches

Peaches became excited when she caught wind of a new pipeline that could withstand the drought. An associate named Malik, who once was her competition in Newark, had the link to a Puerto Rican connect that was still taking large orders. To be able to deliver 10 kilos on demand during a drought was a pipeline worth tapping into. Malik had just purchased six kilos for 215k and was already back in Maryland supplying water to the thirsty. He gave Peaches a pager number and code to reach the supplier and told her to give them a day to get back to her.

She had called the day before and now she was awaiting their response. Although Peaches was happy about the potential pipeline, she understood that unless she figured out a way to tap directly into the South American reservoir, she would always be subjected to the benevolence and whims of others.

Her phone rang a little after midnight. The heavy Puerto Rican accent on the other end of the phone gave her an address and a time to meet. The voice stressed, "Don't bringee no money, just bringee yourself."

She arrived at about 5 p.m. the following day to an unassuming bodega right off of Dyre Avenue in the Bronx. The store was packed with people buying everything from beer to tampons.

To Peaches initial count, there were about seven people working in the store. It was the only indication that there was something more to the store than meets the eye. How could a tiny store employ seven grown men? Besides that, there were no other signs noticeable to Peaches.

The man behind the counter smiled at Peaches, revealing a mouthful of remarkably white teeth, a smile that got her full attention. The man with the pure ivory invitingly asked, "Can I help you, mami?"

Peaches paused trying to remember what her coded response was supposed to be. Finally she uttered, "Pastrami and cheese on wheat, hold the mayo and mustard."

"Would you like a drink to go with it?" He asked, seemingly amused by the game they both must play out.

"Let me get a ginger ale." She paused before saying, "hold the sizzle."

It was the very last command that the man with the remarkably white teeth was waiting for. He smiled again at her, this time more cautious than inviting. "Ok sweetie, give me a second. Someone will be with you."

As if on cue, three of the men in the store walked out. Peaches couldn't even begin to guess their destinations.

She stood patiently in the store for the next 20 minutes. The man behind the counter with the remarkably white teeth went back to servicing his legit customers and uttered not another word to Peaches. Finally, one of the three men that left returned and beckoned for Peaches to follow. He led her back out of the front of the store and into a waiting livery cab. A stab of doubt punctured her thoughts for a brief second before stepping in. It was the first time she had made any move remotely of this nature without having Roc in her corner.

In fact, she followed the instructions she was given to the letter and told no one, including Roc, of this meet. As the cab door closed, she realized that she could be taking her last ride. Malik, her one time competitor in Newark and now friend, may not be a friend after all. The cab driver took off and when Peaches inquired as to their destination he turned up the salsa music—a nonverbal demonstration of the rules.

The driver circled a block a couple of times and Peaches could tell that he was attempting to spot any potential tails. These actions actually made Peaches a little more comfortable. She reasoned that if this was truly a dependable pipeline these precautions were necessary. The cab eventually turned slowly onto a narrow block filled with two and three-story buildings. For all Peaches knew, she could have been in any of the boroughs with the exception of Staten Island. She believed they were still in the Bronx but couldn't be sure. The sun gently began its descent, awakening the streetlights.

The cab stopped in front of a well-lit, two-story building. A man emerged from within and walked directly towards the cab. He opened her door and told Peaches to follow. They walked into the building foyer where they were met by another man and woman. Immediately, Peaches was ordered to strip. They were checking for wires and there was only one way to know for sure.

This didn't put Peaches off; she had gone through this process before. In fact, most pipeline connections started with the same ritual. It was a thorough and necessary search. When it was finally over, Peaches was allowed to get dressed.

The woman spoke for the first time. "Sorry, but you never know," she offered her philosophy apologetically with a shrug. Peaches responded with a forced smile of understanding. She was then ushered through another door and into a cozy, albeit stuffy, looking apartment.

A silky feminine voice spoke from behind her. "Thank you for coming to meet me. Malik said your name is Peaches, am I correct?" A beautiful Latina with ravenous black hair emerged from another room wearing a flowing nightgown that failed at hiding her sculpted silhouette.

Peaches responded, "Yes, that's what they call me."

"Well, what they call you and who you are really are two different things. So who are you really?"

"My name is Precious."

"Precious what? May I ask?"

Peaches grew uncomfortable revealing so much. Being stripped naked was one thing, but being asked her full name felt like a violation. Her hesitation lasted a full 10 seconds before finally lowering her guard.

"Precious Simon," she confessed. The lady smiled knowingly.

"Well it's truly a pleasure to meet you Precious Simon. My name is Martha." She took Peaches by the hand and gently led her towards the living room.

"Martha what? May I ask?" Peaches asked, attempting to gain some kind of parity while breaking the ice.

Martha chuckled at the audacity of Peaches' wittiness before replying with an equally witty response. "Martha-you-glad-you-weren't-wearing-a-wire?" she shot back. Peaches blushed at Martha's humor, thinking *I like this heffa.* Peaches was offered a seat on a plush leather recliner. Martha sat cross-legged like a yoga instructor directly across from her. Peaches doubted that Martha was the supplier, figuring that at the very least she was the middle man or in this case middle-woman.

Almost as if reading Peaches' mind, Martha began with a question. "Are you surprised that I am the supplier?" The mirth in Martha's eyes sparkled with curiosity.

Peaches responded calmly, "I am surprised, but also a tad bit inspired. I've never met a female boss this high up in the food chain." Martha seemed pleased with the answer. "Well, Malik spoke highly of you and since Malik is an honorable business man, I agreed to meet with you. I'm a face-to-face type of person; I need to feel your spirit before I do business with you." Peaches nodded her head knowingly. "I wouldn't have had it any other way."

"So Peaches, tell me why you're here? What's your story?"

"Well, I'm here to establish a connect that can withstand this drought."

Martha waved her off. "Yes yes, I know that but what's your story? We all have a story that explains our path."

Great, a fucking psychologist, Peaches thought.

For the next 40 minutes Peaches spoke about her journey, leaving out all mention of her son Kameek Jr. or her beef with his father. She briefly touched on her stay in Newark and her reason for returning to NYC. Martha was pleased with Peaches' honesty. She knew of course that Peaches was withholding information. They all did. It was the nature of their business. Martha's only concern was hearing Peaches speak. The more a person spoke, the more they revealed.

"Peaches, I accept your friendship and look forward to it blossoming. You can leave now and in a few days you will receive your instructions."

Peaches sat speechless. After being received so warmly, to being dismissed so coldly, she wasn't sure what her response should be.

She wanted to jump up and slap the shit out of Martha, but understood that it would be an impulse that would end her life. Instead, she cracked a smile of confidence and walked out of the apartment.

The cab awaited her. Salsa music was once again turned up.

It took over a week for Peaches to receive any word, but when she did, it was the news she had dreamt about getting. Not only was she tapped into a pipeline, but at the prices she was paying, she would be able to crush the competition. Her only words to Roc were, "It's time celebrate."

Chapter 7: committed to the struggle

A reality I refuse to claim,
that we will oppress each other,
In submission to their game.
For no other reason,
I bow in shame.

JB

1993

Sitting in his mother's kitchen having lunch, JB spoke. "You know, Ma, the statistics don't lie. Our communities are leading in every destructive category you could think of, from HIV infections to infant mortality rates. We're sending more Black and Brown boys to prison than we are to college. The majority of young men entering the prison system are high school dropouts. I mean you would think it would be obvious to these government officials that the high dropout rate equals incarceration. Instead, what they do? They cut school funding in our hoods by 26 percent, while increasing funding for prisons by 15 percent." J.B shook his head in helpless disbelief.

"I know, baby, but what can we do?" Ma Barnes asked her son in a soothing tone. These lunchtime discussions had become a ritual since JB's return home. Ma Barnes knew all too well how this topic would turn out, so she regretted feeding him the question. She didn't want to get him started. He would work himself into hysteria and then get frustrated because there were no immediate solutions.

She wanted to tell her son to let go, that he couldn't be a crusader for people who didn't want to be saved. That the era of martyrs died 20 years prior. That we now, more than ever, lived in a world where every man, woman, family were on their own. Where neighbors weren't neighborly anymore and arrogance was exalted over intelligence. But Ma Barnes could never bring herself to share these sentiments with her son; his passion, however misguided, was too intense. He needed to figure it out on his own, to come to a mature conclusion without the prodding. She just hoped it would happen soon because JB's bitterness would stop him from finding or even keeping a decent job.

"I tell you, Ma, something needs to be done. Someone needs to step up to the plate. I went around the old block yesterday and ran into Mr. Fisher."

"Really? How's ole Stanley doing?"

"He's doing good, still got that strong handshake. After speaking with him for more than an hour, he offered me a classroom in the church."

"Classroom for what?"

"I'm not sure exactly what yet, but I think I want to start getting together like-minded community members and start strategizing."

Ma Barnes wasn't too pleased with the idea; there was a foreboding song attached to it. "Are you sure you want to be hanging around in that neighborhood? I mean, who knows what type of mess your brother's got going on over there."

"Yeah, Ma, I'm good. Besides they love Kameek over there. He's like a hero. It's everywhere else that hates him!" JB chuckled cynically.

"I don't know, son. You be careful over there."

Within months, JB's weekly gatherings were standing-room-only events. He found a vacant storefront and rented the carpeted space for one day a week. His gatherings grew with people attracted to not just JB's insight and fiery delivery, but by his immediate calls to action. JB was an organizer devoted to the minutest of details. For many, JB was a breath of fresh air, a channel for their pent-up energy.

For him, these gatherings offered a sense of belonging, a reason for being, and he reveled in the fact that he was now trying to clean up the community he once played a part in destroying. He addressed this feeling in one of his first speeches:

"I once was a predator in this very community; in fact, on this very avenue. That's right. My two partners and I walked up and down this avenue, and many other avenues, side blocks, and train stations looking for victims. 'Catching herbs' is what we called it. Some of you people in this room today would've been tempting targets.

It was guys like me who made it difficult for people like you to safely walk down the street. And yet, when I was finally captured, I wanted to feel like the victim...as if I had been wronged and the whole ordeal seemed simply unfair. I tell you this because even as a community, we are responsible for our own victimization. Every time we turn a blind eye to an injustice, however small it may be, we are participating in our own victimization. Listen, folks. I'm not trying to get you to put on capes and masks to patrol the community, nor am I trying to get you to become the eyes and ears of the police. What I am saying is that the loiterers, drug dealers, stick-up kids, etc., are your children, neighbors, and neighbor's children. At the very least, let your voice be heard to them. Let them know that you do not approve. Their success as criminals depends on your silence. I know it takes courage, but if we don't act then we're wasting each other's time, 'cause nothing's going to change."

Later that night, still moved by his impassioned speech, he decided to follow his own advice of confronting the wrong by calling Kay-Kay.

"Hello," Kay-Kay answered the phone groggily.

"Hey, lil' bro, you got a sec?"

"Yeah, man. Alicia just finished cooking some banging shrimp étoufée. There's more, if you want to come get some."

"Nah, I'll pass this time, but give my future sis-in-law a big hug for me." JB could hear Kay-Kay in the background addressing Alicia.

"Hey, baby. JB said 'why the fuck you didn't invite him over for dinner?'" JB began to chuckle; he knew his brother like the back of his hand and wasn't surprised at his instigation.

"Man, she said 'fuck you.'" Kay-Kay said sarcastically. JB continued to laugh at his brother's dark sense of humor. He knew that Kay-Kay couldn't help himself when it came to creating awkward moments.

"So, how are your classes coming along, big bro?"

"Well, that's what I want to kick it with you about," JB responded.

"Shit, like I told you, man, anything you need from me just let me know," Kay-Kay offered.

"Well, I need you to hear me out for starters."

Kay-Kay turned the radio down and said, "I'm all ears!"

JB began. "Man, I'm feeling like such a hypocrite. Standing in front of those people talking about standing up to the destroyers of our community and not standing up to my own brother, who has become a recognized name in the field of destruction."

Kay-Kay's baritone laughter echoed through the phone receiver.

"Nah, I'm serious, lil' bro." It was as far as he got before Kay-Kay's violent laughter cut him off mid-sentence.

Then out of nowhere the phone line went dead.

JB cursed out loud. "Did this mothafucka just hang up on me?" He dialed Kay-Kay's number once again. This time the phone rang for a good minute until finally the wistful voice of Alicia spoke. "Hello JB?"

"Hey, Alicia. Where's my brother?"

"You can't hear this fool laughing in the background?" Alicia asked rhetorically. "What did you say that has him laughing so hard? I haven't seen him laugh like this in a long time. He's actually in tears."

"I was about to tell him that he needs to leave those streets behind, to be quite honest!"

Alicia responded with a reflective, "Ahh, well good luck with that one. Kameek, JB is on the phone." Alicia placed the receiver down on what JB could imagine to be the coffee table. The phone sat there for about another minute, while JB continued to listen to Kay-Kay's laughter. Finally Kay-Kay spoke:

"Look, I'ma tell you this once more, then no more. Stay the fuck out my business. What I do with my life is on me. You want to fight the fucking system, be my guest. I'm chasing the paper. That's what I am: a fucking paper-chaser. Now, you're my big brother and I love you, but you're starting to piss me off with this weirdo shit. This ain't comic books. I ain't Magneto and you ain't Professor X. If you stick with the preaching, you should start making some money, but ain't nobody but weirdos gonna drink that Kool-Aid."

"So, I'm a weirdo because I believe in a cause?"

"You're a weirdo because you want to force your beliefs on everyone else," Kay-Kay responded forcefully.

"Yeah well, look man, I can't call you my brother and be about the people..."

Kay-Kay interrupted, "Then don't call me your brother. In fact, don't call me at all." Click.

Once again, JB found himself listening to a dial tone that seemed to grow louder and menacing by the second. He let out an exasperated sigh. He knew that it would take a lot more of these confrontations to reach his brother, but he was determined to do just that.

Like a Jehovah's Witness, JB went door to door preaching his gospel determined to effect a change in his community. He met with Ms. Briggs, the mother who just a month ago lost her 14-year-old son, Demarcus, in a hail of gunfire. Demarcus was walking home from the store when the gun battle erupted. Despite the media coverage and makeshift memorial, no arrests had been made. To add insult to injury, the police interrogated Ms. Briggs like she was their prime suspect. JB's heart went out to her. He wanted to assure her that it would be all right, but such insight was beyond his wisdom. *Would it ever be all right? Would she ever be made whole again? Would there ever be closure to this tragedy?*

JB decided the best thing he could do was to just become an ear, and so, he listened. He listened for hours about a mother's regret, about how she should have moved out of the neighborhood before it claimed her son's life. How could she go on, believing that his death was due to her inaction?

Kay-Kay

I walked in my house one late evening. In fact, the clock had just struck 12, making it the hour of twilight, surprised to find Alicia sitting in front of the office computer. She felt my presence, but still had not turned to greet me. Something was wrong. I knew my babe. When I reached her, I could see the fresh teardrops and the paths they carved down her cheek.

"Babe, what's wrong?" I asked gently hugging her and pressing my cheek against hers.

Finally, she turned to acknowledge me. Alicia was trying her hardest to not completely crack before explaining, "Kameek, I feel like I want to quit."

"Quit what, babe?"

"This school shit."

I was shaking my head vigorously against the notion. She placed her hand in mine and continued. "I know quitting is not an option. We have come too far, we've sacrificed too much, but this is hard, Kameek. The hours upon hours of studying for exams, memorizing terms, the tons of homework, and now the clinicals will be coming soon. It's just overwhelming...that's all."

I nodded my head in understanding because I bore witness to her journey. I put my arm around her shoulder, giving her a cushion to lean back on. We sat in silence for more than an hour, just enjoying each other's company.

Eventually, I reintroduced sound by stating, "I know it's difficult, but all dreams worth pursuing are. I believe they're designed that way so that when we reach it, we appreciate it more."

Alicia shook her head. My philosophy was one that I'm sure she used to motivate herself countless times before. I continued, "Since I met you, you've always wanted to be a doctor. You come alive when you talk about diseases and the human body, medications, and treatments. You were born to heal. I wish I had something I was passionate enough about to fixate on for hours. Something that if I never made a dollar doing, I would still do it every day of my life. You are blessed to be pursuing your passion."

Alicia gave me the 'even a broken clock is right twice a day' look before mouthing the words thank you.

Chapter 8: desperate times, desperate measures

Kay-Kay

1993

Everyone, including me, expected the drought to quickly blow over, but then another shipment of cocaine and heroin was seized and the economy in the hood went into an immediate recession. With crackheads and dope fiends going two to three days without a hit or a fix, the desperation in the hood became visible as the crime rate continued to rise.

Whether you are for or against drugs and the distribution of them, the necessity of their existence in our society, from a wholly financial standpoint, cannot be argued. Drugs have been silent pillars of Wall Street since the days of Prohibition. It's no coincidence that the public was saved from the Great Depression by the ending of Prohibition.

Hustlers are some of the biggest buyers of cars, clothes, electronics, and jewelry. They also open up many small businesses that actually employ legitimate workers. Movie theaters, restaurants, supermarkets, and even cab companies benefit directly from the drug trade. So, again, whether you are for or against it, everyone feels the pinch when it's missing.

Within a few months, the murder rate quadrupled and the community leaders were outraged. They were calling for a greater police presence as if that meant anything to a desperate man. I tried explaining this to JB, but he proved resistant to anything that challenged his moral compass saying, "Man, Kay-Kay, you always trying to justify bullshit. Selling drugs is wrong, point blank."

I decided to lighten up considerably on the sanctions and let the peacocks breathe a little. I didn't want to force desperation. Besides, by this time, I had four legitimate businesses running throughout NYC and another one in Boston. None of them were making any substantial profits, but none were operating at a loss.

JB and I had begun speaking again, and we would have these heated intellectual debates about our opposing worldviews. I actually began enjoying the mental stimulation and felt that, in most of them, I held my own without waiver.

After sharing my humble thoughts on the importance of the drug trade with JB, I made the mistake of deciding to go to hear him speak at his weekly gathering. By this time, his audience had grown to about 60 people, mostly mothers, but still, all in all, I was impressed. Two weeks prior, when Alicia went, she claimed he had over 100 people in attendance. I walked in and a slight nod of his head was his only acknowledgement.

He must have been talking for quite some time prior to my arrival because he was already sweating profusely. Nevertheless, upon seeing me, JB quickly began a new thought:

"There's another thought I would like to share with you today, something that has been bothering me for the past few days. We come to these weekly meetings and discuss the problems that plague our neighborhoods. Which is cool, but there's never any follow through on solutions. We can talk for days about all that's wrong, but I ask you as individuals: what are you doing about it?

When I drive through neighborhoods that are predominantly white, I can't help but notice how clean things are. There's very little trash on the streets. Then I drive through our hoods and there's garbage strewn everywhere. Yeah we know that a lot of this has to do directly with the drug trade. We know that crackheads and dope fiends don't clean up behind themselves. It takes a level of self-esteem and pride to do that. A person has to care what others who see them think, and if they are getting high, they obviously are apathetic to anyone else's opinion.

Drugs are a moral stain on our society. For those of you who are unaware, there is a cocaine and heroin drought going on in our neighborhoods right now. It's been going on for the past few months. This is why the news is reporting an increase in violent crimes, including murders in our communities.

There are some among us who feel that a flourishing drug trade is a good stimulus for our economy—that legitimate businesses prosper and feed off of, be it indirectly or directly, the drug trade. To this, I'm forced to agree."

JB's admission of this point surprised me, but I knew there had to be a catch. There was always a catch with this guy.

"I agree that this is so only because our capitalistic society is diametrically opposed to our moral fiber. We are by nature a communal people, and capitalism, the notion of the 'haves' versus the 'have nots' creates a dissonance or disconnect between our nature and this blood-sucking culture that has been forced on us."

Man, don't ask me what the fuck my brother was talking about. I'm not even sure he knew 'cause he kind of looked around with a damn-I-got-away-with-that look. And, he sure did. The majority of people in the room were nodding their heads affirmatively as if his psychobabble made perfect sense. Or, perhaps it did? For me, it was just rhetoric. It was my brother's way of agreeing with my assessment without conceding to my conclusion.

I left that night once again wondering about my brother. Did he really believe the shit he was kicking? Or was it what we called in the streets 'just another long con?' While selling dope in the hood was the choice of the majority of hustlers, there were a few hustlers with the 'gift of gab' who sold the rest of the people hope—a commodity that required no overhead or re-up.

About a week and a half after attending JB's lecture, I had dinner with an old friend of mine named Ace. We were elementary school buddies who kept in touch with each other periodically throughout the years. Ace and his fraternal twin Reece were inseparable. They had always been each other's crime partners, kind of like how JB and I were before JB flipped the script.

The twins, as I sometimes called them, were exceptional stick-up artists. Having never been arrested for anything, these guys were thorough. For them, arrest was not an option; either they completed the mission or they die trying. They only took on establishments, never people. Both were marksmen with the pistol, so if they fired, they hit.

Ace's short and stocky frame was in direct contrast to Reece's tall and lanky build. Ace always kept a solemn and grave face, while Reece's smile was a permanent fixture, even under pressure. Only their complexion and demeanor indicated their relation. They were the ultimate "Mutt and Jeff" team.

"Kay, this is definitely a big score, I have the inside track on this juxx," Ace explained calmly. "Reece is sexing a shorty who guards the warehouse. There's seven guards per shift; three on the perimeter, four on the inside."

"What about cameras?" I asked.

In anticipation of this question, Ace interrupted, "Six cameras on the perimeter, but due to budget cuts, only three are active. There are another three cameras on the inside, but only one is active. There's a clearance gate on the inside." Ace picked up a napkin, pulled out a pen, and began sketching the floor plans of the warehouse. "Here's the entrance." Ace was pointing to a spot on the diagram. "This police here...we're gonna have to catch the drop on because it's an open space and there's no real strategy for this besides a sudden rush and a little luck. The good thing is that it's isolated. As long as we keep the noise to a minimum it won't affect the mission. The real challenge will be when we reach here..." Not surprisingly, Ace knew the layout by heart. He remained calm throughout his presentation.

"Aight, so let me get this straight, you're saying that there's at least 10 tons of Coast Guard-seized, cocaine and heroin sitting in a warehouse on the piers in Red Hook?" I asked.

"Yeah," Ace responded.

"So how do we move that shit? We're gonna need a huge truck or something."

CENTER OF GRAVITY

Ace was shaking his head dismissively as if to say it's all taken care of. "They have transport trucks on site. We're gonna load a truck up and drive it off the docks. We're gonna change trucks further down by Fort Greene."

I began laughing at the sheer audacity and boldness of the plan.

"So let me get this straight. You want us to run up in a federal warehouse where 10 tons of cocaine and heroin are being held?"

"No less than 10, but maybe more," Ace interrupted.

I continued, "We're gonna tie up the cops, steal a federal truck, load it up with drugs and drive off into the sunset."

Ace arched his eyebrow as if I missed something before giving me his trademark response, "Yeah."

"So where's Reece now?"

"He's putting in the surveillance work. You know how Reece is—he's a stickler for details. He's been on this for more than three months."

"Who's the broad? How far can she be trusted?"

"Well, that's been the thing for us. It's not a matter of can she be trusted, but would you gamble your life on that? We've been assessing whether her information is 100 percent accurate. Trust me, Kay. We have that part of it all worked out. Reece knows how iffy these type of juxxes are, especially when it's coming from an inside source. There's no chance of her flipping the script," Ace answered vehemently. I understood the tough decision and its hidden meaning and decided to leave such decisions to their conscience.

"Is there anything else I'm missing?" I asked.

"Don't forget, all guns will have silencers on them, we're not playing. There's no surrender. Any guard that wants to lose his life for his job will be obliged. Kay, we're coming out of this either multi-millionaires or dead men."

"You said it would be four of us going in, who's the fourth man?" I asked, making sure I was covering all bases.

"June from College Avenue," Ace said. He couldn't have given a better name.

Dewright "June" Johnson was an official stick-up kid out of the Bronx who had pulled off a series of successful airport heists in the mid-80s. I met him in Auburn Correctional Facility where he was finishing up a four-year bid for a gun and vest charge. He was a stand-up dude who kept to himself and stayed out of the limelight. There were rumors that he was a cross-dresser, but no one had any proof. While in prison, the Old God took a liking to him and instructed me to find out if the rumors had any validity upon my return to the streets.

I set my spies on him and, sure enough, they caught him in the act twice. However, neither time was he in the company of anyone else. For all we knew, that could be his surveillance uniform. Whatever his sexual preference or fetish, when it came to getting the job done, he was top notch.

"Who are the drivers?"

"We were hoping you would bring Handbone in on this with you, providing you were in on it."

"Well, you knew my answer before you even asked. Otherwise, you would've never laid the details out to me." Ace smiled at my assessment. To rob the police in their own warehouse—wow, this was going to be fun.

A. C. Clayton

Chapter 9: in search of the source

Kay-Kay
1993

The easy part was making the bread. The hard part is hiding it. I found myself spending a considerable amount of time figuring out ways to protect my assets. I was referred to a guy I was told could help. While sharing with him in superficial detail my efforts to hide my money, he interjected with a proposal for an alternative course. *'The purpose of a dollar bill is similar to the purpose of a virus—it only wants to replicate itself. One dollar should at the very least generate a quarter in interest. And if the need to spend arises, let it be from the interest, never from the dollar.'*

These were the words from my personal accountant the day I hired him. Prior to bringing him on board, I placed a lot of my money into various safety deposits boxes throughout the city. The accountant chuckled at me, *the foolish mortal*, before parceling his advice. "That's like a dog who buries bones. The bones aren't replicating themselves, they're just sitting there entertaining worms. There's a thin line between tax evasion and racketeering. If your money ever comes into question, you want it to be for the former and not the latter. You're hiring me to make you wealthy and I will. But more importantly, I would like to show you how it's done so that the day will come when our relationship will be partners in investments and not client and service provider." From that day on, he became known as the Wizard, and only Alicia knew who he was on sight. He was my hidden hand and the most dangerous associate I had because he knew where the money was and most importantly why it was where it was.

The Wizard was a colorless being who held no allegiance to any race except the race he could win. He was a politician by profession, but an accountant by trade. He kept me abreast to the happenings within City Hall, the Chambers of Commerce, Wall Street, as well as 1 Police Plaza. Through him, I had a window into the inner workings of the respectable crooks, the ones who declared war on drugs even as they sniffed cocaine with prostitutes. They took bribes to look the other way, to stay silent, or yell charges. The Wizard would make the boulders, and any other obstacle, visible to my line of sight. His price tag was steep, but so was my climb.

I couldn't place my finger on where the product was coming from. Whoever was feeding the peacocks was doing a damn good job at concealment. They were definitely keeping a low profile. I had my best eyes and ears out scouting for the lead. I knew that whoever the source was, we were obligated to squeeze.

The most consistent story was that it was an out of town crew bringing the work in. Some believed they were a crew from D. C. or Philadelphia. The problem with both scenarios was that both places were getting their drugs, for the most part, from NYC and then taking it back home. For them, selling product in NYC would be a bad business decision. Even during a time of drought, cocaine prices would be considerably cheaper in NYC than it would be in D.C. or Philly. They could practically double their profits in those two cities, unless they were a crew that had gotten chased out of their own town by rivals, the police, or both. Then they would have no choice but to relocate.

Either way, I was determined to get my share. Yet, I couldn't shake the lingering suspicion that there was more to the story than the million others I had heard, thus far.

In the midst of all that I had going on, I stumbled into another one of JB's lectures. Not sure if it was just for amusement or just wanting to see my big brother's face.

His loud voice filled the crowded room. JB philosophized out loud, "Understand, sisters and brothers, it starts small. We are only 12 percent of the U.S. population; on a national level, our vote can only tip the scale. This is why our votes are wasted when our votes are divided."

A robust woman with too much make-up on raised her hand and JB immediately acknowledged her. "Yes ma'am?"

"I enjoy all that you are saying, Jamal, but many of our leaders are saying that we need to be represented in both parties because if we keep voting for the same party, we have no leverage if the other party wins." JB smiled, his face a mask of deep concentration.

"Yes, I'm intimately familiar with that circular reasoning. This is why we are pushing this grassroots movement so forcefully. It's time we collectively become politically aware of our power. We must break our alliance with the Democratic Party and form a voting bloc. Whichever of the three parties— Republican, Democratic or Independent—agrees to the majority of our demands, wins our vote. It's that simple. This makes sense." JB was pounding the podium to emphasize his message. "Any so-called leader who argues this must have a personal agenda. Voting collectively is our only weapon in this arena."

"Now on a local level, we have the numbers to take control of the borough and ultimately, the city. Understand that whoever controls the Mayor's Office, controls the schools that our children attend, the police that invade our communities at will, the hospitals that fail to provide adequate health care, and transportation that gets us to and from work. Practically every public institution that counts in our day-to-day life falls under the mayor's power. So our focus must be on eventually taking Gracie Mansion."

As I looked around, I saw that everyone in the room was hanging on to every word JB spoke. Even Alicia sat mesmerized. In their eyes, I saw the spark of hope. JB was touching chords in a way that only a few knew how.

My beeper began vibrating, so I reluctantly left the meeting. The call turned out to be Handbone letting me know our target had been captured and placed in a trunk for safekeepings. We would move tonight. My pulse quickened. I had been anxiously awaiting this call. I hung up with Handbone after agreeing to meet him at 9:30 p.m. When I re-entered the auditorium, the meeting had concluded; a crowd of people had JB surrounded, asking him a host of questions.

Alicia was off to the side talking with two other women when she spotted me. After saying farewell to her new friends, she navigated her way over to me, giving me a big hug and lengthy kiss. "Baby, how long have you been here?"

"I was here for a few minutes, listening. I left to make a call. When I got back, it was over. How was the ending?"

"Kameek, your brother is on the right track. I really feel good about this movement."

I looked carefully at Alicia, resisting the urge to put my hand on her forehead and check for a fever.

"Why are you looking at me like I just grew two heads?"

"Who me?"

"Yeah you. Your brother is talking about empowering us."

"Yeah, he's talking it. I'm doing it."

"No Kameek, not that kind of power. Real power."

"Alicia, what kind of power do you think I'm talking about?"

"You're talking that gangsta crap. I'm talking about real political power."

"Alicia, the people in power are gangsters and they keep their power by way of the gun. The rest are nothing but persuasive tactics used in order to avoid using the gun. If they could do what they want without the use of force, they will. But if force is required, they won't hesitate. That's my kind of power, baby."

"Well said, baby bro. Well said."

JB had walked up unexpectedly, obviously hearing my definition. He was grinning.

"So, have you finally decided to join the movement?"

"That's funny, I was about to ask you the same question."

JB began laughing, put his arm around my shoulder and whispered in my ear, "I'm glad you at least came back."

"Yeah after all that talking you did, I'm sure you must be hungry?" I asked.

"Man, I'm famished," he responded.

"One Fish Two Fish, here we come," Alicia giddily interjected.

The call came in and I couldn't resist the urge to leave the early dinner I was having with Alicia and JB.

"Sorry guys, I gotta run."

"Kameek, you're something else. You mean that business can't wait till we finish eating?" Alicia asked exasperated.

"Nah, that's why it's called business baby." I kissed her on the forehead to soften the sarcastic blow.

Rolling her eyes she turned toward JB. "It's probably one of those groupies he's going to meet."

JB smiled. "Baby bro, thanks a lot for coming to hear me speak. Believe it or not, you made my day. Hopefully, you'll swing through next week."

A slick comment was about to roll off my tongue when the sincerity in his words held me silent. Instead, I found myself complimenting JB on his lecture and the overall work he was attempting to do in the hood.

"I enjoyed the speech, even though I still think you are a lil' naïve. At least you're practicing what you preach. When I listen to you speak I know you're sincere, and sincerity always wins out."

"Thanks, Kay. I appreciate that. So can I count on seeing you next week?"

Before I could decline the offer Alicia chimed in. "Yup, JB, Kameek and I will be there."

Alicia's piercing look told me all I needed to know. The decision was final; the compromise was made. To leave in peace, I had to commit to returning next week. I nodded and said, "Yeah man, I'll be back next week to hear what you have to say."

Although it was 20 degrees colder than normal, the cool, early autumn air felt invigorating. It was the right temperature to apply pressure on a peacock. There's something about that crisp autumn chill that reminds them that there's always a grave with their name on it should they choose to rebel.

The sidewalks littered with decaying leaves immediately put me in the zone of serenity. I was falling into my customary trance, focused and heading towards a discussion long overdue. We conducted these specialized gatherings in a cemetery in Queens. Paul Charles, a sophisticated Harlem peacock with a military background, was our latest target.

Unlike so many of his peers, Paul Charles moved a great deal more cautious and deliberate than the rest. It took us well over two months to successfully follow him home. He never took the same route to his pad in Jersey from Harlem. He also made a lot of last minute turns that made following him undetected difficult. But Handbone had a nose like a bloodhound. He kept telling me not to worry and to be patient, that he was closing in on our target. And sure enough, a few days later, his words proved true.

"I got him, Kay," Handbone exclaimed over the phone. "It took us a little while but I'm finally at a payphone about half a mile away from his house."

"Cool, you know the routine, take as many pictures and gather as much info as you can. We need to know how best to squeeze this mothafucka."

Now only minutes away from meeting Paul Charles, my adrenaline was on nitro. This particular meeting meant a little more to me because Paul Charles had started out as a soldier for Papa Doc. He quickly earned his stripes and ventured out into his own hustles, but by all accounts, he'd remained fiercely loyal to Papa Doc. The word on the street was that he paid for Doc's funeral all the while swearing vengeance. Since the funeral, though his rhetoric died down, he was more content with letting the dead stay dead and making his money.

Nevertheless, there was a price to pay in order to play. Today was the day to name that price. There were also rumors that Paul Charles knew who this unseen supplier was. I couldn't wait to squeeze that source for all it had.

Cemeteries are all the same at night. Have you ever walked in one and felt the presence of the un-living? I know it's some spooky shit, right? That's why I chose to have my little chats with the peacocks there. Ironically, it helps to keep them focused on living.

I blinked my flashlight in every direction until I saw what I was looking for. Far to the left of me, a series of flashes blinked in response. Other than the occasional glow of the moonlight sifting through the leafless branches, the graveyard was pitch black. The only sound besides the crunch of my heels was from the crickets and if one listened carefully, the whispers of the dead.

As I approached my destination, I saw that the sophisticated peacock was duct taped and bound. His eyes were wide with fear and recognition. His clothing was disheveled, a clear indication that he didn't surrender without a struggle—my kind of guy.

A. C. Clayton

"You probably wondering what this is all about," I spoke in a low measured tone. "You look as if you recognize my face. Do you know who I am?"

The sophisticated peacock shook his head in affirmation.

"Aight so, there's no need for an introduction. We've been watching you for a good minute, doing our homework and shit, and it's clear to me that you're a great deal more successful than the average peacock. But you're still a peacock. Your shiny jewels, the fur in the winter, the seasonal Benz, though tasteful, is nonetheless telling. You see, that's how I target you mothafuckas. I bet you never knew that. Shit, I do just what the Feds and the police do. I look for the show-offs."

I went on, "So here's the deal. Either you pay and continue to play, or we leave you here tonight in this empty lot. If you agree to pay and then renege on your word, we'll bury you after we bury your family. Yea, we know about your wife and your two pretty little girls, Denia and Dawn. Ah, don't look surprised. I told you we did our homework. It's the nature of the game. So, your fee to continue is eighty grand a month. I don't care about a drought, a pinch, inflation, or recession. I want my money the seventh of every month. The day you can't pay, I expect to hear that you left the game behind for good. If so, then that's a breach of contract and you have to pay a cancellation fee. Only then, will you be free to go. Are we clear? Do you want to give it some thought? Of course not. I know the 80 stacks ain't nothing to a peacock such as yourself. In fact, you should feel honored I'm squeezing you for more than I do the Russians. But that's because I know your hands are in other things besides drugs. I just haven't figured it out yet. I also want to know about this new pipeline that's supplying the streets. I'm very interested to hear what you know."

Handbone ripped the duct tape off of Paul Charles' mouth. The sudden influx of fresh air forced him to choke violently. It was such a natural reaction, one we saw so many times that we just watched him fight to gain his breath. When he finally did, his first words sounded like music to my ears: "What about her do you want to know?"

Even in the dark, the collective smile from my team brought life to the graveyard. "Tell me everything."

Unfortunately, Paul Charles' information proved to be a grave disappointment. He really didn't know shit. He claimed the source was a chick he believed came from Jersey. He only met her once—a brief initial encounter in front of Macy's on 34th Street. Since then, he'd been dealing with a Colombian supplier I already had the squeeze on. The only part that seemed promising was that it was the second or third time that

I heard the supplier might be a female. The most intriguing part was that the connect was made through the *Circle of Friends*.

Chapter 10: return of the king

1993

The four-hour car ride that Kay-Kay and JB agreed to take gave the brothers the opportunity to hang out together and appreciate each other's company. Before taking to the road, they both agreed not to talk about politics, religion, or any other hotbed issues. Instead, they reminisced about their childhood and how much they appreciated their mother.

Kay-Kay expressed his frustration with not being able to connect with her anymore the way he once did and JB was wise enough not to point the finger of blame at Kay-Kay's lifestyle. They talked about aunts and uncles, funny stories, and times that they remembered. Their father came up in the discussion and because JB was older, he had more fond memories of him to cling to.

Their father, the man they knew only as Daddy, walked out of their lives in the middle of the night while they slept and never returned. According to their mother, there had been signs and clues of another woman for months leading up to his disappearance, but if she knew more, she never let on. At nine years old, JB was affected by his departure the most. He idolized his father, and for years afterwards would talk about when his father came back and the things they were going to do.

Kay-Kay was also hurt, but more for his mother than for himself or even for JB. Kay-Kay saw what his father's absence did to his mother's spirit. Though she kept a smile on her face, even at seven years old, he knew that her smile was nothing more than a mask to hide the pain. The truth was in her eyes. She was lost, and even all these years later, her eyes still betrayed her.

Halfway to their destination, Kay-Kay stated his assessment of their father. "Man, Daddy was—and if he's still alive is—a stone cold sucker. I mean, think about it. He left us to live in the gutter, exposed to all the toxins and toxic people. Go figure. As thorough as you and I are, our pops was a sucker who left our mother to fend for herself, who walked away from us when we could barely stand on our own two feet."

Kay-Kay stole a glance at JB just to see if his words were penetrating. "We were just learning balance when he made the ground slippery and shit," he continued. We made it, but it still doesn't take away the fact that he pulled a super sucker move on us. He was a chump who probably never really loved our mother, and therefore couldn't have ever really loved us."

JB listened intently knowing that his little brother held some serious resentment toward the man they knew as Daddy. Their father was guilty of abandoning ship, but what JB never shared with Kay-Kay or their mother was that he spoke with their pops weeks after his departure. "I never told you this, but I saw Daddy about a month after he left."

Kay-Kay's eyes grew wide with confusion as he took his eyes off the road and trained them on JB. "Are you serious? And all these years later you never told me? Do Moms know?"

JB shook his head before saying, "Nah, this is the first time I'm telling anyone about this."

"In-fucking-credible," Kay-Kay shook his head in utter disgust. "You know you're a fucking trip, man. I swear. You think you know what's best for everybody but you don't. In fact, you don't know shit."

"He made me promise not to say anything to ya, because it would just make the pain more unbearable."

The weight of silence that lingered between them was oppressive and prolonged; they rode another 40 minutes before one word was spoken.

"Do you want to know what was said?" JB asked, eager to finally unburden the secret.

"Nope. Fuck him. No justification for abandonment. Fuck him." Kay-Kay was resolute in his thinking. He compared his father's actions to that of a snitch who tries to explain the reasoning behind biting the cheese. "There is no reason except cowardice."

JB shrugged in apathy, but in truth, he was disappointed that he could not unload the secret. "Well, when you're ready, lil' bro."

"I'll never be ready to hear why a sucker chose to be a sucker, or even why a sucker would choose to repeat what a sucker has to say."

JB could not hold back the laughter. "So now I'm sucker?" he asked between convulsions of mirth.

Kay-Kay reluctantly gave in to the humor and smiled, "Maybe you're not a sucker, just his messenger."

For the rest of the ride they kept the conversation light, both afraid of discussing anything that could disrupt the delicate balance of harmony that had been cautiously constructed. Finally, they pulled up to their destination.

Great Meadows Correctional Facility sat brolic and menacing. Both brothers were quietly reminded of the misery they left behind as they looked at the façade of the fortress. Five minutes later, Knee, their brother from another mother, emerged from the castle with a grin the size of Texas plastered across his face. Knee dropped the small net bag that contained his pictures and mail on the floor, folded his arms across his chest, and yelled, "What? This all they had for me?"

The ride home was full of updates. Knee asked question after question, seemingly trying to cram everything in at once. They pulled over a few times to let Knee out of the back seat; he was suffering from motion sickness and his only recourse was to vomit.

"Yo man, I'm ready to get in the mix, Kay," Knee said.

"You ready, big bro?" Kay-Kay responded, excited to hear from Knee what he didn't hear from JB upon his release.

"Am I? I been hearing how you been out here tearing shit up and all I could think about is 'wait till I get home!'"

It was music to Kay-Kay's ears. He was hoping Knee would be ready to rock, and the possibility that eventually JB would come around to his senses just became a real probability. However, that hope was still a long way off. JB just shook his head in disappointment though he didn't really expect anything else from Knee.

Knee seeing JB shaking his head asked, "What's that all about, mothafucka? Why you shaking your head? I know you ain't think I was coming home to join the struggle? I promote violence, not peace."

"Nah, actually I was shaking my head because you just got out and you not even talking about getting some pussy. You're more excited about the streets."

"Tsst," Knee sucked his teeth at JB's stupid assessment. "Pussy? Are you serious?"

"Yeah pussy, I'm dead serious."

"Kay, what's wrong with your brother?" Knee tapped him on the shoulder after asking the question.

Kay-Kay enjoying the debate said, "Leave me out of it."

"Man, pussy is a given. Ain't y'all dropping me off at ya moms house? You know Ms. Barnes is my baby—with her fat ass and all."

If a Black man could turn red in embarrassment, JB turned into a tomato. Kay-Kay's laughter was the only noise that kept the joke harmless.

"Man, I'm really beginning to think that you got the fever for our Moms," Kay-Kay reasoned.

"Damn youngster, you just starting to think that? Fever is an understatement; her picture was the only one on my wall in prison. You know, I got you by five years."

"Fuck is that supposed to mean?"

"It means, I'm old enough to be your father, shot my first load at five. You better respect that, kiddo." Once again, Knee placed his hand on Kay-Kay's shoulder.

"You know, bro, in some circles, talking about mothers is off limits," Kay-Kay said jokingly.

"Man, I'm a mothafuckin' gangsta. It's only two of you in this car, so I ain't worried."

Finally, JB jumped back in the discussion. "Yo seriously, Kay keep this moron away from mommy because if he says something wrong..."

Knee interrupted, "If I say something wrong to my woman, what? It's my woman. I can say what I want." The mush in the back of JB's head was the straw that broke the camel's back. The two friends began play fighting in the car while Kay-Kay drove, loving the moment but hoping that they didn't catch the attention of any state trooper looking to meet a quota.

Kay-Kay

For an entire month, Knee became my shadow. Enthusiastically, I took him everywhere, determined to eventually pass on most of the day-to-day operations to him and Handbone. I wanted time to really concentrate on this real estate hustle I was growing to love. Everywhere I took Knee, his reputation preceded him. Even the cocky peacocks played their position in his presence. While Handbone was as thorough as it gets, he didn't command the type of fear that my name, and now Knee's name, did.

I was thinking about giving Knee his own area to control and do with as he saw fit. But by the end of the month, I had serious doubts about his role in my organization. We were like oil and water, and every day demonstrated the difference. Knee began questioning every move I made, and while I wasn't suffering from an 'I am King' syndrome, it was a kingdom that I fought to build and maintain at all cost. He even began questioning me in front of others. The questioning was always about the use of force.

Knee felt that every transgression, every indiscretion from a peacock, should be met with force. He believed that the only solution to every problem was violence. I tried to explain that more violence, equals more law enforcement, and the more law enforcement, the less money and the bigger the trap. But still the math didn't add up to Knee.

Handbone's take on the situation was best: "Knee's a goon, not a thinker. He's trying to become a thinker, 'cause he sees what you've accomplished. But he's a pygmy when it comes to strategy and will always be reactionary. You gotta be careful, Kay, how you work with him. All it takes is one bonehead move to unravel this tapestry."

Chapter 11: rectifying a wrong

Peaches

1993

Peaches knew that it would be just a matter of time before her and Kay-Kay collided again. To this end, she had no doubt. Already, he had his snoops out trying to figure out who she was. Her whole purpose of lying low was to gather her soldiers and assemble her army. Every piece of profit went to hiring new shooters. She was determined to be ready for the war when it started. Father of her child meant very little. Either they would coexist, or she would exist and he would just become a legend to some and a memory to others. "Take your pick buddy," she thought out loud as she put the finishing touches on with her eyeliner.

1985

She was vexed. Kay-Kay had not returned her calls in two days. He had promised to take her shopping, but that didn't matter to her. She had been building up the courage for the past three weeks to tell him that her period was late and that her period was absolutely never late. She had taken a pregnancy test twice. Both times, the results were the same. Precious was undoubtedly pregnant. She wasn't sure how Kay-Kay would react. In many ways, he was mature beyond his 15 years. But in other ways he was still a little boy. The last night that they were together, the night he came back to her house with a big chain and a wad of cash that he just stole from someone, she was determined to share the news with him. She kept hinting at the subject, but he was so preoccupied with reliving the robbery that he had just pulled off. He barely heard her, or so it seemed.

Right before they went to sleep, she made her boldest hint yet. "Kay-Kay, you wouldn't make a good father. All you do is think about crime."

"That's not true," he replied.

"What else do you think about then?"

"Pussy and food," he chuckled.

At that point, Precious was certain that he knew. There was no way that he didn't catch her hints. She had practically said 'Kay-Kay, I'm pregnant.' It was on him now to decide whether he wanted to be a father or not. Either way, she would have the baby. So his two days of ignoring her calls told her his answer. At first, she felt indifferent but as the second day wore on, her indifference morphed into vengeance. Especially when she found out that the chain belonged to Smooth, the gladiator from her projects. Ever since her 16th birthday, Smooth had been trying to crack her for some ass. She heard Smooth had put a reward out for anyone who knew anything about the chain. Precious figured that with the money Smooth would give her, she would be able to buy baby clothes and supplies. So many years later, she could see how foolish she had been, in so many ways. But at the time, it seemed like the most logical course to take.

Finding Smooth proved to be no problem. He was in front of Tiffany and Shay Shay's building talking to a crackhead. He spotted her walking towards him and immediately his face became a disguise of joyous bewilderment.

A stab of doubt entered her mind. She realized a second before uttering the words, "I know who took your chain," that she was sentencing the father of her unborn child to death.

The next two days went by like a blur. Smooth was only half interested in finding out who Kay-Kay was; his other concern was getting to know her.

"So what's up Shorty, when you gonna let me bless that ass?"

Before Precious knew it, she was in a hotel room with Smooth going for round two. Smooth didn't believe in condoms and so his spills inside of her got her to thinking about an alternative father for her unborn child.

"Shorty, you sure he lives over here by Church Ave?"

Smooth asked skeptically as he, Precious, and a gunman she went to junior high school with named Smiley, were driving in

Smooth's all-black Saab down Church Ave. She pretended that she didn't know where Kay-Kay lived exactly, but she knew what block he was from. She figured that Kay-Kay would be lying low somewhere and so them driving by would be harmless.

"Yea, I'm sure, I was..." she was cut off by Smooth's incredulous proclamation.

"Un-fucking-believable! This lil' nigga got nuts the size of King Kong!"

He was staring at a figure a block away using the pay phone. She couldn't believe what she was seeing. 'How stupid could he be?' she thought. Everyone in the car was staring at Kay-Kay with Smooth's chain dangling from his neck like an anchor. 'What were the odds?' she thought.

To her surprise, Smooth began laughing.

"This little mothafucka's got nuts. He don't know my fucking arms are long? Is that it? He thinks I can't reach out and touch his ass?"

By this time, they were riding past him. Kay-Kay looked directly at the car before looking away, the tints obviously too dark for him to see through.

"Smiley, you better kill that lil' nigga and rip my fucking chain off that pussy's neck." The scene that unfolded did so in slow motion. Precious was proud when she saw Kay-Kay fighting back. Her heart sank when he hit the ground, thinking that he was a goner. But then, he got back up and her heart soared. It was only at that very moment that she realized the depths of her betrayal. The father of her unborn child, and the love of her life, was fighting for his life now because of her.

Fight, baby. Fight. I'm so sorry... she thought.

Then he went down again, and Smiley was running back to the car. A silent prayer escaped her lips. "Please live, Kay-Kay. Please live."

"Shorty, pull him in the car and close the fucking door."

Smooth was referring to his gunman, Smiley, running towards them at breakneck speed. Even before Smiley made it to the car, Precious could see that he had been shot and that realization made her smile.

Word reached Smooth and Precious that Kay-Kay survived the assassination attempt about a week later. Precious was secretly thankful of the news while Smooth flew into a rage, cursing and spewing obscenities at all who would listen.

"This little mothafucka won't survive the next one," Smooth promised assuredly. "I'm gonna personally take care of this one myself."

As if the shooting itself was a unifying force, Precious and Smooth had become inseparable. She wasn't sure how it got so intense so quickly. It wasn't love that kept her by his side, but fear.

Perhaps she was overly paranoid, but she felt trapped, worried that breaking it off from Smooth would prove fatal.

Smooth was a creature obsessed with his possessions. Everything and everyone was his possession. Like the chain Kay-Kay stole, Precious had become just another one of Smooth's trinkets. Precious realized that she might have bit off more than she could chew when it came to Smooth. She thought about her options regarding the fetus that was growing inside of her. There was no doubt; Smooth would put two and two together and figure out that the baby was Kay-Kay's. And who knew what he would do to his enemy's baby.

Precious decided that, for now, it was best if Smooth thought she was pregnant by him. He had a bunch of children already and one more would just add to his possessions. It was either that or an abortion. Though Precious contemplated that alternative, she knew in her heart she would never kill her baby. When she told Smooth she was pregnant with his child, he immediately sent for a couple of cases of Moët to celebrate. He always wanted to have a basketball team of children to carry on his legacy and this baby would ensure that he had at least a starting lineup.

But Precious was troubled. She knew that by telling Smooth about her pregnancy it would buy her some time to figure out another move, but what would that other move be? She had no clue. For six months, Precious plotted her escape. Her plan was to run away, relocate, and never look back. But she couldn't leave her sister, brother, and mother behind. Smooth wasn't the type of person to lose his possessions without a fight. Her family would become his target for revenge.

Precious, Smooth, and Smiley were holed up in one of Smooth's stash houses. It was really nothing more than a two-bedroom apartment, devoid of any real furniture or personality. Smooth had been in the kitchen cooking up eight kilos of cocaine for the past three hours. He transformed the cocaine into huge slabs of crack, slabs that were left to dry before being cut up and packaged for distribution. It was an all-night process and no one would get sleep until the job was completely done. Precious' role would vary throughout the night and into the morning, but at the current moment, she was coming back from Kentucky Fried Chicken with three buckets of chicken.

"What took you so fucking long?" Smooth yelled from the kitchen as Precious walked through the door.

Precious ignored his routine bickering. Smooth always grew verbally abusive when they had this amount of drugs in one place. She dropped the bags of chicken on the kitchen table defiantly. Smooth looked at her as if she grew two heads, "Bitch, don't be slamming shit in my fucking kitchen."

Smiley was standing over the stove slowing stirring cocaine in a pot of boiling water. He began laughing before saying, "I told you, Smooth. She getting out of hand. You're growing soft on her."

Venomously, Precious looked at Smiley. She hated him as much as, if not more, than she despised Smooth.

"See, bitch, you got simple mothafuckas thinking I'm getting soft and shit."

Smooth reached for Precious' arm, but she pulled away. "I'm not a bitch, my fucking name is not Bitch." Precious had had enough.

She attempted to walk past him, but in blinding speed he grabbed her by the throat and slammed her up against the kitchen wall.

"Bitch, your name is whatever I make it." Smooth's grip was rock solid and with very little effort he was squeezing the air out of her windpipe.

"Don't get shit twisted, bitch. I don't give a fuck about you or that fucking baby in your stomach. I'll bury you both and start the fuck all over." Like a rabid dog, Smooth's face was contorted into a mask of insanity. He was frothing at the mouth, spittle leaping from his lips landing on her face like raindrops. "Do you hear me, BITCH?"

Precious could barely breathe. All she could do was nod her head in understanding and hope it would be enough to calm him down. With a shove, he threw her out of the kitchen and kicked her in the ass for final measures.

Precious' mind was made up, now. Her game plan was set and she would not wither from it when the opportunity presented itself.

As she walked in the bathroom, she heard Smiley's warning to Smooth. "Man, you should go get those guns out of the bedroom and bring all of them into the kitchen. That bitch had that sneaky look in her eyes."

Smooth dismissed the notion with a wave. "The bitch knows better. She gonna go sit her ass down in the living room and watch the fucking *Honeymooners*. Stupid bitch can learn a lot from Alice."

That 'learn a lot from Alice' comment tickled Smiley to his core. He began laughing hysterically, annoying Precious even more before finally conceding. "Aight man, you the boss..."

Smiley went back to his measured stirring. Smooth began rummaging through the bags of chicken looking for his dark meat.

"Bitch, where the fuck is the dark meat at? All I see is white meat. Bitch, you hear me talking to you?"

Smooth was yelling at Precious, but received no response. Her ignoring him enraged him. He stormed out of the kitchen *determined to discipline her once again when, suddenly, he was struck in the chest with a deafening punch. In the split second it took for Smooth to realize he was helplessly falling, Precious was moving past him and into the kitchen. Smiley was moving towards the sound of the gunshot, perhaps thinking Smooth had finally flipped his wig completely. The first bullet struck him in the arm as Precious fired wildly. Unfortunately for him, it was his shooting arm and his ability to draw his gun with his other arm was an unnatural motion that required thought and not instinct.*

Perhaps instinct would've saved his life because Precious paused firing long enough to utter the words she dreamt of saying for so long: "Smile now you piece of shit. This is for Kay-Kay." Then she squeezed the trigger twice, ending Smiley's life.

Quickly, she turned back to deal with Smooth. He was on his hands and knees attempting to rise. He looked at her with pleading eyes, but all he saw in hers was an unshakable resolve.

Slowly, she walked up to Smooth and placed the barrel of the gun at the very center of his forehead. With all the strength he could muster, he reached up and grabbed her leg.

"Precious. Please," he began coughing violently, blood pouring from his mouth. "Please, Precious, I'll give you anything you want. We can make this right, baby. I know where we can dump the body." Smooth's pleas fell on deaf ears. "Not like this, Precious. Please..."

"That's where you fucked up. My name ain't Precious. It's 'Bitch,' remember?"

"What about our baby?" Smooth attempted to appeal to her maternal instincts.

"Nigga this is Kay-Kay's baby, you dumb fuck." The final insult and acceptance of Precious' masterful endgame registered in Smooth's eyes right before she pulled the trigger, making sure a Smooth resurrection was impossible.

Meticulously, she began the process of cleaning the apartment as thoroughly as possible. She needed to make sure she left no evidence behind that would one day lead back to her. She took everything of value in that house. The eight kilos of cooked up cocaine, the seven guns, the jewelry that both Smooth and Smiley wore and the 17,000 dollars in cash that she found in the pockets of Smooth and Smiley. Precious knew she had a few days before the streets would start talking and people would begin adding shit up. She knew she had to leave, and her biggest hurdle would be getting her mother to agree to go with her. But now she had some incentives and she would start with those.

Chapter 12: forged in the fires of despair

Kay-Kay

1993

Alicia's older sister, Charlotte, and her brother-in-law, Zach, lived in a luxurious one-bedroom condo in Queens. Zach was a hardworking industrious chap with a proclivity for poker. He was by all accounts a good husband to Charlotte with the exception of the days when he would stay out all night gambling. He usually came back flat broke, but the few times that he did return a winner he wouldn't hesitate to wine and dine his wife the way a queen was supposed to be treated.

Whenever I hung around him at their family functions, he always tried to impress me with the tough guy talk. You know the kind of tough guy who wants you to believe that he's really a loose cannon and has managed to control the cannon from exploding his entire life. I mean, this guy never even jumped the turnstyle. But let him tell it, if he had to use the train he would just walk through the fucking gate and not care who saw him. His tough talk always provided much needed comic relief for me, so I egged him on as much as I could without tipping him to the fact that the joke was on him.

One day Alicia asked that I speak to Zach regarding an incident he had the night before. Apparently, he got into an altercation with some kat at a poker spot in Queens. Zach went home with a swollen eye and split bottom lip. According to Alicia, this same kat accused Zach of cheating a few months prior and smacked the taste buds out of Zach in front of the gambling spot. When I say 'taste buds,' I mean it literally. After getting pimp slapped, Zach went home and told his wife he had difficulty tasting anything. The kat, whose name was Lester if my memory serves me correctly, also robbed Zach of all his winnings that night. But Zach had had enough and was talking himself into retaliation. Alicia and her sister wanted me to talk him down. I agreed to do it only because I knew Zach wasn't built for such conflict—a reality Lester knew as well.

Alicia and I arrived at Zach and Charlotte's place around 7 p.m. the following evening. The overpowering scent of ganja seemed to always be embedded in the walls. Charlotte wasn't a gambler. She was a smoker. Her laid back demeanor was the result of her daily inhalation of cannabis. After a delicious turkey lasagna Charlotte made and small talk about medical school by Alicia, Zach and I stepped out onto their terrace and got down to business.

I listened as Zach relived his humiliation. Lester was a bully who saw Zach as the herb. The more he spoke, the angrier he became. In no time, tears of revenge were rolling down his cheek. Finally he asked, "Did you bring what I asked you for?"

"I did," I responded without moving a muscle. Wiping his tears away with the back of his hand he asked, "How much do I owe you, bro?"

"Nah bro, you don't owe me anything except to hear me out."

"Kay-Kay, if you trying to talk me out of it, it's a waste of time. I know you wouldn't allow a mothafucka to chump you and get away with it, so why should I?" Zach was correct. I would never accept that type of a violation, but Zach and I were two totally different people. He was a civilian, a railroad conductor, an upright citizen who always played by the rules. He was a husband and one day would make a great father because he was mindful and committed. Outside of his gambling habit, he was a man with very few blemishes.

So yeah, we were different and I needed him to listen. "I agree that this dude Lester violated, I wouldn't insult your intelligence and tell you otherwise. But I believe that if I go talk with him, he'll see the light and back off."

"Kay, I've never been a sucker and to have you go fight my battles for me would just..."

I interrupted, raising my hand. "You're getting this all wrong. I'm not fighting a battle for you. I'm dealing with this shit so that you won't have to. I know you ain't a sucker. I know you get busy." I was stroking his ego trying to calm him down before he made a fatal mistake. "The problem is that this dude Lester doesn't know your pedigree, so all I need to do is let him know how official you are and that should do it. Simple shit. Not complicated at all. You said he's a barber? Barbers typically can't afford drama due to their stationary position. They can't afford to have beef and still make money. So this should be an easy sell for me, bro, trust me. I can squash this."

Zach was staring at the ceiling studying the roof's cracks and crevices. "What about Charlotte? If I let you handle this how would she look at me?" Here, he was 100 percent correct and I had told Alicia those exact words the night before. He continued, "I don't know if you know, but a few months ago I had an altercation with Lester and he smacked me so fucking hard I couldn't taste anything for a whole fucking day." It took everything in my power to keep a straight face and it took everything in his power to not break down.

I understood. He felt utterly violated and his back was against the wall. In my heart, I wanted to tell him how best to handle the chump, but my mind told me Zach couldn't stand the repercussions if they came. So I gave him the disclaimer before passing him what he requested from me at 2am the previous morning. "To kill someone is the greatest crime known to man, bro. The finality of murder makes it so. There's no going back to the minute or second before, and there's no giving back what you took. It's final. It's the ultimate robbery. Do you understand this, bro? Do you comprehend that your life will never be the same after you kill this clown? Realize that in killing him, you kill his family's dreams and hopes. You wound an entire family. You punish them in a way that will make it hard for them to ever fully recover. Listen to what I'm saying to you, bro. Even years after your mind figures out how to make sense of the decision, his loved ones will still wake up with broken hearts. It's a haunting that never goes away for them. Are you prepared for this? If I put this hammer in your hand, are you prepared for all the consequences that will accompany your actions?" Like a limousine partition raising unexpectedly, the glaze in Zach's eyes told me that the driver was no longer listening to my directions.

"Yeah man, I am. I don't give a fuck. I'm tired of niggas thinking I'm a joke, a clown or something. Someone they can play with. I'm a mothafucking man, Kay, not a clown!"

"Sitting in prison for the rest of your life is perhaps the most clownish shit I can think of." I responded in one last attempt to steer his thinking back my way.

"So you're saying you never killed anyone, Kay?"

What kind of a meatball question was this? Fuck were we playing, truth or dare? Gangstas don't kiss and tell, especially not about actions where no statutes of limitations exist. So I answered in the only logical way, "Of course not, blood. Whatever you heard in the streets about me is grossly exaggerated. I abhor murder and that's exactly why I'm taking the time to talk to you."

"Yeah, Kay. I appreciate it. But my mind's made up."

I shook my head in resignation. I had a feeling my words would fall on deaf ears even before I uttered them. It was a familiar routine to witness—someone talking himself into doing something that wasn't in him to do. His decision was a grave and unfortunate one. I passed him the Roscoe and walked back into the home and sanctuary he seemed prepared to forfeit.

Chapter 13: a secret kept, a secret revealed

Kay-Kay
1993

The weeks leading up to the caper were full of planning and preparations. We all knew what was at stake and understood that the margin of error was miniscule. I wasn't certain about the others, but for me this was a do or die move. When I wasn't strategizing with them, I was putting my affairs in order. If I didn't come out alive, I didn't want my Moms and Alicia trying to figure out their next move. Alicia sensed the slight shift in my mood and questioned me on it one night at the dinner table.

"Kameek, what's going on with you? You haven't been yourself lately."

"What you mean?" I challenged.

"Come on, baby, don't play games. This is me. I know when you're up to no good."

I smiled at her keen observation. "Alicia, when am I *not* up to no good? I'm always into something." We both began laughing.

"Kameek, you know what I'm talking about. Don't play games. You've been acting real agitated lately. Usually when you're like this, you have something serious on your mind." She was correct and we both knew it.

I didn't want to lie to her, but I had no choice. For her safety, the less she knew, the better. If something went wrong, and the repercussions led to our doorstep, her denials had to be believable.

"Baby, ain't nothing wrong. Ain't nothin' up."

Not only did she know I was lying, she knew I knew she knew I was lying. A sigh of resignation escaped her lips; ripe tears born from my lie welled up in her eyes.

"You know, Kameek, I'm really beginning to wonder if anyone, or their feelings, matter to you."

"Oh brother, here we go!" I quipped.

"Yeah here we go. All you think about is yourself. You're so fucking selfish."

Here we go with this selfish shit, I thought. "You've been hanging around my Moms too much. I see I'm gonna have to start regulating those visits."

"Fuck you!" she yelled. "Everything is a joke with you. It won't be so funny when we have to identify your body."

"Shit no one told you? I'm gonna live forever. I'll ID your body before you do mine."

"Fuck you, Kameek." She was becoming hysterical.

"No, fuck you," I yelled back. "Don't start acting brand new on me now. What happened to 'until the wheels fall off'?"

"Don't run that line on me. There still has to be trust."

"Oh, so you don't trust me now?"

"Trust you? I don't even know you. I only know what you show me, and you don't show me much, but secrets and lies." Alicia was walking away from the table headed toward the bedroom. I knew what that meant—the couch was my bed for the night.

"I'm sorry to hear that," I yelled, refusing to let her get the last word in.

"No," she yelled back. "You're just sorry."

The next morning, I awoke to the sound of my front door slamming. Quickly, I jumped off the couch and ran to my living room window, overlooking the driveway. Alicia was already pulling her car out of the driveway. The nerve of this broad, I thought. We were living in a townhouse in Jersey overlooking the Manhattan skyline and she was driving a $95,000 car—all due to my secrets and lies—and yet she couldn't trust me? Couldn't understand me? She had no problem taking my money and my gifts.

Alicia

Alicia spoke with Ma Barnes with worry and trepidation tickling her vocal chords. She wasn't sure of the role she should be playing in supporting her man. "I ask very little, if anything, about his day to day occupation."

"Why is that? Are you afraid of the answers?" Ma Barnes asked. She always wondered about Alicia, and whether or not Alicia was just down for the ride until the wheels fell off or the crash.

Finally, Alicia was giving her a glimpse into her thinking. "I'm not afraid of the answers because I already accepted his choice."

"His choice or who he is?" Ma Barnes asked. Alicia shook her head dismissively as she gazed at a fourth-grade graduation picture of Kay-Kay. It was encased in a gold frame that sat on the mantelpiece of Ma Barnes' fireplace. In a home fully bought and furnished by Kay-Kay. As reluctant as his mother seemed to be when he bought her the house, she took the gift and many more with very little hesitation. All the while making him feel guilty for his occupation. Alicia tried not to judge. How could she? She would have to then condemn herself for the same crime of selfishness.

"With Kameek, it's not who he is. It's his choice. He believes that this is the only way. That there is an end to the means and that if he does it right, the end will be realized."

Ma Barnes nodded her head in understanding, "That's my son for you. Always justifying his actions." Alicia chuckled at their obvious shared truth.

"I've watched him debate with JB on numerous occasions and there are times when I swear I see consideration for Kameek's philosophy in JB's eyes," Alicia added.

The notion that the bad seed could possibly corrupt the good seed made Ma Barnes uneasy. So she gave no response to Alicia's observation. Instead she inquired, "So what's bothering you, my love?"

"I'm not sure. I guess I'm trying to figure out how to get him out of that life completely without karma destroying him. I worry for him, and I literally can't go to sleep fully until he walks in that door. I'm so afraid for him, but I don't show it because to show it is to make him worry about me. And if he's worried about me, it may make him miss something in the streets that he can't afford to miss."

"So you suffer in silence." Ma Barnes' voice echoed from a corridor of empathy.

"The other day, he walked in on me crying. When he asked me why I was crying, I told him it was because school was hard. But that was only a part of the truth, a small part. I was crying—like I do most long nights—because I'm afraid for him. I'm afraid of one day getting a dreadful call. I tell him that I don't want a baby until we're married, but that's only part of the truth—a small part. The truth is that I don't want to bring a fatherless child into a world ruled by fathers."

Unconsciously, Ma Barnes closed her eyes. It was the only way she could look at the naked truth of her own pain. "I never told you about their dad, did I?"

Alicia shook her head before adding, "You've never even mentioned his existence. I just figured their birth was an immaculate conception."

Ma Barnes found the well-timed and much-needed humor. She was about to open a vault she had kept shut. Its contents held no value to her survival. But perhaps it would provide a historical framework for Alicia to understand her son. "Josiah, their father, was a very resourceful man. He could build or fix anything with his hands. Anything. He was a stonemason by profession, but a jack of all trades by nature. I loved that man to my core and I've never met another who ignited my womanhood the way he did. But he had a love greater than me. He loved the next hustle, the next opportunity, the next chance at making it rich. One day, he came home with $4500 in hard cash. This was in '77, a few days before The Blackout, and he decided we should go on a family vacation. Did Kameek ever tell you about the vacation?"

"Nope. Kameek never mentions his father, ever."

"They had so much fun on that vacation. We went to Disney World in Orlando by car, and laughed and joked the entire time. We were in Florida when the blackout hit New York and we were grateful for escaping that madness. But the $4500, I believe, and I may be wrong, was the price of our family's happiness. When I asked Josiah where the money came from, he told me that it was from stonework he did for a mansion out in Staten Island. He was positive the home belonged to a mafia guy, but wouldn't elaborate on why he thought that or why they would let someone outside of their community do the work for them. I didn't know much about the mafia, so I didn't know the right questions to ask.

As soon as we got back from vacation, Josiah quit the stonemason job and began doing odds-and-ends jobs (his words, not mine) for his Italian boss. At the time, we were living in a run down flat on Herkimer and Kingston. In no time, he had moved us to a spacious two-bedroom on Flatbush. We were the only Black family in our building and one of only four on the entire block. We thought, or at least I thought, that we would be better off living in that neighborhood. But it was hard. The people were unwelcoming and Josiah came home less and less. About a year later, a good friend of his named William was found floating in the Hudson River. Josiah was completely spooked. He wouldn't talk about what spooked him, except to say that it could've been him and not Willie. He was so scared that he made me scared. Every time he came home late I worried. I'm sure not to the degree you're worrying, but I worried nonetheless. I knew just from observation that his fears were all tied to that mobster he mentioned doing work for. I suspect that the odds-and-ends jobs he was doing were illegal, and something, or a sequence of some things, went wrong. He still went out to work, but I could see that the work had become a form of slavery. The money slowed up, but his hours of work didn't. It was as if he was working to pay off a debt.

This is all speculation. I've had years to try to piece things together. I believed for a time that it was another woman and he was paying for two households, but now I really don't know about that. One night, I awoke to something I could only describe as a chill. I looked around and noticed Josiah was no longer in bed. I thought nothing of it and went back to sleep. The next morning was when I realized he was gone. It wasn't until two days later that I found the letter he left under a bra in my draw. The letter was short, and I think the brevity of his words hurt more than the fact that he didn't have the courage to say them to me directly. In the letter, he claimed that I was the only love of his life, but he was choosing to walk away on his terms before his departure was forced to be more permanent."

Ma Barnes' voice grew solemn and regretful. "Every thought you could imagine ran through my mind. Was it another woman? Was it another man? You name it, I thought it. But over time, I've grown to believe that it had something to do with Willie's death and the mobster he got involved with. I think he owed them money and perhaps we were the collateral. I believe this because about a week after he left, a white guy with one of those Bay Ridge Italian accents stopped me on the street asking me about Josiah. I told him that I didn't know where he was and didn't care. I told him when he finds him to tell him to go to hell. After that, on at least two occasions, I thought I saw men watching me from a blue Cadillac. But they never approached again. They just watched. I say all of this to say that I never spoke about this with Kameek. In the beginning, I thought Josiah would work whatever it was out and return to his family. But he never did. And I went from telling Kameek his father was visiting a sick aunt, to 'your dad isn't coming back home.' I wrestled with telling him my suspicion because Kameek, even as a young boy, was the type that would go looking for the mobsters. His anger and stubbornness began surfacing shortly after Josiah left."

"Were they close?" Alicia asked truly intrigued by the story.

"They were a great deal more close than what Kameek will ever admit. Or he may have even blocked it out of his recollection. Josiah doted over both of them, but he always got a real kick out of Kameek's daring nature. His nickname for Kameek was Knievel, as in Evel Knievel, the stuntman. But why now? Why do I share this history with you now?"

Alicia shrugged in confusion and sadness. She was thinking about the two little boys who were abandoned by their champion for no reason. At least there was no reason in their minds. She thought about the two little boys who awaited their champion's return, and the fact that he never found them important enough to do so, or at least that's what they felt. The lump in her throat promised that if she spoke, her tears would betray her. So she kept her mouth shut and remained an ear.

"I told you all of this painful stuff, my stuff, Jamal and Kameek's stuff, because it has unknowingly become your stuff. So, welcome to the family." The smile of affection that Ma Barnes presented to Alicia eased the jumpy lump in her throat a little. "I also told you this for you to understand that their father's abandonment is the source of both Kameek and JB's pain. They both mask the wound differently. One disguises it with the heart, the other disguises it with the head. I'm their mother, and there have been times when I can't tell them apart. But this I know, if you love him, you have to understand the worst thing that could ever happen to Kameek is not prison or death. It's being abandoned by another love he adores and holds dear. If you decide to let go, let him know why." The tears between Alicia and Ma Barnes began to swell, until like Chilean nuns sworn to silence in the face of an inquisition, these quiet tears fell.

"I'm not going anywhere, Ma. I swear. I love your son with all my heart and soul. And I'm not sure how, but we'll make it out together." She hugged her mother-in-law tight and they both held each other for a spell of time long enough to give each other some strength for the task at hand.

Kay-Kay
1993

As the days drew near to the impending caper, our practice intensified. We were growing accustomed to each other's patterns and responses and never once did any of us show up late for rehearsal. Ace and Reece wanted to make sure we were controlling all that we could control. Murphy's Law was an inevitable factor, but with the right preparation, we could still come out on top. June, the cross-dresser, kept the exercises hilarious with his adventurous stories. Every day he would start off a story with, "Ahh shit! This reminds me of the time..." I even asked him about the cross-dressing rumors, even though I knew it was true.

"Yeah, Kay, there's nothing like lace slips and come-fuck-me seven-inch pumps to do top notch reconnaissance. People never suspect a drag for the lineup. Feel me? Ahh shit! Which reminds me of the time when Papa Doc tried hiring me to follow your trail and see where it led." He said it so nonchalantly that it took me a second to fully grasp the implications. Papa Doc was apparently a lot closer to striking first than I initially thought.

"Really? So what happened?"

"Well, I took the job, but never actually had any intention of fulfilling it. I knew that if I would've made an excuse and refused, he would've just found someone else whose allegiance to the Old God wasn't resolute."

Immediately, I understood what June was saying. He was loyal to me because he was loyal to the Old God. Therefore, by taking the assignment from Papa Doc, he had awarded me the time I needed to strike first.

"Damn, you learn something new every day, bro. Word? Thanks for stalling him."

June waived my thanks away. "I knew you would get him, Kay. Papa Doc had grown too comfortable. The nigga started walking around in the streets wearing slippers. Gucci or not, *slippers*, Kay? You gotta be kidding? Come on, man. He didn't deserve to wear that crown any longer, if ever."

I always respected June, but from that day forth, I had a more profound respect for him. In prison, our association was minimal and mostly on the workout court with the Old God acting as the instructor for us both. This was the first time I actually got to gauge his understanding of how this game we played really worked.

Chapter 13 ½ : the poet

1993

The man with the brim hat calmly walked up the six flights of stairs until he reached the third floor. Slowly, he scanned the hallway until he spotted the door he was looking for. Apartment 3D sat the furthest away from the stairwell, tucked into an alcove. He walked to the door and began studying the locks. There were three locks in all, and by the looks of them, they were all inferior brands. He almost grew annoyed with the stupidity of the occupants inside the home. The apartment belonged to his target's mistress.

The target was making money hand over fist, but obviously didn't care to put his mistress in a better situation or location. The man with the brim hat knew that the mistress meant more to the target than his actual wife. The evidence being that the mistress' apartment was where the target spent most of his time when he wasn't in the streets pushing his product.

Before leaving, he placed his ear to the door, listening for signs of life and wondering if the mistress had any kids who lived there. The man with the brim hat had one objective, and that was to take out his target, not to leave casualties of war behind traumatized and scarred for life. He listened at the door, but heard nothing—not a sound, not a peep. And so, just as he had entered the building, he calmly exited. The mistress' apartment would be the theater of war, the arena in which the first target would be eliminated.

Chapter 14: date with fate

Kay-Kay
1993

Alicia was enrolled in Columbia University Medical School. I was picking her up, and then heading to Paco's, a Spanish cuisine restaurant in Yonkers. It was becoming more and more difficult to go places with Alicia without someone spotting me. Most were friendly faces, but still, I didn't want Alicia to eventually become a target. So, in-the-cut spots in Yonkers and Connecticut became our night-out retreats. I was driving my 1993 500E Benz when I felt the vibration on my hip. The beep turned out to be a beckon from Handbone.

Parked in front of Alicia's school 15 minutes early, I had time to walk to a payphone across the street and give Handbone a ring.

"I have some good news," he announced triumphantly.

"I'm all ears, brother."

"We may have a line on that supply train." Handbone spoke magic words to my ears.

Excited, I attempted to remain calm. "How so?"

"Well, Bo Sims swears the connect is a young girl out of Newark named Peaches."

A. C. Clayton

The name Peaches was vaguely familiar to me. "I heard that name before," I replied still trying to remember from where.

Handbone filled in the blanks. "That's the chick who went up against those Philly boys, Abdul and his crew."

"That's right. I remember hearing about that. That wasn't too long ago. The Feds swooped in and snatched everyone left alive, right?"

"Wrong, they swooped in and snatched Abdul and his crew while Peaches and her team vanished."

"Oh wow," was my most insightful response.

"Yeah, I'm thinking the same thing. Either she was and still is working with the Feds or she's a pretty worthy adversary." Handbone articulated my thoughts exactly.

"What makes Bo Sims think this?" I asked.

Bo Sims was an old timer out of the Bronx who owned and operated a handful of gambling spots throughout the city. He was an old friend of Handbone and so our shakedown was pretty minimal. Bo Sims didn't mind paying his monthly tribute; according to him, there's always been a price for doing business. When he first started, it was the Italians he had to pay. And to him, they were beyond disrespectful.

"Well, Bo's nephew Malik knew her from Newark. He's hustling down in Maryland now and claims to be the one who plugged her in with a Puerto Rican supplier up there in the

Bronx. And get this, he claims she was originally from Brooklyn and moved out to Newark a few years back."

"Really?" There was something I wasn't putting my finger on and it kept nagging at me. Aight, so let Bo Sims know we need to sit down with his nephew ASAP."

"I'm already on it, Chief. Bo said his nephew would be back in a week. We could meet him at Bo's clubhouse on Webster Ave."

"Ok, so a week it is then." I paused before completing my thought. "You know, I'm getting this feeling that this could get ugly, like The Three Little Pigs ugly." I was talking about the severed heads of my enemies, the coup d'état that placed me at the top of the food chain.

"I know," Handbone replied.

The clubhouse was Bo Sims' only legit business—his tax justification that kept Uncle Sam off his back. It sat in the middle of Webster Avenue, tucked adjacent to an auto repair spot and a fried chicken joint. There were no signs in front of Bo's clubhouse. It was an unwelcoming place to the casual customers and curious pedestrians. It was a members-only club, where stand-up street guys could be at home amongst their peers, where alcohol and pool were the only past time besides gossip. Yeah, men gossip, too. Especially street kats.

As seedy and neglected as the clubhouse's gloomy façade appeared to be, the inside of the club was anything but rundown. Plush and opulent is the description that comes to mind. The dark cherry cedar wood bar was handcrafted. The rest of the walls were paneled in a light coffee-stained cedar. The contrast naturally drew attention to the bar. There was a station for playing pool with three Olhausen pool tables that were always in use, and a lounge area where comfortable recliners and chairs were set up for relaxation.

There was also a resident barber named Will who still cut hair with scissors and a razor. During fight nights, Bo Sims would pull down the movie screen and the place would become a madhouse. On these days, he would bring local strippers in to serve tables and keep the hustlers spending money at the bar. It was a smooth set up—an idea I was flirting with in Brooklyn—but today I didn't come for that. I came to meet Malik, Bo Sims' nephew.

I arrived at Bo Sims' clubhouse about 45 minutes early, a safety precaution I acquired in prison from an old timer named Rick Martin. "I'm telling you, man, always be early, never late. The early bird springs the trap; the late bird is snared." This old vet out of East New York had sprung plenty of traps in his heyday, but he always relived the one trap that went haywire.

It was not seeing that trap that enslaved him to the Department of Corrections. "I'm telling this moron to hurry up and get under the car because the bozo might come early." Rick's explanation of his downfall was always an animated one. No one ever had a name in Rick stories, only titles like 'one of us,' 'good guy,' 'bozo,' 'moron,' and 'rat bastard.'

"You know what this moron said to me?"

"What?" I asked as if it was my first time hearing this story.

"He said, 'Chill out Rick, you know Black people are never on time!' You believe that shit?"

"Sounds like a bozo to me, Rick." Rick looked at me as if I finally got the point and then flung his hands in the air incredulously.

"Exactly! And here I am, 18 years later, wondering why I didn't blow the rat bastard's head off right then and there."

The story goes that Rick and two accomplices were lining up a moneybag. A moneybag is a person who goes into the mom-and-pop stores, and other local businesses in the neighborhood, and collects their revenue for the day or week. Afterwards, the moneybag takes the money to the banks and deposits it for the stores. The moneybag is usually someone who looks inconspicuous. They are also followed and protected by one or two gunmen whose job it is to protect the money at all cost.

These moneybag operations were initially ran strictly by the mafia, but within the last decade, more and more organizations of color began to muscle in on the action. Rick Martin made a living off of cracking the money trains—a dangerous game he played masterfully—until the day all hell broke loose. Rick found himself dodging a hail of bullets before he even fired one shot. An innocent bystander, a father of five, died in the melee. And though Rick got away, both of his accomplices got caught. One of them— to this day I don't know whether it was bozo or moron—gave Rick up. They even told on past crimes and named him as the mastermind.

They were all sentenced to 25 years to life. The one that told on Rick was found stabbed to death in his cell five years into his bid with a dead mouse stuffed in his mouth. As for Rick, he was stuck in the moment of his downfall. His lesson was timeless; he swore that nothing would've ever went wrong if they were in place on time. I took that, and a lot of other lessons from the old timer, to heart. I was determined never to be someone forced to share the lessons of my downfall in a prison yard.

Rick's lesson on timing was why I was walking through Bo Sims door so early. As usual, the place was empty when Jo-Jo and I arrived. At this point in the game, Handbone and I conducted meetings like this separately. If something were to happen to either one of us, the other's retaliation would be swift and unmerciful. Meanwhile, Jo-Jo my escort was a shoot first ask questions later soldier out of Lefrak City in Queens. I also had another car parked down the block with two more shooters on deck just in case we needed coverage to get up out of there. Their job was to make sure that Jo-Jo and I got away by whatever cost, even if we were running from the cops. For their willing sacrifice and potential occupational hazard, like firefighters, they were paid handsomely.

Bo Sims was, above all else, a smart businessman. The likelihood that he would spring a trap in his own establishment was next to non-existent, but at this stage in the game, my being early was muscle memory. Besides, blood is blood and I was coming to interrogate his nephew, or as Bo Sims put it: 'his sister's only son.' His emphasis on 'only son' was his warning to me that there was a line drawn in the sand when it came to his submission. I respected it, and would have lost respect for him had it been any other way. But I came for answers and if Bo Sims' sister's only son refused to share what he knew, my line would be drawn in the sand, as well.

Nevertheless, we walked into the den, which was unsurprisingly empty of any dead weight. Bo Sims was sitting at the bar with his enforcer Jay and a young kat around my age that I assumed to be his nephew. Bo Sims waved at me smiling, beckoning me to join him at the bar.

"Come, Kay-Kay, let's politic over here."

It was Jo-Jo's first time in the clubhouse, and I could tell by his posture that he was impressed by the layout. As we approached the three men, Bo Sims stood up from his seat and extended his hand to me. We embraced the way warriors do before Bo Sims introduced his nephew Malik. Unlike his uncle, Malik didn't respect protocol; he appeared annoyed and did not get up from the barstool.

"Kay-Kay, this is my nephew, Malik." I extended my hand first and his hesitation told me enough to know that I would have to handle him with an iron fist.

Bo Sims sensed the tension and immediately decided to intervene. "As I was telling you before Kay-Kay walked in, he just wants to know about the Peaches broad."

Malik looked at his uncle with disappointment in his eyes, perhaps seeing a side of Bo Sims he never saw before. Instead of responding, he reached for his glass of dark liquor that was resting on the counter.

I waited, watching him closely as he sipped his courage through a miniature straw. Finally, he put the cup down and I could tell he had built up enough nerve to finally speak.

Before he could, I stole his thunder. "Look nigga," I said in a deadly whisper. "I ain't come all the way to the Bronx to play games. I came for one purpose. I want to know all you know about Peaches. If you think that you are not going to cooperate, then I'm here to crush you. It's that simple, mothafucka. So you decide." Unflinchingly, I looked into his eyes.

He blinked and looked to his uncle for assistance. I suspect my words reached his heart before the liquor. As if on cue, Bo Sims spoke. "Naw Kay, my sister's only son is a team player..."

"So, let him know I hit home runs," I interrupted.

Jo-Jo backed up, ready to draw at the first sign of my bluff being called. Jay, Bo Sims' enforcer, kept his cool refusing to acknowledge Jo-Jo's gun-slinging posture.

Malik spoke for the first time, realizing that this situation was about to get out of hand. His voice cracked in resignation. "Grab a seat, Kay. I'll tell you what I know."

He told me that Peaches was originally from Brooklyn and he was unsure of the reason she ended up in Newark. His description of her fit the profile of no less than a thousand other Black women I see on any given day in NYC. His story started getting interesting when he told us, admiringly, how Peaches held her own against Abdul and his team.

According to him, Abdul was a ruthless sicko who loved seeing the fear in people's eyes more than he loved money. I knew the type well; the city was full of such psychos. Their adrenaline rush was to see people suffering at their hands. Abdul sounded like the type of formidable foe I would have enjoyed squeezing. The story of how Peaches met Abdul head-on and escaped the inferno unscathed was remarkable. I could tell that he was more than an admirer of her work. He was a loyalist. So, I listened to him in anticipation for the punch line.

"If you want, I could set up a meet between you two."

I acted surprised. "Could you?"

"Yea man, I mean I know you're a stand-up dude and she's certified as well. Before it gets ugly, why not reach an agreement? The one thing I do know about Peaches is that she love the money, not the violence."

I pretended to give Malik's proposition some thought while internally I was happier than a kid in the candy store. "Well, I love the money as well..."

"Of course you do."

"Don't cut me off."

"My bad, bad habit."

"If you can arrange a sit-down that will avoid bloodshed, I'm all for it."

He began shaking his head affirmatively. "I'm almost sure I could. Give me a day or two to contact her. Sometimes it take a minute before she responds to a beep."

"Cool."

I wrote down my beeper number on a napkin. "Here's my number. I expect to hear something in three days."

I dismissed him without a second glance. When it comes to this game, it's either play hard or get played. My arrogance was more of a bluff I prayed never got called. It was a necessary tool I used to protect others from feeling my wrath. Bo Sims and I made small talk for another half hour before Jo-Jo and I made our exit. The autumn night's crisp fresh air reenergized me.

"That worked out well," Jo-Jo said.

"Yea, too well. It sounded like a script to me."

"What you mean?" Jo-Jo asked.

"Not sure yet... feels like the hunter has become the hunted."

Jo-Jo sent the signal to our spotters, letting them know we were ready to leave when déjà vu kicked in. I was here before. I stopped dead in my tracks and began really analyzing my terrain. All was in place, yet the hairs on the back of my neck still stood at attention.

"Everything alright, Kay?" Jo-Jo already had his gun out, looking for a target.

"Yea man, put that thing away. Just a feeling, like I been here before, that's all." I patted him on the shoulder for reassurance.

"Since we're in the Bronx, we might as well head over to City Island. I'm in the mood for lobster."

"Shit. Sounds good to me, Kay."

"You treating?"

"Nah buddy, you treating."

Our laughter eased the tension, but the hunted feeling remained.

Peaches

"Did he take the bait?" Peaches inquired.

"Hook, line, and sinker," Malik responded. "It took a lot to hold my tongue with that mothafucka. He really acted like he's some Godfather or something." Malik was venting. "I mean, some real Al Pacino shit. And my punk ass uncle treats this little dude like he really is the Godfather."

Peaches listened quietly. She saw no reason to respond to Malik's opinion. He could believe what he wanted to believe. When it came to Kameek, she knew enough to know that underestimating Kameek had always proven to be a costly, and sometimes deadly, mistake for his opponents. Peaches was on the phone looking out of a second floor window overlooking Bo Sims' clubhouse.

The apartment was one of many Bo Sims owned on the block. It was the apartment that Malik used whenever he was in town. She was standing behind the curtain looking out of the window when she saw Kay-Kay exit the clubhouse. She watched as he slowly made his way to his car. She could tell by his body language that it wasn't the hook, line, and sinker Malik professed it to be. The hook and line might be in place, but the outcome was still exclusively in the hands of fate.

"So, when does he expect to hear from you?" she asked.

"Well, the Godfather gave me three days to get back at him."

"Great, we'll call him in four days to arrange a sit down," Peaches nervously ran her fingers through her hair. "See, Malik, I told you this would be the easiest $10,000 you ever earned."

"Yea, it was definitely a piece of cake. Look, I'm raising up out of NY tonight. You sure you don't want to hang out?"

"Yea I'm sure. Maybe next time." Peaches' mind was on anything but socializing. She had less than a week to prepare for a showdown that was long in the making. She sighed a tired sigh, realizing that her life for the past seven years had been nothing but a series of showdowns.

Peaches' strategy for picking her spots to appear then disappear was affecting her bottom line. Her money was dwindling due to her inconsistent appearances. Hustlers running out of product would beep her and she wouldn't respond for days on end. When she did respond, she was vague as to whether or not she could supply them. And if agreed to, vague as to when and where. Within weeks, her beeper stopped beeping and she found herself sitting on drugs she couldn't get rid of.

She told herself that this setback would only be temporary, that as soon as she dealt with Abdul and his crew she would be right back in the swing of things. But as the days wore on and she had more time to really reflect, she realized that no-matter how the situation with Abdul ended, it was time for her to raise up out of Newark altogether. Her welcome was worn; only death or incarceration was the final destination of this yellow brick road. So it was time to change the scenery and though she contemplated other towns and cities, New York City was the home of her exile. Her return felt stronger than a calling; it was her destiny.

Meanwhile, Abdul made it his business to let his presence be known. He would say to all spectators, especially the ones he suspected of secretly communicating with Peaches, that he was the only one not ducking and hiding. "This can't be a war if one side is ready to fight and the other side chooses to run. The bitch can't be making no money if all she does is run!"

Of course Peaches knew that Abdul was trying to bait her into making a mistake, of striking before she was ready. Perhaps Abdul was more experienced when it came to waging war, but common sense was common sense. She knew she wouldn't strike until it was the right time to do so.

Though Peaches never showed any signs of fear or doubt to her team, the truth was she was petrified. The thought of being gunned down, or worse, kidnapped and tortured, was a frightening possibility to envision. Who would take care of her family if she were gone? What would happen to Kameek Jr.? Would he become an orphan, never knowing his origin, his parents, or even how much he was loved? It was time to leave Newark behind and let her ego go. Too much was at stake, too many precious lives for her to gamble with. Abdul would meet his maker, but Peaches would opt not to be his escort.

Yet the silver coin of fate fell in favor of a showdown. No sooner than Peaches had made the decision to bow out gracefully, or cowardly based on one's perspective, did her pager vibrate. It had been resting on her vanity. Something in her gut told her that if she picked it up, there would be no turning back. So she studied *it carefully for a very long time, weighing her commitments and options.*

She picked it up, and immediately noticed that the pager felt heavier than it ever had before. It was delivering a message that would add to her burdens. Peaches seemed to feel the enormity of the mission in the weight of the pager.

Seven one two was Roc's emergency code, a code he'd never used until today. She immediately called the number that appeared on the pager. It was a payphone number and Roc answered on the first ring. "Just giving you a heads up, it's about to go down."

"What's happening?" Peaches inquired.

"Lil' Boo is in a jam. He's over in Fairmount visiting some broad and Abdul and his crew are camped outside waiting on him. They're actually a block away, out of sight, but one of the broad's friends spotted them as she walked by and knew exactly who they were and why they're there. You know Lil' Boo. He's ready to run out and get to firing, but I told him we're on our way. I got the team loading up and this shit ends, today." Roc spoke with a confident finality.

Her fear and trepidation dissolved and all she could think of was being present on the war front. "Roc, where's Lil' Boo at?"

Roc hesitated, considering if he should tell her and put her in harm's way, or refuse her and feel her wrath later. It was Peaches who Abdul attempted to kidnap and if she was a dude thinking about revenge, Roc would've never hesitated with the information. "He's on South 11th Street between South Orange and 13th Avenue."

"Ok. Wait for me. I'll meet you over on Central and we can catch these suckers by surprise."

It took Peaches approximately 45 minutes to meet up with Roc and the rest of their seven-man crew. They were trained killers, mercenaries, armed with some serious hardware, whose entire objective was to earn their keep. Their loyalty belonged to the bank that was funding them, and this particular bank happened to be Peaches.

Five cars crept through the narrow dilapidated streets of Newark, each car full of occupants who understood their shake. They sat in silence meditating on the task at hand. About four blocks away, they heard the gunfire erupt. The sound of cannons and automatic weapons left no mistake that bullets were being let loose. The five cars sped up heading towards the sound of chaos and uncertainty. Abdul and his team were retreating back to their cars when Peaches pulled up. The gunfire had just stopped when Abdul spotted Peaches and her bodyguards. The surprise he presented to Peaches allowed him the advantage of aiming first and squeezing.

Luckily for Peaches and Roc, Abdul and his crew misfired by a long shot, giving Peaches and her crew the opportunity to return fire. Before the gun smoke gave way to the fresh air, an all-out shootout was underway. Cars were used as shields and clips were reloaded and relied on. Peaches' adrenaline was intoxicating. She was actually enjoying the bang out as she followed Roc from one car to the next. They were trying to get as close to Abdul as they could without being picked off. One of Abdul's men hit the ground in an unusual way and Peaches knew immediately that a hot missile had found its mark.

A whiz and then a ding hitting the wall right by her head reminded her to duck low and keep firing. Even over the gunfire, Abdul was yelling sounds that Peaches could only assume were Arabic. This was all one big game to him and that realization only strengthened her resolve that this madman had to go. Peaches' sharpshooters were closing in and another one of Abdul's men screamed before he buckled.

The shrill of sirens grew more menacing by the second—law enforcement was heading their way. Abdul leaped into the passenger side of a Chevy, all the while returning fire. The Impala took off, and Peaches and Roc knew that they missed their opportunity to end it.

Abdul's two remaining minions jumped into another Chevy and took off in their leader's direction.

"Peaches! We gotta go, NOW." Roc had her arm in a vice grip dragging her to their car. Her shooters were covering their tracks. Peaches watched as they stood over Abdul's two wounded warriors and fired the mercy shots that would ensure their cooperation of silence. This shit wasn't fun; it was real. Peaches reminded herself of that as the car carrying her in the same direction as Abdul's retreat sped off.

Within an hour, the local news chose to cover the shooting as a headline. Peaches watched, in the comfort of her home, the scenery and carnage she just left behind. Three confirmed dead, although Peaches could only recall two. Immediately the thought that perhaps an innocent bystander got caught in the crossfire made Peaches' heart fill with regret. It wasn't until hours later that Roc informed her that the third casualty was Lil' Boo. Lil' Boo had chosen not to wait for Roc, thinking that he could bang his way out of the trap. Had he waited two more minutes, he would've had a better chance of living through the day. Or perhaps, if Peaches didn't slow Roc up by 45 minutes while they waited for her, Lil' Boo would still be alive.

Peaches couldn't wait for round two to commence. She hated Abdul with a passion unparalleled, but could do nothing until he showed his face again. Unfortunately, Peaches' lust for revenge would never materialize. The Feds struck with stealth, in the middle of the night, ensnaring Abdul as he slept in his bed. His trusted grenade, the one that he had almost tossed at Peaches and her crew, sat staring at him on his nightstand as he was hogtied and carried out for the media to witness. The promise that more arrests were imminent sent Peaches in the direction of a new beginning, a new home...her home—New York City.

Chapter 15: prop hunting

Kay-Kay

1993

Knee and I were leaving a mutual friend's surprise birthday party when we ran into a peacock whose code name was Whisper. He was called this because he was better at telling on his fellow peacocks than he was at making money. If the other peacocks knew how much of a sucker he really was, they would've strung him up alive. Every time I saw him he had something to tell me...something or someone to whisper about. I realized early in this game that there was no shortage of these types of characters. They came in all shapes and sizes with grandiose nicknames and titles. These lames had no allegiance to jurisdictions. Like roaches, them mothafuckas traveled and lived everywhere.

It was Knee's first encounter with Whisper, and our running into him so unexpectedly left me no time to put Knee on about this creep. Whisper immediately began in his low conspiratorial tone. "Ahh Kay, I'm glad I ran into you, bro. I was about to beep Jo-Jo and give him a heads up..."

"Really? About what?" I interrupted. Knowing all too well that I was about to enter the Twilight Zone.

Looking around like he was 007, Whisper made sure there were no other spies in the vicinity before continuing. "I just left the gambling spot on Dean. You know, that's the new spot Joe and Goldie operate."

Of course I knew; they paid their monthly tributes, too. But I remained quiet already seeing where this was going. Whisper shared a golden morsel. "One-Eye Stan from Kingston was in there with a few others and he starts talking about being tired of paying what he calls 'punk dues', how everyone else in there should be getting tired, too."

"What was the response from everyone else?" I asked.

"Fuck the response. Is that nigga still in the spot right now?" Knee interjected.

Whisper, confused as to which question to answer first, began stuttering before finally choosing to answer my question. "Wwwwell, no one said a thing. After a while, Big Tone told Stan to shut the fuck up and roll the dice. And yeah, Stan is still there right now, losing a grip."

I had heard enough. Stan was no threat and with all the other shit on my mind he was the least of my worries. But Knee was ready to make an example.

As soon as I got rid of Whisper, Knee began. "Let's go over there right now and make an example out of this clown in front of everybody."

"Nah, we ain't doing that. If we punish everybody who has an opinion against us, we'll wipe out all our money. All those mothafuckas feel the same way Stan does. If we don't allow them an outlet to vent, then eventually they'll explode."

Knee was shaking his head as if I was talking in riddles. "Man, if you're scared to regulate, then buy a fucking dog. Just point me in the right direction and I'll handle it before the sun comes up."

Hearing Knee sound like a dog I could purchase, who only wanted to attack and bite was disappointing to my ears. I was trying to make him a partner. He just wanted to be a soldier. I shook my head dismissing the option. "Nah man, I got it. I'll deal with Stan. Trust me, big bro. It's not a priority right now. I got some really big shit lined up that's gonna change the game for better or worse for us. That's where my focus is. Trust me. This is chess, not checkers!"

Boy, was Knee vexed. He agreed with me reluctantly, so I knew that Stan had just opened up a can of worms he never intended. Stan was a drinker, the type that transforms into a gorilla when he had the right amount of liquid in him. I was pretty sure this was the case: a drunken clown trying to entertain his audience. But Knee was itching to prove his reputation true. He wanted the hood to know that he was back and any example would do. I knew that I would have to sit Knee down and rein him in if we were going to continue to win.

My preoccupation with the heist and the upcoming meet with the elusive supplier was priority and both events carried on their backs the possibility of gunplay. Both events were risky endeavors in which only stellar concentration would ensure that I saw the other side. One-Eye Stan was but a fly buzzing on the web of my construction, but Knee's desire for glory was a problem I would have to deal with if the web was to stay secure.

Chapter 16: build and destroy

Unlocking the mystery of our history,
The path to victory.

JB

Winter 1993

It started out as one of those days where everything that could go wrong did. From the water pipes at the community center exploding the day before the Kwanzaa event, to Darby, the African History professor's flight being stuck in Milwaukee. JB second-guessed his decision to put on a Kwanzaa celebration for the tenth time that day. But to cancel would be to surrender, and JB had already done enough surrendering in his life.

Lately, he found himself questioning a lot of his actions and the true motives behind them. He spent time wondering if it was all worth it. He was committed to helping a people who seemed unappreciative and, at times, resentful of his actions. He reminded himself that the work had to be done and with a steady resolve, JB stayed the course. He headed towards his meeting with the vice president of community affairs at Carver National Bank.

Carver National Bank, the largest Black-owned bank in America, had a long-standing history of making charitable contributions to improve the quality of life in the African-

American community. JB was hoping that Carver's track record would extend to his newly formed non-profit organization.

"Thank you for taking the time, Mr. Jackson, to meet with me today."

"No need for thanks, Mr. Barnes. Here at Carver, we always look for opportunities to assist our community," Mr. Jackson replied.

"I have heard a great deal about your investments in the community and wanted to speak with you today about possibly supporting a more direct and grassroots endeavor." JB spoke with confidence. He had done his research, staying up until the wee hours of the morning studying every philanthropic donation Carver ever gave.

"Mr. Barnes, this Building Young Entrepreneurs, or BYE program, you speak of is really exciting. Please, by all means, elaborate."

"Well, essentially, what I am proposing is a six-week program designed to teach teens from the ages of 13-18 about the world of business and finance. I believe that our crime problem is really an economic problem. And, in a country of unimaginable wealth, the real crime is our lack of knowledge as to how to access or tap into this wealth. What I'm proposing is that, in this endeavor, Carver takes the lead in the informational and educational department. I have the kids and space; you have the know-how and resources. By educating these kids, you are also investing in a future workforce of bankers and business leaders committed to Carver."

Mr. Jackson's sudden overly arched eyebrows were the only giveaway of interest in JB's pitch. "Please tell me more," he requested with sincerity.

For the next half an hour, JB spoke about the logistics of the program, as well as his other business investors who had already committed to the project.

"Mr. Barnes, it may be premature on my part, but I believe that this is a project we will partner with you to champion. Of course, I have to get it approved by the branch president as well as our CFO, but I can be persuasive when I need to be. And I'm going to pull out all stops." Mr. Jackson cracked a winning smile and extended his hand toward JB. It was the first time JB allowed himself to exhale. He shook Mr. Jackson's hand with vigor.

The first person JB shared the promising news with was his girlfriend, Pam. As soon as he walked out of the bank, he found a pay phone and called her at work. Not only was she his woman, she was quickly becoming his number one confidant, even surpassing his mother.

"That's great, baby. I'm so proud of you." Pam's sincere words of encouragement were heartfelt.

"Thanks, baby. I really appreciate it. Let me run. I have to go catch this bakery before it closes and make sure the cake and cupcakes will be ready for tomorrow's celebration. It's the 23rd hour and I feel like I'm behind a day," JB shared.

"JB, the Kwanzaa event will go smoothly, trust me. You have a good team of dedicated and committed people. Have faith in your efforts, baby. Have faith."

"You're right, sugar. You're right. What you doing later on?" he asked.

Pam smiled on the other end of the line. She was hoping JB would ask that very question. She wasn't sure how serious JB was with regards to their relationship, but she had fallen head over heels in love. If she could, she would spend every free moment with him.

"Well, I was thinking about making my man a nice dinner and a hot bath." She chuckled mischievously then began to purr. Her purrs stirred something uncontrollable and primitive in JB and he knew that the conversation had to end immediately.

"Uhm, okay, baby. I'll see you tonight then." Erotic images from previous nights teased his memory.

"Okay, don't keep me waiting." Pam ended the phone call with another purr and JB closed his eyes and envisioned the upcoming evening.

His second and third calls were to his mother and the good reverend. Both expressed their excitement, with the reverend reminding JB that it was all a part of God's divine plan. He wanted to call Kay-Kay, but thought against it at the last moment. Nine times out of 10, Kay-Kay was somewhere in the streets corrupting the very souls that JB was committed to saving.

The Kwanzaa celebration went well. People from all ages and walks of life attended. However, JB was not surprised by the lack of Black men in attendance. The overwhelming majority were women and children, leaving room to speculate as to the whereabouts of the missing crucible in this lopsided equation. He figured some men were home or at work, while some were locked up or in the grave. The rest of them were probably deadbeat dads, deserters of their unit. And with an insurmountable sigh, JB pushed his cynical analysis to the side and focused on the celebration at hand. Kwanzaa was a celebration of culture, of family, and a renewal of commitments. The many beautiful faces in attendance spoke to the resilient spirit of his community.

A. C. Clayton

Professor Javier Medina from Hunter College's African History department took the place of Professor Darby as the guest speaker for the event. He gave a brief history of the origins of Kwanzaa and then spoke on the need to incorporate the seven principles into the daily routines of the listening audience's lives. It was a masterful speech, full of witty analogies and metaphors. Professor Javier was a Puerto Rican man who, in his own words, identified with "his raped great grandmother and not her rapist."

JB was glad that he did not give in to his fears of the event being a bust. He was really close to cancelling it entirely the day before. But now, he watched the kids relish in their face paints and games, while the adults seemed happy off of good food and good vibes. In the sea of faces, he searched to spot one. Pam was on the other side of the gym talking to a well-dressed couple. He decided to be nosey and began walking towards her. The closer he got, the couple's features grew more distinct. He began to laugh when he saw that the couple was none other than Kay-Kay and Alicia. He was not surprised to see Alicia, but Kay-Kay was an entirely different story.

He embraced Alicia affectionately before turning his full attention to his younger brother.

"Glad you could make it, lil' bro. I missed your face," JB said.

Kay-Kay smiled. "Well, I wanted to see what my big brother was devoting all his time to, and like I just told Pam, I'm definitely impressed." JB's smile illuminated the entire gym after hearing his brother's compliment.

Alicia jumped in the discussion. "Pam, JB, you guys definitely did a wonderful job. The decorations aren't over the top, the food is great, the energy is..." She paused searching for the right word.

"Electric," Kay-Kay chimed in with a smile.

"Thank you, Kameek, for finishing my sentence for me. You know, JB, your brother has an annoying habit of doing that." They all began laughing, breaking whatever tension still lingered between them. They were two couples enjoying each other's company for however brief the truce would last.

For the rest of the night, they participated in the festivities together. Kay-Kay kept looking over at the section where the face painting was going on with the kids. Alicia knew what was going through his mind. Kay-Kay was ready to be a father. They spoke often about his desire, but Alicia would not stop taking the pill until she was married and held the title Mrs. Barnes. Since Kay-Kay never addressed getting married, except for the time he proposed to her in the Bahamas, Alicia pushed motherhood out of her mind.

"I will be a wife before I become a mother," was always her resolute response to him.

Almost as if on cue, Pam's "So, when are you guys going to tie the knot?" pierced the solitude of both Alicia's and Kay-Kay's thoughts.

Dramatically, Alicia swiveled her head to look directly at Kay-Kay, as if to say 'ask him.' Kay-Kay took the inquiry in stride; he had become a master at not letting unexpected occurrences rattle him.

Before Kay-Kay could respond with his rehearsed line, JB interjected, "Baby, they'll do it when the time is right."

"Oh, here you go, JB. Coming to your brother's rescue." Alicia's accusation was part serious and part playful. JB pretended to be offended.

Kay-Kay slid back in the conversation. "Actually, Pam, I'm thinking about some time early next year. I want to do something cozy and quaint, just family, you know?"

Alicia playfully rolled her eyes. She had heard that line a million times before and it sounded so rehearsed.

JB followed up with the ultimate conversation changer. "So, how 'bout those Mets?" Once again the laughter erupted between them.

"You're changing the subject like I'm going to ask you when you're going to ask for my hand in marriage," Pam said teasingly.

"Marriage." JB grabbed hold of his own throat as if he was choking on a chicken bone.

Pam caught him with a playful slap to the back of his head, before declaring, "You know you love me."

A gamble she felt, she had to take. She needed to know whether she was the only one drowning in such an intense emotion. JB stopped his theatrics long enough to look Pam deeply in her eyes. "I do, baby."

"You do what?" she asked, wanting clarity.

As if caught with his hand in the cookie jar, JB sheepishly repeated himself.

"I do... love you. In fact, I'm in awe of you."

"Aww," Alicia teased.

"Ahh no, big bro. You know you done committed yourself to figuring out corny lines to say from here on out, right?"

JB's eyes were trained on his prize. Kay-Kay's cynicism appeared to be completely ignored as Pam reached up with a seemingly sacred purpose and gently rub his face. It was a magic moment where time stood still, and Alicia and Kay-Kay were blessed to be spectators. JB knew he had found the woman of his dreams.

At 4'11, Pam was the tiniest woman JB had ever dated. Her petite yet well-proportioned frame complemented her height perfectly. Symmetrically a masterpiece in his eyes, her smooth maple syrup complexion tasted as good as it looked. When asked about her, JB spoke briefly on her physical beauty before speaking on the sexiest part of her. For him, her mind and spirit were hypnotic forces. When in her presence, he was drawn inextricably toward her and could focus on nothing else but her. He compared her presence to that of a fountain of clear cool water that never overflowed or stopped, inviting the worthy to drink and savor her purity.

Pam was a native of Barbados who moved to NYC with her parents at the age of eight. Her parents had been married for 25 years and their genuine happiness together was still a love to be admired. Pam bragged about her father as being the greatest man she ever knew. He was loving and genuine to her and her mother. He had been a nurturer, provider, friend, and teacher to Pam every waking day of her life. JB knew that to win Pam completely over, he had to walk the path of a giant or get lost in the titan's shadow.

Chapter 17: baboons talk

In the jungle, even the baboons grow silent when the lion roars.
-O.G. Bible

Kay-Kay
1993

I must admit, I was taken aback when I walked into the Kwanzaa event with Alicia. In the days leading up to the event, I found myself being reminded insistently about it. It was made clear that if I skipped out on this, there would be no peace in my home for at least a week. So to keep the peace, I went. To my surprise, the event went smoothly and without drama. I actually left knowing a great deal more than I had about Kwanzaa and its origins.

The next morning, while sitting inside of Ruben's Diner in Flatbush, I began telling Handbone and my man Kush about the event and all that I learned. Kush was a loudmouth Mr. Know-It-All. He came home after doing six years in prison, a scholar in all areas under the sun. I enjoyed his company when it came to just hanging out, but I refused to let him into my world in any other way. He talked too much; not about people or gossip, but just in general. He couldn't stand silence. It was like his mortal enemy.

I feel like people who enjoy talking for the sake of talking cannot be given sensitive subjects to talk about, even accidently.

Nevertheless, the discussion about Kwanzaa quickly grew heated. Kush and Ruben, the diner's owner began calling the founder of Kwanzaa, Dr. Mualana Karenga, a rat, saying that there was no reason to honor anything a rat created. I had heard this argument in prison way too often to find it anything more than entertaining. But Handbone found their position flawed.

"First off, there ain't any proof that Karenga ratted. Second off..." Handbone's words were cut short by Kush's interruption.

"What do you mean there's no proof? He admitted he ratted!"

"Never! Where did you read that Karenga admitted to ratting?" Handbone challenged.

"I can't remember the book, but I know I read it."

"So what exactly were his words? Do you recall?"

"Nah. It's been a couple a years since I read the book, but I know he admitted it."

Ruben wisely steered away from that position. "I never read that, but everything I ever heard was that he ratted."

"Okay so, let's say for a second that this is true. Should we condemn the gift?"

"Hell yeah, we should condemn it," Kush replied.

"So, somehow celebrating Kwanzaa would be like working with the police? Is that what you're saying? And that Karenga and Kwanzaa are one and the same?"

Ruben chimed in. "I just feel like it's not right, so I don't celebrate it."

"Kush, you went to jail for what?" Handbone inquired, ignoring Ruben's logic.

"Bank robbery," Kush proudly responded.

"So, you committed a crime against society. Is that not the ultimate betrayal?"

"Betrayal? I didn't rob anyone. I robbed an institution that robs people, and I'm the closest you'll ever get to meeting the real Robin Hood. A bank job and ratting—what does one thing have to do with the other?"

"Everything!! Ratting is despised because it's an act of betrayal to others and most importantly yourself. It's despised because you mutilate your own spirit by doing it."

"Okay so, that's my point. He mutilated his own spirit by doing it," Kush reasoned.

"Well if he did rat, then yea. But what about someone who resorts to robbing a bank? Is that not a mutilation?"

"No, 'cause my crimeys got away. I was the only one who got caught and I took the weight."

"But the act itself was a mutilation."

"C'mon, Handbone. Don't act like your hands are clean."

"Boy, I went to war. I was in war before you were born, so hell no my hands aren't clean. No one walks through life with clean hands—that's exactly my point. If we hold everyone to their worst, then we leave no room for their best."

"So, what you saying? Kwanzaa was Karenga's redemption?"

"I'm saying I don't know what dirt he did, but Kwanzaa was definitely his gift to his people. Why not accept the gift?"

Ruben jumped in. "Man, you old timers just don't get it. That's why we fucked up now. Ya'll Civil Rights niggas sold us out."

Handbone dismissed Ruben's comment with a wave. I chuckled to myself because I knew he wanted to respond, but realized Ruben was baiting him.

While Handbone was stewing with a strong urge to respond, I jumped in and changed the subject. "I see the police been playing the hood a lot more lately."

Ruben simply shrugged, clearly disappointed that Handbone didn't take the bait.

Kush, on the other hand, could not fight his nature to talk. "I think it has something to do with that kat Touchy who just came home. The whole hood talking about how he's running around giving dudes ultimatums and shit."

"Ultimatums?" I inquired. "What type of ultimatums?"

"He calls it the 'get-down or lay-down' ultimatum. And he's been pressing all the scramblers. From what I'm hearing, the murder that went down on Regent the other day was a lay down move."

I feigned surprise. "Damn, Touchy ain't wasting no time putting that work in. He's only been home about three months and he's already causing tidal waves?" I shook my head in disbelief. Kush couldn't help himself; his need to be heard was overwhelming his senses.

"Yea, man. And I was up North with Touchy. We were in Elmira together and he was on some Christian shit. I used to try to get him to fuck with the click, but he was all about the church. Now he comes home and he's a gorilla. Shit be incredible to me."

"I heard Touchy got a complete reversal on his case. That's how he got home," I added.

"Yeah, I heard that, too," Ruben interjected. "I don't know how Touchy was in Elmira, but since we were shorties, he's always been...what's the word I'm looking for, uhmmm... touched." Ruben's words and his timely outburst brought a serenade of laughter to the diner.

"Yeah, Touchy has always been a hot head," I added. That's just how some mothafuckas are wired."

"Yeah, but don't do the religious shit in prison and come out a gorilla, that's all I'm saying." Kush would not let up.

Handbone peered at his watch and gave me a nod. It was our prearranged signal. "We gotta go, Kay," was all he said. Ruben gave a quick salute to Handbone and then went back to serving a customer. Kush stood up from his stool and gave us dap.

When we shook hands, I pulled him close and spoke in an octave above a whisper. "Sound travels on a magical carpet called matter at the terrific speed of 1,125 miles per second. If the sound connects to the wrong eardrums, it activates the war drums and nothing else will matter. Be mindful of that." It was a departing warning to a reckless associate.

A riddle he caught but decided to overlook. "Nah, Kay, I'm on point. I'm expressing my feelings amongst comrades. I'm not running around and exposing homeboy. He want to perform a Billy the Kid role, that's on him. As long as he stay over there with it, we cool." I nodded my head in understanding; I understood his weak tongue would be his ruin.

"That kid can't help himself. His mouth is gonna bury him," Handbone said as we walked out of the diner. I shook my head in agreement. "I'm surprised he lasted this long. He just don't get it." We were walking toward my car enjoying the unusually warm winter air on this particular morning. The diner had been a detour; my visit had been a favor to Ruben. He called me the night before asking me to speak with Kush. Apparently, Touchy caught wind of Kush's words and was preparing to 'lay 'em down.'

The only reason Kush was still breathing was because Ruben and Touchy were once partners in crime. Touchy reached out to Ruben and then Ruben reached out to me. Ruben had not said a word to Kush regarding his potential demise for fear that Kush would run his mouth out of fear, and make matters worse. After hearing Kush firsthand, I knew Ruben made the right call. Touchy wasn't hustling drugs, he was shaking up drug dealers. His 'get down or lay down' ultimatum was basically a pay up or die choice.

It was I who had paid for Touchy's appellate lawyer, once I was sure that he would definitely make it home. I gave Touchy Flatbush to do with as he pleased, as long as my monthly tributes stayed the course. The misplaced rhetoric of kats like Kush made fools bold. Bold fools equalled extreme examples, and extreme examples equaled more police. The strange thing about it was, as far as I knew, Kush had no dealings with the streets. Since he came home, he had been working odds-and-ends jobs to get by. There was no reason for him to be commenting on a game he wasn't playing.

I was once again reminded of a quote from the O.G. Bible that read: *"In the jungle, even the baboons grow silent when the lion roars."* Touchy's roar was growing louder by the day and yet there was one baboon that refused to submit to its command. I decided to talk to Touchy personally about this one. The twins, grace and mercy, were on Kush's side. In the spirit of Kwanzaa, I was determined to save a life—even if that life belonged to a stubborn baboon.

The wizardry of the Wizard was in his ability to make the money invisible, yet still present. At first, he simply advised me on which investments to make and the traps I needed to avoid. But over time, the way a master does with his apprentice, he began to confide in me some secrets of his craft. He was a genius clothed convincingly in the disguise of mediocrity. He relished the opportunity to reveal his skills to a worthy student. "Making the money disappear is easy, young man. The real magic comes into play if your audience one day turns on you. Can you make yourself disappear? This is why you send that money out of the country. When escape becomes your only option, you have a few comfortable ones to choose from." Similar to my tutelage under the Old God, the Wizard taught me how to study.

Over time, I learned how to invest in stocks and bonds. I was required to read at least five newspapers daily. I was instructed to sift through the gossip, tragedies, and sensationalism, and find the gems in the stories. The gems the Wizard alluded to were indications of simple investments. War on the horizon meant investments in technology and defense. A new strain of the flu meant investments in pharmaceuticals. For me, the newspapers were homework assignments to show me how the world really worked. The Wizard had inside scoops on investments. It's what they called insider trading. It was such a racket. I marveled at its simplicity. Here I was scraping the pavement for crumbs, putting my life at risk every day while others were stealing 10 times the amount I was making, with just the click of a button or a head nod in the right direction. Like the music industry, the game was rigged for the insiders to win. They were shaving from the top, sharing secret paths to the wealth. Crimes with high stakes and minimal consequences were discussed openly in swank restaurants over shots of bourbon and seductive waitresses. It was a world the Wizard painted for me, a world he would only allow me to see from behind a one-way mirror.

I could see the players and the game, but the players couldn't see me. I could only bet on the game, not be in it. It was the way the Wizard wanted it, keeping me beholden to his benevolence. It was a ritual of control, his methodology of dominance. I appreciated the lessons and the rewards. My money was secured and replicating itself here and abroad. But the leash of dependence didn't sit well in my gut. I needed a few more big scores before I would give the Wizard an option he, like my peacocks, would be wise to accept. This heist, if successful, would pull me three moves closer to declaring checkmate.

CENTER OF GRAVITY

Chapter 18: example must be made

*drinking on an empty stomach
the actions of an idiot*

Knee
1994

Knee was disappointed in Kay-Kay's decision to let the violation slide. In Knee's opinion, small violations led to big violations. And since Knee refused to let any sucka score points on him, he felt that a lesson had to be taught. Increasingly, he grew less confident in Kay-Kay's ability to make decisive calls. Some circumstances dictated strong responses, yet Kay-Kay wanted to *'think things through'* all the time. It was an annoying trait he'd picked up somewhere along the way. He compared everything to chess, but some of this shit wasn't that complicated. In fact, it was as simple as checkers or even Connect Four. Knee called his trusted driver Turtle.

"Yo boy, what you doing?" Knee shouted into the phone receiver. "Come pick me up outside the Lightning Lounge," Knee continued before Turtle had a chance to respond. Turtle, true to form, never disobeyed or hesitated on a command. "I'll be there in a half."

167

A half an hour was good, since Knee was about 15 blocks away from the lounge. He would walk for exercise sake and also to get his mind and nerves primed for the task at hand. Turtle would bring the gloves, gun, and mask.

The feeling of having the power of life and death over another person was mind boggling in its intoxication. Knee felt god-like—an unmerciful god. He was determined to show Kay-Kay how the fuck shit was supposed to be done. One-Eye Stan was about to regret the game he chose to play.

As always, Turtle was on time. Knee climbed in the passenger side and reclined his head. The plush leather interior of Turtle's 325i always had the potential to put Knee to sleep.

"Aight, so where to?" Turtle asked.

"We're going to pay Stan a visit in Kingston Park," Knee replied.

Turtle responded with his customary words of bafflement. "Ahh, the joy of a kangaroo jumping through the forest."

Knee was determined to, just for once, make sense of Turtle's metaphors, but realized that this kangaroo shit wouldn't be the one he figured out. "Park on Pacific and Kingston. I'll walk the rest."

"The park will be packed," Turtle interjected in recognition of the unusually warm winter weather.

"Yeah, I want this message to be understood by all," Knee responded matter-of-factly.

"The banjo was created in slavery," Turtle countered.

Knee just shook his head in disbelief. Turtle had to be the funniest philosopher Knee ever knew. Not that he knew a lot to begin with.

The shooting of One-Eye Stan in broad daylight became the topic of discussion for weeks afterwards. It was reported that Stan was brain dead and in a coma, and that his mother refused to pull the plug. The truth was that Stan was in rehab trying to get back his motor skills. A masked gunman shot him five times in his stomach and legs before fleeing the park. Everyone speculated who the gunman was, but Stan knew the hit came from Kay-Kay. He felt lucky to be alive and contemplating revenge just didn't seem as important as figuring out how to walk again.

Kay-Kay was livid when he heard about the botched shooting of Stan. Immediately, he sent for Knee. They met on the Coney Island boardwalk. Knee arrived first, accompanied by Turtle. Kay-Kay appeared alone 15 minutes later. They embraced like old warriors meeting on yet another battlefield. Kay-Kay acknowledged Turtle with nothing more than a nod.

Knee and Kay-Kay began walking down the boardwalk leaving Turtle behind.

"So, Stan is still alive," Kay-Kay uttered.

"I didn't shoot to kill."

"Who doesn't shoot to kill?" Kay-Kay asked incredulously.

"It was a light lesson, like an-eye-for-an-eye type situation."

"You're fucking crazy," Kay-Kay responded.

They walked on, both warriors consumed momentarily in their own fragmented thoughts. Kay-Kay took the moment of silence to observe, not for the first time, the waves in the ocean. There was no other place that reminded Kay-Kay of freedom like the vastness of the sea. There were no barbwires or walls, just a limitless horizon.

Kay-Kay understood that the streets were a game of longevity, of remaining under the radar. *Low key equals longevity.* Knee refused to grasp the axiom. He wanted to go down in the annals of hood folklore. His name destined to die with the memories of the people who knew him. But Kay-Kay was determined to be immortal, to leave behind a legacy bigger than the hood itself, and Knee could only jeopardize his mission.

"I thought I asked you to leave Stan be?"

"Yeah, but it wasn't a good call."

"Don't matter. It was my call to give."

"I think you getting too soft around the edges with this, honestly."

"There's a time and place for everything and handling Stan at this time wasn't a part of the plan. You have to understand that I make the plans, not you..."

Knee interrupted with force. "Man, you getting too soft. We can't let niggas run all over us."

Kay-Kay stopped walking and looked Knee square in the eyes, not surprised at all by what they held. A smokeless fire of ruthless disregard was present. "And since you can't respect that I make the calls for this team, it's time we go our separate ways."

Knee stared at Kay-Kay for at least 20 seconds, assessing the full implications of Kay-Kay's words. "Man, you wanted to do that since the day I came out. You never wanted a real nigga on your team to begin with. You like keeping old men and scary mothafuckas around."

"Nah, I like keeping thinkers around, not fools."

"You calling me a fool?"

"That's nothing new. You always have been a fool." Both men refused to break eye contact. "You always been a fool, but you always been my brother as well. And before it gets to the point where I can't stand the sight of my brother, I'd rather us part ways," Kay-Kay concluded.

Knee secretly began to panic. His meal ticket was slipping through his fingers. "So how are we brothers, when you're leaving me in the cold?" Knee challenged.

"I would never leave you in the cold. I got 100 stacks for you as a severance package to do with as you will. That's providing that you understand to stay out of my lane. My hustle can't be your hustle." Kay-Kay was referring to the extortion game. He also knew that without giving Knee a severance package, he would eventually have to deal with him in a more calculated and dishonorable way.

As for Knee, 100 stacks was an unbelievable amount of money. He had no idea Kay-Kay had that type of money to just give away. For the first time, he saw Kay-Kay in a totally different light. Sadly, it was too late. Knee was never the type of person to give too much forethought to his own action and he wouldn't start now. A hundred stacks would go a long way in the coke game. It was just the right boost he needed. "When will I have the money?" he asked trying not to sound too thirsty.

Kay-Kay smiled; he was glad this would be painless. "I have the money with me." Just then, Handbone emerged from underneath the boardwalk carrying a backpack.

'Of course Kay-Kay wouldn't be alone,' Knee thought to himself, and for the second time in less than five minutes he saw Kay-Kay in a unnervingly different light.

A. C. Clayton

Chapter 19: imperfect math

1994

Knee had a love for shooting pool. His earliest recollection of spending time with his father was at Poppa's pool hall in Bed-Stuy. He was about nine years old and even at that age, Poppa's seemed like a place for the cool guys. Shooting pool was a game of finesse, skill, and accuracy.

Knee's father was considered a pool shark. On that day, his father taught him how to hold the cues and look for the angles. Knee was a fast learner and by the end of the day, he felt comfortable enough to call some basic cut shots. Though that was Knee's only opportunity to play the game with his father, he never forgot the moment. Billiards became his escape, the one constant he held control over. When he was not in the streets, he was in a pool hall.

As for his father, the funny thing about sharks is that they wear out their welcome in a town quickly. And though NYC was big, the world of billiards was tiny. As a result, his father had to continuously leave town for stints of time to let his victims recover from his swindle. He would always say, "It's time to take the show on the road."

The last time he said that Knee was about 11 years old. His father packed a suitcase and said he'd be back in a couple of months. He had heard that there were some good marks in Buffalo and Rochester, and he was going to show the "Billies" up North a thing or two. Knee never heard from his father again. But the lesson of that day always stuck. He remembered his father's words like it was yesterday. "See, it's all about taking aim. See the shot and the results before you take it."

The problem for Knee when it came to anything but pool was that he always saw the shot, but didn't care too much about seeing the results. Kay-Kay's withdrawal was an unintended consequence. Knee initially felt a sense of betrayal on the boardwalk as Kay-Kay severed ties with him. The way Knee saw it, he was the one who introduced Kay-Kay to the game. It was his reputation that protected Kay-Kay in prison. And the first chance Kay-Kay had, he cut Knee off.

But as the days went by, he began to see things differently. Knee realized that Kay-Kay was afraid of losing control over his organization. Though Knee never had any intentions of doing so, he realized that eventually Kay's soldiers would want him to lead instead of Kay.

Kay-Kay moved like them politician niggas: cautious and nervous. Knee saw himself as a general through and through. "I'm always in the trenches," was one of his favorite sayings. So yeah, Kay-Kay made the right move, because a handover of power would've been inevitable had Knee stayed.

Knee contemplated these thoughts as he shot a game of pool with his right-hand-man, Turtle. They were at the billiards hall on Flatbush Avenue, awaiting JB's arrival. Since the day Knee came home, every other Sunday afternoon belonged to him and JB. They would play a couple of games of pool and just catch up. JB's conversion to "Mr. Save the World" was an unfortunate fact of life. He wasn't that surprised because JB had always been a square at heart. He never had any real fire in his belly for the street.

As always, JB arrived at 3 p.m. on the dot, as if he stood right outside the door until the clock struck three before walking in. Turtle spoke up first. "If I was a betting man, I would bet on the trinity." Both JB and Knee looked perplexed at the comment, but not surprised. JB knew that Turtle was Knee's gofer, and that was the only reason he kept him around. But what JB couldn't understand was why Knee allowed him to say the most asinine things.

JB and Knee quickly embraced as only brothers would. Turtle was given the customary dap and head nod of recognition. "What's up, Killer Knee?" was JB's ritual greeting.

"I'm good. How's moms doing?"

"She's doing good. Hanging in there, waiting for retirement," JB responded.

Knee's mother had passed right before Knee made it home from prison. The fact that he would have made it home to see her alive if he had only chilled out in prison for six months was a sore spot for him.

"Yo, Turtle, give me and JB a few minutes to catch up."

Turtle was already in motion before Knee could finish his words. "Man, I was waiting for you to ask. I see those honeys over there." Turtle was pointing to a group of women sitting at the bar enjoying each other's company. "It looks like they need a bee in their lives."

"How's little Robert Jr. doing?" JB asked shaking his head.

Knee shook his head in uncertainty. His relationship with his son, Robert Jr., was an uncomfortable one to say the least. The boy was so different from what Knee imagined a product of his loins would be. At eight years old, his son didn't like sports or fighting. He liked video games and playing with what Knee called dolls. They were superhero figures, but to Knee it was all the same. The fact that Knee could not recall ever playing with "dolls" never made him question his upbringing. In fact, he was glad that his brothers had him playing with guns instead of dolls. So how could his child be cut from such a different cloth?

"Man, you should be happy that your seed is growing up correctly," JB reasoned.

"What you talking about growing correctly? He's playing with fucking dolls, JB."

"They're not dolls, they're *action figures*," JB corrected.

"It's the same thing, my man."

"No, it's not. You bugging. He's a good kid. You should be happy she's raising him the right way."

"For a revolutionary who wants to save the people, I could see your point. But I ain't a revolutionary. I could care less about any of that shit. I promote violence, that's what I do."

"So, what's that have to do with your son? You really want that for your son, bro?" JB asked incredulously. Knee remained silent. JB shook his head in disbelief, chalked up his cue, and took a shot. He missed his mark completely.

"Don't judge me, JB," Knee warned in a brotherly tone.

"Man, I'm judging the fact that you are actually judging your eight-year-old son. If you don't like to be judged, how do you do it to your own child?"

"Man, fuck you with that reverse psychology shit."

JB could tell that talking to Knee about his son would only ruin the day, so he shifted the subject to a more comical matter.

"Yo, Knee, what's up with your boy Turtle? Why is he always thinking his riddles are deep?"

"Man, I don't know. I tell you this though," Knee paused midsentence as he grabbed a cue and began studying its balance. Once satisfied with his pick he continued. "If he ever gets knocked and decides to cooperate with the law, as soon as he opens his mouth, they'll place him in a psych ward. So..."

JB began laughing profusely, his hand held in midair trying to stop Knee from continuing. Knee shook his head in resistance, determined to explain his logic. "So I encourage him to talk like that. As long as we understand each other, that's all that matters. He can get lost in that shit for all I care."

JB never lost interest in Knee's logic. He would keep an idiotic philosopher around so that, if the logician ever decided to betray his master, no one would ever believe his equations. For many, Knee seemed out of control, especially if they only studied his first layer. But when the layers were peeled, you could see an imperfect math begin to add up.

Chapter 20: politicizing the struggle

1994

Sinclair Monroe was a seven-time state senator for District 21 in Flatbush, Brooklyn. He prided himself on his ability to charm people into seeing things his way. He stood impressively at 6'5 and 264 pounds, an imposing yet pleasing presence to most people. His new position as the chairman of the senate's finance committee placed all eyes, and to a large extent, hopes on him.

He was now in a position to channel funds directly into his community for its revitalization. Many business and community leaders were seeking an audience with him in hopes of being included in the economic growth of his community. At the urging of his good friend Reverend Frost, he agreed to meet with a young upcoming community leader named Jamal Barnes. The young man's name had come to his attention as someone to keep an eye out for. Jamal Barnes was a rising star who could prove to be an ally or enemy.

Due to Jamal's criminal record, he would never be able to run against Sinclair, but Jamal's potential endorsement of an opponent could prove detrimental to Sinclair. So the meeting today was one of neutralization. Sinclair was willing to throw

Jamal a few crumbs, if he would agree to pledge his allegiance to Sinclair. All these thoughts raced through the politician's mind as he sat behind his massive mahogany desk in his modest Flatbush headquarters.

Expectedly, the phone began to ring. He knew it was his assistant informing him that Jamal had arrived. Sinclair picked up the phone and instructed his assistant to have Mr. Barnes wait for 15 minutes before sending him in. Like all astute politicians, Sinclair prided himself on being a master at adhering to the rules of engagement. Sinclair ran through his thinning gray hair with a finetooth comb, adjusted his Marc Jacobs tie, which had been a gift from a special benefactor, pulled out his pen and pad, and prepared to feign interest in the upcoming meeting.

Meanwhile, JB waited patiently in the senator's reception area, admiring the lawmaker's taste in African-American art. There were two pieces from Nathaniel Quinn that he recognized immediately. *One day, I'll be able to afford nice artwork,* JB thought with hopeful anticipation.

"Mr. Barnes? Senator Sinclair will see you now."

Jamal walked into the senator's chamber with great reverence and humility. He stole quick glances at the trappings of power, curious to discover any secrets to success. He noticed a few more paintings of notable African-American artists, a wall full of degrees and other notable accomplishments. Two four-foot Kemetic statues stood as sentries in front his massive bookshelf. At least five hundred books were lined by size and category, with two entire rows dedicated to books JB knew all too well. New York State second edition law books containing words composed in a crafty English, revealing wormholes that carried its readers both in and out of the black holes of justice. He took a deep breath before shaking the lawmaker's hand.

The handshake was firm and assertive. *A rare and admirable sign of a confident man; such a missing quality in young Black men nowadays,* the Senator thought to himself with pity and shame.

"Mr. Barnes, it's my pleasure to finally meet you. I've heard glowing reports from many people in our community regarding you."

"The pleasure is all mine, Senator. You've been a champion for our community for over 20 years."

Senator Sinclair smiled at the obvious truth in JB's word. "Well, young man, I'm not sure if champion is a good title, but I've definitely been a soldier for the cause. Enough about me, though. It's about the next generation of warriors such as yourself, and how can we make sure the baton is passed on correctly. So please, have a seat and let's chat."

The conversation lasted more than an hour. They were like two warriors studying each other's strengths. For JB, the whole experience was surreal. Only two years ago, he was an inmate in a correctional facility, and now he had the undivided attention of a man he saw speak on television his whole life.

As for Senator Sinclair, he was a great deal more impressed with JB than he originally thought he would be. This young man really had his fingers on the pulse of problems and the solutions facing their community. Of course, the young man was naïve and a tad bit nostalgic when it came to the reality of politics and power. However, Sinclair Monroe was confident that he would be able to groom the young lion, who preferred to be called JB, into becoming an effective tool to wield against Sinclair's opponents.

"JB, I can see that this meeting is only the beginning of a long and prosperous relationship that will help our community in a profound way." JB and Sinclair Monroe parted ways with the promise of lunch early the following week.

Later that night, JB explained the promising news to both Pam and his mother.

"Be careful with that one, boy. He's a slippery character," was Ma Barnes' cautionary advice.

"Ma, you say that about every politician," JB replied with a straight face.

"And I'm right about every one of them, especially the Black ones."

JB looked confused after hearing his mother's comment. "You lost me with that one. How are Black politicians more slippery than the rest? That just sounded like some real self-hate issues going on."

"Oh, don't try that self-hatred mumbo jumbo with me, JB. I'm too old to be guilt-tripped into wanting to sound politically correct. The truth is the truth, and the devil is a liar. And Black politicians will lie because Black people have short memories. They know we won't hold them accountable for their lies and false promises."

As much as JB was ready for a debate, he realized that she had a solid argument. His only response was, "Yeah well, that's why I'm doing what I'm doing. If not us then who, Ma? Who protects the babies? Do we continue to rely on a system that has proven to never work in our favor? If he's as slippery as you say he is, then trust that I'll spot it."

"And when you spot it, then what?"

"Then on to the next alliance. The work gotta get done."

Ma Barnes shook her head in disagreement, more out of reflex than wisdom. She couldn't put a finger on her discomfort with her son's decision to want to make a difference in his community.

Pam sat quietly throughout the exchange between JB and Ma Barnes. She was wrestling with a dilemma of her own. Her period was late by weeks and her period was never late. Pam didn't believe in abortion, but she knew that financially her and JB were not in a position to have a baby. She worked as a paralegal in a prestigious and reputable law firm, but while the work was exciting and challenging, the pay was meager to say the least. JB was in no better of a situation. His commitment to his community was honorable, but not profitable. "Revolutionaries don't make money," her Papa had reminded her. Pam lived in a modest one-bedroom apartment and JB still lived with his mother. They never spoke about their future together. She knew that they were in love, but the depths of that love had never been explored. Having an abortion seemed like the only logical course of action to take, but she still shuddered when she thought of the regrets she would have to live with.

Chapter 21: ruins of the reckless

Knee
1994

Knee was excited to finally be on his own. His initial reservations about parting ways with Kay-Kay quickly gave way to relief. The more he thought about it, the more he realized that if he had remained with Kay-Kay, a collision between the two would have been inevitable. If that had happened, neither one of them would have been able to walk away from the outcome with their heads held high. He realized that their styles were different and that Kay-Kay was more leery about getting caught. For Knee, the name of the game was to make money and live like a king; getting caught was an occupational hazard that you could accept or resist.

Within a month, Knee was entrenched in his old Flatbush neighborhood selling weights of cocaine to the smaller hustlers who were then being extorted by Knee's accomplice, Touchy. Knee would inform Touchy of exactly how much each dealer purchased so that Touchy knew exactly how much to squeeze for. Touchy would then give Knee a small percentage of his score. The unsuspecting dealers had no idea of this covert alliance and simply went along with the flow.

Knee began recruiting a lot of dudes fresh out of prison. He stocked his team with what he considered "tried and tested" warriors. One of his top lieutenants was Spank, a mercenary out of Tilden projects in Brownsville. Both Kay-Kay and Touchy had tried to recruit Spank as soon as he came home, but in the end he chose to roll with Knee.

For Spank, it was a tough decision. Kay-Kay was the richest, but he already had his core team in place, and in that organization Spank would just be another spoke in the wheel. Touchy, on the other hand, was moving like a stone cold madman. The body count was rising by at least one every single week. Eventually, it would catch up to Touchy, and Spank didn't want to walk into any indictments in the making. Knee, though a little off his damn self, was the most logical choice for Spank. In Knee's organization, Spank saw his best opportunity to strike gold. He quickly became Knee's enforcer and the middleman between Knee and Touchy.

Within three months, Spank was cruising around in his own two-toned Lexus LS400 series with 19" chrome rims relishing the attention of those who recognized his status by virtue of his car. Spank savored his newfound celebrity and felt it was well earned. "Why should only the suckers eat?" he asked himself.

Knee believed in rewarding his team and paid Spank handsomely for his hard work and dedication.

One day, after having lunch with Kay-Kay, Spank received a beep from Knee.

Immediately, he called Knee back from the first payphone he saw. "Yeah, what's up?" he asked.

"Meet me at the stash spot ASAP," was all Knee said before the line went dead.

Spank arrived in no time and was surprised to see Touchy reclined on the sofa, laughing at a Budweiser commercial on the TV. Knee emerged from the kitchen a few seconds later wearing an apron and rubber gloves. Knee smiled that sinister 'wait till you hear this one' smile. Spank looked at Knee's attire once more, attempting to glean a hint of what was coming next. He knew that the rubber gloves meant that Knee was in the process of packaging cocaine. It was a task that, no matter the quantity or the size, Knee trusted no one but himself and his righthand man Turtle to take care of. Spank quickly ruled out a packaging assignment. Whatever was coming, Spank knew he wouldn't wonder for long. Knee peeled off his rubber gloves as he walked nonchalantly towards Spank.

He began to speak, with very little patience for small talk. "We have a slight problem, but a better solution," he sighed.

Knee began to explain to Spank how a lot of the clients have been buying very small quantities from them as of late. "At first, I thought it was just a slow period, nothing to be concerned about. But this shit's been going on for the last three weeks. Then Touchy called me and said he had an interesting story to share with me."

As if on cue Touchy jumped in. "Bredren, mi nah gonna focus on petty petty details. Let's just say one of my men may be working with Babylon. Dis same coward dat started tipping off de hustla dem to our business." Touchy was indicating the relationship between him and Knee. "Mi nah sure 'bout the Babylon link, but definitely sure 'bout di uddah stuff. Either way, he a dead man."

Knee chimed back in. "The problem is that we're not sure if Touchy is being watched yet by the po-po. So when this shit goes down, Touchy needs to be somewhere far from it."

Spank knew what this meant. He had anticipated Knee giving him an assignment of such magnitude sooner or later. While he would've preferred it later, he wouldn't hesitate to do what he had to now.

His lunch with Kay-Kay ran through his mind. "How's shit going with Knee?" Kay-Kay had asked jokingly. "He ain't asking you to kill nobody for him yet?"

Perhaps Kay-Kay knew something or this was some form of an omen he should not ignore. But an immediate response was called for. "Aight," Spank replied with a false bravado to Knee's request. "Give me the details and I'll handle the rest."

"My man," Knee said with a huge smile.

The killing of Peter Wonder was felt throughout Flatbush. He was one of Touchy's top lieutenants, yet Touchy showed no sign of anger or grief. In fact, he was spotted on the corner of Newkirk Ave—the very street Peter Wonder lived and grew up on—popping bottles of Dom Pérignon and singing "Another One Bites the Dust" while offering a drink to anyone who wanted one. For many, that was confirmation that Touchy orchestrated the murder, and a handful of people believed they knew exactly why.

Meanwhile, Knee, the unseen hand in all of this, congratulated Spank for a job well done by sending him to Vegas to see his Brownsville alum Riddick Bowe take centerstage. Little did either one of them know that it would be the last fond memories Spank would ever hold dear.

While Spank was enjoying himself in Vegas, Knee unexpectedly found himself in damage control. Apparently, the killing of Peter Wonder sent the opposite message than the one they had intended. Where both Knee and Touchy figured there would be fear, they found nothing but anger and calls for revenge. At first, the calls for revenge were directed at Touchy, but many suspected Knee had a hand in the affair. When word reached the hood that the police lifted a set of fingerprints from the crime scene that belonged to Knee's enforcer, and that there was an eyewitness that saw the same enforcer leaving the scene of the crime, Knee knew that his name was about to take a beating.

Although Peter Wonder ran with Touchy, he was still a well-liked individual in the hood. Most of the upcoming stars looked up to Peter Wonder more than they did Touchy. Word on the street quickly spread that Touchy had Peter killed out of jealousy and out of fear that Peter was going to eventually takeover.

As for Touchy, the gravity of his oversight failed to register as he continued business as usual. The danger he faced remained hidden in plain sight until it was almost too late for him to avoid. Touchy was driving his Nissan Pathfinder down Beverly Road in Flatbush when he pulled up at a red light. He was staring at the car in front of him when his instincts told him to look in his driver side mirror.

The two gunmen were less than 20 feet away, converging on both sides of the car. Quickly, Touchy threw the car in reverse and hit the gas, slamming into the car behind him with such force that a spasm of whiplash engulfed his senses. Sensing that Touchy was about to escape, the gunmen opened fire on the Pathfinder. Bullets shattered the back windshield with resounding force.

By this time, Touchy had shifted back into drive and was ramming his way free, yelling, "Fuck! Fuck! Fuck!" The road was in chaos. People were running in all directions, unsure where the shots were coming from or whom they were intended for. More shots hit the vehicle and a bullet tore a burning path through Touchy's ear before shattering the front windshield. A pathway opened up and Touchy took advantage. He hit the accelerator once more and like a rocket, his Pathfinder blasted off into the unknown. More shots rang out and bullets ricocheted off the metal on the van. Touchy knew he was hit when he felt the searing pain burning in the back of his right shoulder, but wasn't sure how bad it was. With pure adrenaline coursing through his veins, Touchy drove like a madman from death's call.

He ditched the Pathfinder five blocks away. The shrill of police sirens grew louder by the second. The gun on his waist had proven no use in defending against the assassination attempt, but it would definitely aid in his escape. Touchy jumped in the backseat of the first taxi he could flag down and gave the driver an address before lying down. He needed to avoid being seen by passing cars or pedestrians. His shoulder throbbed in nauseating pain. The blood was not slowing down.

Initially, Ahmed the taxi driver failed to register the complexity of the situation. He was accustomed to weird passengers, but when he looked through the rearview mirror and saw Touchy wincing in apparent delirium, he panicked, slammed on the brakes and yelled, "Oh no, oh no, my friend. I got a wife and three kids. I don't want to get involved..."

Before Ahmed could finish, Touchy sat back up pointing his 9mm Berretta at Ahmed's temple before saying, "Take mi to di address I give you, and you will see ya wife and pickney again. Bredren, trust me, any uddah way is death. No time fah chatter bredren. Drive." Motivated by Touchy's words or the point of his gun, Ahmed coolly delivered Touchy out of danger and into a doctor's care. The doctor was one of those unique and very rare doctors who specialized in treating patients who'd rather not report gunshot wounds to the hospital and, ultimately, the police.

While Touchy was being attended to, someone notified the police of two of Touchy's hideouts and within hours, Touchy's face was plastered on every local news channel in the Tri-State area. The raids on his hideouts netted the police a cache of guns, grenades, two Kevlar vests, and more than $106,000 in cash. According to the news, there was other incriminating evidence inside the apartments, but the police were not releasing those details to the public.

A profile of Touchy appeared on the evening news describing Touchy as "an ex-con suspected in the killings of more than 11 rivals and just as many kidnappings." The morning newspaper went a step further and labeled him the "get down or lay down killer." It was obvious to Knee that someone pretty close to Touchy was spilling his guts to the police. There were too many details of the crimes being described in the paper for there not to be someone talking. This worried Knee. If they were that close to Touchy, then perhaps they also knew about Knee's business dealings with him. Knee decided to lay low, not leaving his honeycomb hideout for any reason. He wished Touchy the best, but felt no obligation to go down with a sinking ship.

Kay-Kay

When I received the call from my doctor buddy telling me that Touchy was at his clinic being treated for a gunshot wound, I just shook my head and went back to thinking about my own daily drama. It wasn't until I saw the nightly news reports that the gravity of Touchy's situation really hit home. I was so upset with this dude because just less than two weeks ago, I had sat Touchy down and told him that the murders were out of control. I told him that it seemed like he was doing this shit more for the thrill than for the money.

I was upset because I knew it was now on me to get him out of town safely. It was obvious that no one Touchy dealt with could be trusted, so it would have to be exclusively my resources at work here. When I arrived at the makeshift clinic that sat in the basement of my good friend's Park Slope brownstone, Touchy was heavily sedated. Apparently the bullet tore through Touchy's right shoulder before lodging itself into his shoulder bone. The wound itself wasn't life threatening, but Touchy's severe anemia and the loss of a tremendous amount of blood almost did him in. By 3 a.m., Touchy awoke and groggily began to fill me in on everything that had led up to that point.

The more I listened, the more upset I grew. I was disappointed at myself for letting this moron run rampant without any supervision, and for being so caught up in my own drama that I failed to pay attention to how other people's performance could end up affecting me. I was upset with Touchy for being a moron. I had to put my head in my hands as soon as I heard about Knee's involvement and how they dragged poor Spank into it. Everything in my mind told me to just kill this mothafucka right there in the hospital, but there was honor amongst thieves, an unsaid commitment I felt duty bound to uphold.

Touchy must've read the conflict in my eyes because he quickly began scanning the room in search of his trusted gun.

I handed it to him and spoke. "It makes no sense to say I told you so, so I won't. We gotta get you out of the country, bro, quickly."

Touchy looked away in hopes that his suspicion wasn't apparent before responding. "Bredren, I'll never forget this. For as long as I live, I'll never forget this." When he looked back at me, there were tears in his eyes. He was afraid and I was his only salvation.

It took me a couple of days to get him a passport that would withstand any scrutiny. Touchy also trusted me to go to his real stash house. He had more than $276,000 in cash, about another $70,000 worth of jewelry, and more guns. We agreed that I would wire the money to him in increments. He was going back to Jamaica and that amount of dough would definitely give him a cushion to get established out there.

When the smoke cleared, we moved Touchy in the trunk of a pimped out Cadillac from Brooklyn to Boston. Then, Touchy boarded a bus from Boston to Cleveland, where he caught a plane from Cleveland to Miami. In Miami, he caught a helicopter ride to the Bahamas, where he chilled for about a month to make sure that his trail was a cold one.

Touchy arrived in Kingston and linked up with some childhood friends who were happy to have another boss on the scene. It would take me an entire year to get all of Touchy's money to him, but shortly after I sent the last payment, I got wind that he was fleeing Jamaica headed to London by way of Barbados. To this day, Touchy is one of the most feared but seldom seen gangsters in England. While I was able to help Touchy escape the jaws of justice, Spank's capture caught me off guard completely.

Chapter 22: impoverished realities

JB

1994

"Baby, we're not ready to have a baby. I mean, financially we just..."

Pam placed her finger on JB's lips to quiet him. They sat on her couch, Pam's head nestled snugly on his lap. She was looking up studying the lines of worry that creased his face. "JB, I know we're not ready and I didn't tell you about my pregnancy to pressure you in any way. I told you because I never want to hold secrets from you. I'll set up the date for the abortion and we'll never regret this decision."

JB placed his hand on Pam's cheek and began caressing her skin, not to stir lust but to convey adoration. Gently, he stroked as if the genie in the lamp would appear and make this pregnancy a joyous moment and not a dilemma. Pam reached for his face, determined to catch the tear welling up in his eye, but it never fell. It just sat there like activists on a hunger strike, sacrificing its own appetite for a greater good. He bowed his head, placing it on the top of hers thinking, *Heaven can't possibly feel anything like this.* Slowly, he broke the connection, lifted his head and looked directly into Pam's eyes. Her naked soul stared back, inviting his entry.

"Baby, I'm going to build a life for us, I promise. We will never have to make a decision like this again."

Tears began welling up in Pam's eyes, liquid mirrors, opaque and just out of reach. She hugged him harder, attempting to reassure him of her faith in his words. But it was hard to see how a community activist could ever make such a guarantee. Still, she loved him to his core and could not fathom a life without him. So she hugged harder, willing herself to believe.

"Never again, baby. I promise." He whispered a chant that put her to sleep.

JB's back was against the wall. There could be no doubt about it. As much as he felt he was making a difference in his community, he was pretty much penniless. Meanwhile, his kid brother and best friend were destroying the hood and were rich for doing so. It just didn't seem fair, but it appeared to be the norm. It was a paradox of ruling contradictions. He felt like a child lost in a wilderness of bewilderment.

A. C. Clayton

Chapter 23: the meet

Peaches

1994

In the week leading up to her meeting with Kay-Kay, Peaches found concentrating on anything other than the meet impossible. It wasn't the fact that she was meeting a worthy rival, as much as it was seeing the father of her child whom she loved but left for dead on a Brooklyn street corner. Emotions she held in check for close to nine years were now threatening to unravel her well-laid plan. *What if he chooses war,* she pondered with a heavy heart. Why did she choose to come back to New York City? She could've easily gone to another state in America. Why go to the one place where the clouds of uncertainty were the thickest? No other reason could be given except the fact that Kay-Kay wasn't in any other city. Was it a death wish or a desire for forgiveness that motivated her?

Roc sensed the tension in Peaches. He had been with her long enough to know that this upcoming meeting was anything but routine. There was a great deal about Peaches' past that Roc didn't know—and never desired to inquire about—but this somehow seemed different.

Roc brought the topic up while driving Peaches to her private spa appointment in Astoria, Queens. "So, this meeting with this dude Kay-Kay on Saturday, it's more than just business, huh?"

Sitting in the passenger seat, Peaches could see Roc's inquisitive stare out of her peripheral. She chose not to meet his gaze, instead focusing on the traffic signs they passed. "Yea, Roc, he's my son's father."

"Who? Lil' Kameek?" Roc's rhetorical question was more of a statement. "Damn, Peaches. When were you gonna tell me this?"

Peaches remained silent, fixated on a thought beyond Roc's question. Roc was used to her secretive ways, but this took the cake.

"Do we need bigger guns, Peaches?"

Peaches' indecision was reflected in her silence. She felt as if she were sailing in unchartered waters. Would bigger guns bring victory or conquest? For her, victory was forgiveness from Kay-Kay; conquest meant his submission or death. Though he didn't realize it, Roc was asking for clarification on the objective, and even in the ninth hour, Peaches was still conflicted as to her end game.

"We have enough guns. If, or when, it gets ugly I'm pretty sure it won't be at the meet." The raising of his eyebrows and the shaking of his head were the only visible signs of Roc's discomfort. Everything in his head told him more guns were needed, but his general made the call. His job was to follow her call.

She dressed meticulously for the meet, making sure that all of her accessories were in place. Her nerves sat precariously on edge. The anticipation was spooking her. "Pull it together, girl. We got a job to do," she said to herself, trying to soothe the butterflies flying aimlessly in her stomach. It had been nine years since she set up and left the father of her then unborn child fighting for his life on a street corner.

Why Peaches chose to confront her demon head-on remained a mystery to her. This meeting could end ugly. Kay-Kay wasn't the "forgive and forget" type, but it was a meet she needed to happen for her own sanity. She needed to know exactly where they stood—not for her sake, but for their son, Kameek Jr. Her son needed to at least know his father, and Kay-Kay needed to know his son. She told herself that this was the reason for her orchestrating this showdown. But deep inside she knew that there was a hidden truth, a truth she fought not to accept: she still loved him and needed his forgiveness.

It had been her obsession for the last nine years. Not a day had gone by without thoughts of her son's father entering her mind. Peaches played the scenes back, trying to rationalize her thinking at the time of his shooting. Her conclusion was always the same—she wasn't thinking. Then she would reminisce on the feeling of falling in love even though he was younger. Recalling the very first time she realized her feelings had grown so intense.

They were in her tiny bedroom playing checkers on her twin-sized mattress. On Kay-Kay's face sat a stern mask of pure concentration. His inability to beat her frustrated him tremendously. For the life of him he couldn't figure out the strategy to victory. Peaches always seemed to be two steps ahead of him.

"Fuck!" he yelled, sensing that a move was about to be made, but unable to figure out where it was coming from.

Peaches had learned how to play from her Uncle Chad. He had taught her the secret to the game, and from that day forth, she only lost to others who knew the secret. Unlike chess, checkers had some sure-fire moves to victory, but Kay-Kay treated it like a guessing game. Unfortunately for him, his guesses were always wrong.

She watched his frustration mount, and felt sorry for him. It was such an alien feeling to want her competitor to win. She shook her head trying to dislodge the notion, but the harder she shook the stronger it stuck. The move was hers to make and if she took the square that controlled the board, victory was once again hers. Instead, she took another square, one that would allow her to jump a man, but nothing much else. By the look on Kay-Kay's face, he was oblivious to her gift that appeared to be a blunder. The game would be his if he took the square that she left behind, but instead he took another. She grimaced at his lack of foresight, reminding herself of her mother's words: Boys are a lot slower than girls, baby. At least from this display she couldn't agree more....

"Peaches, you ready to roll?" Roc yelled from downstairs. "We have a date with fate."

He was referring to the dinner they were about to have with Kay-Kay.

"Date with fate," Peaches mumbled under her breath in resignation of the irony. "I guess you're right. A date with fate!"

Kay-Kay

"Handbone, talk to me."

"The restaurant is clear. We have the artillery in place and exits are all secure."

"Ok, great to hear. I'll see you there."

Handbone's reference to exits was the most important part. I was finally headed to meet with the elusive Peaches, a rival of sorts who had been feeding my peacocks without paying her taxes. She had also went up against a heavy hitter in Jersey, so we were making sure the deck was stacked in our favor, not hers. I was prepared to leave a firm example behind for all who needed firm examples to understand the order of operations.

'Exits all secure' meant my escape was assured, so this chick Peaches better be ready to talk submission or her last rites.

I arrived at the restaurant 15 minutes before the scheduled time. The place had a few customers sprinkled about. Our booth was next to the emergency exit doors, and the camera inside the establishment had been shut off for the evening. I sat down and ordered a glass of champagne. Both Jay T and Ras, my human shields for the night, sat across from me at another booth. Whenever Peaches arrived she would be escorted to my booth and her two bodyguards would join my two at their booth.

Everyone would be armed, hammers unlocked and off safety. So it would really be a matter of who gets the drop first. The edge went to us because the waiter was also ours, and at an agreed upon sign from me, he would commence to taking out the bodyguards while I handled Peaches personally.

"Kay, they're here," Jay T informed.

My adrenaline was on high; I lived for this shit, man, I tell you. One of her bodyguards came through the door first, and the maître d' pointed in our direction. The bodyguard walked across the room, taking the whole scenery in without seeming too.

Pretty impressive, I thought to myself. It was a reminder that she wasn't the typical adversary and that this showdown might be surprisingly fun.

The bodyguard noticed the position of the booth and its close proximity to the exit—his expression momentarily registered alarm. Immediately regaining his composure, he met with my team before coming over and shaking my hand.

"Everything seems good. I'm going back out to get Peaches."

"Cool. I'm right here," I responded.

His eyes darted back to the exit door once more before turning and heading to get Peaches.

"The exit door seemed to peak his interest," I said to my human shield.

"Yeah, he seems like he knows what he's doing."

"That just means he's the first to get slumped," I responded.

Moments later a beautiful snake...an unspeakable apparition that defied belief, slithered through the door. Could it really be her?

Chapter 24: tough decisions

JB

1994

It was 8:30 a.m. and already the line of people in front of the building awaiting its opening grew longer by the minute. While most stood in line in silent contemplation, there were a few who acted as if they were there for free concert tickets. JB immediately recognized these as the veterans. For these vets, this entire process was nothing more than an occupational hazard. He glanced at Pam and saw strength in her demeanor, but he knew deep down inside she was in turmoil. He grabbed her hand as a gesture of support and comfort. She appreciated the thought behind the action despite the circumstances. The doors to the abortion clinic opened and the line began to move. Pam's hold on JB's hand tightened as she braced herself for what must be. They spoke into the wee hours of the morning before heading to the clinic, discussing the reasons for this abortion.

The primary reason for both was financial; they simply couldn't afford to bring a life into this world at this time. They were both still young and agreed that in a few years they would be better suited to be parents. Also, time would give them the opportunity to know for certain if this love affair was for a lifetime or a season. JB didn't want to just be a baby daddy and Pam didn't want to be a baby mamma. For JB, single parenting went against all of his teachings. He felt that it was hard—not impossible, but hard—for single parents to raise well-rounded children. Either the child grows up lacking compassion or discipline or both. Either empathy or motivation ended up missing from their upbringing.

JB understood this firsthand. His mother's Herculean effort of raising them when their father left could not be waved off. She did her best, yet both of her children ended up in the penitentiary. This was not just her story; it was the story of single Black and Brown parents clear across the country.

JB knew that when he finally did decide to cloak the hood of a father, he would never forsake the sacredness of the office. Pam understood and agreed wholeheartedly with him. Unlike JB, Pam grew up with both parents, active and loving in her life. She knew from experience what having both a mother and father present meant. She loved JB for appreciating the enormity of becoming a father and accepting that it was a responsibility he wasn't prepared for.

Though Pam understood all of the logical reasons why having a baby at this time did not make sense, she still felt an unshakeable sense of guilt and dread knotting in her stomach the closer she got to her number being called. Before she looked up, there were only two other women in front of her. One was unshaken and the second seemed full of regrets.

JB sat next to Pam, uncomfortable in his seat. He was looking around, taking the madness in. This was such a place of pity and despair. The words *butcher's shop* illuminated in his thoughts like a neon sign. *There's life inside these wombs, defenseless and precious and yet they're slated for slaughter. Why? Why should they be?* The reasoning wasn't congruent with its summary.

He knew he couldn't afford to follow this path of thinking for too long. He had to pull it together. He wouldn't let that voice alter his actions. So he reminded himself of the facts. They weren't ready to be parents. They couldn't afford it. They weren't where they needed to be in life professionally at the moment.

Yet every justification that worked the previous night sounded like nothing more than an excuse echoing in his ears today. They were about to make a permanent decision based on temporary obstacles.

Pam beat him to punch. "JB, I'm sorry, baby... but I just can't go through with this. At least not today." Her inflection and facial expression matched her plea.

JB stood up, took a very deep breath and extended his hand, palm up as a sign of rescue. Pam grabbed hold of it tightly. It was a firm hand pulling her from a hole she could've never found her way out of alone.

"Baby, we've been blessed with this gift and we'll humbly accept it. Let's go. Let's get out of here." JB's words were soothing to her soul.

As they walked through the clinic, they could see the mixture of emotions etched on the faces of despair. The women could sense that JB and Pam had changed their minds. It served as a painful reminder that it wasn't too late. For some, the choice was engraved in stone; abortion was the only option. But there were a few who weren't too sure and their decision was now being challenged by a second guess. An older woman touched Pam's hand gently and mouthed the words *God Bless*.

No sooner had they stepped out of the door did Pam collapse into JB arms. She began crying uncontrollably. "Oh my god, JB. What did we almost do?"

JB hugged her, holding back his own tears as he looked towards the sky for a sign. "A mistake, baby. A mistake we'll never consider again!"

Chapter 25: the ace

Peaches

Peaches saw the surprise on Kay-Kay's face as she walked through the door. Slowly, his surprised expression gave way to hatred and contempt. The situation was about to explode before she had a chance to say a word. *Roc was right, more guns were needed,* she thought. Immediately, she raised both her hands in surrender and said, "Give me a chance to explain."

Her body language seemed to disarm him ever so slightly before he replied, "Explain?"

Both of Kay-Kay's bodyguards were in utter bewilderment, unsure as to what this new wrinkle meant or didn't mean. Even Peaches' bodyguard, who first came in as a scout, seemed baffled. The only other person in the room beside Kay-Kay and Peaches who knew what was taking place was Roc, and he immediately understood that this situation was about to get really ugly.

"Explain?" Kay-Kay repeated.

Peaches yelled back matching Kay-Kay's aggression. "Yeah, explain! Let me fucking explain."

Her response was timely and loud, drawing the attention of the sprinkle of customers enjoying their meal. Kay-Kay looked around, taking it all in as the wisps of a smoldering thought emanated imperceptibly from the canyons of his ears. Kay-Kay was standing hunched over the table holding on to the edge; his body language suggested attack mode and at any second, the table could become his first weapon.

Peaches did not break her stride; she continued to walk towards him. Their eyes locked in a combination that would not be cracked. *Date with fate* drew Peaches near the fire until finally she stood directly in front of him, then slowly and deliberately sat down. Her theatrics did not impress Kay-Kay one bit.

Kay-Kay

Explain! Did this bitch just say explain? My mind immediately began sizing up my surroundings. I saw that too many eyes were watching us. If I snapped, there would be way too many witnesses to discredit. My mind registered the need to grow calm, but my blood boiled in a raw unspeakable rage. She sat before me like a lamb willingly surrendering to the slaughter, and yet a part of me needed to hear the explanation. Was a few dollars worth leaving me for dead? The slaughter was there for the taking, but the explanation would bring me a reason. So I sat and kept my gaze on the snake.

"So, Precious is Peaches?" I asked rhetorically.

"Precious is Peaches," she confirmed.

We looked at one another and silence, a force greater than gravity, lingered between us.

"Kay-Kay, I'm not sure where to begin…"

I remained silent, wrestling with the urge to reach across the table and snap her fucking neck. *Take the neck, Kameek. It's yours.*

"I thought you was avoiding my calls because you were abandoning your responsibility," she continued.

I cut in. "I robbed that nigga, Smooth. I took the risk my damn self. Not you, me. I promised to take you shopping, because you were my girl. I wasn't fucking obligated to do shit for you, so what the fuck you mean 'abandoning my responsibility?'"

Precious, Peaches, whatever the fuck her real name was, sat looking at me as if I had grown two heads. "Is that what you believed, Kay-Kay, for all these years? That I snaked you because you didn't buy me a fucking Gucci bag or some Jordans?"

It was my turn to just look at her.

"You started avoiding my calls after I gave you all the hints," she continued.

"Hints? What hints?" I challenged in a whisper. This bitch was beating around the bush and, witnesses or not, the urge to crush was growing stronger by the second. *Take the neck, Kameek, it's yours!*

Peaches turned to one of her bodyguards and said, "Roc, bring in the gift."

"I don't have time for the games," I warned in another deadly murmur.

"Kay-Kay, please." She attempted to touch my arm and I recoiled in disgust. For the first time, she put her head down and studied her lap.

The door to the restaurant opened and the guy she called Roc walked in. At his side was a young boy who, upon seeing Precious, broke free of Roc and ran into her arms. She kissed him on the forehead before turning him to face me.

As if lightning truly strikes twice in the same place, for the second time in one day, my heart stopped and my world froze. Before Peaches was able to utter the words, I knew I was looking at a face all too familiar. A face I had watched for 24 years. The face was mine.

"Kay-Kay, meet your son. His name is KJ. Kameek Jr."

A revolution of emotions took hold of me, leaving me paralyzed and confused. The one gift Alicia refused to give me— the snake, Precious, had just delivered.

Blood test?

The boy is mine.

It's like looking in a mirror.

I'm still gonna kill this bitch.

Hug her for bringing him to me?

Hug him?

Speak, Kameek, say something.

Yet, despite the inner voice urging me to respond, I still remained speechless—stupefied to be exact.

It was my replica who broke the silence. Looking me directly in my eyes, Kameek Jr. asked, "Are you my father?"

My eyes welled up with tears from a reservoir I knew nothing about. How could I deny the obvious and be just as bad or no better than my father? Finally, my tongue no longer weighed a ton. In fact, it grew wings. "Yes, I believe so. I'm happy to meet you." I extended my hand to him awkwardly, not sure if I should give him a handshake or a hug.

The snake chimed in, hissing and shit. "KJ, give your father a hug." She nudged him towards me, and like a toy racecar that needed just a push, he ran into my arms and my world suddenly became vibrant in color. After a minute, she hissed again. "Ok, KJ. Mommy and Daddy have to talk." She reached for Kameek Jr. prying him from my arms. Her bodyguard, the one she called Roc, walked Kameek Jr. away and towards the table where the other bodyguards were sitting. As soon as Kameek Jr. left my world faded back into black and white.

I stared at Precious for a good while as I gained my composure. "So, let me get this straight? You lured them to me, and then left me for dead, because you thought I was avoiding a talk with you about your pregnancy? For dead! You left me for dead. You stuck that arm out of that car for a reason. You wanted me to know who was behind it." Peaches glanced down in shame as I continued. "Now, nine years later, you wanna talk? Bitch...leave while you can still crawl off on all fours."

Peaches

Peaches once again stared into Kay-Kay's eyes. "I didn't go through all of this to be dismissed," she informed him.

"Leave." His own calm scared him. Never before had both sides of his conscience been in full agreement. Both called for blood, but then it wouldn't be revenge. It would just be a release.

"There hasn't been a day that I didn't regret my mistake. I really thought you was trying to play me, and my emotions took me there."

Kay-Kay stared through her, playing the different scenarios of her demise in his mind. Deciding which would bring the best satisfaction. The intensity in his look conned Peaches into thinking she had his undivided attention.

"Kay-Kay," she continued. "Try to remember how crazy my life was at the time."

She was referring to her mother's drug addiction and the countless hours her and Kay-Kay spent talking about it. A nightmare they tried to make sense of together.

"I was a wreck and my recklessness almost cost you your life. There hasn't been a day since then that I haven't lived with that regret."

"Of my survival?"

"No. That you almost died because of me. Kay-Kay... I'm sorry."

His face contorted into a mask of confusion. He was pretending to be wrestling with forgiveness. He looked over at the little boy who looked like him, but even he was just a focus for his distraction, for his mind to wander and ponder his revenge.

Kay-Kay

"So you think you got me checkmated?" I asked.

It was a rhetorical question that needed no response. Of course I was checkmated, at least for the moment. Even though my mind screamed, *crush her*, would I in front of her son? In front of *our* son? With Kameek Jr. placed strategically at the tables with the shooters, the chance for a shooting to occur was effectively neutralized.

For the time being she was the safest rival that ever stood before me. The look of confidence in her eyes that said she knew the advantage went to her added insult to injury.

With a new found air of cockiness, the snake hissed again. She was ready to negotiate and with the assuredness of a sharp shooter she revealed her cards. "So, can we talk business now?"

"Hmm," I shook my head in disbelief at the audacity of this chick. To me, she was a ghost who refused to accept that she was already dead, a denial that left her trapped in a world she no longer belonged to. I would play along with her haunting for only a spell.

"Can we talk business, Kay-Kay?" she asked again before I cut her crazy ass off.

"Business? This shit ain't 'bout business! This shit has always been personal with you." The truth made her uncomfortable; her body language betrayed her. "Now you want to act like it's about business?"

"It *is* about business," she interjected feebly.

"Get the fuck out of here with that. You left me for dead, because you thought I didn't get your hint. Why give a hint? Why not just say you was pregnant?"

"Kay-Kay, you weren't stupid. You had to get the hints."

"Bitch, you're crazy."

It was clear that this line of interrogation without a hammer pounding away at her fingers or toes was going to be an exercise in futility—so I decided to play her game.

"Okay, let's talk business. What the fuck do you want?"

"I want to keep doing business without your interference," she answered.

"See, it's always personal with you. You waltz in here with a child that might be mine, expecting preferential treatment in *business* because of something *personal*."

Peaches grew visibly annoyed.

"Might be yours? Huh. Well either that or we go to war," she declared.

War! Now she was talking my language. "Bitch, you ain't ready for war, not by a long shot. I don't play games in these streets. This ain't the little Kay-Kay you knew 10 years ago. I run these streets." I said, simply explaining the facts.

"Well I don't want to run the streets, I just want to flood them," she avoided the bait.

"And in return for you flooding them, what's my percentage?" She couldn't possibly think I was going to budge on her paying.

But she did. It was obvious. I saw it in her face, but she regrouped quickly and said, "Yeah well, considering I raised our son for eight years without a dime, I was figuring that the 20 percent you tax everyone else should be greatly reduced. Kinda like backed-up child support."

I couldn't help but laugh at the audacity of this broad. "How much less are we talking?" I asked.

"I'd be willing to go 10 percent," she quickly responded.

I thought about it, pretending to contemplate far longer than was necessary. Ten percent would work until her expiration date.

"Ten percent and I get to spend time with my son, whenever I want to," my resolute stipulation.

"Now who's getting personal?" she asked.

"Precious," I called her the name her Moms gave her.

"Peaches," she corrected.

"Whatever, I..."

"Peaches," she said with conviction. Determined to define and defend her essence. "You can see your son whenever you want. You may not believe me, but that's all I ever wanted."

Making her suffer was all I wanted. It had been a fantasy of mine for close to a decade and finally the dream was mere breaths away from becoming a reality.

I left the restaurant with the mystery of Peaches answered. I now knew that the broad I had imagined exacting revenge on for years, was the mother of my only child. How would I play this? Immediately, I thought about knocking her head off and filing for custody. But then, I thought about the attachment lil' man obviously felt towards her. I had no clear answer on what my course of action should be. This broad had an unbeatable hand, it seemed. I decided for the time being, I would simply go with the flow until an opening presented itself. I also realized quickly that while she was a supplier, she wasn't the one I had been in search of. Over the years of my hunt, I realized that the supplier I was looking for had to be Spanish. Being able to withstand a drought meant the plantation where the coke was being cultivated belonged to the supplier or someone real close. Precious was neither. I suspected she was the link to the source, but anything short of torture would not make Precious give up the connect. *In due time, the torture will occur, and the connect will be revealed,* I thought. *In due time.*

Meanwhile, I had to go explain this new wrinkle to Alicia. I needed her take on it. She was the most grounded person I knew. Alicia knew very little about Precious, except that she was my mortal enemy—the snake she could never put a face to. What would her reaction be to this life-changing reality?

Alicia was at her mother's house, spending the day with some relatives who arrived the night before from Georgia. As tempted as I was to disrupt her reunion, I decided against being selfish for once. Instead, I made a rare spur-of-the-moment detour to my mom's crib.

The surprised look on my mom's face when I walked through her door told me how rare an unexpected visit from me really was. I felt bad about not visiting more frequently, but her home was no longer a place of refuge for me. It had become a courtroom over the past few years, and I was the helpless defendant. But since JB wasn't present, the judge herself would handle my prosecution—at least that's what I expected.

Instead, my Mom surprised me by grabbing my face in her hands and looking me square in the eyes, telling me that she loved me. The shiver down my spine was the only warning that her words hit me directly in the gut. Her message was perfectly timed. I needed the comfort that her soothing words offered.

Her next sentence really did the trick. "Boy, are you hungry? Come sit down. Let me fix my baby a plate!"

For the rest of the day, we talked like two adults and not mother and child. She listened more than she spoke and in return, I spoke about shit I never intended for my mother to know. She listened without judgment about how I, like Alice in Wonderland, had fallen down the rabbit hole and was unable to fully find my way out. I explained to her how a part of me wanted to walk away from the streets, but the other part took pride in all that I had built and accomplished, that the money I counted in a month was the equivalent to a surgeon's salary for an entire year.

When I told her the numbers, her eyes lit up in panic. It was obvious that she really didn't know the level I was on. I saw the surprise in her eyes, but I also saw the fear. I understood her fear, because it was a reflection of mine. If anyone in the streets ever tells you anything different from what I'm about to say then they're either delusional, a stone cold liar, or worse, a rat with a "get out of jail free card" attached to his tongue.

But here's the gritty truth: We live in a state of constant fear. Fear that any misstep will be our undoing. Fear of a foe disguised as a friend. Fear of not covering our tracks and leaving a trail of crumbs to our doorsteps. Fear of the envious, the over ambitious, the ruthless, the weak, the petty and yet we persevere. We navigate, trusting the nature and habits of the characters we surround ourselves with, but never trusting the characters themselves.

We're actors in a movie. A movie of which we are unaware of the ending or even if our characters will make it to the end. Yet we persevere, because the role we play is prominent. We are the leading characters; it's our movie and walking away or turning our back on the script just seems unheard of. Unless, of course, you figure out how to change the script and direct your own ending. I was moving in this direction and I needed my mother to understand that I knew the perils and feared the challenges. But a path out of the rabbit hole was becoming visible. Faint but visible.

After sharing the news with Moms about her potential grandson, I realized that I had to break the news to Alicia. If Kameek Jr. was in fact my son, and by the looks of it he was, then Alicia and I both had a serious adjustment to make in our lives.

Would she resent Kameek Jr.? So many thoughts were swirling through my dome as I navigated through the side blocks, and not the highway, on my way to her mom's crib. The highway would've gotten me there in minutes; by the side blocks the trip was nothing less than an hour. I needed the time to get it all together in my head. This bitch, Precious, or Peaches, or whatever the fuck else her name was, once again left me stumped.

Peaches

Peaches left the meet with Kay-Kay in a state of disbelief. The fact that she had gone through with the actual confrontation surprised her a little. Though she was the one to put the wheels in motion for this day to occur, a part of her had doubted she would actually go through with it. But she had gone through with it, and what she hoped for seemed to be shaping up to go her way. She wanted to be in Kay-Kay's life once more, somehow, some way. And for the past nine years she had longed to be able to speak with him again. The fool in her told her that he may forgive her and take her back, but she knew that his forgiveness would never be pure because her betrayal could never be pardoned.

She prayed that he wouldn't order a death sentence that would force her to pull the lever first. She hoped that her display of force and her track record was enough to convince Kay-Kay that she was ready for the collision if there was no other choice.

"So what are you thinking?" Roc asked noncommittally.

"A lot of shit, Roc. A lot of shit." Peaches' far away response told Roc not to push the conversation, but Peaches continued. "He understands that we're here to stay and I understand that we gotta pay to continue to play. That's the business discussion. As far as the personal stuff, he knows it's his child, but he still wants a DNA test for KJ."

Roc held his tongue, determined to remain apathetic. "I know you thought, and probably still think, this is a bad idea. But, I really felt like I had to confront my demon. This demon! It felt like I've been living in a witness protection program for the last nine years. The ducking and hiding is over."

Roc's admiration for Peaches' courage was top grade, but not until this very moment did his pride in his boss soar to breathtaking heights. She was not a little girl playing in a big man's game. She was a she-wolf, leading a pack of ferocious but fiercely loyal hounds.

Kay-Kay

By the time I picked Alicia up, I was weary from thinking.

"You drive. I'm tired," I said. I tossed her the keys before opening the driver side door for her.

"You must really be tired to let me drive your favorite toy," she replied and winked before caressing my cheek. Alicia always knew when I needed the extra affection to help lighten my load. I suppose that's why a lot of kats resort to alcohol or drugs when life's pressure begins to mount. They lack the caress of a soul mate who, in that simple but attentive gesture, says 'no matter what's going on, we will be alright.' An art mastered by Alicia.

I sat in the passenger seat and immediately reclined to the fullest extent possible.

"Where to?" she quipped, adjusting the mirrors to fit her comfort.

"Let's roll up to that seafood spot up in Rhode Island," I suggested with my eyes closed.

"Rhode Island, huh? Must be something serious if you're letting me drive this thing for two hours while you sleep."

I pretended to already be drifting off and gave her no response.

With my silence she had her answer. The warmth of her hand on the back of mine once again communicated her message, 'No matter what's going on, we'll be alright.' My woman was behind the wheel and without opening my eyes, I felt myself floating through the eight million stories of the naked city as she transported us to a place more serene and calming.

"So, you think just by looking at him you can tell he's yours?"

"He looks like my twin."

"With the facial hair and all?" Alicia's sarcasm was an attempt to mask her skepticism. We were finishing up the king crab legs, while waiting for our to-go bags.

"He looks exactly how I did at eight years old."

She remained silent, studying the last crab leg in her hand, perhaps counting its spikes. With the concentration of a doctor, she was examining the problem.

"So, let's say the test comes back and he *is* your child. How involved do you plan to be in his life?"

I understood the question, but the perplexity in my facial expression must've thrown her off.

"I guess what I'm asking is..."

I cut her off, "Nah, I understand your question. I would like to get to know him, definitely. If the bitch don't play games with me and let me be a part of his life, I think I'm ready. My biggest concern right now is you. How do you feel about all of this?"

"Honestly?"

"Yeah, honestly."

"I'm leery about Precious."

"Peaches," I jokingly corrected trying to lighten the conversation.

She continued without pause. "From your descriptions of her, I only see her in a negative light. I know she was the one who set you up to get shot, and now you're telling me the reason for the shooting was because she thought you were ducking your responsibility to be a father? If that's not a vindictive mind, I don't know what is. With all the other stuff you are dealing with in those streets, adding one more ruthless element so close to your bosom doesn't sound like the smartest move. But, I also understand your sense of honor. If that's your child, then even the devil herself won't prevent you from being in his life. And as your woman, hopefully one day your wife, I'm rolling with you."

To this day I'm not sure why I thought there might have been a different response, but her answer was who she was to the core and that's why I loved her so much.

Chapter 26:the agony of desperation

The agony of desperation,
I was grappling for air.
All was lost and
no one cared.

Kay-Kay

1994

It was a grim conversation to have—sitting with Spank on the visiting floor the day after he blew trial. I knew I had to get to him before the reality of his situation truly sank in. There's a numbness that overtakes the condemned moments after the sentence is rendered. Spank walked onto the visiting floor stoically chipper; go figure, a smiling zombie. His facial expression was not matching his body language. He was trying to make sense of what had occurred. Our eyes met, he smiled and though I did my best not to, I winced, and my failure was all that mattered. He sat down in front of me, quickly folding his hands. "Damn, Kay. I don't believe I blew. What the fuck happened?"

His question was the only one I could expect and the only one I had no answer for. "Your lawyer put up a damn good fight, but the evidence was overwhelming. Especially the rat boy taking the stand." I was referring to one of Touchy's lieutenants who testified that Touchy personally told him Spank was the shooter. This was the same rat boy who sent the police to most of Touchy's stash houses. It was revealed in trial that the sucker had been a confidential informer for two years and had successfully helped to bring down two different operations in the Bronx before being assigned to infiltrating Touchy.

"Man, this is only the first battle, bro. We have a war ahead of us."

Spank looked unconvinced. "I knew I should have fucked with you, Kay. Fucking with Knee..."

I needed to keep him grounded and so I pushed back, "You're a grown man, brodie. You understood the risk with this shit. Neither Knee nor Touchy put a gun to your head and told you to perform. You could've said no. Or better yet, you could've wore gloves and your own signature would've never been used against you."

"What's your point?" Spank interrupted, obviously not appreciating my insight in his time of despair.

"My point is that the grave wasn't dug by Knee; it was dug by you. And so, if you have to sit in it for the next 25 years, than do it with no regrets. Do it with a spine."

A dam worth of dreams and hopes watered up in Spank's eyes, promising to escape its cage. He tried to hold on and keep it together. He nodded his head in agreement, surrendered to my words and then they fell. Huge tears of acceptance cascaded down his cheeks. He cried in silence, all the while looking me directly in the eyes. He was hurting, badly, but the message he sent in silence was clear. He was ready for the war, but understood that his immediate future was, in all likelihood, its first casualty.

The rest of the visit went by like a blur. Though the evidence against Spank was strong, we both kept going back to the rat boy's testimony and how prideful he was in testifying against Spank. He held his head with dignity, as he looked at the jurors, honored by his occupation, unafraid of the consequences. And why should he be afraid, he was working for the occupiers, protected by their might. The hood would still embrace him while whispering behind his back.

Knee, who wore sunglasses in a windowless courtroom got up and walked out during his testimony. I didn't need to see him to feel his disgust. I knew the conversation that would follow: could we get to rat boy, and if so, how soon. But this was a discussion for Knee and I, not Spank. For Spank, I assured him that his appellant lawyer would be taken care of, and his commissary and packages would always be on time. But, I also informed him that my visits would be few and far between. The financial commitment I made to Spank—from his lawyer fees to seeing to his comfort while locked up—was based on rules of honor. I considered him a friend, so he wouldn't be forsaken. But I didn't lose sight that he joined Knee over me, a high stake gamble over the sure fire bet. My obligation as his friend would be sealed in honor, but suffering the indignities of metal detectors and disrespectful guards was reserved for a chosen few. Since Spank, as a free man, made his choice... Shit, need I say more?

While exiting the jam-packed visiting floor, I heard my name being called by a familiar voice. It was distant, but strong. I stopped and scanned the room until I spotted a hand waving at me. It was Zach, Alicia's brother in law. He was sitting with an older lady that I could only assume was his mother. He was smiling and trying to mouth something to me, but I couldn't make it out. The prison guard was behind me doing his job ushering me and a few other visitors toward the exit. I threw up a salute sign to Zach before making my departure.

I thought about Zach and the decision he made that landed him in prison. About a month after our talk, he confronted Lester inside of the barbershop where Lester worked. Lester, apparently not respecting Zach's desire to be heard, turned his back on Zach midsentence, and continued cutting a client's head. According to the witnesses, before Lester had a chance to regret his under-estimation, Zach calmly placed the gun to the back of Lester's head and pulled the trigger. Afterwards, Zach waited outside in front of the barbershop for the police to arrive. He had no intentions of running; his case was a slam-dunk for the prosecution. Charlotte was devastated, and at some point in the very first days of his arrest, she wrestled out of Zach the fact that I had given him the gun. To say that she was livid would be an understatement.

"How could you, Kameek? How could you give Zach that gun? You ruined my life. You ruined our life."

"I didn't think he would really go through with it."

"He wouldn't have if you didn't give him the damn gun, Kameek. All I asked you to do was talk to him, to try and talk sense into him. Instead, you talk him into being a wannabe gangster."

"Charlotte, listen, I did try to talk him down. I told him the fucking consequences. I even offered to take care of the situation for him."

"Oh did you? Did you really?"

"Yeah, really I did."

"You know, you got my sister fooled, but I see through you. You are a selfish piece of shit. You don't care about anything or anyone except yourself."

"So now it's my fault your husband decided to grow balls?"

"Fuck you, nigga. I hope you die slow, but until then, don't ever say shit to me ever again."

As I walked off the visiting floor, my discussion with Charlotte replayed in my mind. We hadn't spoke since that conversation and would probably never speak again for as long as either of us lived. She was devastated by what she perceived to be my betrayal. Alicia was clueless to the cutoff. Charlotte didn't say a word about my obvious blunder to Alicia, and I saw no need to give her one more thing to worry about.

While I understood Charlotte's pain, I refused to accept responsibility for her husband's decision. Especially when he still chose to go through with it after I warned him of the potential outcome. Zach telling Charlotte where he had gotten the gun troubled me. I immediately got word to him within those *walls of regrets* that some secrets were sealed in blood and could only be broken through additional bloodshed. He sent word back that he understood the warning and apologized for his wife's anger.

He believed that she would eventually simmer down. Her simmering down was of very little concern to me. The potential running of his mouth was of greater importance. When I first heard of his arrest, a top-notch lawyer was placed on standby. But as soon as Charlotte revealed her husband's recklessness to me, it was a wrap on my assistance.

Charlotte couldn't understand why I had given him a gun. I wrestled with the thought of trying to explain to her how he would've probably bought a hot one in the streets with five or six bodies on it. That he most likely would become a snitch, trying to explain to the police why the other murders connected to that gun weren't his. Or the purchased gun could've been defective and backfired on his stupid ass, or jammed and instead of being in prison for murder, he could have killed himself. She should have been thanking me for recognizing what stood before him. To ensure that he at least had a fighting chance, I had armed him.

He was gifted with a brand new cannon to harbor his burdens and mistakes. Should I have explained the code to her? That when a friend asks for arms, no matter what, if he is a friend, you arm him. When it was all said and done, I decided to let her encode me in her mind as the villain. I was the safe reason for her to go to bed at night alone. Who the fuck was I to steal her placebo?

She was running from the truth. I saw it in the jovial smile Zach sent my way as I exited the visit. Although he was facing life, he was at peace with his decision. He was at peace with finally finding his perceived manhood. If that meant a life without Charlotte, obviously it wasn't the end of the world to him. And so, I felt no guilt or regrets. If sis and I never acknowledged each other again... Shit, need I say more?

After leaving the visiting floor with Spank, I decided to stop by my mom's. I thought the conversation I had with my mother a week earlier was the talk that settled the conflict between us. I popped up at her house expecting the same energy. What I got was a lecture on my unhappiness. Miss Cleo had nothing on my mother when it came to psychic abilities.

"Despite the money, you don't look happy. You came out of my womb, so I know. You're in trouble and you can feel it."

I laughed, not disrespectfully but comically. She was uncomfortably close to the truth. The stakes of the game I played and the level I was on made every second of my life speak to a reason. If I didn't take the time out every night before I shut my eyes to reflect back on the day, I would have been finished years earlier. There is a key to the game and it's called homework. A rule taught to me by the Old God in the prison yard of Auburn. Even though I did it well, I knew Lady Luck was in my favor.

Mom's logic was the only one I couldn't climb over. She asked me about Alica and if I ever intended on making her an honest woman. She admired Alicia's intelligence as well as her commitment to me. But I was being selfish. My mom's usual argument was, "You haven't reached that level of maturity yet... You're incapable of being happy until you address the cause of your pain...." Blah blah blah. She was convinced that my father's abandonment was the hidden factor behind my occupational decisions—that I was afraid to let go of my anger and afraid to grow up. "You gotta walk away from those streets before you marry that girl. You can't be married to both her and the streets; that's adultery, son. You understand that, right?"

"I know what I'm doing, Ma. I got this. Trust me, I got this."

"For you, but what about her? You obviously feel you can handle the repercussion of your action, but what about her, son?"

"I got it, Ma...." It was like swatting at a persistent housefly.

"After all these years, you're still selfish," was her final verdict.

A. C. Clayton

Chapter 27: quiet jack

Kay-Kay
1994

I was chilling at Ruben's diner with a handful of childhood friends. The old fashioned gates were drawn down obscuring any signs of life inside and we were enjoying each other's company. I knew everyone's story. I had watched their stories play out through the years. They knew they could count on me to assist when they needed it, and most of them had utilized my helping hand.

Besides my man Brook, who made a killing selling prescription drugs, and Jaycee, who sold small quantities of weed, everyone else in the diner had legit jobs. There was Ray. I used to hump his younger sister, Dawn, on the roof when we were kids—until their father caught us one day and threatened to throw me off the roof if I so much as looked at her again. Unsatisfied with my response to his threat, he made Ray, who was older than me by three years, beat me up. Ray did the chore with very little effort. But then, JB found out what happened and beat the shit out of Ray in front of Ray's father.

There was Naquan, the fast talker who always talked about nothing. He was the only child from an over-protective mother.

She did well at keeping him out of jail, but he still lived at home and had no intentions of leaving.

To my left was my man Chaz. Chaz and Knee had always been super tight. One day they got locked up for breaking a kid's jaw in school. Chaz swore it was Knee and Knee swore it was Chaz, but they both told the police that the punch had come from an invisible man. No, literally, that was their story. A fucking invisible man did it. What more could you expect from fifth graders? As the years went by their interest changed. Chaz loved basketball and rapping. Knee loved the streets. Knee never tried to pull Chaz in, but Chaz always tried to pull Knee out. Whenever they got together, the jokes would be endless.

Onederful, my example of an honorable gladiator, was talking on the payphone bending up some female's ear with chivalrous talk. He was a kat of moral renown. In the streets, he took his licks like everyone else, but throughout all the trials his principles stood firm. If there was anyone in that diner whose words I held in high regard, it was him. Ever since I was a little boy, I knew he had my best interest at heart. Onederful was a Five Percenter who lived his lessons, unwaveringly. He didn't drink, smoke, or partake in any criminal activity. But more importantly, he didn't judge those who did, so his words carried the weight of a father, even to men much older than him.

Then there was Quiet Jack, whose stoic and aloof demeanor had given him the title 'quiet' for as long as I could remember. Quiet Jack and JB had always been close. The only time I ever saw him say anything more than a few words was when he was around JB. The funny thing was that the shit he would be talking about was always insightful.

Quiet Jack's father was a retired police officer who used to warn my mother about her sons' transgressions. We always suspected Quiet Jack of not being so quiet when he got around his pops so, even though he was a part of the crew, everyone—including the guys in the diner—talked sports and politics around him for the most part. Even though his father had been five years into his retirement, old habits were hard to change.

Iquan was the hot head of the lot. He grew up in severe conditions; both his mother and father were dope fiends whose nodding and scratching in the middle of the street were, unfortunately, usual occurrences.

Iquan was the youngest of us present in the diner. He was under me by two years. His little sister, Jan, got rescued early. An aunt of theirs who lived in Maryland scooped her, but left Iquan behind. Not having Jan around to be responsible for worked in reverse of what perhaps was intended. He became a lonely kid living in a nightmare and his only daily companion became his anger. My mother felt sorry for him and gave him an open invitation to come eat and sleep whenever he wanted to. I became his big brother and he relished in my hand-me-down clothes the same way I did with JB's.

One day a gold chain of my mother's went missing out her bedroom and when she confronted him about it, Iquan exploded and cursed her out. It took very little time for me to catch him in the park playing basketball as if nothing happened. As soon as he saw me coming he took off running. I chased that little mothafucka down and beat him senseless.

What I admired about him that day was that he fought back and never stopped fighting. Even after his eyes were swollen and his mouth bloody, my knuckles were hurting and I was dead tired, he still invited me to his private part while calling me every name in the book.

His parents heard about the beating and decided it was only right to chastise me, but in the middle of their lecture the heroin kicked in and I was able to walk away leaving them both suspended on a lean, defying gravity. When I returned 15 minutes later, they were still nodding and scratching, suspended in mid air.

My mother eventually forgave Iquan, but the trust was never the same. While I was in prison, Iquan had grown into a terror. Some fool gave him a gun and he decided to correct every wrong he could recall with it. His murder trial was big news in the hood. He killed a dealer named Duke, who years before, had beat Iquan's mother mercilessly over some stolen drugs in front of him. The beating was similar to the one I had given him over the stolen chain.

Initially, there were witnesses who said Iquan walked up to Duke in front of the laundromat and shot him eight times at point blank range before calmly walking off, like he was going for a stroll in the park. Yet, by the time trial began the witnesses had recanted their statements. They were no longer sure Iquan was the shooter.

Of course the hood had gotten to them and explained the reality of what they had witnessed. A young lion coming of age and correcting a wrong the only way he knew how. The acquittal strengthened the hood, in my opinion. It said that there were rules and consequences for a ruthless hand.

Iquan came home about five months before my return and on a couple of occasions. I gave him minor jobs that required a little muscle. I used him sparingly because I didn't want to wake a sleeping giant and be the cause of his downfall. He was working as a painter's apprentice and was satisfied with getting that paycheck. Everyone knew what he was capable of, though. And I knew that he was always on call whenever I needed him.

The last person was my good friend Ruben. He was the glue that held everyone in the diner together, the one constant in a hood of change. About a year after my release, Ruben came to me with the idea of opening a diner in the hood. After showing me his idea on paper, I agreed to finance it. In less than six months, I had been paid back in full and his spot had become a place of refuge for many.

The talk was primarily about Michael Jordan, a topic I gave less than two fucks about, but it felt good just to be around no hidden agendas or larceny.

The conversation took an interesting turn when Ruben asked, "Did ya hear that there were letters found at both Big Chance's and Rico's murder scenes?"

I perked up immediately. Ruben was really only talking to me, but if his store was under surveillance, the casual conversation could not be considered a conspiracy. He continued. "A friend of mine with ties to the NYPD," a quick glance in Quiet Jack's direction told me where it was coming from. "Told me they suspect that there may be a vigilante-type serial killer on the loose. Killing hustlers."

"What did the letters say?" I asked with great interest.

"Oh, from what I'm hearing, the investigators are being tight-lipped about it. I hear they've nicknamed the killer 'The Poet.' I can only imagine that the letters are poems."

Ruben was doing his math. I nodded my head in agreement then in disbelief. "This shit sounds like something straight from a movie," I commented fully engaged. "Man, Big Chance got murdered in his side chick's bed, so his wife refused to even attend his funeral."

"Ah, that's fucked up," Naquan interjected.

A resounding "Yeah" went around the room. With that, the conversation went back to sports.

But my wheels began turning. I thought it coincidental that two of the peacocks I had been squeezing both got murdered in their cribs and not in the streets. In both instances, I figured it would just be a matter of time before the wife—or in Big Chance's case, the mistress—would eventually be charged for the crime. *It's always the wife,* I remember thinking. But obviously, whatever was being written on those letters found at the murder scenes had the pigs oinking otherwise.

Chapter 28: the summons

Corrupting an unguarded soul is child's play

JB
1994

JB was summoned to the senator's home for an important reason, but hadn't a clue of what the reason was. Ordinarily they met at the senator's office during daytime hours. This meeting was nocturnal, nestled in the privacy of the lawmaker's castle.

"Jamal, you have been a very stable and resonate voice in our community over the last two years," the senator began. "Your tireless efforts on behalf of my constituents have not gone unnoticed by me. I always try to acknowledge and reward loyalty to the best of my abilities..." The graying senator paused and stared directly at JB as if contemplation of his words were actually being considered. "...Whenever the opportunity to do so presents itself." His smile broadened, revealing his full arsenal of pearly whites. "The upcoming mayoral election is, once again, upon us and due to expiring term limits, we will have a new mayor. Most of our constituents will either vote for the Black or Hispanic candidate that they recognize or can relate to the most. Here's the dilemma," the lawmaker continued in a low conspirator's tone. "They can't win! They will be going up against a billionaire media magnate and his billionaire media magnate friends. They will spend the bread to divide our vote. We will begin to squabble amongst ourselves and the rest is history."

JB felt Sinclair's assessment should be challenged and so he spoke. "So if you know this can potentially happen..."

"Not 'potentially happen.' It will happen," Sinclair interrupted.

"If you know it *will* happen, then why not work to prevent the division?"

Even before JB finished his question, Sinclair's head was shaking profusely at such a question. "You know, JB, sometimes your naïvety borders on moronic outburst. Let me explain how the real world works, as opposed to the comic books. Black people, like all other people, are creatures of habit and conditioning. It starts in the homes, but is cultivated and incubated in the schools; we are conditioned as a people to be divided. So even when we know our division plays into other people's agendas, we still find a way to justify its presence. This political process is no different than the street shit you grew up in. The only difference is, where you guys risked it all for chump change and fleeting reps, we play for real bread and honorable legacies. This is the game you've placed yourself in. This is the arena you choose to test your swords in. We feed families and communities." Sinclair became animated. His calm and cool demeanor was lost. His hands, as if bolts of wisdom were discharging from his fingers, helped to emphasize every word. JB found himself in conflict.

"Sacrifices must be made," the senator continued. "Tough decisions based on practicality, not fantasy, must be adhered to. You have to decide: do you want to continue to be a poor, struggling, community leader? Or do you want to be a true power player, representing more than the interest of a 20-block radius? It's up to you, brother. But before I go on any further I need to know that I can count you in."

The question, which sounded more like a challenge, became the elephant in the room. JB's heart raced. His parched mouth kept his lips sealed. He realized a minute too late that he had walked into a squeeze play and his decision, which had to be made now, would affect his immediate future.

He thought about Pam and the fetus growing in her womb. He barely had the money to take care of himself and now a baby was on its way. Since he had been home, he had been a selfless servant of the people and he would have remained a servant.

But now things were different, he thought, with his growing family in mind.

JB looked Sinclair firmly in his eyes and said, "I'm in."

Sinclair smiled appraisingly. "Well, good for you, young man. So now, let's talk business. Here's the game plan. We endorse no one until the division severs alliances. After that, we will say due to the division we choose to get behind the person who, with the most practical agenda of moving this great city, blah blah blah."

JB cringed before asking, "And that person will be the republican candidate?"

"Oh wow, you are on a roll tonight," Sinclair said. "But here's the trade-off: We will get 17 posts to which I will give you five!"

Confused, JB interrupted. "Posts?"

Once again Sinclair looked annoyed. "Yes, posts. Major job positions with governmental administrative levels. 'Deputy Director of This,' and 'Assistant Director of That,' or 'Managing Supervisor,' etc."

Sinclair waved his hand into infinity, yet JB was still confused. "What would I do with five jobs?"

Sinclair restrained his chuckle as best he could, realizing that JB really was more childlike than he previously suspected. Immediately, Sinclair regretted offering JB the five posts, figuring he probably could have gotten away with giving the fool only two. Sinclair overestimated JB's intelligence and made a mental note of his slip. It was a mistake he was determined never to make again.

"Well, you have five posts and two options. You can give posts away to allies who have the credentials, or you can sell the post to allies or potential allies who have the credentials."

"Sell them?" JB asked, as the realization of what was being offered slowly began to take root.

"Yes, sell them."

"For how much?"

"Hmm, well the prices vary, but anywhere from 10k to 75k depending on the post."

"Are you serious?" JB questioned with renewed enthusiasm.

"Son, what do you think it means to endorse a candidate? It means, 'I'll scratch your back, you scratch mine.' It means unfettered access to the person you help elect. And since the rules say the candidate cannot solicit your support with money or gifts, they bargain with the only capital they can use, which is key positions for your people in their administration, and accessibility. This is how the game is played. Sharpton, Jesse, you name 'em, they play it."

A. C. Clayton

Chapter 29: secret rendezvous

Kay-Kay

1994

Alicia's friend Shaun was stealth. Secretly, we met in restaurants and hotels careful to remain undetected. I knew Shaun just as long as I did Alicia; in fact, I met them together. It was a Sunday afternoon in a roller-skating rink in Brooklyn called Empire. On Sundays, teens from all over Brooklyn congregated in Empire to show off everything including their skills on skates. It was also a place where neighborhood posses formed alliances for the sole purpose of claiming dominion over the rink.

Me and my crimey Kev went every week religiously, indifferent to the idiots roving around in packs. Kev was a shooter who never hesitated on the draw, a fact well known by all. We went every week for the broads. There was no other place in Brooklyn where the pick of the litter sat so invitingly.

Alicia, Shaun, and another friend I can't recall her name, were enjoying themselves. They were rolling around the rink like professionals showing off their skills. Shaun was by far the baddest chick on wheels, with Alicia coming in a distant second. At 17, Shaun had the body of a grown woman and every eye driven by testosterone paid close lustful attention to her every move. Her chocolate skin glistened under the colorful lights of the glimmering disco ball. Her graceful moves were of a majestic design; her crossover turns and backwards gliding made my erection impossible to restrain. I wanted her badly, but I watched her turn down attempt after attempt. Secretly, I built up the nerve, prepping myself for the approach and the potential rejection. Finally, just when I felt ready to go in for the conquest, Kev swooped in and scooped her with a corny joke.

Before I knew it, he was all in her ear and she was blushing in surrender. Kev introduced me to Shaun and Shaun introduced me to Alicia. It was then that I noticed Alicia's beauty. She was a redbone with green eyes. While her body was nowhere near Shaun's, her smile and the radiance of laughter in her eyes drew me in. I was willing to settle for the silver knowing that at least it was my home team that got the gold.

Alicia and I exchanged phone numbers and by the following weekend we were on a double date with Kev and Shaun. We took them to the movie theater in Times Square, but Kev and Shaun argued like a married couple the entire time. They argued about butter on the popcorn, Kev telling the plot of the movie, his getting too close too fast, and on and on. Finally, Kev had enough and called Shaun every kind of bum bitch he could think of in the book.

A. C. Clayton

We parted ways that night, Alicia and I, both siding with our friend. Kev continued to call Shaun every name under the sun the entire train ride home, and I sat there and agreed with him but I was secretly happier than my Puerto Rican buddies at a Menudo concert. I was already scheming on how to dump Alicia and get to Shaun.

Now all these years later, Shaun still possessed the curves of a racetrack. Heads still turned, as every path she walked was a runway of her design. I was seated at the Hilton Hotel's bar, sipping on cranberry juice when she walked up and gave me a light kiss on the cheek.

"Alicia is getting suspicious," she said as she sat down next to me. I disagreed but found it pointless to object. "I feel so guilty doing this," she said and smiled. I smiled back and slid her a manila envelope covering her fee. She was professional at what she did. We left the bar and headed to the room I had reserved for us. So far, the tab was close to 90 grand and climbing, but it was worth every penny.

Chapter 30: Reparations

We remember the beaten,
While our hearts kept on beating,
Refusing to quit, fucker,
Until we get even.

Kay-Kay

1994

The day finally arrived. I awoke fully charged to the sound of a low but harmonious snore. I sat upright in my bed and took in a sight of beauty other men would die to behold. Alicia slept— such a masterpiece. Her rhythm of breathing was unhurried and tranquil, while a slight smile of naughty thoughts creased her lips. Was I the cause of that smile? Though our bodies were close, our spirits were light years apart. Looking at Alicia in such a peaceful and worry-free sleep was like looking at a distant planet and wondering what life would be like there. I glanced at the clock; its neon orange light read the time: 12:18 a.m. I took a deep breath as I watched my babe sleeping for what could be the last time.

The repetitive and thunderous knock at the door of my chest cavity sounded like the propellers of a helicopter upon landing. I now understood the importance of the war drums, they mimicked the pulse of a heart that has only two choices: fight or flight. With Alicia, I could flee into the arms of assimilation and conformity, fall into the role of a doctor's husband whose checkered past was a thing of the past. Or I could risk everything for the freedom that a victorious heist could deliver.

The war drum thumped, an option for cowards—flee and be safe. I looked once more at Alicia as she slept oblivious to the choice I must make. I kissed her on the cheek gently, so as to not wake her or disturb her smile. She was a gentle soul who touched my life. I silently prayed for her understanding if this heist went wrong and my consequence was the morgue. It was the call of the drums living in my chest that issued the challenge, a challenge I was powerless to decline. *Steal what I feel is a need, or else why breathe.* It was a tough predicament and she slept without knowing. She would either awake to news of a nightmare or my victorious voice, unable to share with her the truth of what I won. I left my sleeping beauty asleep in her beauty. For me it was time to get ugly. It was time to rob the dragons in their own lair.

Hypervigilant

The itsy, bitsy spider scaled down the warehouse's façade. He wore all black to blend seamlessly with the night. The coordinates were correct and the cameras, which hung from the building of interest, were aimed at the street. They would never see it coming. They would never see him coming. Electronic eyes were the mainline of defense, the only thing that would alarm the targets of the assault team's arrival. The snip of the wire that sat directly above the camera itself needed to occur, and so good money was spent to ensure that it was taken care of.

The assault team patiently awaited the coast-is-clear sign, adrenaline racing through their veins at a terrifying speed; they were men amped to a higher wattage. The moment of truth and grit stood before them. Slowly they lowered the masks over their faces, transforming themselves into superheroes of the D.C. and Marvel kind. The masks were for their alter egos and reminders that they were the liberators, not the villains.

Ironman nodded his head at something Superman suggested. Both were in agreement pointing to a shining light at the edge of the pier that was never in the plans or rehearsal. Ironman spoke to the Black Panther in a low whisper. "I'll be back. I'm going to check that out. Hopefully, it's nothing. But, it's better to be safe than sorry."

The Black Panther gave no response; his adrenaline could not be dissuaded. The assault was going down tonight. The coast-is-clear sign penetrated the darkness. The assault was going down now.

Ironman returned a few seconds later. "It was nothing but a garage light left on—probably by accident."

Superman spoke, "Let's shake."

Kay-Kay

The smell of rusty metal and river sewage sat in my nostrils like weed smoke that refuses to leave. I pulled the rubber Black Panther mask down completely altering my appearance. I chose this character because he represented a cause bigger than himself. A nation depended on him, just as the hood depended on the success of this heist. Ironman and Superman, the twins of different stature and weight, had planned this to a tee. They could care less about ending a drought. Their only concern was the millions of dollars this score would yield. Certified and determined, an unstoppable combination, we were entering this arena with our game faces on. If the juxx went wrong, if the alphabet boys refused to read our handwriting, then this move would truly become one for the record books and carnage would be its title. With the first line of defense taken care of, our march toward the second perimeter was quick and easy.

On The Brink

The itsy, bitsy spider joined the team just as they made their way around the massive warehouse divide that separated the transport dock from the administrative center. He now wore a night crawler mask, an irony not lost on the Black Panther whenever he thought about his friend, cross-dressing June. Their well-oiled guns were resting in their hands. Screwed-on silencers made them a couple ounces heavier and the trajectory of their shots, a little lower if they didn't take the difference into consideration. It was a point of emphasis that Reece stressed during every rehearsal.

They hit the corner with stealth and precision, catching two FBI agents off-guard playing cards. Their startled looks said it all. Never in a million years did the sight before their eyes ever present itself as a possibility—superheroes with silencers. Instinctively, their arms went into the air—out numbered and caught off-guard made the guns on their hips useless and just for show. Nightcrawler and the Black Panther moved quickly; gags and ropes ensured that the next and final level, which was undoubtedly the most difficult, would not be burdened by a failure to secure the second one.

A. C. Clayton

Kay-Kay

So far, so fucking good, thought Kay-Kay. We were moving with perfect timing. Our hours of training and Reece's recognizance were proving true blue. While June and I worked the ropes and gags, securing the bases stolen, Superman was already moving toward the nerve center.

Liberation Is Ours

The evil villains never knew what hit them. A sleeping sentinel was monitoring the one camera that promised them a fighting chance. His snoring wasn't an act. He was temporarily out of commission, making the superheroes job a guaranteed score. The remaining guards were also caught with leisurely dispositions, from reading magazines to watching *The Honeymooners* on a portable television. The startled and perplexed looks on all five of their faces were practically identical to each other. Only one guard, a young, round clone of Tom Cruise, who clearly skipped out on quite a few workout sessions, found the nerve to articulate their expression. "What the fuck are you doing? Do you know where you are?"

The Black Panther spoke, "We're in a leprechaun hole, ready to kill for the Gold, so shut the fuck up chubby and get down on your knees with the rest of them."

The guard showed resistance, evaluating his options or perhaps his chances.

Ironman took deadly aim at the guard's left eyeball with his handheld cannon, and prepared to squeeze the trigger.

The heist was about to become a homicide, and the homicide would turn into a massacre. An eternity of limited seconds presented themselves, the only time afforded as Ironman contemplated putting a bullet into fat boy's skull.

No sooner had fat boy puffed up his chest did a bullet muffled by a silencer send him to the floor. The shot didn't come from Ironman, though. It came from Nightcrawler. And instead of it being a headshot, it was a blast that shattered fat boy's kneecap.

Ironman took a long look at Nightcrawler; even the mask couldn't contain the anger and heat escaping through its open portals. Both Ironman and Superman were visibly furious. The rule, "what we shoot, we kill," had just been broken. In such a high stake game like the one we were playing, rules had to be adhered to.

The guard crumbled like a deflated balloon, howling in pain and cursing the heroes to damnation or justice.

I broke the tension and perhaps saved the mission from implosion. "The next shot is the death shot. If you have something or someone to live for, I suggest you begin considering their grief. All you mothafuckas listen up. None of this shit belongs to you. None of it. You are nothing but guard dogs. To die for it, makes no sense. If you make the news, it won't be because you foiled this—it will just be your pictures on a screen and news anchors talking about how you died bravely in the line of duty. It's your choice, but I assure you, every scenario has us coming out on top."

Superman yanked the agent who had the key to the property gate to his feet. Nightcrawler accompanied them as they marched him toward the goodies.

With all the guards gagged and secured, including Tom Cruise who was falling in and out of consciousness from the waves of pain that engulfed him, the loading of the FBI truck took under 40 minutes. Not only did the superheroes clear the warehouse of what they came for, they also took a massive arsenal of firearms, evidence that would never make it into the testimonies at a dozen or more upcoming trials.

Slowly the superheroes drove the truck off the compound, careful not to draw any suspicion due to unusual activity. Reece was in the driver's seat, his Superman mask sat next to him, ready for use at the drop of a dime if the need for a disguise arose. The three other superheroes sat in the back with the booty, masks already off, replaced by grins engraved on their faces. The kind you see on high stakes gamblers, rewarded for their heart and their risk.

The unloading of the truck and transportation was handled with equal stealth and professionalism. Handbone and Ace drove the new truck carrying the cargo to a designated location in Hunts Point. While Reece and June drove the FBI truck to a pier in Williamsburg, where they ditched it behind some brush and abandoned buildings. It would be found in a day or two, but would yield no evidence against them. Kay-Kay followed in a car that Reece and June quickly jumped into. With seatbelts secure, the three of them rode through Brooklyn cautiously obeying the traffic laws, thinking of the money they were about to divide.

Kay-Kay

The days after the caper were really quiet, too quiet for my taste. There was no mention of the heist on any news channel or paper. The FBI was playing this close to their chest either out of embarrassment or because they were working an angle. The five of us met in the Hunts Point garage to divvy up the goods. Ace and Reece already had a buyer for their portion and had plans on relocating out of the country as soon as the sale was final. Handbone and I decided to sit on our product for a little while.

The FBI would undoubtedly have their confidential informers wired up for surround sound and closed captioning for the foreseeable future. Handbone and I would eventually slow leak the product back into the streets through a few trusted suppliers. But in the meantime, I had a couple of other pressing issues that needed to be settled, so we would be patient. As for the guns, they were my idea to grab and because they were hot, no one else wanted to deal with them. They were all mine to do with as I pleased, so Handbone and I took the tedious task of breaking them down and destroying them. The missing guns would guarantee that a few good men would make it home, but I refused to put these weapons back into the hood. There were more than enough already threatening the innocent; I wouldn't be one to add any more.

June was taking his product to a Colombian supplier I had on the squeeze. I told June that he needed to hold up and wait awhile, but he shrugged my suggestion off before rendering this outlook. "It's easy for you to say when this lick was just another score for you, but this was my bread and butter, my retirement move. I'm about to lay up, buy a beautiful house, find me a broad I can trust, make some babies, and get fat off of good food."

I laughed because I knew he was dead serious, but I also saw the conflict in Ace's eyes as he watched June speak. Reece with his customary smile remained aloof, but he too was gauging the dialogue, wrestling with his own inner voices. June didn't stick around for long. He packed the trunk of his Land Rover, wished us all the best, and escaped the potential inferno.

No sooner had he departed did Reece speak. "I'm a little worried about that one there." The customary smile never leaving his face.

We all nodded in agreement.

"Why did he rush to save that mothafucka?" Ace asked seemingly perplexed. "He knew the rule, 'what we shoot, we kill.' Why did he block my shot?"

Handbone, the only one who had no clue what Ace was referring to, remained silent.

"Exactly!" Reece chimed in, "What the fuck was that all about?" Fear and trepidation crept into the question.

"I haven't been able to make sense out of it myself, and I've been thinking about it since the moment it happened. Maybe he just has a good heart?" I offered.

"Or maybe there's another reason we're overlooking," Reece countered. "Look, Kay-Kay. We're out of the country within a week and we may never come back to this rat hole, but we did bring him in. And before we leave, if you want us to take him out to keep it on the safe side, we would."

I'm not going to front. I truly considered taking Reece up on the offer. That move June did, shooting the agent in the leg wasn't a mercy move consistent with his character. The thought that he didn't want to hit someone who was probably on the same team as him invaded all of our thinking. But it could all be paranoia, the type that keeps us alive while also keeping us in fear.

"Nah, bro. I admit it was a weird move, but I don't think y'all made a mistake bringing him in on the juxx. No one else would've been able to disable that camera the way he did. I think it was just a loner move."

"A cross-dressing move, you think?" Ace questioned with a smirk, before finishing his thought. "Just be careful, Kay. I swear it's taken everything in my power to not drop him."

"I will, bro. And I'll definitely keep an eye on him." We looked at each other once more before saying our goodbyes. It saddened me to think that this was possibly the last time I would ever see my childhood buddies, but at least the goodbyes weren't at a cemetery or prison. We were departing as millionaires, a triumph of thieves.

To play on the safe side, Handbone and I moved our portion of the product just like everyone else that very day. I understood Ace and Reeces' concern completely. To override a rule we all agreed on left some serious unanswered questions.

Was June a rebel or a double agent? Either one was deadly because they were two faces of the same coin. If you don't respect agreed upon rules then what would make you respect the rules against ratting and cooperation?

Sometimes, the most successful of us connects dots in complex ways. The game we played presented a labyrinth of possibilities that leaves no room for doubt or second guesses. I would keep my eyes and ears on June from here on out. The first sign that he possibly crossed over, I wouldn't hesitate to uphold the law and administer justice.

Chapter 31: matter of principle

In the sea of suckers,
Gangsters drown in honor

Knee

1995

With winds pushing close to 48 miles per hour, an arctic breath of the Most High enveloped New York City. Only people who needed to brave the cold did so with great reluctance. Knee, however, was oblivious to the weather and, for that matter, any other form of distraction. His adrenaline was working as an internal heating system. His black leather gloves were worn not to protect his hands from the cold, but to disrupt his prints from leaving any trace. Knee was a man with a singular purpose: to destroy the rat bastard who chose to become a paid informant and bury his boy Spank.

Kay-Kay's warning that the Feds would be watching fell on deaf ears. Knee reasoned that dudes like Kay-Kay always pretended to see bigger pictures, but the game was all fucked up because mothafuckas was *seeing* bigger pictures instead of painting them.

"Watch the fucking Picasso I paint tonight," Knee mumbled to himself. The rat was definitely in his hole. Turtle had been staked out in Red Hook for more than a week carefully watching the vermin's movements. Today was the first time Turtle saw the rat unaccompanied.

"He's finally all alone," were Turtle's only words into the receiver of the pay phone before the line went dead and Knee was on his way.

Now on this cold winter night in hell, Knee was standing in front of the informant's apartment. He took one last look to make sure there were no visible cameras in the hallway before reaching into his brown paper bag. A handful of cloth strips were the prize he dug for. After lighting the strips one by one he began strategically placing them along the cracks of the rat's apartment door. As the smoke began to gather, Knee carefully began fanning it into the cracks. He didn't want the smoke to enter any other apartment but the rat's. A few times he had to douse the flames to control the direction of the smoke. But finally, the smoke alarm inside the apartment began to wail. It was like music to his ears. Knee heard the muffled cursing from the rodent inside; he was looking for the cause of the smoke. The trail led him to the door and, ultimately, his death.

The rat squirmed for his life, pleading with Knee not to shoot. "Take what you want, man. I have money, coke, please man. Oh god, please, not like this."

Yet the black mask covering Knee's face was impenetrable. Only the fire in Knee's eyes told his victim that there would be no intercession on his behalf. Knee's first and final words were, "This is for Spank."

The getaway car was warm and cozy. Turtle had been sitting idle for the past hour waiting for his general to return. Only after climbing into the passenger seat did Knee finally dare to acknowledge the temperature outside. "Damn, it's cold out there."

He tossed a small duffle bag into the back seat and grinned at Turtle. "The rat had a stash of cheese."

It took two whole days before the victim's girlfriend found the body. In no time, top brass, as well as a team of federal agents, were moving in and out of the apartment. The nature of their business calloused them to seeing dead bodies, even when the victims were on their payroll. As one federal agent put it, "This cocksucker took out a promising star." But what caught their attention more than the loss of their beloved informant was the message directed to them—a message almost mocking them. There was a chunk of cheese lodged in the mouth of the deceased and a note placed in his hands. The note was viewed as a personal affront to the agents, one that they swore would

eventually be avenged. The content of the note would be spoken of in law enforcement circles to this very day:

> The price rats must pay
> for playing in the mud with pigs!

A. C. Clayton

Chapter 32: a little girl's dream

Spring 1995

I surprised Alicia the day before her spring break. Told her to pack her bags because we were heading to Hawaii.

"What? Where? Tomorrow? How?"

"Damn, babe, you asking too many questions. Acting like you don't want to go or something." I grabbed her waist, pulling her close to me. "We need to get away and go somewhere majestic."

"You're such a romantic. *Majestic*, huh?" Alicia mockingly replied.

"I mean, we did the Bahamas already. Hawaii has to be as beautiful, if not more."

She nodded her head in agreement, her eyes already glossing over dreamily.

"You've been studying so hard for your mid-term exams, it's time to take a break."

"But I don't have a new bathing suit. My hair is not done."

I attempted to silence her with a kiss but she kept right on with the worrying. "I have to get my nails done, my feet done... Oh my god, look how horrible my feet look! I can't go anywhere looking like this."

"Relax baby, here's some bread. Go take care of everything you need."

She shook her head vigorously. "Kameek, you are always so full of surprises."

"Baby, don't wait up tonight for me. I have a lot of running around to do, and a lot of shit to put in order before we leave. Our flight leaves at 10:30 a.m., so be ready."

"Oh my god, Kameek! Be ready? How long are we staying out there?"

"About a week, but don't pack too heavy. You can buy whatever else you need out there."

Alicia left in haste, talking to herself, mumbling under her breath about all the things she needed to get done within the next 24 hours. Undoubtedly, she would call her friends with the exciting news, and her parents would also know within the hour. I figured it was the least I could do to make her happy.

It had been nearly two years since I took her to the Bahamas. That meant it was two years since I proposed to her. Since that trip, I hadn't been susceptible to any wedding dates and avoided taking trips with her for fear of her bringing up the discussion of marriage. But the signs of discontent were there. She was growing restless.

One day, I overheard her talking to her childhood friend, Hotdog, about me not being agreeable with the wedding date. So, I figured she would think this Hawaii trip might buy me some more time. She was all I needed in a woman. My hesitation to get married was only a financial one, and not a hesitation born out of second guesses. There was no question of my love for Alicia. I just wanted to make sure my money was buoyant enough for any blows that might come our way. I needed to know that if I walked away, completely and utterly from the streets, that my investments would be enough to sustain us. The risky, but successful, heist my superheros and I pulled off with perfection ensured that I was ready for any unusual storm.

When I walked into the house at 7:45 a.m., Alicia had our bags packed and was ready to roll. I took a quick shower and we headed to the airport.

The plane ride was long to say the least. Five hours to Los Angeles, then another five hours to Honolulu International Airport. We immediately boarded a small Cessna and flew to the northern tip of the main island, to an exclusive and secluded resort.

"Aloha," was sung by a chorus of tanned smiling faces.

A beautiful Polynesian woman by the name of Moana approached us. She introduced herself as our host and promised an experience of a lifetime. Necklaces of flowers called leis were placed around our necks and on our shoulders, a welcoming gift from a land of beauty.

Moana led us down a dirt road away from the landing strip. The road grew narrow as we entered a thicket of exotic flowers. The air was fresh and relaxing. A cool but steady breeze sang a melody of serenity.

Alicia's face was worry free for the first time. I grabbed hold of Alicia's hand as Moana guided us towards our bungalow.

"Don't worry, your bags will follow shortly," Moana assured.

Our bungalow sat in the middle of a group of other bungalows in the heart of a grassy, tropical terrain. Mammoth, movie-like palm trees created a canopy of shade. From a distance, we could see people gathering all around our designated bungalow.

"What's going on?" Alicia asked Moana. "Why are those people there?"

Before Moana could answer, I chimed in. "Damn, baby, that lady in the flower dress looks a lot like your moms."

By this time, the crowd had swelled and we had moved close enough to make out faces. Alicia suddenly stopped dead in her tracks and asked, "What the hell is going on?"

I tried to look surprised. "What do you mean?"

The crowd continued walking toward us, and Alicia's eyes began to water.

"Oh, them" I replied. "They're here for our wedding."

Alicia looked at the smiling faces. She saw everyone—from the faces she would expect, to the ones she would have never guessed. Her parents and two younger brothers were present. The only one missing from her immediate family was her older sister, Charlotte. My mother, JB, his pregnant girlfriend Pam, and my uncle were walking together. Alicia's friends Shaun, Desiree, Hotdog and Shalunda made up another cluster. My old friend Handbone and Robert Jr., Knee's son, walked side by side. All of these faces were expected, but then there was Sunshine, Alicia's hairstylist, Mr. Wilson, her fifth-grade teacher who told her she would be a doctor one day and wrote her a recommendation letter to enter medical school. There was her cousin Pam from Seattle, who she had not seen since she was seven, and nurse Elaine, the kind woman who helped nurse me back to good health after being shot years earlier.

It cost me a pretty penny to fly everyone out, but we only live once and tomorrow is not guaranteed to any man. So our todays are, in truth, the most important. Shaun had organized this wedding down to a tee, and so far it was running as smoothly as I could have imagined. The countless hours of planning and organizing, looking at fabric and color samples in hotel rooms with Shaun was paying off.

The crowd engulfed us. I felt like a politician shaking so many hands. Alicia was jumping up and down hugging everyone who came up to her.

After about five minutes of congratulations, Shaun's voice crescendoed above the crowd. "Okay, people, let the lovebirds go in and rest. We have a lot more celebrating to do before this is all over."

Slowly, the crowd of loved ones dispersed, heading to their destinations of choice. I paid for the entire resort so every bungalow belonged to one of our guests. Shaun and Moana were the only two still at our sides as we walked toward Bungalow No. 7.

Alicia looked at Shaun in disbelief for a long time before saying, "Girl you knew all about this and didn't say jack?"

"Babe, not only did she know, she planned every detail," I said.

"Well, actually, Moana helped. She was my eyes and ears on this side of the pond. Without her this wouldn't have been possible," Shaun clarified.

Moana blushed in appreciation. Alicia hugged both Moana and Shaun affectionately.

Shaun gave Alicia that all too familiar coy smile before saying, "Girl, get freshened up. We've got a busy day ahead."

Our bungalow appeared to be made out of sugar cane and straw. Its true structure, I discovered later, was bamboo thatch and palm leaf. We stepped onto its deck like two conquerors of love. I expected to hear the wooden floors creak in response to our every step. Instead, each step created its own comforting feeling that reminded me of walking on pillows. Never had I felt so light. I suspected that my burdens had decided to take a vacation, as well.

As soon as I closed the white French doors, I was struck in the face with a pillow.

"Kameek Barnes you are something else." Alicia's tears of joy began flowing down her face. She took both my hands into hers. They were moist and warm like her insides. We gazed at each other in silence. We belonged to each other and no one else.

I lifted her up off her feet. *So this is the weight of my heart?* Gently, I placed her on the bed. *Behold, my masterpiece.*

Shaun had organized a private luau for our guests that evening. Hand in hand, smile for smile, Alicia and I arrived right before the festivities began.

Hula dancers, elegant and graceful, guided masterfully by Tahitian drummers, told beautiful stories of vibrant Polynesian folklore. Santa-bellied Samoan fire dancers left me in awe; human dragons stood before us. Lomi salmon dissolved in my mouth like cotton candy. A cold dish's flavor, a cross between unbelievable and astonishing, made my aversion to onions and tomatoes a thing of the past. Free-flowing Mai Tai's relaxed my spirit and cured my jetlag. I wasn't a drinker or smoker, so the effects of alcohol kicked in a lot sooner on me than it did the rest.

My family enjoyed the unfamiliarity of my laughter. A hug from my mother, and dap from my brother, spoke to their pride and support for such a grown man move. They knew I had it in me, and here I was delivering.

Being only a day shy of making a commitment to the one I loved in front of everyone that she and I love seemed surreal. How many gladiators are blessed to live out this dream? The sights and sounds were alive. It felt as if I was living in a painting full of color while sleeping in a song of wonder.

Alicia

Alicia still could not believe Kay-Kay pulled this off without her having a clue. Or how her best friend Shaun could remain stone-faced for months, all the while plotting and conspiring on Alicia's happiness. It was a wonderful blessing to have such a friend. Kay-Kay had transported her and all of her loved ones to a paradise for a reason. He was about to honor her with his vow of forever; the sometimes elusive dream that every little girl envisions as her birthright.

Hugs and kisses flowed like the liquor—freely. Alicia felt somewhat uncomfortable being at the center of the joy. So many of the faces that surrounded her and Kay-Kay had hoped for this moment, but had also began questioning its eventuality. Perhaps Kay-Kay wasn't mature enough, they began hinting at in discussions. Alicia had stopped her defense of Kay-Kay when the topic arose because her own doubts had grown stronger than theirs. But as she gazed at her future husband, laughing with his uncle and Handbone, her heart felt wrapped in a blanket of warmth and belonging.

Her mother, father, and Ma Barnes sat off on the side, away from the cacophony of laughter and music. They were holding a heavy, but mirthful discussion. All three were shaking their heads in what appeared to be collective relief. Alicia's happiness at such a sight was dampened slightly by the sad news that her big sister couldn't make it. No reason was given for her absence, but Alicia felt she knew why.

Charlotte was no longer the same since her husband went to prison for murder. She had become a recluse who Alicia only saw on special occasions. Each time Alicia found herself around her sister, she left wondering if her sister was secretly wrestling with depression. But thinking of Charlotte and her sadness in the midst of so much happiness felt like a defeat of purpose. Alicia pushed her sister's absence out of her mind. When she made it back to New York, she would go and sit with her sister and find out how best to help. The scenery that stood before her was a memory she refused to forget. Mental snapshots captured the festivities, and she looked towards the photographer wondering who was capturing the better pictures, her mind or his machine?

JB

JB was amazed at the beauty of Hawaii. He was even more amazed at the obvious expense Kay-Kay must have shelled out to make this a reality for so many people. Perhaps it was a trait of the poor, but JB couldn't help but attempt to tally up prices in his mind. He even shared some of his calculations aloud to Pam. "Damn you can't tell me my brother spent anything less than $50,000 on flying everyone out here. That alone had to be around 50," he argued with himself.

Pam did not want to study someone else's expenses, but understood the reasoning behind JB's need to do so. She grabbed hold of his hand and acknowledged his observation, "You're right, babe. At least that much. I would say that he spent over $100,000 easy for all of this."

Smiling from ear to ear, shaking his head in utter disbelief, JB couldn't help but to render this judgment. "Babe, do you know what he could've done for our community, for the kids in our community with that type of money? With so many people fighting evictions, so many kids starving because of empty refrigerators?"

"One hundred thousand dollars is not a lot of money, Jamal. It's not enough to save the hood with," Pam interjected.

"Yeah, but it could be better served..."

Pam interrupted once more. "Please, babe, this is your brother's blessing. He brought us out here to celebrate it with him. Let's appreciate the gift. You said it yourself you don't remember seeing him this happy in forever. Why not suspend the self-righteousness for a while and just enjoy yourself."

"Self-righteousness? That's how I sound?" JB asked a bit surprised at her description.

Pam responded with a 'knock it off' look before cupping his cheeks in both hands and whispering, "Enjoy yourself. Let go of the judgments."

After the chin check from Pam, JB did find relaxation a great deal easier. Due to Pam's pregnancy, she was unable to do much of anything except become a beach bum and soak in the sun. Her and Ma Barnes sat next to one another on the beach chairs and talked for hours.

Knee, who flew in on the second day, joined Kay-Kay and JB, along with Alicia and some of her friends, on a volcano hike to a place called Kīlauea.

Kay-Kay

I was glad that Knee decided to attend the wedding. Initially, he'd declined, stating that he didn't believe in attending 'sentencing days.' He argued that marriage for a thug was a form of castration; that we couldn't be married to the streets and a wife.

I understood his point and wrestled with that very dilemma. But the heart sets its own path and if I were forced to give one up, it would be the streets, not Alicia.

I think Knee decided to come out of guilt. His own son was there and his absence would've made an already strained relationship between the two of us a lot more difficult. It was the first time that the Knee, JB, and I went on an adventure together that didn't require us looking for herbs. We weren't out stalking alleyways for victims; we were hiking inside of craters, solidified lava lakes, witnessing actual lava flows and gas eruption belching from the earth. Like little kids in a city pool, we were in wonder.

The volcano belched or at least that's the story we decided to stick with. We heard a loud grumble followed by, "Oh shit. What was that?" coming from Knee. He looked ready to dive for cover and he wasn't the only one. In fact, everyone except Alicia's friend Hotdog and I remained unfazed.

After calming everyone's nerves, our guide explained the noise in scientific terms that boiled down to the fact that every now and then the volcano makes noise. Something about the sulfur and carbon, but I was only half listening. I was enjoying the escape from the concrete too much to be shook by a sound.

The green fertile mountains were peppered with yellow and red homes sitting on their cliffs. What an escape from the steel and concrete that defined the New York City landscape.

Alicia

There was a king-sized hot tub, which sat snugly in a crevice of a mountain that overlooked the vast Pacific. Alicia and her friends mingled with Kay-Kay and his small group. With the champagne flowing and the laughter bubbly, comfortable conversation became a feat easily accomplished.

Knee was enjoying himself immensely as he studied Alicia's friends. He was looking to see which one might be up for a Hawaiian fling. So far they all seemed to be satisfied, the look of abstinence did not appear in any of their eyes. But as the night wore on, Knee was sure the champagne would eventually reveal one sexually dissatisfied vagina awaiting conquest.

Shalunda, one of Alicia's best friends asked the two lovebirds a question she already knew the answer to. "So how did you two meet again?"

Alicia was a split second faster than her friend Shaun. "We met in the Empire roller skating rink. Kameek didn't even notice me; he noticed Shaun. But his friend beat him to the punch and he had to settle for me."

Kay-Kay chuckled, shaking his head at the absurdity of the hypothesis before replying. "Where do you get *that* from?"

"Oh knock it off, you know I'm right. You got beat to the punch by... what's that guy's name again? Kev, I believe was his name."

Shaun found the fact amusing. It was a sisterhood joke that Alicia never let go of. "Whatever happened to your friend Kev?" Shaun asked, as if remembering the double date for the first time in years.

"Kev got deported to Jamaica a few years after you met him."

"Ahh," Shaun begain to recall the situation. "I liked him until he started calling me a 'bum bitch.'"

The group responded with a spicy mixture of sympathetic moans and chuckles of disbelief.

"Yea, that sorry son-of-a-you-know-what sure did call me a bum bitch. And if I hadn't seen Chucky in his eyes, I might have tried his jaw," Shaun said calmly, as she reflected on the wisdom of her choice. "'Cause he was sure enough crazy."

"But what kills me is when they feel rejected, they start calling us names," Hotdog added.

"So what exactly is a bum bitch?" Shalunda challenged the men as if they were co-defendants being held for interrogation. At least that's how Kay-Kay felt. It was a slippery slope they were asking him to climb and who knew what lay in waiting at the bottom if he fell. But a challenge was made, so a challenge was accepted. He hesitated long enough to appear unsure, confused, and apprehensive.

The women began to smell blood, their shoulders pointing towards their prey. Two of them, Shalunda and Hotdog, even began licking their lips in anticipation of his stumble. But his nervousness was just a feign, he met them with brutal honesty.

"A 'bum bitch' is a woman who on first appearance or conversation seems to have it all together..."

"No one has it all together," Shalunda chimed in.

"Of course not," Kay-Kay dismissively countered. "That's why I said *appears*. It's because they try so hard to hide their flaws. They also value gossip over any other form of communication; they gossip about their friends, family or celebrities."

"They choose men and clubs over their kids," JB chimed in, willing to plunge into the losing argument in defense of his brother.

"They're one paycheck away from being homeless, yet still find a way to get a name-brand bag," Knee followed suit.

The brothers began stacking their thoughts one on top of the other. On this topic, they spoke as one.

Kay-Kay continued. "But here's the part that makes 'em 'bum bitches' in my book. It's that they take pride in that behavior and don't even see the lack of respect men have for them. The only question we ask ourselves when we answer their calls is: 'Is the pussy good?'"

Both Knee and JB nodded their heads.

"And if it is good, then we tolerate their silliness for a spell. Maybe buy them a handbag or two—conquest for a conquest, fair exchange and no robbery."

Knee felt a clarification was in order. "A 'bum bitch' will give up the pussy for a handbag or some shoes." Like a prosecutor's closing argument, the look of satisfaction in their accusation left no chance for a conclusion of reasonable doubt.

An uncomfortable shift occurred in the hot tub; the jurors in the juror box began searching their inner souls for any signs of guilt.

The morning of the wedding began late with a light, misty drizzle of warm rain. It was just enough of a distraction to become a topic filled with questions; the main one being, "Will the rain put a damper on the wedding?"

Kay-Kay saw it differently. The rain for him represented all that he and Alicia had gone through while still not skipping a heartbeat of love for one another. They had gone through drizzles, but not storms. To him, storms were the battles with cancer and other deadly diseases, serial infidelity, physical abuse, or drug dependencies. Those were storms. What he and Alicia lived through were light, misty, warm drizzles. He appreciated God's benevolence. Kay-Kay also had no doubt that, come time for the reading of the vows, the sun's rays would be the only memory their guests would keep—besides his kiss of the bride.

A light lunch consisting of a spread of sandwiches, fruits, and salads was delivered to each of the bungalows. This allowed everyone to move throughout the day at their own pace and convenience.

Alicia was relaxing and taking it all in. Her early morning massage and pedicure was rivaled only by the manicure and facial that followed. She felt beautiful—almost like a new woman—as she sipped champagne and glided around her bungalow in her fluffy slippers and silk caftan. Her hair was pinned up in curls that would fall only as she received a headdress styled in the likes of the African goddess of love. Moments later she would hold her father's hand for that sacred walk.

Without a cloud in the sky, the sun's rays illuminated the sacred space. Contemporary jazz gently surfed the wind. White Dupioni silk with an iridescent effect hung delicately from the bamboo-framed wedding canopy. Behind it sat the altar, and behind the altar sat the mouth of an infinity pool that overlooked the vast and seemingly endless Pacific Ocean. Colorful wao akua birds were trained and set free to hover in a coordinated fashion over the wedding like a floating halo over an angel.

The guests sat anxiously, in awe of the paradise they had found themselves in. This was something for the story books, and smiles in appreciation of God's creation could be seen on all faces. Kay-Kay and his best man, JB, accompanied the officiator to the altar.

Dressed in all white from his crown to his sandals the officiator, a Babalawo of the Yoruban vein, was the only aspect of this wedding that Kay-Kay insisted on. "No colonial priest will oversee this day," was Kay-Kay's instruction to Shaun.

He spoke briefly with the priest, thanking him in advance for his service.

Kay-Kay also wore all white, as did the rest of the groomsmen.

Luther Vandross' "Here and Now" began playing, signaling Kay-Kay's undivided attention. A murmur of excitement from the guests became a language of its own.

The bridemaids, escorted by the groomsmen, walked hand-in-hand down the purple Phoenician runner. The ring-bearer, Alicia's eight-year-old cousin Brandon walked with a purpose of responsibility and honor. He was followed by the two adorable flower girls, Makayla and Makira. They were dressed identically in white lace knee-length dresses with purple satin belts.

Radiant smiles were seen on their faces as they sprinkled rose petals, as if in a ritual of seed sowing.

The stage was finally set. The sun, clouds, and birds all conspired to make this moment unforgettable. And then Prince's "Adore" began to play.

Kay-Kay

Then she appeared, not too far away, holding her father's arm. My nerves began to betray me. My hands began to shake. How could I love someone this strongly? My weakness, my Achilles Heel, began walking toward me.

Alicia

There he stands. Not slumped, but standing. My king who gently rules the kingdom of my heart. I'm coming, my king. I want to run to the altar, but I waited this long, what's a few seconds more?

Her floor-length white chiffon beach wedding dress fit perfectly. Her curvaceous body brought life to the gown. It was as if the dress was made exclusively for her. She allowed her father to guide her symbolically. The passing of the prize was about to take place, from the hands of the first man she ever loved, to the hands of the only other man she will forever love.

A. C. Clayton

As she approached the altar, she could see Kay-Kay brimming with tears. Like a yawn, his tears became contagious and before she knew it, her eyes mirrored his.

A gentle smile creased both their lips at the very same moment, as if mind reading was a secret science they had figured out together.

"Finally," he whispered to her.

"Finally," she whispered back. Kay-Kay took her hand as her father faded into the background.

The priest spoke. "The spiritual union of these two destined souls is also a union of two families and two sets of friends. We are here to witness the union of two dreams becoming one. Of two hopes, of two fears, of two questions, and two paths, all becoming one. Can we ponder the enormity? That we are blessed, today, to be here to bear witness to a union of such love and purpose. Now is the time to share your vows."

Kay-Kay spoke first, looking the love of his life directly in her eyes: "Alicia, my queen, my friend, this marriage is but a seal placed on the oath of my commitment. My thoughts are forever on you and what I must do in order to protect you."

Alicia smiled at the secret poet, and replied, "Kameek, my partner, my lover, my protector and most importantly my friend. You never cease to amaze me and today I promise to honor, love, and cherish you... until the sun burns out."

Kay-Kay and Alicia were then given four separate flavors to taste from. In the order of vinegar, lemon, cayenne pepper, and honey. These flavors represented the bitter, sour, hot, and sweet stages of life and marriage. The priest explained to Kay-Kay and Alicia that marriage can only succeed if they were both prepared to stomach each flavor. To which they replied in unison, "We will."

"The two become one," the priest declared. A leather string was handed to Kay-Kay from JB and he proceeded to wrap the string around Alicia's right wrist. He then tied the other end to his wrist before looking to the priest for approval. "The leather string represents the two becoming one. It is symbolic of an umbilical chord from God to the children of his creation. Where love and the willingness to unify resides, we find God. Now let us pray..."

The wedding concluded with Alicia and Kay-Kay jumping the broom. Nine white doves were released into the sky, sent as messengers to the Most High that the union was a success.

Chapter 33: It's a girl!

JB

Ashe Auset Barnes entered the world nine minutes after midnight during the seventh sign in the zodiac. Weighing six pounds three ounces and 17 inches in length, she was by far the tiniest bundle of joy JB had ever held in his hands.

She peeked at him through one eye tucked under her unibrow, studied his blurry face as if checking to see if the face matched the voice she envisioned for nine months. Seemingly satisfied, she cracked a smile of relief and went to sleep.

Throughout the day, both Pam and JB's family visited in celebration. Huge bouquets of flowers decorated the hospital room, turning a sterile place into a garden of vibrant colors and smells of sweetness.

The flowers were sent from Kay-Kay. He wanted his princess to learn the scent of beauty early. Though both brothers were back to barely speaking to each other for a reason neither could actually explain, when it came to Ashe's birth, Kay-Kay made it clear that he was her proud uncle.

The baby shower that took place two weeks prior was quaint. Aside from their immediate family members, the only other people in attendance were Pam's co-workers and friends.

Though now a public figure, JB wanted to keep this joyous occasion private.

A U-Haul bearing gifts arrived just before the cutting of the cake and two men began unloading the crib, strollers, playpen, high chair and a few other necessary items for the couple. Alicia was responsible for organizing and throwing the baby shower, as well as, making the registry. She didn't bother to put any of the 'big ticket' items on the list because she knew Kay-Kay was going to cover it all. And so he did.

Pam hugged Kay-Kay and Alicia with unbridled tears streaming down her face. Shortly after Alicia and Kay-Kay's wedding, Pam confided in Alicia about how close she and JB had been to getting an abortion.

Alicia was mortified and asked why.

"Financial, no other reason."

Alicia understood immediately and hugged Pam tightly.

"You made the right decision, sis. Everything will be alright."

Pam knew that Alicia would tell Kay-Kay. She knew that they needed his help, and JB was too darn stubborn to ask or even accept the help. As his woman and the soon-to-be mother of their daughter she had to make an executive decision.

Financial blessings unrelated to Kay-Kay's benevolence also began falling into their laps. Two local stores donated nine thousand dollars a piece to assist JB's organization. Senator Sinclair Monroe convinced him to use the money to purchase an apartment and buy furniture for their new home. "You are a grown man and your responsibility is first and foremost to your family," he explained. "Even revolutionaries have to earn a living."

JB reluctantly followed his advice. Secretly, he felt good about being able to feed and provide shelter for his newly formed family.

Chapter 34: black wolves

JB

1995

It seemed the gang culture bore flesh in New York City overnight. Flatbush was no exception. In 1985, it was crack. Now a different form of self-destruction was manifesting itself. JB shook his head in ironic disbelief. Gangs had always played their part to rot the core of the Big Apple. But where it was once territorial and profit driven, it was now driven by colors.

'Dick riders' were the first words that came to mind when JB searched his mind for answers. A number of movies and documentaries depicting the red and blue war in L.A. had recently done well in the box office. Shortly after, NYC was jumping into a beef they knew nothing about.

Knee told him that in NYC's case, it started in prison. The few live wires that were in leadership positions basically used their positions as tools of manipulation, while the majority of the flock were simple-minded soldiers just wanting to be a part of something bigger than themselves. Now the gangs were in Flatbush, and the heads of both gangs were meatballs disguised as whoppers.

These leaders watched him, Knee, and Kay-Kay from the sideline, admiring their heart and wishing they could locate their own. Soon they found a vehicle to substitute what was missing. They controlled a score of young kids, hungry for fame and respect, even if it sent them to an early grave.

JB pondered a solution to this new problem. He thought back to the crack epidemic and wondered how different his community would be if, instead of embracing the distribution and usage of the drug, the men in his hood would have stood up and taken arms against it? How many innocent lives would have been saved? How many families kept in tact? JB knew that this new gang threat was just as dangerous, and if allowed to go unchecked, would become another cancer resistant to treatment.

It took JB seven months to assemble a five-man team. In prison, he had studied all the revolutionary books and knew that in every movement there existed a military arm separate from the political one. While the political arm showed its face and shared its message to the public, the military arm demonstrated the alternative. He accepted the harsh historical reality that no substantial change could occur without bloodshed.

He had met with the five men separately, but now they were all together. The back of Ruben's diner became their meeting place, a sanctuary for them to congregate in secret.

JB spoke to them in a pleading, passionate tone. "So, I asked all of you to meet with me today because I wanted each of you to look around and see the faces of sacrifice. Take a good look. You brothers have been chosen to defend your community. We cannot depend on others to defend and protect our women and babies." A peculiar stillness controlled the temperature in the room, a silence that only existed in the face of imminent danger. "Though I've spoken with each one of you guys separately about this, I want to make sure we are all on the same page collectively." JB stared into the eyes of each man. "I can't say that I know how all of this will turn out or to what extent we will be successful. The repercussions could very well be prison or the grave. With every stand comes sacrifice, and I'm asking you to stand up against the senseless killings, even if the only alternative is a sensible killing."

The gravity of his meaning weighed heavy on their faces. "There are some things that we can't stop, things that we won't be able to stop. Our mission is only to stop the senseless killings. We don't want to dismantle the gangs. We want to stop the killing. First by talking, then by warning, and lastly," he paused for a pregnant second before continuing. "Lastly, and this is where you guys come in, if all else fails, we stop this shit by force. We can't expect *massa* to do it for us. This is our community, our responsibility." JB looked at his army and saw no fear in their eyes, only a weary resolve.

Chapter 35:

Only when trauma touches your core,
can you possibly abhor it for others.

1995

The man with the brim hat always felt most alive during the hunt. Once his target was captured and eliminated, his feeling of euphoria quickly evaporated and the reality of his actions led him to search for justification. He continuously reminded himself that he killed for a purpose and not just for the sport. It was a silent mantra that he'd been telling himself since his early childhood days when he practiced his hunting on stray dogs and alley cats. Back then, he would imagine that the dogs carried rabies and if left to roam, they would bite some innocent kid whose death would then be on his hands.

The allure was always the hunt. He would lure the animals to one elaborate trap after the other, perfecting his stealth and cunning. Only once was he discovered. A younger kid, whom he knew well, followed him and watched in bewilderment as he bludgeoned a sickly dog to death. The frightened little boy swore to never tell a soul what he saw.

The young boy was now a man. They kept in touch with one another, but from that day on there was a flicker of bone-chilling fear whenever he looked into the eyes of his friend who witnessed his craft.

The man with the brim hat sat on the roof looking down on the street below, allowing his mind to wander away from the true task at hand. For an entire three months, he'd stalked his prey, studying its habits. It never failed that the prey would almost always get caught slipping at the home of the mistress. Where there's a mistress, there's a soft target. So far, he had been picking off soft targets. Perfecting his craft, studying its nuances.

He knew that the hunt would become increasingly difficult each time he put his brim hat on. The size of the game would get bigger and so would its force. If the man with the brim hat didn't prove lethal in his first strike, all other strikes would be in defense against a unified force, one stronger than he could ever be alone.

He was thinking about the police; they would surely come if he ever slipped. Slipping wasn't an option. He left poetic lessons behind, not to taunt for the purpose of teasing, rather to annoy his pursuers into making their own mistakes. It was the only way to win.

The man with the brim hat had stalked this particular prey for months, finally deciding on the place and the time of the execution. The man slated for death controlled a large part of the heroin moving in East New York, Brooklyn. His death would be talked about by most, but mourned by very few. Those who mourned would be the few he fed. The tears would be for the free meal that was lost, not the soul that was freed from its shell. A mad scramble would ensue to fill the void left by the deceased. The man with the brim hat didn't care about who would, or could, step up to the plate. The only thing that mattered was the message: the plate cost.

His entry into the mistress' home was simple—too simple. The silly chick opened her door for UPS with no expectations of a pending delivery. Once inside, he sat on her living room couch in quiet contemplation of the task at hand. The mistress, bound and gagged, lay placidly on her queen size bed. She hadn't been touched in a sexual way, but by the end of the night she would feel the touch of sorrow. The married man she had decided to love would be dead, in her home, on her watch.

As the man with the brim hat sat silently in the chaos of his own thoughts, he fought the urge to abort the mission. The fact that he considered, even for a fraction of a second, what the lady in the next room was feeling, seemed like an omen, warning him to cease the operation. But he'd heard about that whisper that taunts some into a second guess. He decided to block the whisper by creating his own whisper. *'This sacrifice, my homage,*' he repeated over and over again to calm his mind and keep him focused. He heard a metallic sound of keys followed by a voice full of vulgarity and unproven bravado. His prey was about to enter a death chamber called karma. It was his time to go and the grim reaper with the brim hat had waited long enough.

The king of the castle walked into the smack of a hammer that rendered him unconscious. The man with the brim hat had decided to change his method of law and order for this particular task. He decided to bludgeon his sacrificial lamb. He swung his hammer over and over regardless of his prey being close to death after the first swing. The sound of bone cracking like walnuts after each blow ensured a closed casket. With each swing, more blood splattered until the hammer got stuck somewhere between the jawbone and the cheek.

The man with the brim hat yanked the hammer free and noticed his masterpiece of abstract design. Written all over the walls and furniture was his signature of carnage. His heaving chest rose as if a cardiac arrest was imminent. He could hear the echoes of whimpering from the adjacent bedroom.

The blinding thrill was primeval; it belonged to a distant place and time, not civilization, not now. But the man with the brim hat had just accepted a rare collect-call from the wild; a call he answered on the first ring. He slowly began the process of allowing clarity to re-enter his vision.

The man with the brim hat dug into his bloodied jacket pocket and retrieved a small plastic bag. He extracted the chalk from within the bag as if it was nitroglycerin. For the next 15 minutes, he outlined the body with the opposite hand he used for writing. The outline was for the police. They would once again walk away empty-handed on account of the poet, who walked with a brim hat.

This murder was personal, and law enforcement would be able to tell right off the bat. But all roads would still lead to a dead end. They would have to wait for him to slip. However, with each kill, his mistakes grew less perceptible. They would have to call in Scotland Yard and Sherlock himself to connect any dots beyond the obvious.

Another note was left behind for the investigators to ponder, along with another body for the coroner.

Deep in the bowels of Brooklyn
There exists a place...
Where men kill for the sport
Just to say they did it

Part Two

Chapter 36: a flame of resistance

1997

In 1931, a small farming town in Attica, New York opened the doors of a dungeon for the condemned. For decades after its grand opening, the harsh sadistic conditions and treatment of its citizenry remained a secret to all outside its walls until September 9, 1971 when the inhabitants rose in the face of tyranny. Though many died in a hail of bullets, the tragic event brought attention to the plight of the condemned.

To this day, it is still a dungeon. Now, however, it is a haunted one that carries in its very arteries a heaviness and cruelness of demonic proportion. It is a prison that houses perhaps just as many of the innocent as it does the guilty—and that count is before factoring in its prisoners.

It was the Old God's third time in the more than 30 years since he had been transferred to its bowels. In all that time, the lifelessness of the place had never changed. It was a punitive prison, designed to break the spirit. During slavery, certain islands and plantations were designated as 'breakers.' These were the places the rebellious and recalcitrant slaves were sent to be broken. If not broken, they would be made examples of in order to break the rest. Only after being broken would they be sold to more "humane" plantations. Attica was the breaker prison, and everyone from the governor down to the civilians who worked there turned a blind eye to its practice of brutality.

Knowing all of this, the Old God still walked unfazed through its corridors, as he made his way to the visiting floor. He had walked through countless shadows of death and when the true shadow came, he would meet it with his spine erect.

The humiliation for a visitor reminded JB of why it took so long to make this visit. Being made to feel like visiting a loved one was a crime in itself disturbed him profoundly. He watched as women with small children were manhandled and spoken to with hostility and contempt. Like him, most visitors travelled by bus for over eight hours. They were tired and exhausted by the trip, but they were determined to see their loved ones at any cost. They accepted the humiliation with little to no complaints because to reject the contemptuous treatment would place the visit in jeopardy.

JB went through the process in silence like everyone else, for the same reason as the rest. For the twentieth time, he reminded himself why he would never visit another one of these hellholes again. But this visit was important. He was visiting purgatory for a purpose. He was there to tap the mind of a sage.

The Old God was somewhat surprised when he walked onto the visiting floor and caught sight of his visitor. When he saw the last name Barnes on the visiting slip, he didn't bother to read any further, automatically assuming it was Kay-Kay. Though he was wrong in his guess, he was still pleasantly surprised to see that it was JB.

The handshake was firm, their smiles genuine. For years, they corresponded through letters, after the very first letter JB sent to the Old God thanking him for keeping his little brother safe. Over time, their letters grew to become more socially conscious in nature. For JB, his communication with the Old God was similar to a correspondence with a college professor. JB's insight and perspective on the problems and solutions facing their communities had been gleaned from the man standing before him. He smiled, glad to meet his hero in person with no censor or filters.

The two men stared at each other in honor of the mirror that stood before them. The head smiled at the heart. JB sat only after the Old God did, as a sign of respect.

"What a surprise. I thought it was your brother coming to see an old man."

"Nah, I've been meaning to make it up here to meet you in person for a while."

A. C. Clayton

The Old God studied JB, weighing the validity of his words. Finally, nodding his head in acceptance, he replied. "Well, here you are. We only have seven hours, let's get to work."

The two men spoke about everything under the sun. They tackled the topics of love, family, fears, and triumphs. Finally, the discussion turned to Senator Sinclair Monroe.

"So, what is it like working with such a character?"

"Enlightening, definitely. He's shown me how the system *really* works," JB replied.

"You mean the crooked shit?" the Old God interrupted.

"Yeah that, too." Both men chuckled at such a cynical reality. The Old God chose to share some clarity and insight with the young warrior.

"It's hard to stay true to the people's needs when our own desires and passions go unchecked. That's what happens to a lot of our so-called leaders who start off with the right intentions. They partake in a system of compromise. Nothing wrong with compromising, except that what they agree to compromise is the principle that should never be bargained. Integrity is a quality that should never be a bargaining chip. But these leaders of ours, especially the political ones, check their integrity at the door. From the moment they swear their oaths, they put their hats in their hands and begin the skinning and grinning. They speak well, so they dazzle the masses. Our people love tough talk, but no longer have the stomach to match it with action.

"We seem to have forgotten that this is not truly a country of equality and justice for all. And since it's not, then they're in breach of contract. That constitution of theirs, the one that governs this land, the wording of that document reveals the trick; it's an illusion of freedom. A prism on a defective lens and they control the angle that we're viewing it from. This is not the land of the free and brave, unless that's a code for master and slave. But these leaders never challenge the contract's breach; they feed us the illusion of peaceful protest and conciliatory gestures. They blame the system, because to do so absolves the hands that make the system operate. Their fluency in quoting acronyms becomes the trademark of their genius. According to those at the top, it is because of JJD or BBT or some other acronym as the reason for the dilemmas our communities face. They want us to believe they truly grasp the problem. That's what they want *us* to think? But what they want *massa* to think is an entirely different message. They want to assure *massa* that it's safe for him to sleep peacefully at night. Meanwhile, our kids will kill each other for sneakers, but not for their education."

The Old God paused, before continuing on. "It's a twisted logic that we accept as normal, because we have been trained to see it as such. *Massa* will pay us enormous amounts of money to make songs that justify our slaughter. If 'niggas and bitches' is all we are... 'killers and pimps,' 'hustlers and savages,' then why not gun us down in the streets like dogs? Why not bury us in prisons disproportionately? It makes sense then. It becomes the only reasonable solution." The Old God spoke from an observation deck perched on the veranda of a jail cell. His wisdom was flawless because his entire being was committed to one purpose—the resurrection of his people.

"Never lose sight of the hand behind our destruction. Sadly, these politicians and civil rights leaders have. They are neutralized through legitimacy. The enemy legitimizes them as responsible leaders then they rock us to sleep for the slaughter. They're committed to making sure, better still...their job is to ensure that Nat Turner and Denmark Vesey are never resurrected. I'm talking to you. It's time the wolf sheds the disguise of the sheep. It's finally time to take a closer look at the matador standing in front of us and not the red cape he holds."

The Old God grew quiet, allowing time for his slow methodical words to marinate. JB simply listened to these words of confirmation. "I've read some of your speeches," he continued. "I can see that you're being real particular with your wording. I can't help but wonder whether you're biding your time or if you drank the Kool-Aid?"

A reserved smile creased JB's face. "What kind of Kool-Aid?" he asked.

"The cowardly type; its ingredients make you scared to talk truth to power. The safe drink," the Old God explained, searching for a sign of life in JB's eyes.

JB remained silent. "You have a following. People actually travel in order to hear you speak. So what do you speak about? A safe revolution? A struggle that bares no teeth? The script of a chump or a champ? Which one?"

JB unconsciously held his clinched fist over his lips, a habit whenever he was in serious contemplation. Finally, he spoke, using his pointer finger; its similarity to a music conductor's baton—accentuating his words. "Many years ago, when I was still in Green Haven, you wrote me a letter with a list of books. I still remember every book, because I studied them over and over until they became a part of me. But it was the very first book that you sent to me that made my transformation possible. The book's simplicity grew more complex the more I learned. You're smiling because you knew the power of that book." JB was referring to the O.G. Bible. The book of revolution and not revelation. The book of acceptance and not meditation.

"My speeches, the ones you've read, mimic the way I was taught. The simplicity grows more complex by the degree of the chapters. They come to hear me speak because my words are easy to grasp and digest, but there will be a time when they will be forced to accept or reject the message. I understand the book. I understand its message. The *flame is greater than the name*, and we must not let it burn out. No matter the size or the might of our opposition."

The Old God smiled in satisfaction, pride, and resignation. He had grown old, tired, and weary, but his job was finally done. The seeds were planted; the harvest was assured not just in one brother named Barnes but both. The "flame is greater than the name" slogan recited by the initiates was only true if there was someone with a name to pass the flame to.

The Old God had been waiting for this day when he could finally pass the torch on to a worthy soul. "Then speak truth to power. Resurrect the dead. Let your words awaken the warriors. Pass on the flame. My job is done." The aged man proclaimed with a slow nod of assurance.

"Your job is done!" JB agreed, his hands motioning the closing of a chapter, as he accepted the symbolic and sacred torch.

The Old God rose. He gently placed his fingertips to his forehead and then to his heart before tilting his bald head in a subtle gesture of farewell. JB, still seated, sat with the heaviness of the burden now placed squarely in his lap. He touched his

head and then his heart as he watched his hero return triumphantly back into the furnace of despair.

Chapter 37: keeping the peace

Kay –Kay
1998

In this game, it is paramount that you study niggas' patterns. They all have patterns. Same scripts, same shit, nothing too different. Some get stuck, fascinated by the reruns. They love reliving the reruns, as if opening their minds to the future is too scary a prospect to face.

AG was one such hustler. He was as stubborn as they come when it came to change. He was the type of hustler who still kept his money in shoeboxes under his bed or behind the shoe rack in his closet. Though I never asked him if it was true, rumor had it that he still took the time, every night, to iron his money on an ironing board.

AG was 10 years my senior and yet, despite the age and style differences, he was one of my most trusted allies. He was one of a handful of scramblers I never attempted to apply pressure to. In fact, it was through his frequenting of the strip clubs that I came across a stripper named Chamomile. She was the brown-skinned, doe-eyed beauty who led me to Papa Doc's castle and, ultimately, my victory.

Ruben's diner was becoming my unofficial meeting place to discuss light issues with trusted friends. My meeting with AG was to chat about an incident that occurred the week prior, between him and one of JB's righteous followers. Apparently the follower, whose name was Mark, approached AG on a crowded street corner in the middle of the day and began calling him 'an enemy of his people' and 'a cowardly traitor.'

Mark's attempt at public humiliation didn't last more than the time it took for AG to realize what the hell was going on. AG quickly pulled his gun out and began gun-butting Mark. When the incident was over, Mark laid crumbled in a puddle of his own blood from gash wounds to his head and face. He was lucky that it was the middle of the day and that he escaped the stunt alive. What was strange was that Mark refused to identify AG to the police as the culprit. It was as if he was saying what started in the streets would remain in the streets, a rule that typically applies to those who pledge their allegiance to the streets. But it was a code seldom honored by regular civilians.

AG walked into the diner in an altered state of mind, as usual. He reeked of high-grade exotics and his eyes were bloodshot red. Like I said, the same script and the same shit with this dude. When it came to his drug use, it was to be expected. He smoked like a chimney and snorted more than

Lawrence Taylor. He was a functioning addict who, every now and then, went on a cocaine binge and would sniff himself into a paranoid zombie-like trance. His wife, Jeannette, would then call me, afraid that he was about to do something stupid. I found myself talking him down and away from the demons he faced at all hours of the night.

He would thank me the next day for holding him down, but would never address the drug abuse and neither did I. It was his battle, and the last thing I would be to him was an addiction counselor.

"You're late as usual," I observed.

"Man, the parking sucks around here," he countered.

"Must be some good shit you smoking, 'cause there's a space right out front and it's been there for the last 20 minutes."

"Ahh, fuck you, Kay. There you go with that Sherlock Holmes shit."

I laughed at his reference. "Sherlock Holmes?"

"Yeah man, you can't just take a lie and let it be. You got to prove a mothafucka wrong and shit. I can only imagine the shit your mind might come up with if you took a pull."

"I'm high on life, bro. You know that."

"Yeah so I hear, but we all have our addictions, lil' bro. You're no different."

The conviction in his voice made me accept the challenge. "So, what's my addiction?" I asked.

AG looked at me for a long time, I suspect contemplating just how far he dared go with this line of conversation. "Your most obvious addiction is your reputation. You take pride in this Godfather shit. You even talk like a Godfather. I be wondering what kind of theme music be playing in your fucking skull. Like right now, for real, what music is playing in your head? Some Godfather shit, I bet."

All I could do was laugh. "Nigga, you bugging," was my only response. But he didn't back down.

"Nah, you know I'm dead right. You go everywhere with shooters."

As if to prove his point, AG stole a glance to his right and left acknowledging my assistants who were sitting nearby. "Securing perimeters and shit, even this meeting we're having today is some Godfather shit."

"How so?" I asked, amused at the direction of this discussion.

"Come on, lil' bro, I knew you was going to reach out to me about JB's flunky. What was the clown's name?"

"Mark."

"Yeah, Mark. The funny thing is, if he weren't a part of JB's cult, we wouldn't be having this meeting. You don't call me to have a meeting just to kick it like comrades. You're calling me to tell me to lay off, so that I don't get into conflict with your brother and ultimately with you. I get it, lil' bro. I got it. So, don't say it. Don't do that Godfather shit to me today. I'll lay off his cult, but do me one favor?"

"What?"

'Tell JB to sic his guardian angels on another sucka. I love you, lil' bro, but I'm not playing with no sucka nigga yelling at me in the middle of the street."

"Fair enough," was all I could say.

"Fuck you," his reply dripped with sarcasm.

"Fuck me? I didn't say anything but 'fair enough.'"

"Yeah, but you know you mad that I cut you off from giving me your Godfather speech."

I couldn't help but laugh; these kinds of conversations kept me grounded. To AG, I was just another gladiator out here putting in work. He wouldn't allow me to have a big head in his presence.

The rest of our meeting was full of laughs and street gossip. Eventually, the topic of the mysterious murders arose.

"Man, I'm hearing that whoever's doing it is leaving fucking notes on the bodies." AG was scratching his head as if he was trying to make sense out of the bizarre occurrences. "I'm hearing they're poems, not letters, and the police named him 'the Poet.'"

"Really?"

"Really."

"How do you know it's a he? Could be a broad for all we know?"

I thought about devious ass Peaches and shook my head at the possibilities. "You right about that. It could be, but it probably ain't. A woman would be wasting kats with cyanide or some cunning shit like that. Bullets to the head seems more like something a man would do. Just my opinion."

"All of them are kats that was paying punk dues to you, correct?"

"Doing business fees, not punk dues."

AG dismissed my correction with a backhanded wave. "Semantics. My point is that at some point, shit could start looking like you had a hand in it. You're a common denominator in these kats' lives."

What could I say? AG spoke to a concern that had been growing for a couple of years. This killer was picking off peacocks from my farm and leaving poems for the police to discover. At what point would the police discover my connection to the colorful and begin training their lenses on me?

"Yeah man," was the only response I could muster.

The very next day I met up with JB in front of his apartment building. I had just pulled up when he came walking out.

"Get in," I yelled. "I'll take you where you need to go."

Reluctantly, he accepted. "This is a nice ride. I never seen you in this one."

I was driving my new money-green Coup Infinity. One of the many toys that my status demanded I have.

"Thanks. It's yours whenever you want it." I was dead serious, even though I knew he would never accept my offer.

"No, thank you," he declined with as much contempt as those three words could muster.

"Where to?" I asked growing more annoyed by the second.

"Take me to the train station. It's a couple of blocks away."

I told him I would take him where he needed to go, yet he still chose the iron horse. Fine. I got straight to the point. "I spoke with AG yesterday."

"Yeah, so?" JB responded with sincere indifference.

"So, I told him to lay off your peoples."

"You want me to say thanks, is that it?" He wasn't making this conversation easy.

"Nope, but I'm expecting you to do the same."

He laughed with a snort. "What's that?"

"Fall back, Jamal."

"Jamal? You must be upset. You always call me *Jamal* when you're mad. One of my friends got *hurt*," his emphasis on the word hurt resonated. "And you're mad at me?" A statement filled with disappointment. "You're so far gone, lil' bro."

"That's funny, 'cause I feel the same way about you." I wasn't going to back down this time. Since his return, I had been avoiding this conversation as best as I could, but his attitude needed to be challenged. Arrogance is only admirable to the misinformed. I knew his arrogance was going to end up getting one of his followers killed. "You're bugging with this meatball shit." I argued.

"What meatball shit?"

"This civil rights shit. This dumb shit. You're wasting time, Jamal."

"So the victory is theirs? That's what you'll have me believe?"

"Who's *theirs*?" I challenged, expecting him to imply my drug-dealing friends.

But he curve-balled me with a sneaky one instead. "Your master."

A. C. Clayton

"My master?" I sarcastically repeated.

"Yeah, mothafucka, the system of minds that unify to keep you oppressed. You mothafuckas accept defeat from them, but then declare war on your own community, predators to your own kind. But you call me a meatball?"

The truth in his words felt like a physical blow to my body. No rebuttal entered my mind quick enough. A crook caught red-handed and placed in handcuffs, I followed my training and remained silent.

"I refuse to do to you what our dad did to us."

I still couldn't speak, but my facial expression must have shaped into a question mark so he answered. "I refuse to not show you the true definition of a man. You may be a big shot to them clowns, but you'll always be my little brother and I'm telling you, you're fighting the wrong fight."

My senses finally returned and I was able to take the offensive again. "I know who the oppressor is, but I also know you can't beat them with marches and rhetoric. You're not sending your cult followers to stand in front of the precinct and call the cops pigs. But you'll send them to AG? Some revolutionary!" It was his turn to feel the handcuffs of silence squeeze tightly. "You're becoming an embarrassment to me, but you kidding yourself into believing you're making me proud. Like you're the teacher and I'm the dumb student, you feel your sacred mission is to school me. Get the fuck outta here. I ain't buying it. Practice your weekly speech on someone else. Just fall back before you get one of your cult followers hurt." I knew my words had pierced him deeply. I didn't hold back from the jugular; he needed to know I wasn't drinking the Kool-Aid and that I never would.

The conversation didn't get any better and we didn't say a word to each other for months afterwards. On the rare occasions that we would find ourselves together at our mother's house, we avoided each other completely. If our mother knew what was going on, she never said a word. Knowing her, she probably felt like it was something we had to work out on our own time.

I knew we would talk eventually, but for the time being, it was best we kept apart. Alicia still attended his meetings, but because of the awkwardness it caused between us, she kept her participation in his cult to herself. I wanted no part in it. I was done entertaining the discussion. If it was not about dollars, I could not afford volunteering my attention. My thoughts were always restless. Adding more stupid shit to the mix could tip the scale out of my favor. Being on top meant there was always a plot that needed to be foiled and my very life depended on me being focused enough to foil the plots.

Chapter 38: criminal empire

1998

Knee

Knee met with his old friend Sony, who now went by the rap moniker of Rushie Rush or Rushie for short. Rushie was an established rap artist who recently walked away from the record label that made him a star. He was also a kat who had done time with Knee on Riker's Island back in the day. Rushie was considered a gangster rapper who supposedly used his 11-month Riker's Island stint and two-year prison bid to validate his authenticity.

Never mind that his entire time on Riker's was spent reciting songs for any live wire who commanded him to do so.

"Knee, I'm telling you, man, I walked away from the million dollar re-signing deal with the label because I realized they are nothing but a bank with a high interest loan. I'm starting my own label and I want you to be my partner."

Knee had not a clue of what Sony would say, but the prospect of starting his own label appealed to his ego immediately. Having a well known, established artist on board was too good to be true. Knee knew that the drug game couldn't last forever, and hip-hop was a lane that, within the last few years, had surpassed the distribution of narcotics.

"Man, I don't know much about that shit. Walk me through it. What does starting our own label mean? How do I win?"

After hearing Sony out, Knee was astonished to discover that although Sony was an established platinum-selling artist, who drove a Ferrari and owned a mini mansion in New Jersey, he didn't have the money to create a label on his own. The more Knee tried to make sense out of this, the more confused he became.

"So you sold a couple million records, correct?"

"Correct."

"But you're *not* a millionaire, correct?"

The question—an interrogation of sorts—did not sit well with Sony, so he chose to let the evidence speak for itself.

Knee shook his head in bewilderment, perplexed at the unbelievable, not understanding how anyone could sell over a million pieces of a product and not be a millionaire. It slowly became apparent to Knee, by the look on Sony's face, that Sony was just as confused.

"Aight, so what do you need from me?"

A. C. Clayton

After hearing the game plan, Knee gave serious thought to Sony's proposition. All the real money appeared to be being made in the music industry. A lot of suckers were winning, while the true livewires sat on the sideline. The few steppers who did bully their way into the industry found success. Knee decided he wanted in, but he realized that he knew very little about the industry and didn't want to rely strictly on Sony's word.

Kay-Kay would be able to lay out a blueprint for Knee to follow. The thought of going to Mr. Know It All for advice was not an appealing notion, but in this instance Mr. Know It All knew enough to be of benefit. This endeavor could be the way out of the streets for both him and Kay-Kay. The hurdle would be in convincing Kay-Kay that this was an opportunity that needed to be explored.

Kay-Kay

My reasoning for avoiding the rap game altogether was obvious. It was the ultimate sport of the peacock. It was a look-at-me game; the more colorful the feathers, the more money they made. Dudes were making millions of dollars for literally saying nothing. The simplicity of the hustle became so attractive to the lazy that before you knew it, every goon in America suddenly had rap star aspirations. Shit, let them tell it, it had always been their dreams. But I knew the truth. Most of them wanted the fame more than the money. They wanted the attention that a successful rap career would promise. They envisioned a yellow brick road to an unlimited vagina supply, and were convinced that their rap skills would get them there.

I also found it amusing to see these wannabes tell my story convincingly. They rapped about drug deals gone bad, gun plays that left the right men dead, and heists that were so epic the media was forced to remain silent. These wannabes glorified our story, and capitalized handsomely off of our courage, without claiming the perils that came with it. It was our story, but how could the guilty raise their hands in public? Bloody hands dare not sit under a spotlight.

Throughout the years, quite a few budding artists looking for a sponsor had approached me. Every time, I turned them down without a second thought. But as the years went on, I began to question my reluctance. Perhaps the investment was worth it and with a platinum-selling artist on deck, the investment could be my way out of the streets altogether. For me, being the invisible hand would be the only approach that would work. Any knowledge of my involvement in the label would only draw an unwanted light.

Knee

"So you're sure you want to fuck with Sony on this? Are you sure that he won't flip-flop in the ninth inning?" Kay-Kay challenged.

"Of course I'm sure. Come on, man. Don't quiz me like I'm your son."

"I'm not. It's just an exercise of due diligence. That's all, big bro."

Knee took a deep breath to calm his defenses. "Yeah, Sony won't flake. If he does, then I'm going to put in that work. It's that simple. I know he understands this, so there's no reason to even say it. Just like you should know that whatever you choose to invest is going to be safe."

Kay-Kay studied Knee's words, searching for his confidence. He needed to hear the hunger and devotion in Knee's voice and he thought he heard it, that declaration of victory.

The next day, Kay-Kay and Knee were given a tour of Sony's mansion in New Jersey. The spacious palace was the reward for Sony's lyrics. *'A wordsmith of rare talent'* is what one reporter wrote when describing Sony.

"So this is what a 'wordsmith' earns?" Kay-Kay remarked.

"This is something light compared to some other homes owned by my colleagues. Man, Kay-Kay, this hip-hop shit is where the money is at."

"I don't doubt it. But at what cost? I never been one to smile in fake kats' faces," Kay-Kay replied offhandedly.

Sony nodded his head in understanding, wondering if Kay-Kay considered him one of the fake kats he had just referenced.

Knee chimed in sensing the awkwardness but not sure of its cause. "It's definitely a money maker, and I want in. I brought Kay-Kay along because he's agreed to be a silent partner."

"Knee told me you guys were considering starting this label with a war chest of $250,000," Kay-Kay interjected. "That made me wonder how committed to the success you are. Because, that's not enough to really make a label take flight."

"But, I'm hot right now," Sony replied. "And I'll be our first artist. Every album I drop, I'm guaranteed at least gold."

"I understand. I get it. And that's why I'm willing to invest," Kay-Kay said. "But, if we're gonna play, we need to play big. I'm willing to put up a mil' if you both agree to my accountants and my lawyers representing this company."

Both Knee and Sony's eyes grew big. Knee had no idea Kay-Kay was thinking on that scale. He thought Kay-Kay was considering 50 or even 100 grand, but one million would be a game changer. And by the look on Sony's face, he obviously saw the same.

Needless to say, the agreement was sealed with a handshake. The paperwork would be taken care of within the month. The label would be called Criminal Empire, despite Kay-Kay and Sony's reservations about Knee's name choice. Knee even changed his name that very day to Cream, arguing that if he was going to be a CEO in the rap game, he needed a name that reflected his purpose.

Chapter 39: gun talk

1998

The first single off of Rushie Rush's album was called "Gun Talk." Its platinum achievement the very first week in circulation shattered industry expectations. Rushie was equally surprised; he truly believed that the song would flop. Rushie had completed 24 songs, but knew that only 12 could make the album. He took all 24 songs to Cream seeking a new ear.

Cream closed his eyes and listened to each song without showing a hint of emotion or excitement. After hearing all 24 songs, Cream insisted that Rushie's first single should be "Gun Talk." Rushie vehemently disagreed. He wanted to lead with a club song that talked about smoking weed next to the club's speakers.

A meeting of the executive team was called to allow all voices to be heard. Even Kay-Kay attended, though he told Cream that he would remain silent throughout it all. Other than Cream, only Rushie knew Kay-Kay's role in the company. Everyone else just assumed that the carte blanche access he had to every meeting and room in the company was a direct result of being good friends with Cream and Rushie. It was how Kay-

Kay designed it to appear and it was working to perfection. Rushie began his argument, speaking to the conference room full of the company's A&Rs and executive team.

"We see that the formula right now is making music that appeals to the clubs, or music that talks about getting high. I made a song that talks about both, with a beat that's going to crush the clubs. I've never sold anything less than gold and I can guarantee that this song will be another one. I've been doing this for over six years now; I know what works and what doesn't. It's that simple." The air of authority in Rushie's voice ticked Cream off.

Cream had agreed to the meeting to allow the illusion of a democracy. But after hearing Rushie's condescending argument, Cream decided to suspend the constitutional rights and turn the democracy into a dictatorship.

"Look man, that shit is stupid. This is not just your first independent song; this is Criminal Empire's *first* song. Either we come out the gate on some meatball shit talking about getting high next to some fucking speakers, or we come out preaching a fucking gospel of the streets. There's really no debate. 'Gun Talk' is the first song out the gate. Period. You should put that meatball shit on a mixtape and name the mixtape *Homoerotic*. Real talk."

Cream was no longer talking to Rushie. His gaze now fell on everyone else. "What else could he be thinking about standing next to a loud ass speaker smoking a blunt?"

Kay-Kay rubbed his eyes in disbelief. Cream didn't only attack Rushie's plans, he attacked his sense of manhood in front of the decision makers.

Cream didn't let up. "Fuck is going to be your next song? 'Wet Dreams'? Nah, nigga, this record label is called Criminal Empire and not Party City for a reason. I don't care about the fucking clubs. I care about the cars. I care about those mothafuckas taking road trips for hours at a time to get at the money. We want those college kids who gotta finish that paper at 2 a.m., who need that 'crush all obstacles, defy all odds' music. The little kid on punishment, sitting in his room plotting on his freedom; the revolutionaries out there evoking the spirit of Malcolm. Let Pacific Records appeal to the junkies and the clubs. This ain't a club label. We're letting the world know we're here."

"Hello says Batman to Robin." The timely and philosophical response from Turtle eased the tension and brought a low murmur of laughter to the conference room.

Rushie quickly scanned the faces in the room. He could tell that all present were in agreement with Cream. He looked towards Kay-Kay for any sign of support, but Kay-Kay was staring out the window obviously in a distant thought.

Fuck it. If the shit fails, it's mostly their money blown, Rushie thought.

Kay-Kay

It took every fiber of self-control to look out the window and not into the eyes of the defeated. The power play came early; Cream wasted no time. He would be CEO not just in name but also in practice. I remember thinking to myself that this might be the role Cream was destined to play.

Cream

Sure enough Cream's words proved true. "Gun Talk" took the industry by surprise and Rushie was once again a household name. Though Cream was satisfied with the success of the song and album, he knew that if he relied exclusively on Rushie's music to carry the label, the label was destined to fail.

A young artist by the name of Folklore was considered the best lyricist in the game by many. However, his project sat on the shelf over at Pacific Records because the label didn't approve of his revolutionary content. Folklore's first album was a commercial success, but after establishing himself as a rising star, he wanted to make music that was more thought-provoking.

John Stephenson, the president of urban music at Pacific Records, did not approve. And after a series of heated exchanges between Folklore and Stephenson, it was decided that Folklore needed to be taught a lesson. His album release date was pushed back three consecutive times, until finally they decided to just put it on the shelf indefinitely.

Cream was willing to gamble with Folklore. He reached out to Stephenson to figure out a way to get Pacific to release him. But Pacific Records took the tension between them and Folklore to heart, and refused to allow Folklore to go somewhere else to win. Cream was considered an infant in the game, and Stephenson's flat-out refusal to even sit down with Cream spoke volumes. Pacific had no regard for Criminal Empire.

JB

During a lecture at Lincoln University, a historically Black college in Pennsylvania, JB felt the need to clarify his position on the state of hip-hop. A couple of well-known rap artists had recently took offense to his view that hip-hop was being used as a tool for destruction rather than empowerment. They argued

A. C. Clayton

that hip-hop was employing many young Black men and providing honest money for their families. One artist even accused JB of being jealous of their success and secretly wishing he could live in a mansion.

In response, JB spoke to the crowd. "Some ask why I'm so hard on today's hip-hop. Why I'm so critical on the over-arching messages. It is because I truly understand what music is. Imagine for a second a planet without water, barren and desolate—a wasteland. Where there is no water there is no life. Our bodies are similar to planets and music is a spiritual current that carries streams of consciousness that flow like water through us and gives us life. Music is in everything that we do. We ride the train to music, drive to it, work out to it, cook to it, make babies to it, and even wage war to it. We pray with it, using chants and hymns that rhyme and evoke spirits within us.

"So, in essence, music is spiritual. And the powers that control our music—I'm talking about the devils who make the decisions to put the money behind certain projects—know the power of music. They put millions behind certain artists like they put millions behind certain politicians. Just as they rig elections, they rig music selections. These artists or candidates run on platforms that are demonic. These rappers are more influential than all of us speaking from a podium or a pulpit combined. Their lyrics mold the minds of our youth. Their lyrics are scepters of immense power. These scepters can be used as tools for us or against us, to uplift us or destroy us.

"When every song is in some way dedicated to our destruction, or at the very least, our exploitation, who are we but cowards not to speak out against it? Let a Jewish rapper talk about killing his fellow Jews over money and cars. Or have his Jewish women walk on stage with dog collars around their necks attached to leashes. If he's lucky, he ends up in an insane asylum diagnosed with a severe psychosis.

"Just as I speak out against the local drug dealers for peddling poison to our kids, I take the same position against these radio disc jockeys who knowingly promote and push songs that exalt our annihilation. Yeah, I get it. Just like drug dealers, their logic is, 'If we don't sell it, another disc jockey or radio station will.' And who owns these stations? Who pays these salaries? Who truly benefits? Is it the same people who have benefited from our labor and genius for centuries? We must always keep the matador in focus. I'm condemned, so it seems, by my own people, for exposing our enemies."

A. C. Clayton

Chapter 40: a reason for the layers

Peaches
1998

The currency was powder. Its flow, more majestic and reliable than a river's inundation, allowed Peaches and her team to name their price without a second guess. Her prices were the highest on the market, as was the quality of her product. *'You pay for the best,'* was her team's mantra. It was recited like gospel whenever anyone dared to question the margin of her profit.

Ever since her early days in Newark, Peaches had adopted the practice of creating layers between her and the product she distributed. A rule she took from a discussion she had with Palmer, a mentor of sorts, who successfully distributed cars and cocaine while remaining completely off the radar. In the daytime, Palmer ran a successful Audi dealership. At night, he oversaw the cocaine that ran rampant in Trenton. Yet very few people knew his Mr. Hyde side; he hid it well.

"See, little sis, the trick is being invisible in an occupation that can't stand the scrutiny of lights. Unwanted attention will bring about our downfall."

"How do we do that? How do you do that?" Peaches asked.

"Well, for starters, you take the product out of your hands as quick as possible. It's about creating layers. By the time my product reaches the street, it has gone through two or three layers, with only the layer underneath knowing the direct layer above."

For a long time after that discussion, Peaches found herself confused by his logic. But over time, as Peaches employed the practice, her appreciation for Palmer's advice grew. It was no wonder that he had retired and was now a beach bum in Key West, having never encountered any run-ins with the law.

Peaches' pyramid design was simple. She would get the product from Martha's top layer and pass it on to her top layer, Roc. He would then move it on to Soldier, a good friend of Peaches from her high school days.

Soldier was from the Fort Greene housing projects in Brooklyn. He was a living legend in his hood, whose reputation transcended reality. He was a known gunman, the type to handle his business in broad daylight. All of his shootings were public and spectacular. Yet, every one of his trials ended in acquittal due to lack of evidence. It took a lot of convincing and outright bribery for Peaches to win Soldier over. But with Soldier on deck, she knew that her pipeline to the streets was secure from the average stickup kids. They would think twice knowing that Soldier would seek to even the score anywhere and anytime. Thus, the streets saw Soldier, Soldier saw Roc, and Roc answered to her.

With the money flowing like a New York City fire hydrant in the middle of August, she felt comfortable enough, for the first time, to take a much-needed vacation. She decided to take her family, along with Roc and his woman, to Atlantis in the Bahamas. "We deserve this getaway," was her pep talk to Roc. It was only then that she discovered that he had never been on any form of a vacation. Roc had spent his entire life inside the Tri-State area. "That's why I told you to get your passport together. We're heading to some fun in the sun for two weeks."

When she told Kay-Kay that she would be taking Kameek Jr. to Atlantis for two weeks, he grew suspicious and asked for the proof.

"What you mean you want proof? You're not my father or my husband. I ain't gotta show you shit. You lucky I even told you."

Kay-Kay knew as soon as he asked for proof that he had played himself. The last thing he wanted to do was show her how strong his attachment had grown for Kameek Jr. "Yeah, you right. Enjoy yourself one thousand percent and I'll see ya when ya get back." He hugged Kameek Jr. one more time, whispered something in his son's ear and walked away without so much as a goodbye to her or a glance back.

Roc's tropical getaway with Peaches and her family was unreal. Never before had he experienced anything like it. His girlfriend Chrissy, on the other hand, didn't enjoy herself at all. She was jealous of Roc and Peaches' relationship to begin with, but the trip solidified her feelings. Roc seemed to worship Peaches in a weird kind of way. He always seemed to be at her beck and call.

When they first started dating, Roc told Chrissy that Peaches was his partner. Chrissy quickly discovered that their relationship wasn't a partnership; it was more like an occult leader and her lone disciple. Chrissy liked Roc, especially his willingness to spend money on her and her six-year-old son Kyle, but after seeing his adoration for Peaches firsthand, she knew that competing with his idol would never be an option. He would always be on standby for his boss, and his aspirations of calling his own shots one day couldn't be taken seriously.

Chrissy couldn't do it any longer. As soon as their trip was over, she broke the news to Roc. He didn't seem surprised. It was almost as if he knew the day would come. When he told Peaches about the breakup, her response was, "Good. I thought I was gonna have to throw the bitch in front of a train. She wasn't your type. You can do better."

Roc wanted to ask Peaches for an example of better, but held his tongue.

As if the topic were unworthy of further discussion, Peaches changed the subject completely. Her thoughts were once more on Palmer, whose teachings kept her grounded. One time, while they were watching a fellow hustler lose all his money in a gambling spot, Palmer shared an observation. *"See it's time for him to walk away. Fortune is not on his side today. You see gambling, it's just like the hustle game. It's a game of longevity. The money will always be there, the question is... will you?"*

"We have a shipment of 60 bricks coming in tomorrow and I'm pretty sure we will be done with that before the week is out with the way Soldier and Rico are moving them things," Peaches said to Roc. I'm thinking we need to slow it down after this one, just to make sure we're not heating up too much. At least three weeks of nothing from us."

Peaches realized that her ability to move 60 or more keys in less than an entire week was not the pace for long distance running. They had to slow down to complete the marathon.

"I could use a couple of weeks to just chill, so don't expect me to argue," Roc replied in agreement.

Three months after the time off, Peaches was alarmed when she realized that Soldier was getting rid of whatever she opened up to the market within days and on two occasions within hours. At first, she figured Soldier had found his niche and had the Midas touch. But her conversation with Roc raised suspicion.

"Our boy Soldier is moving them things like it ain't nothing," she commented from an angle of pride.

"Yeah, he's actually working with two buyers out of Connecticut. They're buying up all the shit."

"Connecticut?" Peaches asked, her curiosity building slowly.

"That's what I said when Soldier told me, but he stands by them."

Peaches had nothing against kats from Connecticut, but at the rate they were buying up her product she couldn't help but wonder if the two friends were supplying the entire state. "How did he meet them?" she asked, excited by the possibilities.

"Not sure. He told me, but I was half listening. We were both in a rush, so the convo was brief."

"Hmm, I need you to find out everything. This could potentially be a serious score. The way they're buying, we might create a whole separate line for them. See, I knew Soldier would deliver like no other."

Three days later, while walking through the Palisades Mall with lil' Kameek Jr. in tow, Roc began filling Peaches in on all that Soldier shared with him. According to Soldier, the two friends, Rick and Dominic, were the two designated buyers for a team of suppliers in both Hartford and Danbury. The suppliers would pool their resources together and send Rick and Dominic to New York to cop.

Peaches was familiar with that type of approach. Her friend Ducky and his crew from Far Rockaway used to cop like that before transporting their drugs out to Columbus, Ohio.

They would essentially buy the cocaine in bulk to ensure a discount. They would buy so much that a kilo or two was practically given for free. Unfortunately for Ducky, jealousy and internecine warfare decimated his team right around the time millionaire status was about to be theirs to claim.

"Soldier also said that they've been asking to meet with me."

"That's strange. Why?"

"Not sure. They think they can get a better deal from me, I guess?"

"Hmm," was all Peaches could offer. They walked in silence, both playing the information over in their minds. Peaches distracted herself with Kameek Jr. and his inquisitive mind.

Roc reignited the discussion. "They just bought about 22 of the 40 we had last week."

"Hmm."

Roc continued. "Soldier has gotten so cool with them that they actually brought him up to one of their houses up there in Connecticut."

"They actually brought him to their house?" Peaches asked a bit baffled.

"Yep. He met the dude's wife and son, from what he's telling me."

"That's super sloppy on their part," Peaches pointed out. Roc just nodded his head, but Peaches needed to see more than his head nod in agreement. "You do realize that it's super sloppy on their behalf to let a stranger into their crib and have him around their family, right?" Roc not being the brightest crayon in the box finally caught what she was saying and agreed with her logic.

"Tell Soldier to be careful with them. Yeah, they spending good money, but all money ain't good. Especially if it's attached to fools. Either... what's these guys names again?"

"Rick and Dominic."

"Yeah, Rick and Dominic. So either Rick and Dominic are stupid mothafuckas or they're playing an entirely different game. *You*," she pointed at Roc directly to emphasize her command. "Definitely *do no* business with them. They're too sloppy."

Roc thought Peaches was once again overreacting, but he respected the fact that her paranoia had taken them this far. He fought hard to always make sure his second guess never made it to a third.

Rick and Dominic slowed up their purchases for a few months claiming that they found a cheaper, though less consistent, supply. Soldier, greedy to keep his meal ticket in the fold, asked them what could be done to keep them coming.

"Bring us to the source, bro," Dominic insisted. "We need to get better numbers. We'll cut you in on a percentage as well. We just feel like we're buying a lot and our business is not being appreciated."

"Nah, never that. It's appreciated. It's just that the good shit is limited, so the prices are going to be high." Soldier, talking from a position of greed, couldn't see the game that stood before him. "Let me talk to my peoples again and see if we can arrange that meeting."

"Well, if you can, then we're ready to really talk. My crew is ready to cop about 80 of those things from you," Dominic threw out.

Soldier's eyes grew to the size of half dollars envisioning the Ferrari that he felt was his birthright.

After talking with Roc and getting nowhere, he reached out to Peaches directly.

"So what's up, Soldier?" Peaches said in a tone designed to remind him of his position in the structure.

"These Connecticut niggas I been fucking with hard body is ready to cop 80 birds in one shot. The only thing is, they want a discount from you or Roc."

"Me or Roc? Did you tell them our names?"

"Of course not. I'm not stupid. I'm just saying that's a nice little score to catch."

"You're right, but why are they trying to bypass you? Whatever deal we decide on, you will be able to offer it to them. They don't need to know about Roc or me."

Soldier was shaking his head in disagreement. "I know if I was buying eighty birds, I would want to speak to the supplier as well."

Peaches fought the urge to say, 'That's why you ain't buying 80 birds and probably never will.' Instead she deferred to a more tactical approach. "But that's just my point, bro. You're not buying. You're the supplier. That's all they need and should want to know. The fact that they want to know more doesn't raise an alarm in your head?"

Soldier did not appreciate the snooty tone she spoke with; it was time for a truthful warning. "Peaches, when alarms go off in my head, people die." He spoke with no malice in his voice. But he was disappointed that she had mistaken him for anything less than a general.

"Well, that's my point, bro. I would hate for alarm bells to go off and for people have to die." Her double meaning had not escaped Soldier's wit, but instead of responding he just smirked.

"Your call, Peaches."

Satisfied that once more rank had been established, she continued. "If they got the bread and they really want it, they gotta go through you, bottom line. I promise, the best deal I would personally give to them if I were dealing with them directly, will be the same deal you can give them. If that's not cool, then no hard feelings. Let them go somewhere else. We're not in a race. The pipeline is endless and that means we'll always have clients."

Soldier's explanation to Rick and Dominic that they would have to deal strictly with him didn't seem to faze them in the least. Strangely, after stressing him for months about meeting his supplier, they suddenly seemed content with working with him. It was then that his alarm began pulsating from deep. They insisted on buying the 80 kilos as soon as possible. But Soldier began stalling them. He told them that the Coast Guard had snatched a shipment, and he was waiting on a new one to arrive.

Rick and Dominic seemed desperate to close the deal, claiming that they were uncomfortable sitting on that much money. Soldier suggested that they go somewhere else and cop if they couldn't wait.

"Perhaps we will," Rick said, considering Soldier's challenge.

For two straight weeks Soldier heard no more from them. Then, as if their last conversation had never occurred, they were back asking to close the deal.

Soldier met with Roc, explaining his suspicion. Roc was clueless on how to proceed and so a sit down with Peaches was needed. They met in a friend's basement that Peaches termed 'the bunker,' on account that it resembled a wartime bunker. In the bunker, there were foam and metal insulated walls and shelves stocked from ceiling to floor with water and canned goods of all kinds. Two battery-operated back-up generators and a boom box radio sat with a bunch of other gadgets.

Soldier detailed his concerns as Peaches listened.

"Definitely police. I don't even think they're CI's." She was referring to confidential informers, a sub-species of humans who trade information to law enforcement as an occupation. "Or maybe one is the cop and the other is the CI."

"Who linked them to you?"

"You mean, who introduced me to them?"

"Yeah."

"This nigga Dumar out of the Bronx."

"How much have you sold them since you started dealing with them?"

"Not sure, but a whole lot."

Peaches wasn't sure either, but her estimate was close to 100 kilos over the past year. She knew she had some top-notch lawyers, but even they wouldn't be able free Soldier from the hole he would surely be calling home from for at least a decade.

These were the days when this hustle truly taxed the spirit. There was no easy choice to make for anyone in the room, especially Soldier. He could wait for them to nab him and begin the process of a legal defense, which Peaches would pay for without hesitation. Or he could run, relocate, and lay low. She would talk with Kay-Kay and see if he knew how to get Soldier out of the country.

But Soldier dismissed all options. "I got it, Peaches. I know how to handle these mothafuckas."

"What does that mean, Soldier? That's too vague. There's a lot more at stake than just you."

Soldier stared at Peaches, daring her implication to cross the line. When he was satisfied that an understanding between the two had been reached he spoke. "Never question my honor." Soldier firmly beat the palm of his hand over his heart as he continued, "This... is my Morerall. My name is Soldier for a reason. Becoming a prisoner of war is not in my future. My trial by fire will be held on the battlefield, not in a courtroom. That's our problem. When the heat finally comes, we roll over and surrender. There's a cost to play in this game, but it doesn't always have to be one-sided. They choose to play, they choose to pay."

Soldier gave his good friend Dumar a call. It was Dumar who introduced and vouched for Dominic and Rick. On Dumar's word of honor, Soldier embraced the enemies. Dumar had to be held accountable for betraying the code. He answered on the second ring.

"Boy boy, what's up?"

"Got great news, man."

"Talk to me. What's up?"

"The ship has docked. My grandma's cruise was successful."

"Damn that was a long ride. How old is she again?"

"She just turned 80. It's celebration time and I want you to come to the party."

"Word?" A bit of suspicion crept into Dumar's voice. "To the party?" His second question confirmed his CI status. Why else would Dumar be reluctant to be a part of a 2.4 million dollar score?

"Yeah fool, to the party. You made the link. You're going to get a piece on this. Not a lot, of course, because my points ain't that big. But definitely, I'm gonna break you off. My only concern is that these niggas was bluffing all along and they money ain't really right."

"Nah... Soldier, I wouldn't..." Dumar paused for a long time, his conscience attempting to break free from its captor.

"You wouldn't what?" Soldier asked hoping that the slave made it to freedom. But the hounds caught him before he made it to the river, so his larceny stood. "I... wouldn't worry about the bread, they definitely got it."

"Saying that shit is one thing, seeing it is another, bro. I'm just saying, you never know."

"Nah, Soldier. Trust me, man. I fucks with them. I know their money is long."

"You fucks with them, huh?" The difficulty in that question was hard for Soldier to disguise.

It gave pause to Dumar and once again a chance was provided for him to run free and follow the North Star, but this time he hugged the plantation with conviction. "Yeah, I fucks with them. It's on you if you want the lick, but I'm telling you, they good."

"Aight, man. If you say they're good, then it is what it is. I'll give 'em a call and tell 'em where the party is going to be held."

"Aight, bro, I'm there. See you then."

Rick, Dumar, and Dominic met Soldier on Prince Street, in front of a nerve center the police called Central Booking. It was also the side entrance to the Fort Greene projects. Dominic had initially objected to the last minute change of the meeting place, arguing that he was uncomfortable carrying that much cash into the projects. Soldier argued back that Fort Greene was the only place he felt safe sitting on 80 kilos. A last-minute compromise was reached. Dominic and Rick would bring half the cash, and in exchange, Soldier would give them the entire package.

Soldier would then meet them in Midtown for the remainder of the money later that evening. On Dumar's word, the second half of the money was guaranteed. "You've sold us about 110 keys within the last year already and our money has never been short," they had argued.

"I can't argue with that logic," Soldier replied. "Especially when it's the truth."

The four men greeted each other like long lost friends, complimenting one another on the obvious effects of good living. Only Soldier seemed in shape. The other three had clearly seen better days.

"Damn," Rick observed. "These projects don't seem as bad as they've been portrayed."

Soldier quickly corrected the naivety of Rick's comment. "Only cause you walking with me, bro. This is my domain." Soldier's words left no room for doubt.

With great leisure, they walked towards the heart of the kingdom. Occasionally, they stopped as Soldier spoke to one of his subjects.

A group of little kids riding dirt bikes—the leader no older than 10—saw Soldier and raced to him. Every bike skidded to attention less than five feet in front of Soldier.

"What's up with my little soldiers?" he asked.

The leader, a light-skinned giant named Kaliph spoke for the rest. "We just practicing our wheelies and teaching Damir how to bunny hop."

Soldier looked at one of the babies of the bunch, the child called Damir. His mother, Amira, was Soldier's best friend growing up. "Damir, you don't know how to bunny hop?" Soldier asked in a tone of comedy, designed to make Damir comfortable in answering without shame.

Damir, always the quiet type, unlike his momma, stayed true to his nature. He bit his bottom lip and just shook his head from side to side.

"What? Impossible. Let me see that bike." Soldier pointed to Sulamin. A tall lanky kid of nine, he had the most fancy and biggest bike in the group. Soldier took Sulamin's bike, determined to give instruction to Damir on how to bunny hop.

Rick, Dumar, and Dominic seemed uncomfortable yet amused. They were sitting in the middle of the projects with a million and a half dollars in cold cash stuffed in three book bags and Soldier seemed determined to give bunny hop lessons to the kids.

"Soldier, don't hurt yourself trying to show off for your friends." The female voice came from above. The two beautiful sisters, Sarita and Brenda were hanging out the window anticipating the comedy show. Soldier just smiled, knowing that their laughs wouldn't be at his expense.

"See, Damir?" he said with great concentration. "It's all about balance and concentration." Soldier began lifting the bike, making it hop like a frog, in circles.

The kids looked on, deep in study, trying to get the technique down pat. Rieffie and Amari, another two of the youngsters and the dearest to Soldier, began mimicking his movement and then the rest followed. Even Damir began doing it after a few sloppy tries, and finally started hopping away. By this time, Soldier was tired and had played with his little buddies long enough. He passed the bike back to Sulamin and asked the little rascals, "Where's Jamal and Shawn?"

In unison, the group all yelled, "On punishment."

Soldier found that funny. Of course they were. Those little bad asses were always in trouble. "Aight, y'all. I gotta roll."

The kids, led by Kaliph, dropped their bikes on the floor and jumped in line.

Soldier began handing them money. He gave $20 to each one of them only after they touched their head and their heart, as a display of allegiance to an unbreakable bond. The kids jumped back on their bikes and took off racing toward the corner. They were headed to the game room, a place that also doubled as a weed spot for the adults.

"Give us some money," Brenda yelled jokingly from the window.

"Get a life!" Soldier countered back without looking.

The four men began walking once more.

"Damn, you weren't kidding. They love you out here." Rick's observation sounded clouded with second thoughts. *Was he about to take a villain or a hero off the streets?* he wondered to himself. As an upstanding member of society, one sworn to uphold the law in his own community, he never got a greeting remotely similar to what Soldier was receiving. *Why was that? How could a criminal like Soldier be more a part of a community than an officer of the law?* Rick knew he had to do what he had to do. He couldn't question his oath, only uphold it. Soldier was selling poison, probably to this very same community that loved him. There was no time for questioning his actions. Soldier's takedown had to happen.

As they passed the basketball court, a group of young men stopped the game to shout Soldier out.

"Ayeee, Ayo," one guy named Maurice yelled. "Didn't you say Soldier was talking about spotting me 20 points the next time we play?"

Ayo started laughing before saying, "He sure did."

Soldier waved them off. "Y'all lucky I got company!" he yelled in their direction.

"They could get it, too," Rashaun, the 6'6 giant, declared with assurance. The entire court erupted in laughter before resuming their intense competition.

"You play ball, too?" Dominic asked, for the sake of conversation.

"Yeah, I used to be nice. Had a wicked jump-shot, but now... ahh, I'm able to score now and then if they leave me open long enough."

The three men nodded their heads. None of them were spring chickens.

They finally reached their destination. Sixteen Fleet Walk sat in an alcove of withered grass and careless debris. Soldier reached for the entrance doorknob, but before his hand made contact, two beautiful young ladies emerged exiting the building in great haste. Sakinah and Aleah were clearly on their way to a celebration or date, seemingly running late. They wore dresses, eye-catching in their splendor. Their shapes were a distraction to even the most trained eye. And that was the plan all along— the distraction.

Rick, Dumar, and Dominic, all felt comfortable enough to compliment the ladies and it was the only distraction Soldier needed. He drew off his hip like a cowboy from an Old Western movie. The difference here was that this wasn't a movie and it wasn't a six-shooter.

The Glock 380, a dragon in concealment, revealed its fire to the slave called Dumar first. He fell in the rhythm of wrong. Dominic fell a close second. Only Rick had enough time to attempt a reaction and he was the only one who knew why he died. The gun was a smoking hot dragon waiting for another belly rub, yearning to belch more fire.

Soldier had no time to waste. He knew that the Feds would be on the move. They must have heard the shots and they knew their plan went terribly wrong.

Soldier had gambled that the Feds would stay on the project's perimeter until the deal was made, out of fear that entering too soon would have tipped him off. He was right. This gave Soldier the seconds he needed to put these suckers in their graves. He let off one last shot at Dumar's face, ensuring that his funeral would be one with a closed casket. Quickly, Soldier tossed a set of keys to Aleah. She caught them in mid-air and buried them deep in her voluptuous bosom. Before the two ladies began screaming at the top of their lungs, they touched their head and their heart and whispered goodbye to Soldier. He returned the gesture with sadness, not at his actions, but at the fact that he would never look upon them again. Such is the heavy price of war.

Soldier took the book bags off the bodies and ran into the building. He jammed the door, guaranteeing at least a 30-second delay.

He took to the stairs, five steps at a time, until he made it to the fifth floor. He could still hear Sakinah and Aleah's screams, but now he heard the sirens as well.

Apartment 5D was empty. It was under renovation. He unlocked the door with the master key he had to every empty apartment in his kingdom. He emptied a bag and a half of money into the hallway closet. It was his deposit to Aleah and the rest of his family's future. He then snatched an AK-47 out of the same closet. Rivaling the speed of light, he ran back out of the apartment, wiped the doorknob clean of any fingerprints in anticipation of a future dusting and locked the door quickly. Law enforcement could be heard downstairs attempting to get pass his door wedge. The incinerator swallowed the master key as he continued down the hallway. They would never find that clue on his body.

Only then did he slow up and take a deep breath. This was the moment of truth. All he could do now was live in the moment. One deep breath and then he surrendered to the calm.

Soldier made his way to the roof and spotted the helicopter at the same time the helicopter spotted him. Great, they knew where he was. The AK-47 blasted two quick rounds, sending the helicopter into a startled retreat. He then took aim at the ants dressed in Kevlar flap jackets covering the sidewalk. They scattered in all directions surprised at his response. Within minutes, more helicopters came hovering at a safe distance. Soldier believed he could spot at least two news helicopters, though far. The All-Seeing Eye and the Peacock were there to bare witness. Soldier watched from the roof as the entire building was evacuated. Families were being ushered from their homes to secured perimeters.

The wind was picking up and the final part of Soldier's plan was executed. Soldier went to the ledge and began emptying out the contents of both bags. Bills, the Ben Franklin kind, hovered like tiny green kites as they began to fly. Spectators looking out their windows began cheering his name. Many would never again in their lives see a true warrior in action, and though they knew what the eventual outcome would be, they applauded the spirit and the example. He was one man, a soldier, standing up to an army that they loathed and feared. They cheered enthusiastically for the courage they wished they had.

But Soldier was running out of bullets, so it was just a matter of time. A voice from a bullhorn could be heard, attempting to reason with him. In response, Soldier sent his last rounds towards the armored trucks that the ants now hid behind. From a distant, he caught a glare reflecting from a point on the closest helicopter.

His brain yelled 'scope' and he knew that it was his time to salute. Milliseconds later, Soldier was down. The shot captured by the media for the whole world to see came from one of the many helicopters that hovered just outside of his assault rifle's 300-meter range. The transmission sent over the walkie-talkies of 'suspect down' sent an inundation of law enforcement onto the roof.

More shots were delivered to his corpse and the truth behind the additional shots would never leave the roof. The sniper's shot was the one that did it, the only one that was needed. The 11 other shots that entered Soldier's body postmortem were shots of anger and desecration—revenge for the death of two of their own and their loyal rat.

Chapter 41: a general's farewell

So the true and living Soldier
is but a ship alone in a sea.
Navigating boldly,
outnumbered exponentially

1998

Soldier's sendoff was presidential, not just by hood standards, but by all standards. Peaches and Kay-Kay spared no expense to honor the fallen warrior. Even the local hip-hop stations promoted the location of the wake and funeral. Scores of people made their way to the funeral home to view what was, to many, the last of a dying breed. From the time the doors opened at 10 a.m. until they closed at 10 p.m., streams of people went to pay their respects.

The police, viewing this show of support as an affront to their authority, were initially prepared to harass all who attended. That was until word came from the Feds to stand down.

The Feds had a team of agents and confidential informers who would be working the crowd. They were searching for clues to the rest of Soldier's team, as well as, any street alliances they did not know existed. Soldier's funeral would provide a

A. C. Clayton

treasure trove of information that they would not allow the NYPD to disrupt. The previous night, federal agents broke into the funeral parlor to make sure that whatever their eyes and ears might miss, the concealed cameras facing Soldier's corpse wouldn't.

Just as expected, gangsters from all over came to pay homage to a Rambo. Soldier was dressed in his customary army fatigue from head to toe. On the top of his right shoulder sat six stars stitched to perfection. It was the hood's way of acknowledging his rank, a livewire from start to finish.

The procession to view his body was deliberately slow; two mammoths dressed in matching fatigues controlled the traffic, ushering the viewers along. Whether brief or lengthy, everyone who took the time to stand over Soldier, departed only after placing their hands on their forehead and their heart before signing off in a gesture of military salutation.

Around 7 p.m., a large but orderly entourage made their way to view Soldier. The buzz that this crowd generated elevated the level of importance and prestige to dizzying heights. Sony, the platinum-selling rap artist, along with a slew of other well-known artists made up the contingent. Even inside the funeral home, cameras began snapping. After viewing the body for all of a minute, the group of artists opened its rank, allowing Cream to view the body. A human shield of artists had blocked the view of the onlookers, and the planted agents, from seeing what Cream said or did.

They did not see him whisper a combination of words designed by Tehuti to resurrect and arm the spirit for its future return. Not even the artists themselves understood this warrior's chant. Having completed the mission he had come for, Cream departed, but not before placing the flag of allegiance (that both he and Soldier pledged to uphold) inside the casket. He placed it on top of the left breast pocket, above the heart. Death was a concept of the defeated and not the victorious. For the victorious, death was just the moment when the baton was passed to the next warrior, entrusted with the sacred duty to uphold the laws of identity and purpose.

That night, the FBI's eastern division chief poured over 13 hours of video footage with his tech crew on hand. They were looking for anything out of the ordinary that would provide a clue as to who and what Soldier had been a part of. The entire wake and funeral service were done on the same day.

It was a comical affair to the chief. "You would think this guy was Martin Luther King Jr. or something the way they're honoring him."

The footage didn't get interesting for the chief until the 1900-hour mark when the entourage of "hip-hoppers" made their way to the coffin, and one of the hip-hoppers, who clearly stood out from the rest, began whispering in the ear of the dead. The chief's antenna really stood up when the whisperer placed some sort of object on the left breast of Soldier before leaving.

"What is that?" he asked his entire staff.

The answer to his question was met with expected silence.

"Zoom in on that as best as you can!"

The camera's pixilation left a lot to be desired, but they were able to see that what was left behind was some sort of fraternal pin, placed above the heart.

"What is that?" he repeated more from a rhetorical vantage point than anything else.

Finally, a reply worthy of note came from the rookie in the group. "It looks like some type of bird clutching a rodent."

The chief pointed to the rookie and a vet of 20 years. "You and you, I want an actual picture of that pin by the morning. Do not let that body be buried without a clear and concise image."

The rookie and the vet took their leave.

The hand gestures of many who attended the funeral now made sense. The chief dismissed the rest of the team before placing an important call. The voice on the other end belonged to a man of power and authority.

The chief spoke with no patience for small talk. "Do you remember that homicide that happened a while back in Red Hook? A confidential informant was killed and left with a rat in his mouth and a letter attached to it? Do you remember the symbol that was at the end of the letter?"

"I do," the voice on the other end responded.

"I think we finally have a lead on the author."

A. C. Clayton

Chapter 42: the point of it all

Kay-Kay
1999

After serving nine years in prison, my man Big Sha from Brownsville found himself liberated in more ways than one. For the past five years, he had been living upstate in the city of Rochester. He had met and married the sister of another prisoner who introduced the two on a visit. Prison bars do not always stop love from blooming, and before Big Sha made it home, he had become the father of two little girls.

Sha was a reformed man and his decision to move up to Rochester was a good one in my opinion. His reputation in Brownsville would have made his change difficult to maintain. The lure of the streets would have pulled him back in.

I went to visit Big Sha and meet his wife and kids. His wife was a nurse and Sha found a job unloading freights for Kodak. They had a cozy one family house that sat on the outskirts of the hood. Rochester had seen better days, but I could tell it was still a lively city.

"Man, I'm telling you, Kay, there's a lot of potential up here," Sha was filling me in on a nightclub idea he had that only required the capital.

I actually liked the idea. But even if I didn't, the money he was asking me to invest was the money I had planned on giving him regardless, simply because his friendship never waivered.

His wife Rose's hospitality was better than a five-star hotel. She was excited to finally have someone from Sha's side of the family come to their home and visit. His little girls, ages eight and six, were adorably witty. My brother was happy. He was beating the odds and statistics, and I was proud for him.

I watched Big Sha, the bully of C-74, read a bedtime story to his girls that put them to sleep. It wasn't an act for my sake. I could tell this was their routine.

After his wife went to bed, Sha and I sat at the kitchen table and popped a bottle of Moët in celebration. We talked for hours, catching up on each other's lives and struggles. I told Sha that his idea of opening a nightclub would become a reality, and that piece of information seemed to elevate his shoulders by degrees.

At one point in our conversation, I mentioned how proud I was of him for creating this life he was now living.

"Kay, I'm not going to lie. Financially, it's been a struggle. But, bro, I wouldn't change it for the world. You know me and my sister never grew up with any man in our lives for more than a weekend? Unless it was a holiday, and those niggas never paid us no mind unless they were giving us some funds to get rid of us for a while. So this life I'm living is foreign to me. I never saw it before. But my wife, she's the general in this. She's the one who put this all together and then said, 'Okay, big guy, here's the script.' And man, I love following it. I love waking my kids up in the morning and getting them ready for the day. I love coming home at night after a hard work day and have my babies dive into my arms. I love the doctor appointments, the family trips to the zoo, all of it. But most importantly, I love being able to walk the streets with my family freely and not look over my shoulders because I might run into a bandit, feel me?"

All I could do was nod in envy. His reality was so foreign to me and if I thought that money was the answer, then how was I to explain this anomaly?

He continued. "I decided when Akira was born that I would rather study my kid than study a bid, sitting back in a cell like 'Damn, you missed it.'"

"Missed what?" I asked, curiosity getting the better of me.

"The point of it all, the responsibility. This peaceful space you see is a result of both my wife and I working to create this for our children. There's nothing more important to me than making sure my kids don't grow up deprived of love and guidance the way I did. I feel like when a man becomes a father he can no longer risk his freedom, because his freedom is now tied to the protection of his children. If I'm out the picture who guarantees their protection?"

Again all I could do is nod, but this time I was nodding in shame.

My ride home allowed me the time to absorb my discussion with Big Sha. I was now the father of a 14-year-old who I barely knew. And while I provided for and spent time with him, Sha got me thinking about the quality of that time, and more importantly, its frequency. I never really spent any undivided time with Kameek Jr. I always had someone around us whenever I spent time with him. I still conducted business in his presence, as if nothing had changed. Alicia spent more one-on-one time with him than I did. I found myself trying to justify why my body was present, but my mind was always distracted by the streets. Big Sha had me thinking about my responsibilities to the heartbeats that weren't mine.

Yet, the closer I got to NYC, the less I had time to think about the fairy tale that Big Sha's life was turning out to be. Perhaps it was the polluted air that seemed to sit over the city like a pregnant cloud, or the filth and debris that littered its arteries, but pure, clean thoughts were difficult to entertain. By the time I hit the Bronx, Kool G Rap's "Road to the Riches" was bumping in my system and all that was on my mind was peacocks and their colorful feathers.

Chapter 43: war begins when ideas collide

2000

JB's quest for balance was as complicated as walking a tight wire suspended 1,000 feet in the air. He knew that his connection to the senator stifled his true feelings. He couldn't really express to his audience his sentiments on a number of topics. Senator Sinclair Monroe was a systems man, a responsible negro who preferred begging and bartering for equity and fairness than really getting his hands dirty.

JB knew that at some point in the senator's political career, Monroe had become content with making the money and having access to the power. He may have started off with the best of intentions for his people, but it only took him long enough to understand how the system worked before making it work for him. According to the senator, there were no clean hands in politics. It was all about favors and blind eyes, selective amnesia and calculated back-rubbing.

JB quickly discovered that the game of politics was more treacherous than the streets; a disheartening fact that left him in turmoil and astonishment. The suit and ties disguised the villains, tailored them to look respectable.

JB knew that he wouldn't be able to continue faking in this politician-in-training role. He was a revolutionary, a warrior. His spirit's affinity was more akin to Che Guevara than Al Sharpton. He respected Al for keeping the issues present, but there was no counter balance to Al. Martin had Malcolm to play the boogieman. Sharpton had no one, so he attempted to play dual roles: the man of reason and the angry Black man.

Both were just acts in JB's opinion, because no true change ever really materialized. Sharpton had recently gone from being the most hated by the oppressor to the face at the negotiating table. Sharpton had cleaned up his image. Word was he even hired a publicist to make his message more conciliatory and cautious. JB wouldn't be surprised if Sharpton eventually landed a movie role. That's how the enemy co-opts, he surmised. They work to turn revolutionaries into court jesters.

JB refused to become neutralized through legitimacy. JB was the alternate script, and if Senator Sinclair Monroe or any other politician thought it wise to try to control him, they had sadly miscalculated.

"Brothers and sisters," JB began. "While sitting in a town hall meeting in Jamaica, Queens the other day, the discussion came around to improving the educational system in New York City. But this is not an education system, it's a triage. Let's call it and see it for what it is. It's an experiment to see how well they can kill our minds and replace it with consumerism and impulse. The system ain't broken. It works just as it was designed to.

"If you eliminate charter schools, you get rid of the evidence exposed by its presence. That's why they never teach true history in these public schools. They deliberately distort the facts or downplay the truth because history explains it all. I would much rather talk about how we can change the entire system. How do we make this system work? And if we can't then how do we scrap it?"

JB was in rare form. The crowd hanging on his every word was not mesmerized by his eloquence, but by the simplicity of his logic. His implied threat was directed at those whose sole purpose for being present was to spy and report. At this point, JB knew there had to be a couple of agents in the audience.

Hypnotically, he repeated himself as if he was amazed at what he just heard. "Then, how do we scrap it? That's where I would like our discussion to move to. Let's take away their choices; our children's minds are not theirs to destroy. Making a businessman the head of an educational institution is like going to a bar and asking for tea." A chuckle made its way through the room. "Or since we're talking about bars, it's like knowingly putting a drunk behind the wheel and patting him on the back for making it home without crashing. It doesn't make sense unless your purpose for putting him in the car is to calculate the eventuality of a crash. It's just a matter of time. It's the same as this public school system with outdated materials and antiquated teaching methods. It can never equal success. I refuse to accept this and I hope you do the same."

The speech electrified the crowd. So much so that Sinclair Monroe was hearing about it well before its conclusion. What disturbed the senator wasn't the fact that the kid was picking an unnecessary and useless fight as much as it was the revolutionary undertones. As JB's benefactor and mentor, Sinclair Monroe knew that he needed to quell that fire before it consumed them both.

The meeting took place the next day in his Flatbush office.

"JB, you knew the media was in attendance and you still chose to address what could've, and should've, been addressed behind closed doors."

"Says who?" JB challenged.

"Our concentration is on negotiating a better school system! Overthrowing and starting a new system is just fiery talk, but it's not practical!"

JB, with his face contorted in disappointment, fired back at what he saw as cowardice. "That's the problem right there. The people we appoint to be our voices are afraid to yell charge."

"Oh don't give me that bullshit pitch. Before you were born, I was in these trenches fighting for my people. When you get 30 years in and you can look back, then you tell me about how well you used your voice. That's when you can judge me. Until then, either you accept my guidance or we separate."

JB remained calm realizing that his words had hit the mark they were intended to. *Bullseye, mothafucka*, he thought. Silence consumed the room. Both men weighing and appreciating the juncture they found themselves in. Would their paths continue to entwine or had the point of dissection been reached?

The answer hung on JB's shoulders like an exhausted teammate. A slow grin slid across his face. Their division wouldn't be today. JB accepted that the hour glass was almost up on Sinclair Monroe's usefulness. However, a few more ducks needed to be lined up before he would respectfully say farewell. For now, he would remain under the wing of the most powerful Black politician in Brooklyn.

"I always have accepted and appreciated your guidance and nothing has changed. Let's move on." For some reason the command in JB's tone didn't settle well with Sinclair Monroe.

"We don't move on until you retract your statements in public."

"Absolutely not. That's a game changer."

Sinclair Monroe grew enraged. How dare the little gutter brat he had picked out of the trash and attempted to clean up and civilize, have the nerve to show his ingratitude? "Then we are done. I'm not fucking playing these hoe games with you. Get the fuck out. Come back when you've found your senses." With a wave of his hand, he dismissed JB without a second glance.

JB hadn't wanted to sever ties this soon, but he felt his hand being forced. Skillfully, he controlled the response that his heart demanded, choosing instead to follow his intelligence. "I'm sorry that we couldn't see eye to eye on this issue, and that the ultimatum is etched in stone. I've learned a lot from you and thank you for the help that you've provided."

Sinclair Monroe found JB's words to be insincere and sarcastic. His refusal to respond or look in JB's direction was enough of an indication for them both that the association had ended.

Chapter 44: awakenings

Kay-Kay
2000

When I heard about the split between my brother and his mentor, the bullshit artist Sinclair Monroe, I was not surprised. I knew that JB would eventually have to separate himself from that joker if he wanted to keep the grease from sticking to his name. But when Alicia told me the split was over JB's education speech and the nature of his speech, I thought back to a discussion I had many years before.

Many went away to college not only to learn about complex ideas, equations, and systems, but to also begin to discover themselves. Unfortunately for me, that experience was not in my cards—at least not in the traditional sense.

My college was encased in 30-foot concrete walls and steel meshing, designed to shred the flesh off of any who dared to envision freedom as something more than just a wish. If I had to say what I majored in, I would have to say it was the psychology of the neglected mind. And if I had to name my greatest professor, I would have to name the Old God.

"I'm giving you this book. It's called the *Pedagogy of the Oppressed*. Pedagogy means education, or better yet, instruction. Take your time and read it. It's not a Donald Goines book, but it still has some substance," the Old God told me.

It took me about three weeks to fully digest it, but as soon as I did, I brought it back ready to discuss the book with him. Instead, the Old God began talking about the institution we currently found ourselves in.

"It's a hell of a mind fuck to be able to convince so many people to just go along with whatever, don't you think? I mean, men with nothing to lose, humbled and castrated into the profession of court jesters. It's impossible for that type of submission to happen overnight."

"I'm lost," I replied, truly not understanding exactly what the Old God was referring to.

"Of course you are. The system wouldn't work if you weren't confused. The book you read explained the why and how, but what we're analyzing now is the evidence. Look around and tell me if this is a coincidence."

Still confused I asked, "If what is a coincidence?"

"That even though Black and Brown is a minority in the state, we're a majority in the prison. How is this anomaly possible without training? It's like teaching an elephant how to ride a tricycle. Unless you buy into the notion that we are genetically inferior and our very blueprint, our DNA makes us more susceptible to commit crime. This is why we study statistics."

"Statistics?"

"Yes, statistics. It's the mathematical fingerprints left behind."

I remember scratching my head, trying to figure out what he was talking about. He saw my confusion and adjusted his approach. "I see I need to simplify this shit for you. Okay, here it goes. The failure of the public school system ensures the success of the prison system. The failure of the public school system guarantees that those who are privileged will always be privileged and we, who are not privileged, will always be fighting for an increase in minimum wage. We will always be begging for more crumbs. When, after great protest and pickets, they finally say, 'Okay, here are your crumbs,' we jump for joy because a victory was won. Meanwhile, inflation rises and minimum wage is still too low."

"Inflation?" I asked, truly attempting to grasp the bigger picture.

"Yep, inflation. That's your word for the night. Tomorrow morning, I'm expecting you to know and understand its definition."

Chapter 45: boiling point

JB

2000

"Brothers and sisters, just the other day I was asked a series of questions by a local news reporter who was trying to get me to say something disparaging about my mentor Sinclair Monroe. They asked me, as if I don't recall the trap they put Malcolm in."

"Speak, brother, speak," a voice from the jam-packed crowd interrupted.

"While Senator Monroe and I are no longer working hand in hand, make no mistake about it, he's still my mentor and his commitment to our people's political well-being can never be questioned. However, there is a distinction between the senator and myself. He's a politician. I am not." Laughter erupted before JB's hands silenced the crowd.

"Don't take what I'm saying as a diss, because it's not. Politicians are needed on the warfront. I'm just not needed to be a politician. We all play our roles and my role is simply to assist you in remembering to fight. I was asked by this same reporter 'Why have you started talking that 'fight the power' stuff?' My answer seemed to throw her off. Do you want to know what I said?" The crowd was in a frenzy. He had them hook, line and sinker. He asked again to make sure their interest was truly invested in the answer. "Do you want to know what I said?"

A collective "Yes!" sent vibrations throughout the building.

"The answer is simple. If it's the people in power who are destroying our future, then they're the only power worth fighting. What other power or force should we be focused on except the force that's threatening to destroy us if we do not act? Come on, soldiers, talk to me. I need to hear the warriors!"

Later in the same speech, JB hit another nerve. "Our relationship with law enforcement has never changed. Since the days when law enforcement wore all white. Their disposition has always been outright contempt. They hate that their engagement with us has to even appear to be civil—something other than what it is. Because what it *is* would mean bloodshed. An unshakable truth we try to avoid at all cost. We forget that our shared history has pitted us against each other for over six thousand years. We've always harbored conflicting worldviews, yet now we pretend that our philosophies have been reconciled and are now one and the same. Or is it important for my people to forget that these different approaches are distinct for a reason? I'm just thinking out loud and I know that some of us are afraid to even do that, afraid to think out loud. We prefer instruction on how not to step out of line from our so-called leaders.

"Asking for a script change will never work. Here's what will. We gotta take back the institutions that mold our children's minds. There are many battles, but this one affects all the rest. If our children, our *tomorrows,* are educated properly, ahh, man what would that look like? How beautiful would our future be? They make that kind of future nearly impossible. They overwork and underpay the teachers of our children. The design of this equation is to ensure that the institution attracts not the brightest, but the best at teaching mediocrity or failure. Yet we act like we don't see the scam, like we're really okay with losing our babies..."

Senator Sinclair Monroe read the entire speech the next day in the *Daily Challenge* under the title "Fight the Power" and grew nauseous. In one breath, JB called the senator his mentor, and in the next, he sounded like he was calling on armed insurrection. All morning, Sinclair found himself on the phone assuring many of his allies that JB had gone rogue and by no means did JB represent any of Sinclair's views. Many of the established civil rights leaders in New York City encouraged Sinclair to denounce JB's message as misguided, irresponsible, and naïve. They reasoned, ever so passionately, that JB was oversimplifying the struggle to simple people and that's why they were attracted to his messaging.

Sinclair agreed, and by midday he had denounced JB's comments not in the *Daily Challenge,* but the *Daily News* and the *NY Post.* Sinclair knew that to not do so would mean the death of his own political career. His opponents would pounce on his relationship with this radical who spilled hatred and destruction toward the very system Sinclair took an oath to protect and preserve. JB had become a liability, and it was time to let everyone know that Senator Sinclair Monroe was not the culprit that poured the toxins into JB's polluted mind.

Winter
2001

JB's visit to see the Old God in Attica was a boost to his morale. He struggled with the question of whether or not he was becoming too radical too fast. But according to the Old God, JB had not been moving fast enough. The litmus test for the Old God was simple: if you have people traveling to hear you speak, why waste the message?

JB agreed and having the senator's backing seemed less important than having the Old God's blessing. The torch had been passed and JB was determined not to disappoint.

"Brothers and sisters, I held my tongue as I watched lunacy steal our attention. The towers fell two months ago. America is about to invade Afghanistan and when we blink, they will invade Iraq. Over 2,000 people perished at the hands of mad men on a mission. But what mission could be so important to inflict such a wound on humanity? How could 19 deranged men find each other and unite to pull this off? A conspiracy of such a magnitude went undetected by the greatest snoops in history. How is that possible? Were these villains geniuses or lucky? These are the questions people are afraid to ask.

"What could make people hate so intensely? They call us the big Satan. Why? Because we love freedom and fairness? Or is it because we are oppressors in practice? So now, the media's job is to ensure that the madness and sadness of 9/11 gets reduced to 19 deranged men taking orders from a psycho who lives in caves. What a hell of a script, a twisted sitcom of epic proportions. The architects of this story are better authors than Donald Goines and Shakespeare. Perhaps, they are just as good as the authors of the Bible, because what they're writing has real consequences for real people. My people, I'm not sure you guys see what's happening. The laws are about to change; it will be rewritten to justify the chains. The attack on the fourth and second amendments by this government, are strategies to weaken the populace, to disarm the rights of its cattle. The authors will once again spin a story that makes you agree to be weakened. It's an evil genius at work manipulating millions, but to what end? Why write such a sinister script, yet claim to work for God?"

JB was in a zone, tiny prisms of light reflected off the sweat beads on his forehead. His heart was racing. He knew that he would become a target, but he was committed to a silly notion called freedom of speech. "Don't expect me to tip-toe around the truth. I have nothing to fear but the truth."

Senator Sinclair Monroe stared at the transcripts placed in front of him by a hand that belonged to a wise man. A secret meeting of civil rights leaders had convened in the senator's spacious office to discuss Jamal Barnes. They were afraid of the attention he was attracting. If they did not come out as a unified front and vehemently denounce him publicly, the magnifying glass would eventually focus on them.

"Sinclair, do you see the fire your protégé is causing?" The elder statesman of the group asked in his customary fashion.

"He's no longer my protégé," Sinclair reminded the group. "I denounced him six months ago, remember?"

"Still, you vouched for him to begin with," an aspiring senate rival corrected.

"What are we? Mobsters? What's this shit about vouching for someone?" with a tinge of disgust Sinclair stood his ground.

"Calm down, Sinclair," the elder of the group chimed in. "Nobody is saying..."

"Like hell he's not," Sinclair said pointing at the politician poised to unseat him. "This fucking guy's been watching entirely too many mafia movies."

Before there could be a counter by his rival, another voice was heard. "Let's not waste time pointing fingers. Let's focus on the fix. What can you tell us about this young man?" The mother and leader of the group asked Sinclair pointedly.

For the next three hours, the eight established civil right leaders in New York City discussed ways to silence JB's voice.

After an exhaustive litigation, they agreed that the most proficient way was to assassinate his character. They decided that his criminal history would be the tool they would use to discredit his message. They would spread the story that JB was a thug at heart and anyone who listened to him was devoid of any real intelligence. The great eight, as they were sometimes called, would call in favors. The media would become their weapon. Considering the validation of JB's words never entered their minds. To them, his voice was sinister because it was becoming louder than theirs and people were beginning to listen. Their quality of life and comfort were being threatened, and an agreed response to the threat had unanimously been reached.

Kay-Kay

I felt bad for my brother for about five days straight. I watched the media, and his so-called civil rights *peers,* dig up every rock they could on him. The cameras he was once quick to get in front of, now denied him the opportunity to respond. I knew he was hurt about the betrayal of Sinclair's crew, but what did he expect them to do? Agree with him in speaking out against the mightiest gangsters on the planet? That was, in their eyes, equivalent to committing suicide.

But then I began to see a change occur. The attack on his character was obvious and rejected. JB's popularity began to soar in the hoods. The enemy of their enemy became their friend. JB's reputation as their champion finally crystalized. I wondered if this had been my brother's strategy all along? If so, then he was playing one hell of a chess game.

A. C. Clayton

Chapter 46: when the masses decide

JB

2001

JB laughed. Never doubting for a second the response that would be brought about by his speech. He knew Sinclair's crew would make it their business to articulate the line of difference. What he wasn't sure about, and in truth had been a bit apprehensive about, was how the people he was fighting for would view him. At the end of the day, he regretted ever doubting them.

The community embraced JB as their own, while Sinclair's crew found themselves answering accusations of treason within the community. This power shift was slight, but sudden. With the instincts of a topnotch stripper in a strip club, the press gravitated to the new money.

Jamal Barnes was the name that sold the news, and as a result, his opinions on even the most trivial of issues became the headline of the day. With his newfound celebrity came a spotlight that, he realized too late, he wasn't truly ready for. Almost immediately, the death threats began pouring in. The spirit of the Klan had a new target, a new voice and face to hate above the rest. But they were enemies of the expected kind, so they were of very little surprise. It was the unexpected ones who left him massaging his eyelids at night, milking them for relief.

The 'great eight' were rendered voiceless when it came to critiquing JB. But the countless other community activists and leaders, who had been in the trenches for years vying for the attention JB was now receiving, were not. They felt their platforms of reform were more realistic, more palpable, and JB was nothing more than a rabble-rouser, speaking to the people's emotions and not their intellect. Many of the voices he considered to be his allies less than a month prior, now spoke out against him. JB had broken bread with them in their homes, discussed hotbed issues as well as trivial ones. They talked sports and good movies, but all were passionate about the elevation of their people. So why were they on the attack now?

The only logical reason was jealousy. That smokeless fire could consume the righteous as easily as it did the grime balls. If JB allowed himself to spend a great deal of his day ducking and dodging their direct and indirect slanders, he would be a useless voice. Heavy is the head that wears the crown, and JB's respect for the crown that sat on Sharpton's head grew immensely.

JB was still a local voice; Sharpton was a national one. So Sharpton's detractors were multiplied exponentially. He began to admire the reverend for having thick skin, even though he disagreed with Sharpton's tactics. JB decided that a meeting of the minds must be called to avoid the obvious traps caused by division. He would reach out to those he believed really and truly wanted liberation for their people. But first, he had some loose ends in his immediate circle that needed to be tied together, or clipped.

Chapter 47: poet's clue

Kay-Kay

2002

I received another call from AG's wife, Jeanette, one night. It was past 2 a.m. so I knew she was calling me to tell me that AG was drugged out his mind somewhere again and she needed my help. I looked at the phone for a long time before deciding to ignore its ring. I was exhausted and didn't have it in me to talk him off the ledge. It was a selfish act on my part, but, hey, I'm just being honest. Unfortunately, the calls kept coming. Jeanette was blowing up my phone so much that I realized I had no choice but to answer.

"Hello," I said in the groggiest voice I could muster.

"Oh God, Kameek..." was all I understood. Jeanette was crying uncontrollably. It took me five minutes to piece together what she was saying and then another 40 minutes at 90 miles an hour on the highway to get to their house in Freeport, Long Island.

Jeanette opened the door as soon as I pulled into the driveway. She jumped into my arms crying uncontrollably.

"You didn't call the police, right?" was the first thing I asked before entering her house.

"No. You were the only person I called," Jeanette managed to moan between sobs and hiccups.

"Where is he?" I asked preparing myself for the ugly truth.

Jeanette couldn't find her voice, so she just pointed and stepped aside.

As I walked into the work den, the presence of the un-living was noticeable. AG was sprawled over his leather La-Z-Boy rocking chair with a gaping hole the size of a quarter drilled into his forehead. There was very little blood. It was as if the bullet itself was being used as a stopper. AG was in his silk pajamas, and a glass of white wine sat undisturbed on the coffee table next to him.

"Did you touch anything? Move anything out of place?" I asked.

"No. I was too scared to even come in the room. I was upstairs in the bedroom and I didn't hear anything."

The hairs on my arms stood up. Was Jeanette lying to me? How could she not hear or see anything? No sooner had I thought her a suspect did I spot it on the floor next to the remote control.

I bent down and picked it up. It was a note and immediately I knew that the rumors of a serial killer were true. The police nicknamed the killer 'The Poet,' and as I read what was on the note I understood why.

Written in red, the poem mocked AG's life. So much so that I still remember what it said:

When you died, were you high?
Did you see the truth or did you see the lie?
I wonder, why would they cry?
When it's evident all lessons are relevant,
When you can taste the smell of it
to determine fact from fiction
the proof or religion,
Were you a man or an
addiction?

I immediately thought about Knee and how he had left a note behind at the rat boy's crib, but that was something different. Entirely different... Or was it?

I folded the letter and put it into my pocket. "My God, Kay, what does it say?" Jeanette asked.

"You don't want to read this, 'Nette. It's only going to hurt more."

"Kay, please don't do me like this. That's my fucking husband lying there." Jeanette was pointing at the body that once housed AG. "I need to know what happened."

I was looking down at the floor trying to wrap my mind around my suspicions, trying to fit the pieces together. I could feel her eyes transfixed on the pocket the note was in. Reluctantly, I handed the note over and waited. Her collapse came quicker than I thought, but not quick enough for me to miss her fall.

I caught her on the way down. "I told you, 'Nette. It's only going to hurt more."

I held her providing comfort, but my thoughts were everywhere but in her grief.

"So it wasn't a robbery. Whoever did this, came here just to do this." Jeanette concluded with the first coherent sentence I had heard all night.

"'Nette, listen to me. You have to trust me now. Are there any drugs or money in this house?"

She hesitated before responding. "No. Not that I know of." Her hands were trembling and her eyes were looking for any place to focus on except on me.

"'Nette, listen. When the police come they are going to do a thorough search of the house. Whatever they find will, when it's all said and done, somehow be used against you. It's up to you. I can take whatever is in the house and when the suspicion dies down, I can give it back to you. Or I can get rid of it for you and give you the nest egg."

It took her a few seconds to see the logic, but once she did she escorted me to AG's stash. There were a number of small handguns and one AR-15 with an extended clip. There was less than 50 thousand in cash and what appeared to be half of a kilo in cocaine. I was happy to know that AG was smart enough to not keep his real stash where he lived.

I placed the note back on the floor realizing that without it, Jeanette would be the prime suspect. With the letter, the police would be able to compare it to the others and realize that it was the work of the same killer. My leather gloves ensured that my presence would also be untraceable, unless Jeanette folded under interrogation. It seemed Jeanette was more angry than hurt after reading the note. The fire in her eyes and the thirst for revenge were perhaps why AG loved her so much.

"Don't worry, Kay. You were never here."

"I'll have Alicia help out with the funeral arrangements and I'll cover all the expenses."

The finality of losing another ally to this game descended on me in the worst way. I couldn't help but to replay in my mind the first few questions in the note: *When you died, were you high? Did you see the truth or did you see the lie?* Knowing AG and his love for stimulants, I couldn't help but hope that he was sober for the weighing of the scales.

The Poet had already killed three of my peacocks and now he'd taken the life of one of my friends. I wasn't sure what his total body count was, but I was sure of one thing: I had a big problem on my hands.

Chapter 48: born to betray

2002

Peaches was confused about the summons. It was so unexpected and out of the ordinary that she hoped Martha was okay. Ranaldo, Martha's right-hand and the point person between Martha and Peaches had contacted her in the middle of the night. He told Peaches she needed to be at Martha's within the next two hours. That was approximately 90 minutes ago.

Now, Peaches was being escorted into the apartment where they first met so many years prior, and where Martha still conducted all of her business.

Peaches walked in and was immediately elated to see Martha alive and vibrant.

"Peaches," Martha called out opening her arms wide inviting Peaches in for a warm embrace.

So far, so good, Peaches thought, growing unsure of what was going on by the second. She decided to simply go with the flow. Ranaldo normally excused himself from these meetings, leaving the two women to speak privately. But not today. Ranaldo was posted up next to the entrance of the kitchen while the ladies sat directly across from one another at the tiny kitchen table. They were drinking tea, which had become the ritual whenever the two met.

Martha was a tea aficionado. She was always giving Peaches a different type of tea to try. "What flavor do you taste?" Martha teased Peaches' palate per usual.

"I think there's a hint of ginger and something a little more bitter that I've never tasted before."

"Ahh, you are getting better. You are beginning to be able to distinguish the flavors that conflict from the ones that blend. This is good, because what we must discuss is a similar issue."

Peaches remained quiet, happy that Martha was finally moving towards whatever the hell her point was.

"Peaches, why didn't you tell me? In all the years I've known you, all the years that I have given you transparency and solid business, why didn't you tell me that the legendary Kay-Kay is none other than the father of that handsome little boy of yours?"

With feline quickness Peaches responded, "I never thought it mattered much who my son's father is."

Martha studied Peaches, admiring her heart but disappointed in the obvious deception that had taken place for so many years. She sipped her tea allowing time to help dissipate her distaste for Peaches' decision. "So you didn't think that an extortionist who has been looking for me for the past 10 years, who *also* happens to be your baby daddy, is important?"

Remembering Ranaldo's presence, Peaches chose her words carefully. "Kay-Kay and I just share a son together. A son that, for the most part, he's just now getting to know. I pay my monthly share just like everybody else. Kay-Kay doesn't see me as someone special. And I feel the same way about him. I didn't think anything of it because I would never tell him who you are. The fact that I've been dealing with you for years and Kay-Kay still has no clue of your identity should speak to my loyalty."

Martha, still trying to remove her distaste for Peaches, nodded her head in agreement, rocking Peaches to sleep ever so gently, disarming her with a display of understanding. "So what do we do about this, Peaches? How do we fix this?"

Martha's ultimatum was not a difficult one to understand. Kay-Kay was getting close to Martha's operation and the only logical recourse was to eliminate Kay-Kay. The only thing that didn't sit well with Peaches was the question of how Martha knew of her connection to him? It was a secret that both Kay-Kay and Peaches kept secure within their inner circles. It wasn't just a pipeline at stake, if Peaches didn't follow the plot to the letter, her son's life could possibly be held in sacrifice. The threat was just too great to second-guess what had to be done.

A. C. Clayton

Peaches thought long and hard about her current dilemma, figuring that it would all boil down to which one would cross the other first. From the day she and Kay-Kay met in the restaurant, she knew by the look in his eyes that he would never understand or even forgive her betrayal. Since that meeting, she has felt that she was functioning on borrowed time. She felt that as soon as he figured out a way to get rid of her and keep his son, he would. Now the opportunity for her to ensure her longevity had been delivered on a silver platter. No one could judge the decision she made. Oxygen was an important element to her; she decided she'd like to continue inhaling it.

Peaches followed the letter of instructions laid out for her without hesitation. Too much was at stake for her to waiver. She could not figure out how Martha discovered the connection between her and Kay-Kay. Now that the cat was out of the bag, the only thing she could do was make sure that her son would be free from any harm related to his father. She cared deeply for Kay-Kay, but she cared more for their son. Aside from uprooting once more and leaving town, her options were limited.

In a cozy hamlet just outside of Teaneck, New Jersey, sat a modest Victorian one family, two-story house. Its well-manicured lawn never saw a day of dishevelment. A tea garden sat on the side of the house next to a white cedar fence that separated the Victorian from the neighboring house. The neighboring house's state of disrepair was cause for gossip and concern. The fact that the owners of the house were faceless added to the speculation around it. Its disrepair devalued all twenty-two of the other houses nestled in the suburban pocket.

What none of the homeowners knew was that both houses, the house of disrepair and the one with the cozy tea garden, belonged to the same woman. The owner kept a house full of servants as if she were wealthy, yet chose to live in humble surroundings. Neighbors knew her as Maria, a beautiful middle-aged Latina widow who always had a kind word and enthusiastic smile. Her tea garden produced some of the most exotic and potent leaves. Maria shared freely from the wonders of her garden, but there was a dark side to Maria that no one in the neighborhood would ever know or believe.

"This is perhaps the greatest disguise I've ever witnessed," Kay-Kay remarked, genuinely impressed with his surroundings. "You blended in so nicely. There's so much I would have loved to learn from you. So much money we could've made together..."

Kay-Kay was imagining what could have been. A shift in her body position snagged his attention returning him to the present. "Your maid, who is not really your maid, told me that the stash house is next door and that there's an underground tunnel that can get us there and back without attention from nosey neighbors. So here are the options: you can tell me how to access the tunnel and if successful, your death and the death of Ranaldo here," Kay-Kay pointed to the unconscious man, tied up in a heap on the floor, "will be quick and painless. The rest of your mules and pigeons will be let go. But if you refuse, we will figure out how to get in that house undetected, just as we did this one. You and him will die painfully, and the rest of your mules and pigeons will be euthanized."

Kay-Kay spoke nonchalantly as he and his assault team stood in a living room full of rare masterpieces and one-of-a-kind decor. The modest façade of the house disguised the wealth that lived within. *So this is the type of shit a million a week could do*, Kay-Kay thought as he looked at his adversary who refused to look back at him. His million-a-week estimate was just an estimate. He wouldn't be surprised to learn that it was a lot more.

He had been searching for this particular supplier for years; he was always close but never close enough. All he wanted to do was squeeze, drain her like pus and make her pay, like the peacocks. That dream had remained elusive until now.

The supplier of suppliers sat comfortably on her mink couch, hands folded in her lap like an innocent schoolgirl, her steady gaze off to the right of Kay-Kay full of unbound hatred.

Martha, who was known as Maria in respectable circles, refused to blink as she and Peaches gazed into one another's eyes. The victor and the defeated faced each other at the table of life. Like witnessing a sunrise, it was a priceless moment as they both acknowledged their respective truths.

Without averting her focus from Peaches, Martha finally spoke to Kay-Kay. "I've avoided confrontation with you for as long as I could, hoping that eventually you would grow content with the ones you were able to reach. When I discovered Peaches' connection to you and what I believed to be her hatred for you or yours for her, I had to take the opportunity to eliminate the weed in my garden. It was never personal. It was business. I will tell you what you want to know, because where I am going I will have no use for it. But, understand that my connections are beyond your imagination. My death is the entrance to your hell..."

"I'm not into poetry," Kay-Kay interrupted. "I admire your spunk, though. It's unfortunate that we couldn't be on the same side..."

"Before I tell you what you want to know, I have one final request." Martha cut Kay-Kay off the way a parent does a child, or a master does an initiate who has not comprehended the lesson. Kay-Kay could never deny the final request of the condemned, so he listened.

Martha finally disconnected the stare between her and Peaches, looked at Kay-Kay for the very first time and spoke. "I fought hard since a little girl to be respected by men. To not be objectified or taken for granted. I clawed my way to the top. I didn't sleep my way here. What I saw in Peaches, the younger version of me, I wanted to cultivate. I wanted to truly make her my apprentice, my daughter." Martha wiped a fraught tear from her eye. The type that both Peaches and Kay-Kay suspected did not come from sentiment. "I do not want a man to dishonor all that I have built by being the one to pull the trigger. I ask that it be her, and I ask that she looks me directly in the eye when she does it. Let me die knowing that all I clawed for was not in vain."

Kay-Kay

It was such a boss move Martha pulled on Peaches and me on her way out. Such a boss move!

Martha told us what we needed to know and all proved true. My team was excited on the score. The house next door was a warehouse with a stash that rivaled the federal one I took down some years before and a bank full of money that challenged belief. The loyalty of my team was put on trial. If anyone were to go rogue and show a different side, this would be the moment in time for them to do it. But they all remained true, and we waited till nightfall before we slowly began the extraction of the goods.

Everyone on my assault team understood that if they weren't before, they were now millionaires a few times over.

Peaches

Peaches didn't hesitate to step up to the plate and accept the challenge. She liked Martha, but Martha made the mistake or miscalculation of including Kameek Jr. in the equation. Even if Peaches considered setting Kay-Kay up, Kameek Jr. would be the carrot she used the next time she needed something. That shit about becoming Martha's apprentice was just that: shit, bullshit. What Martha really meant was that Peaches would've become a puppet and Martha the puppeteer.

The piece Peaches held against Martha's forehead, as they looked each other in the eye, seemed to be generating its own heat.

"You asked me to betray all that I love," Peaches felt the need to explain.

Martha smiled in understanding before replying with her final words that would stay with Peaches forever. "I didn't ask you to betray. I asked you to embrace the truth that I had to embrace when I was your age."

Although she knew that she had been baited into asking the question, Peaches took the bait. "What truth is that?" she whispered cynically.

Martha's silky voice grew softer than cotton as she shared her truth to the final ear: "Love is loneliness for a lioness, my friend."

Peaches slowly closed her eyes and allowed the wand she was holding to do its magic.

Chapter 49: betrayal lies within the heart

Peaches

It didn't take a great deal of investigation or deduction to realize who had leaked Peaches and Kay-Kay's relationship to Martha. For Kay-Kay, the *who* was all that mattered. For Peaches, the *how* and the *why* became the puzzle to piece together.

The move against Martha was the first time since the days of Smooth and Smiley that Peaches had used artillery without her Roc by her side,. It felt strange, like a part of her was missing, but it had to be that way to ensure that the mission not be compromised. It was Roc who had told Martha. But Peaches had to know why.

The empty bedroom was covered in black plastic from ceiling to floor. Even the windows were covered, blocking out the curious eyes of the sun. There was no furniture in the bedroom, save a lone metal chair. The chair sat in the middle of the floor. A tied-up Roc was its occupant. His fear had already been demonstrated twice with the uncontrollable release of his bladder. Fear and urine didn't mix well. Both smells were acrid and acidic. Combined with sweaty plastic, the entire room smelled like a leaky, wet diaper.

Peaches walked in and Roc's eyes grew wide in astonishment. Slowly they gave way to understanding and acceptance. She removed his gag, allowing him to once again breathe the normal way.

She looked at him, holding back her emotions out of fear that they would lead her to indecision. They attempted to speak at the same time, but Peaches' question overrode the chatter.

"What were you thinking?"

The one question Roc never hoped to hear from Peaches had just been uttered. His eyes welled up with genuine tears of regret. Was his answer as simple as "love"? Should he dare tell her now what he had wrestled with for such a long time? That he loved Peaches unconditionally and yet her love and fixation with Kay-Kay was the only fulfillment she sought? That he'd thought that perhaps if Kay-Kay were eliminated, she would finally see him as someone more than just her shadow.

But even at the eleventh hour, Roc could not reveal his secret. "Peaches, I'm sorry," he said instead. "I never intended for Martha to use little KJ as a bargaining chip."

"How could you not know that was a possibility, Roc?" Peaches asked growing angrier by the second. "What were you thinking?"

Roc began crying uncontrollably because there was no answer but the truth. He betrayed her out of love and would die for it now. Accepting that this was possibly the end of his life, the harness on his heart malfunctioned and the dialect of amour came spilling out. "I did it because I love you," he uttered in a whisper.

Peaches could barely make out what Roc was saying. She asked him to repeat himself. It was as if the finding of his voice, the freeing of his feelings, had liberated him from bondage and the fear of death.

Roc began proclaiming his truth for all present in the room to hear. "I love you," he yelled over and over. "I love you. I love you. That mothafucka will never love you. He will never appreciate you. I did what I had to do. I needed to protect you from him, Peaches. I did it to protect that beautiful heart from him. My only regret is that it didn't work. I love you. So there, there's your reason. Your loyal dog was trying to protect his master." And with those words of honor, Roc bowed his crown.

Peaches' hand was covering her mouth as he spoke. *Of course he loved her!* Deep down she knew it all along. She saw it in his eyes during the unguarded moments. It appeared while on vacation, hanging out with her and Kameek Jr., in the moments without worry. She had seen it, but had always denied what she saw because she wanted Kay-Kay.

Now, standing in front of Roc, she thought of what life would be like without him and it scared her to the core. *Love is loneliness for a lioness*, Peaches recalled. *Damn that woman*, she thought as the hands of Martha's wisdom reached out from the grave.

Peaches had sought the full picture. She wanted to know the truth, but the truth didn't fuel her anger as she had expected it to. Instead, it erased her anger and replaced it with regret— for Roc and for herself. She regretted what could've been and what must now be. She placed her hand over her mouth to muffle her sobs and shook her head ever so slightly in defeat.

The entire time, two men leaned on the wall behind Roc's chair. The side-chick syndrome that had just played out was amusing to them. They were privy to the discussion, though its content made not a shred of difference in the outcome. Peaches' slight nod was the signal awaited. One of the men broke away from the wall with a wire of metal in his hands.

Roc had spoken the truth. He had done it to protect her. He had tried to protect her heart, but what he sought to protect he had broken. His death and her life without him was a deathblow to them both.

The wire dug deep into Roc's throat cutting off all possibilities of air and hope. With his hands and feet tied to the chair, Roc's barbaric strength served no purpose. As his eyes bulged Peaches' sobs shrilled like a siren, the alarm of a little girl seeking asylum from the madness. As Roc's resistance grew weaker by the second, so, too, did Peaches' legs. One minute she was standing firm, the next she was on her knees in prostration begging the escaping soul for forgiveness. Peaches' ears registered Roc's last gasp and a heaviness of regrets claimed her heart. For several long agonizing minutes afterwards, she cried the cry of the condemned.

Still clinging to the floor for balance, she noticed the second man on the wall begin slowly walking toward her. She could hear the rubber of his boots and the plastic on the floor collided. Each collision grew louder bringing him one step closer.

She was powerless to react and was not surprised that her death was next. She braced herself. Refusing to give her killer the satisfaction of looking her in the eyes, she kept her head down and focused to the ground.

The second man from the wall got down on his knees next to her. He grabbed her by the shoulder and whispered in her ear. "It's time. Let's go. I forgive you. May not mean much, but I forgive you."

Chapter 50: the ties that bind

Peaches

Powerful arms lifted her off the ground and onto her feet. A handkerchief to absorb her tears was handed to her. As she attempted to wipe away her sorrow, the voice spoke. "It was the only call you could have made. He did it to himself. If you want to cry, cry for his stupidity. This life we live is not for the stupid."

Peaches looked back at the corpse tied to a chair. Her heaving chest exhaled the final winds of a torturous decision. As they began to exit the room, a piece of paper and a photo was handed to her.

"What's this?" she asked, apathetic to his mind games.

"One of the reasons you're still standing," he responded in brutal honesty.

Hotep. I hope this scripture paints a triumphant picture. Just wanted to touch base with you and let you know that, as you can see by the address on the letter, they moved me once more. Yeah, I'm back in Auburn. Sadistically, they placed me back in the same cell I left from.

A. C. Clayton

Nevertheless, what's going on with you out there? I haven't heard your name circulating through these prison vents and kites in a minute. Apparently, you're doing something right because you're still alive, free, and accessible. Old man Stanley and Tank send their regards. Tank claims he finally knows how to clean Jack Mack. Besides that, it's the same old routines in here. Same daily battle for dignity and respect. Same stale air and weighted souls wondering why they can't fly. I would like to tell them why, but this is still a barbaric setting where the messenger is killed for delivering the message.

Oh, that KKK cop Snow died the other night in a violent car crash. Apparently, he discovered that his wife had been cheating on him with a Black man or 'Nigra,' as they call us in these parts. The thought of genetically inferior sperm touching her lips must've been too much. So he went to a local bar and got pissy drunk. The bar kicked him out, but didn't send him home in a cab. Now the community is blaming the bar and calling for a boycott. (Yeah, they're probably reading this and if in a day or two my commissary slip goes missing or my water stops running or flushing, or the hot water bucket skips my cell, I'll know why.) All the pigs are in mourning and are looking for any excuse to bust some heads. I told this one young buck to fall back because I saw them lining him for an example. Sure enough, he disregarded my advice and got spanked severely.

Anyhow, I did receive your letter and read your concerns. They were lengthy, but not irrational. You speak of challenges to your success. Most don't realize that the greatest challenge to success is distraction. Everything that's not part of the agenda is a distraction. Do you remember the exercises I gave you when it was your turn to wash the pots? I told you focus exclusively on washing the pots and to be mindful of the difficulty in doing so. Do you recall how hard it was to stop the mind from wandering? How you expressed your amazement of how little control you had over your own thoughts? Then after about a month of practice, you were able to keep the focus for an entire minute. The same rule applies out there in the "free society." Don't deviate from the daily plans, except to enhance them. That's the secret: discipline. Train yourself to not fail. If I had one wish that could be granted, it would be to understand all that I do now, at your age and outside this cage. Ahh, the tremors that would warn of my coming. But, alas, I've accepted my destiny and the fact that I will most likely (barring a miracle or a prison break) die in here amongst the broken. Where every victory regardless of size, speed, or shape is a delectable morsel I savor with care.

Case in point, I recently received a letter from my only daughter. Believe it or not, it's the first of its kind in 26 years. The letter, though brief, is her stubborn way of apologizing. Even when she was a little girl, she would get caught red-handed and deny the hot hand was actually hers. She would be so convincing that you would begin to question your own senses. Like "I know this is weed I smell and that's a joint in between your fingers." I mean, clear-as-day type scenarios, and her response would be "Weed? Joint? Fingers? Who are you?" Haha. After reading her letter, I can see that she has changed very little. My son has kept me informed and updated with regards to her throughout the years and I know that she has become a crack addict. My oldest granddaughter, who is 34 or 35 now, has been holding her siblings down. She has even given me my first great-grandchild. Which leads me to this humble request. I would like to get to know my grands and great-grand before I die in here. I'm 81 years old and my situation is what it is. I ask for no quarter, nor expect any. But I do ask that you find my grands and bring them to me. Here's the only picture of them I have. My daughter just sent it to me, but it's obviously a couple of years old. Their names are on the back of the picture along with my daughter's address in Jersey.

Peaches remembered the picture immediately. It was her 25th birthday and her little sister Jazmeen's graduation day from high school. The whole gang was there; her mother, brother, sister, and a six-year-old Kameek Jr. were standing in front of the entrance to Dorney Park. She knew that her grandfather was in prison serving life, but had never met him. Her mother spoke sparingly of him throughout her childhood. Peaches never had a desire to learn anything about him and yet somehow, more than three decades later, her grandfather's words were saving her life. Her death sentence was commuted to a lifetime of probation by a judge who was clueless of her crime.

"This is my grandfather," Peaches confirmed. "Who is he to you?" she asked.

Kay-Kay remained quiet as he searched for a definition, but no one word would suffice. "He is the man who saved my life and trained me. He is the reason I think things through. There's no request that he can make that I won't try my best to deliver on. To you, he is a long-lost grandfather. To me, he is the Old God.

Chapter 51: goodnight to civil rights

*If we could read the minds of men
we would go insane
From the truths buried within
or the labyrinth of lies
the truth uses to conceal itself.*

Winter 2002

Senator Sinclair Monroe's corpse would be found neatly in his own king-sized bed. His death was the result of one well-placed bullet to his head. That's all it took to eliminate the problem. That's all it ever took.

The man with the brim hat, who was known in law enforcement circles as 'The Poet,' stood over the senator, staring at the lifeless body in quiet solitude. He did this with every corpse he helped separate from its soul. He wasn't obsessed with killing. He didn't enjoy it, but he understood the necessity for it.

A familiar voice spoke from behind him, a voice that brought a smile to his face. *Finally*, he thought.

"So, you're The Poet?" Kay-Kay asked rhetorically.

"I am what I am," the man with the brim hat replied poetically.

Kay-Kay rubbed his eyes. Senator Sinclair Monroe, aka the Wizard, was dead. Kay-Kay shook his head in bewilderment, wondering if the land of Oz would ever be the same? He thought about the day he suggested that the Wizard take JB under his wing. The Wizard was reluctant, but agreed to at least meet him.

"Kay-Kay, your brother is a zealot," the senator had said. "It's either black or white with him. It's never green. I'm afraid of zealots." Now he was dead, and Kay-Kay wasn't sure all the secrets had died with him.

"Man, you are fucking good. I swear you had me fooled with all this sanctimonious shit."

The man with the brim hat smiled before turning to face Kay-Kay and finally taking a seat on the edge of the bed. Sinclair's wife was out of town, so there was no concern of her being startled.

"How did you figure me out? And how did you know I would be here?"

Kay-Kay took his time before speaking. The gravity of this moment was surreal. "The note you left on AG. I remember a rap song you wrote when we were kids," Kay-Kay replied to his big brother, the man with a brim hat.

JB recited the verse, "'Did you see the truth or did you see the lie?' I didn't expect you to read that one, but they were all for you."

"All for me, huh?"

"Yes. All for you. I knew you would eventually use your resources to figure this out."

"What's with the hat?" Kay-Kay asked.

"I don't know. It kind of makes me feel mysterious. It's like a Dr. Jekyll and Mr. Hyde thing." He chuckled before continuing. "So ask away. What's going on in your mind?"

"Why, JB? What's the end game with this? Are you a serial killer for a righteous cause? Is that what you are going to say?"

"Exactly what I'm going to say. I'm no psycho. I'm a revolutionary. I'm committed to bringing about a change. I told you when you came to my graduation in prison years ago that I was coming. That we were coming. Every man that has died at my hands has committed crimes against our communities that could not go unpunished."

"So, what? You plan on killing every drug dealer with a little more than lunch money?"

"It wasn't the drugs that were sold that ended their lives. It was the selfishness that accompanied them. They didn't give back a red cent to the hoods they poisoned. Innocent people died because of their recklessness. I consoled the mother who lost her son to a hail of bullets that weren't intended for him. The scumbag who was responsible for her suffering didn't deserve prison; he deserved a closed casket. When the revolution starts, the selfish mothafuckas feeling they have so much to lose will be the ones who cooperate with law enforcement. I'm just eliminating the leeches.

"This guy right here," JB pointed to Senator Sinclair Monroe's lifeless corpse. "He became a numerical value void of substance." JB spoke like a mathematician. "He was worse than all of them. He was the worst kind of mercenary, a whore for the establishment. His death sentence was placed on him the moment I met him. But everything takes time, so he had the time to repent. Instead, he dug deeper into the trenches, deeper into siding with the enemy. Understand who he is, lil bro. Understand what we are up against. Let's put it in perspective. He comes from a place," JB squinted his eyes as he began tapping his own forehead to indicate that the place he was referring to existed in the senator's mind. "A place where religion gave God an image. Then made sure the image didn't look anything like him. How could we effect any real change in our community with that kind of damage being done to the minds of our so-called heroes who are leading the charge? Who would the mercy be on, if we kept him alive, them or us?

Anyone who chooses to serve the system that serves us death—deserves death. Point blank, end of discussion."

Like a rap artist delivering bars in a booth, JB gesticulated his gospel. This was the most animated Kay-Kay had seen his brother since the days when JB would create a graffiti masterpiece for Kay-Kay's eyes only.

"You know what has bugged me since I been home? How you thought I was just going to be some picket sign maker." Kay-Kay remained quiet, unsure of an appropriate response to discovering the truth.

"We gotta clean up our own backyard first, lil bro. That's the only way it will work. We can't expect others to treat us with respect, if we don't hold each other accountable. If we act like niggers to each other, how can we get mad when outsiders call us by our actions? For too long, law and order has been missing in our hoods. My actions are but a small contribution to correcting the paradigm."

Still Kay-Kay remained silent as he played back the clues and buried memories. He remembered JB killing a dog in front of him. It wasn't the act itself that unnerved Kay-Kay, as much as it was the pleasure he saw in his brother's eyes when the dog took its last whimper.

"So now you know. And here we stand. Either we are going to stand together or we are going to stand apart. Either we are brothers or strangers. For me there's only one true option, but it's time I know where you stand." Taking his brim hat in his hand, JB rose like a phoenix to face his little brother head on. "Talk to me, Kay. Say something."

A. C. Clayton

Chapter 52: blindsided

Kay-Kay
2003

My arrest for Sinclair's murder caught me by surprise. I left no trace entering or leaving his home. And, according to JB's thorough inspection of the house, as well as my own, we departed pretty certain that there were no cameras. Yet, I was being charged for Sinclair's death, and because he was a state official, it would be a capital murder charge. The four million dollar ransom they called bail was an obvious attempt to locate a money source. Bait that only a fool would take. So I sat in involuntary administrative segregation for the first month following my arrest. Even my high-powered and well-connected attorney was clueless as to what was going on or the evidence against me.

Knee wanted to post the bail, using our record label Criminal Empire for collateral. I sent word to him that I had enough real estate to cover the bail, but in my gut I knew that this was an unusual arrest and there was more going on than what our eyes could see. The irony of it all was that the Wizard would usually be the one to peer into his crystal ball and tell me what or who stood right around the corner. Without him and his crystal ball, I was a mere mortal without clairvoyance.

As a security precaution, I restricted my visits to only my immediate family and my lawyer. I did not want to reveal any of my connections to whoever was watching. Then, in the middle of the night under the cloak of darkness, I was transferred by helicopter from city jail to federal custody. I was placed in isolation for two days before my lawyer was even aware of my transfer.

The following day, a sealed indictment unfurled like a king's decree. I was charged with racketeering, extortion, and ongoing enterprise with special circumstances. I was glad that I didn't post the bail. They were obviously digging for evidence. Though my real estate and record label were legitimate enterprises, the attention and scrutiny they would be under would add more pressure to an already head-twisting case.

The next day, my face and name, alongside JB's, made the cover of every newspaper in NYC. They nicknamed us Dr. Jekyll and Mr. Hyde. JB was the champion of his community, while his brother was the community's greatest villain. How could two brothers turn out so differently? By virtue of my arrest, JB's credibility took a beating.

"How could he not have known about his little brother's underworld ties and criminal activities?" was the quote in the *New York Post* by a community leader out of Far Rockaway.

"This is what happens when you allow thugs into politics," was another in the *New York Times* from one of the more established and prominent Black leaders—as if politics were anything but thuggery.

As for JB, he had not been arrested for Sinclair's murder or any of the other executions. This was a good thing. That fact told me that there were no witnesses hiding in a closet or under a bed that had been overlooked by us. There was no hidden camera concealed beyond our detection.

The bad thing was the letter that was found on Sinclair's body. Because of that letter, the authorities were able to connect eight similar murders to the serial killer they named 'The Poet,' and then charged me with them all. Details of the other murders mysteriously made their way into the press and this case went from a local sensation to a national one. Within weeks, it was an international phenomenon.

If that wasn't enough of an eye-opener for me, a revelation of true biblical proportions followed like a sequel. Truthfully, all I could do was laugh at my own stupidity. I should have posted the bail and exited the country immediately. I had the means to leave. I had places I could go where American jurisdiction didn't trump money. The entire case against me, from the ongoing criminal enterprise, racketeering, and murders stemmed from one witness and one witness only. The witness was none other than Senator Sinclair Monroe, aka the Wizard.

Apparently, the Wizard had kept a file on me. The file spanned 13 years of my involvement with him, but had only been written in the past year. Ever since he and JB had their fallout, Sinclair was obviously afraid that his all-out war with my brother was a dangerous declaration to make. To be fair, given his circumstances, he was correct in his thinking.

The documents he left behind told a story that made for a good movie or, at the very least, a great novel. Excerpts were leaked to the press, all designed to taint the pool of potential jurors. Though the accusations were extraordinary, and in some instances very detailed, the evidence sat strictly on a dead man's word. He was a charlatan, who only revealed his decades of hypocrisy and deceit out of fear, not out of a struggle with his conscience. The system would have to prove beyond a reasonable doubt that I was all they claimed me to be. Their case would be based on the words of an admitted crook's confession to bigger crooks about a crook that admitted nothing. The irony of it all!

A. C. Clayton

Dear [redacted],

Should I die in any way outside of natural causes then I am instructing you, my dear friend, to give this to the proper authorities. I trust that you will know which ones. I want to first apologize for my role in allowing this monster, this criminal mastermind, to corrupt and blemish all that I have held dear for most of my adult life. Even in my death, the disgrace of dishonoring my senate seat and my constituents will haunt me. Even now as I write these words, I am ashamed. With that said, here are the facts...

The monster I am referring to is disguised as a young man named Kameek Barnes. You may be familiar with the name Barnes because he is the younger brother of my former protégé Jamal Barnes. I met Kameek Barnes (Kay-Kay) through a mutual acquaintance [redacted]. At that time, he was a young drug dealer looking to find legit investments to clean up his cash. My initial assessment had him sitting on a little less than two million dollars in a number of safety deposit boxes throughout the Tri-State area.

I immediately took him on as a client and began moving his money into legitimate streams. I created two dummy companies [redacted] and [redacted] for Kameek Barnes. Over time, our friendship grew and through my greed, he was able to solicit favors from me. Some of these favors were informational in nature. For instance, throughout the 13 years I've known him, on a number of occasions I was asked to look up (through my first-grade detective sources at 1 Police Plaza) names and addresses of individuals. Who, for one reason or another, he needed. I never asked for particulars, I just followed orders. Other requests along the same vein were to have names run through the database to see if they were informants. I'm pretty sure this allowed him to stay ahead of the game he was playing. The name and location of one individual he got from me I know for certain ended up dead.

My detective friend grew real nervous after a confidential informant in Red Hook ended up dead with a rat in his mouth, following him giving me the informant's home address. It took a great deal of Kameek's money to calm the detective's nerves.

Another incident I believe Kameek had a part in, was a heist that went unreported to the media. This was the heist of a federal warehouse holding cocaine and a cache of confiscated guns. During the heist, a federal agent was shot in the leg and almost died from a loss of significant blood. I believe Kameek had a hand in it because I was asked to confirm the warehouse's existence three months before the heist went down.

About five months after the heist, Kameek had me wire 1.9 million to an offshore account. I know that as law enforcement, you will be scratching your head trying to figure out a way to *prove my accusations. Especially the tracing of the money, because I'm sure that just as quickly as I moved it for him, he moved it again. He used me for the first leg of the journey of his money, but certainly not the last. Nevertheless, here is the routing coordination of that transfer [redacted].*

The key to all of my accusations, I believe, will be in getting your confidential informants to verify.

Another wrinkle presented itself early: 'Nette, AG's wife, upon learning that I was being charged with AG's death, began speaking negatively about me in circles still loyal to me. She was calling me a snake for killing AG. And saying that she hoped the death penalty would be my reward. So far, she hadn't spoke to the police about my visit to her home on the night of the murder, but it would only be a matter of time before she decided to do so.

I understood her pain. And I understood how everything that was going on would appear to her. I was facing a dilemma: do I send a messenger or a death horse her way? I decided on both options. The death horse would act as a messenger who would be given the instructions to use his own discretion if she didn't receive the message correctly. The message was simple: I'm absolutely innocent of my comrade's death.

I poured over the 34 pages of the Wizard's accusations, admiring his detective skills. Though I never told him much about what I did, he was able to connect the dots and fill in obvious blanks. He was correct in his warning. His skills were the first step, but they weren't the only. All the paths he was sending them on led to nowhere beyond a question mark.

Back in 1992, Kay-Kay asked me for a simple favor. He wanted me to meet his older brother Jamal Barnes, who at the time was a local community leader out of my constituency. In Kay-Kay's words, JB "needed a Rabbi." Kay-Kay wanted me to take his brother under my wing and guide him to the light. By which he meant the money. My initial assessment of JB was that of a young man who had learned the theoretical aspect of a defeated cause, yet refused to accept defeat. I personally felt my job was to wake him up to the reality of our situation.

Kay-Kay devised a plan to funnel money to his brother's cause without his brother knowing. JB did not approve of whatever Kay-Kay was doing in the streets and would not allow Kay-Kay's taint to rub off on him. Kay-Kay approached a number of local bodegas and a few clothing stores, giving them each 10K. He then would have them donate 9K to JB's organization and they would pocket 1K for themselves. He spread this out in intervals as not to raise suspicion from JB. It worked, not only financially, but it also provided a moral boost for JB during times when he seemed ready to throw in the towel.

Kay-Kay would see to these types of secret fraternal forms of affection, even when JB would barely talk to him. It is because of this that I am compelled now to believe that, with all that's going on between JB and myself now, Kameek Barnes would undoubtedly kill or have me killed for his brother.

I swear this weasel's words sounded convincing. He made me seem like a mastermind. Like I was some sort of mind bender that he couldn't resist. Like he hadn't suggested the ways to funnel money to my brother's cause? His words made it seem like I came up with these things all by myself. The Wizard had to know that, at the very least with these accusations, he would make the invisible visible.

I had prided myself on staying under the radar. But now, my name had become synonymous to the spotting of Big Foot. A mythical creature they all knew existed, but the evidence could only be seen on the A&E channel. Now they had an eyewitness who not only claimed to have seen me, but added that he assisted the boogieman. And society just might believe his accusations.

Most of the pages documented financial transactions to different countries and international banks. They detailed not only the transactions, but the reasoning behind each one. It was the Wizard who taught me how to make the money disappear, how to stay one step ahead of the game. I wasn't worried about them tracing the money, but I was sure that wasn't the Wizard's intent. He was more concerned with my exposure.

Another verification Kay-Kay asked for was that of the serial killer nicknamed 'The Poet' by law enforcement. I handed him a dossier of all that was known at the time, including copies of the poems themselves. For this information alone, he paid 25K. He appeared to be really concerned with the investigation being put into finding this serial killer. So much so that I asked him why he would spend so much on the information? His excuse was that he was doing research for a friend; she was an author trying to get a lead on a true crime story. I laughed and so did he. Knowingly we were laughing at each other with each other.

The last time I spoke with Kay-Kay was in person at my office in DC. He came to discuss JB and what it would take to make the situation right between JB and myself. I explained to him that JB's rhetoric made reconciliation between the two of us impossible. That it would be political suicide for me to stop denouncing him every chance I got.

Kay-Kay seemed disappointed and began talking to me in a riddle. He spoke about an adulterous minister who fucked every woman in the congregation except the one woman who refused his advances in the name of the God they both claimed to believe in. This woman was named Wisdom. The minister grew so enraged that he denounced Wisdom in front of the congregation. The congregation sided with the minister at first, but as the facts came to light, the women in the congregation recalled their own seduction and sided with the woman named Wisdom. I got his message and knew that he was referring to me. Over the years, Kay-Kay was always sharing these types of anecdotal stories from some book he calls the "OG Bible". I had always gotten a kick out of them, so I asked him jokingly what happened to the minister.

Kay-Kay looked at me and smiled. He said that the minister was visited by an angel and told to edify the woman and make her the prophet.

I asked what happened if the minister refused and he replied with the following:

"According to the double-sided coin of fate, two scenarios presented themselves. In the first scenario, the minister rallies behind Wisdom in repentance and follows her because she was the only one in true submission of God. Together, they were able to heal the congregation. In the second scenario, the minister mocked the angel and as a result was struck down by God in the most violent and painful way imaginable."

It was after this discussion with Kay-Kay that I decided to write this journal in fear for my life.

Most of the accusations hurled at me in this journal never made it to the jury's eyes during trial. It was hearsay. Since the hearsay could not be cross-examined on account of the author being dead, the judge did not allow it in the trial. But that didn't stop the desperate prosecutors from leaking excerpts to the media every chance they got. Their case was based on trying to verify the accusations without mentioning their origins.

It was an uphill battle for the prosecution. They canvassed the streets and leaned on their confidential informants to take the stand, trying to nail me to the cross. But the streets and most of the informants refused the path of Judas. Either they loved me more than their masters or they feared me more. Either way, my presence and force were still being exerted while I sat in a tin cell of isolation, pleading my case to the jury—the only one that matters.

The prosecution paraded more than 32 witnesses before the judge, from forensic scientists to so-called drug dealers. Law enforcement spoke about securing crime scenes and their frustration with what they perceived to be a dead-end investigation. Even with me in custody their paid informants refused to testify when my name was mentioned. The few drug dealers they did call to the stand were clearly low-level hustlers who were given a script to recite to the jury. They testified fanciful rumors about heads being dismembered and sent to my adversaries. My lawyer ripped them to shreds, but I wasn't sure if any of it made a difference in the eyes of the jury.

The media had done a great job in painting the picture of me being a Godfather-type figure. The challenge was dispelling the myth.

Alicia's sister Charlotte took the stand. She was the only character witness the prosecution presented that really stung to the core. The larceny in her eyes was filled with misplaced vengeance. She volunteered on her own accord to testify against me. While she couldn't confirm any criminal activities, she did say that her entire family, including her sister, knew that I was a criminal.

She began crying hysterically when she recounted the story of her husband, who was now serving a life sentence in prison for murder. She told the jury that I gave him the gun and talked him into committing the crime. She even told the jury that she confronted me about it and I admitted to not only giving him the gun, but also talking him into the killing. As she spoke, I could feel Alicia's eyes burning into the back of my skull.

All I could do was shake my head at the unbelievable mess her testimony was causing. Alicia had been scratching her head for years trying to figure out her sister's sudden withdrawal. Now she and the rest of her family knew why—or at least Charlotte's version of what happened.

The following day of trial Alicia was a no-show. Though they paraded a bunch of useless rats to the stand for theatrical purposes, it was by far my worst day at trial. Alicia, my rock, was not behind me.

Peaches, who had not missed a day of my trial, came from the back of the courtroom and sat in Alicia's seat next to my mother and our son. She understood that I needed the extra support that day, that my armor had been pierced, but the enemy could not be allowed to see the hole.

The next day, Alicia was back. A reassuring smile creased her face as she looked at me with sad but enduring eyes. Her eyes spoke a language only I understood. For better or worse is what they conveyed. We were currently sitting in a storm of the worst kind.

Peaches sat back in the corner of the courtroom, providing her silent but rock solid moral encouragement. I knew that there would be no testimony that would shake Peaches' support. The fact that I couldn't say the same about Alicia, disturbed my spirit greatly. It was also the day of my brother's testimony.

Transcript from the courtroom:

DA: So Mr. Barnes, is JB short for Jamal Barnes?

JB: Yes it is.

DA: Thank you. I just wanted to make sure.

JB: (interrupts) Well JB is a pretty common name.

DA: Yes, agreed, but I just want to establish that you're one of the many. So the name Kay-Kay refers to your brother Kameek Barnes.

JB: Is that a question or a statement?

DA: Question.

JB: Well, I call him Kay-Kay, but I'm not sure what everyone else calls him. My moms calls him Boo-Boo, but I'm sure no one else calls him that.

<Audible laughs in the courtroom>

DA: Well, I'm glad you feel the need to entertain us here today. Your witty sarcasm is duly noted. But please keep in mind that your brother is facing serious charges and your testimony can bring some clarity to the courtroom.

JB: I'm still not sure how my testimony is of any importance, except for political reasons.

D.A: Political reasons?

JB: Yes. You are trying to discredit me in the eyes of my community.

D.A: Is that what you truly believe? That this whole trial is about discrediting your... rhetoric?

JB: I believe this farce that you have put my brother and my family through is exactly for political gain.

D.A: I'm glad the jury can see narcissism on display. Thank you... for the demonstration. Now can we get to the facts?

JB: Sure.

DA: Great. So can you tell us the relationship between you and the man in the blue suit sitting at the defense table?

JB: That's my brother Kameek Barnes.

DA: Thank you. Now let's get to the point. How would you best describe your relationship with your brother over the past few years?

JB: We have no relationship outside of family functions.

DA: And why is that?

JB: No particular reason. I guess we just grew apart.

DA: Is it fair to say that your relationship with your brother is a tumultuous one?

JB: No sir, that wouldn't be fair at all.

DA: Why not?

JB: Because it's not true.

DA: Isn't it true that you disapprove of his secret lifestyle?

JB: Secret lifestyle? What are you implying? That my brother is gay?

DA: His gangster lifestyle and affiliations.

JB: I know nothing of that.

DA: Be careful, Mr. Barnes. Perjury is a serious offense. Now, let me ask you in a different way. Have you ever expressed your disapproval of Kameek's criminal lifestyle and his running of a criminal empire as 'a black eye to the community' over the phone to anyone?

<Long pause>

DA: Do you understand the question, Mr. Barnes?

JB: Yes I do.

DA: Do you care to answer?

JB: I may have said something to that effect at some point.

DA: Well, let me be more specific. It is true that after the murders, you and Kameek stopped speaking?

JB: What murders are you referring to sir?

DA: What murders am I referring to? July 6th, after an associate of Kameek, a Thurston (Touchy) Pilgrim, eludes capture, there are a number of deaths of low level drug dealers that are tied to this Touchy character. This takes place in the heart of your constituency, in the neighborhood that you claim to protect...

JB: (interrupts) I do not claim to protect any neighborhood.

DA: In the neighborhood that you work out of. These deaths had you upset. Is this a fact?

JB: I vaguely recall expressing that.

DA: You may be interested to know that this isn't the first time the name Kay-Kay appears on wiretaps. In fact, law enforcement had been trying to put a face or real name to Kay-Kay since at least two years prior when his name first began circulating in phone conversations of the dealers we were monitoring. But it wasn't until your wiretap, that we were able to connect that the elusive Kay-Kay was none other than your little brother.

JB: There are many people nicknamed Kay-Kay, so what's your point?

DA: The timing coincides with the chatter surrounding the disappearance of his friend Touchy and you directly linking him to, in your own words 'the chaos in your community.'

Defense: Objection, Your Honor, prosecution is suggesting...

Judge: Sustained. Counsel I've warned you before about making inferences.

DA: My apologies, Your Honor. It won't happen again.

Judge: Proceed.

DA: Mr. Barnes, is it safe to say that at some point you no longer accepted Kameek's assistance in your organization?

JB: Yes, that's true.

DA: Can you tell us why?

JB: I...

DA: Bear in mind, Mr. Barnes, you are under oath. Did Kameek ever speak to you about possibly donating to your cause?

JB: How so?

D.A: I mean, your brother was, or rather is, a very successful real estate guy. So, did he ever offer you any donations or even space to operate out of?

JB: Actually, he did.

DA: And did you accept?

JB: I turned him down.

DA: Why?

JB: Because... Because he was my kid brother who was successfully selling and owning property and my pride would not allow me to take a handout from him. We always had an unhealthy dose of competition. I will admit I was jealous of him.

DA: You were jealous of him? So, you are saying that there was no suspicion that the bulk of his money didn't come from real estate?

JB: I still have none. None at all.

DA: Interesting. Mr. Barnes, you are a leader in your community. The hardworking honest people look up to you.

JB: They do, and your point is?

DA: Are you being loyal to them or your brother?

JB: I didn't know there were two sides. My brother is a successful businessman from our community.

DA: Did Kameek ever tell you in all these years that he knew Senator Monroe?

JB: He never told me that. Did he tell you that?

DA: I'm the one doing the questioning here, Mr. Barnes.

JB: Oh yeah I forgot. You're in control.

DA: It's not about being in control, Mr. Barnes. It's about...

JB: Sure it's about control; it's always about control.

DA: Mr. Barnes have you ever confronted your brother about illegal activities?

JB: No, I haven't. And if you have any witnesses that say contrary, then *they* are committing perjury.

DA: I'm going to be honest with you, Mr. Barnes. I knew you would come in here today and cover your brother's tracks. I just wanted the jury to see how strong his influence is.

JB: My apologies, but this has been a complete waste of time and taxpayers dollars.

DA: How so, Mr. Barnes?

JB: My brother is absolutely innocent and meanwhile the real killer is out there somewhere putting my community in danger. If this killer was bold enough to kill a state senator in cold blood, then who can be next? Perhaps it's me; perhaps it's you. Perhaps it's the judge. I'm just saying, it's not my brother and therefore, the killer is still at large.

DA: Or perhaps the killer is in custody and has been for the past 18 months. Is it possible that the killer is in this courtroom, Mr. Barnes?

JB: Yes, perhaps the killer is in this courtroom. Anything is possible, sir. But I'm sure it ain't my brother.

DA: Mr. Barnes, I admire the fact that you're convinced that your kid brother is innocent. Thank you. No further questions at this time, Your Honor.

JB's taking of the stand didn't shift the needle one bit in any direction. But what happened next was a game changer.

Chapter 53: the absurdity of it all

He took pride in ensuring the demise.
Committed he was to stopping the God's rise.
(Hip Hop)

2003

John Stephenson, the famous and extremely rich record executive from Pacific Records, was found dead in the bedroom of his lover's Upper Eastside apartment. One neatly placed bullet to the forehead was the cause of death. The line of cocaine found in the crease of a folded $100 bill obscured Benjamin Franklin's face. It sat on the bedroom nightstand next to his keys, wallet, and phone.

His lover was a man and his wife was in a state of disbelief. No one was sure if the disbelief was because he was cheating with someone of the same sex or that he was dead. The police didn't care one bit about his sexual preference; it was the letter found at the crime scene that rattled their cage.

It was still too early to be certain, but the letter appeared to be a poem and the poem appeared to be consistent in every way with that of The Poet's signature. If The Poet was indeed behind the murder, what of Kameek Barnes? What of the sensational trial that had been underway for close to a month, a trial that was only days away from finally wrapping up.

John Stephenson, age 44, was pronounced dead on arrival at Lenox Hill Hospital in the Upper East Side. John was one of the biggest names in hip-hop, especially gangsta hip-hop. He was responsible for the signing and promotion of artists such as Lil' Uzi, Cocaine, and Bombs Away. Bombs Away, with his platinum single, 'Kill a Nigga Quick,' won best album of the year at the BET Music Awards. John Stephenson was labeled one of the most instrumental and powerful influences on pop culture by *TIME* magazine the previous year.

The irony of it all did not go unnoticed by some. The man who played a major role in polluting the true poetic expression of hip-hop was now dead at the hands of The Poet. As much as the police wanted to keep the details of his murder hush-hush until after Kay-Kay's conviction, they knew that they wouldn't be able to withhold the truth. The poem that was left on the body was also sent, along with a picture of John's corpse, to all of the major news outlets in the Tri-State area. The poem read:

> Hip-hop provides a platform to be heard.
> Oh what genius he was
> to ensure
> that what was heard,
> was absurd.

Kay-Kay

Secretly, I laughed when I learned of my brother's strike. For 18 months, I knew that he would figure out a way to assist in my liberation. However, it wasn't until his testimony, when he said that The Poet could strike again that I understood his game plan. The only thing I wondered was who would be his target.

My lawyer rushed to the bullpens where they held me while awaiting my entrance into the courtroom. He was excited beyond belief. "Kameek, I really don't know where to begin," he said truly perplexed. "I mean I have been practicing law for 23 years and never before have I witnessed such a timely turn of events."

"What's up?" I asked.

"He struck again."

"Who?"

"The Poet, the real fucking Poet!" As if realizing his surroundings, my lawyer lowered his voice to an audible whisper. "He's killed again and this time it was a famous White man. I just left the judge's chambers; forensics and the handwriting analysis team both confirmed that it is indeed the Poet. It's the same person who killed the eight previous victims. They are dismissing the murder charges against you, and if the accusations made by Sinclair Monroe are really the only accusations that connects you to crimes, then the rest of the indictment can't stand. Or if it does stand, and the jury completes the case and finds you guilty, we will immediately move for a 30/30 motion to set aside the verdict and move toward a dismissal. I guess what I'm trying to say is that you are, barring some strange occurrence, walking out this courtroom a free man pretty shortly."

I laughed the laugh of a cynic who realized that there actually does exist an honor amongst thieves. As long as my brothers were free, I would be, too.

The judge dropped all the murder charges and allowed the jury to deliberate on the rest. They asked for testimony read-backs on JB, Charlotte, and some hustler who went by the name of Grand. Conspiracy charges in America are easy enough to find convictions on, as long as they had hearsay witnesses who sounded convincing. The jury was not allowed to read a lot of the Wizard's allegations, but there were a few excerpts that made it. His final entry was one of them:

This young man, Kameek Barnes, is truly one of a kind. I may not have given you the evidence you need to convict without corroborative proof. And in that, I think of the 18th century astronomers who argued about the centrifugal force of the sun and its gravitational pull on all the planets, moons, and asteroids in our solar system. These astronomers were called heretic and quacks. I now find myself in the same dilemma as these men. Kameek (aka Kay-Kay) Barnes has a gravitational pull on all that he comes in contact with. He is human, but with a force like that of the sun. Many lives depend and orbit around him. He has been hidden, but through the lenses of my telescope, I hope you see him for what he truly is: a center of gravity that must be stopped.

Chapter 54: the price of freedom

"We the jury find Defendant Kameek Barnes not guilty on all counts of the indictment."

I took a deep breath and exhaled. I hugged my lawyer, Alicia, and, finally, my moms. Handshakes and pats on my back reassured me that this wasn't a dream. I was free to walk out the door. I looked into the eyes of Kameek Jr. and Robert Jr. It was there that I saw a fire burning in a forest amidst oxygen and timber. These young men were ready for training. Finally, a quick glance to the back of the courtroom revealed the smile of a warrior. There she was, sitting aglow in the knowledge that the center of her devotion would no longer be boxed in a cage. I smiled back.

I had Criminal Empire to help build and operate. With the death of John Stephenson, our number one rival, the industry was ripe for a hostile takeover. Pacific Records had been shaken to its core. Plastered on the front page of the three most prominent newspapers were articles citing a source within the NYPD who had detailed poems that had been sent to each one of the remaining Pacific Records executives, promising a repeat of The Poet's last performance. It was the perfect assist from a floor general who only wanted to win.

Though I understood with a certainty that I was no longer under the prosecutor's gun, I also knew that law enforcement would not stop until they could prove me guilty of something. That would be their trap to configure and mine to dismantle. The war never stopped. The only change my brothers and I conspired to teach is that the casualties will no longer be one-sided.

Epilogue

So here we are, my imaginary friend, who has toiled with me in this cell for the past 18 months. Here we are, just minutes away from my release due to an unexpected mistrial. Yeah, they'll find a way to try me again. I appreciate that you listened carefully to all the evidence and withheld your judgment up until this point.

But here's the dilemma you now face, how much of my story can you believe? I mean, yeah, the major events happened. Those are all facts that can be verified. But the belief that JB, Knee, and I ever operated as anything but one would make you a little naïve, don't you think? That our reach for true power could work without unity? That The Poet was ever a mystery to me? Or that Knee's recklessness wasn't a calculated agreement? Could it be that you believed the disunity because that's all you ever saw from Black men? Even to you, my most trusted and endearing friend, did you believe I would sit here and confess?

Perhaps all that I said is true, and perhaps there's a scarier thought to consider. And I'll leave you, my friend, with this to ponder:
Could it be that you just bore witness to the fact that there does exist an honor amongst thieves?

I gotta go. It's once again time to shake, but thanks for listening.

Book Three: Black Wolves

FBI headquarters: joint session

"Gentlemen and Gentle-ladies," the balding potbellied, middle-aged man spoke. "We have a unique situation on our hands that has garnered the attention of the media as well as top brass in Homeland Security. I have been instructed to put together this joint task force to first see if a cancer really does exist. And if it does, to then discover how deep and how far it has spread. Finally, we determine how to eradicate the threat.

"Before I go further, I would ask that everyone in this room identify yourself and the agency you represent. Please no acronyms, I'm getting old and I can't remember their meanings."

Chuckles and laughter made their way around the room.

A thin freckle-faced man who looked as though he'd never seen the sun raised his hand and spoke first. "Jonah Beil, Deputy Commissioner New York Police Department's Anti-Terrorist Division."

"David McCullah, Federal Bureau of Investigation"

"Mark Gates, Bureau of Alcohol, Tobacco, Firearms and Explosives."

"Manuel Rodriguez, Detective First Grade New York Police Department's Gang and Hip-Hop Division"

"Ozzie Smith, Senior Advisor to the Pentagon and a bunch of other agencies that only have acronyms."

The men at the table were pretty much strangers to each other, but they were all familiar with Ozzie "Damage Control" Smith. He was a political operative with no allegiance to any party. He bled red, white, and blue, and operated for any party in power without a second thought.

"So, I guess that leaves me," the balding, potbellied, middle-aged man spoke as he adjusted the projection monitor that sat in the middle of the conference table. "As you all should know, I am Wellington White, East Coast Bureau Chief of the Federal Bureau of Investigation. Once again, welcome and thank you for coming on such short notice. Allow me to get to the point. We have reason to believe that the serial killer's future threats to Pacific Record that concluded the trial of Kameek Barnes were not empty. Even our well-placed informants have nothing to share regarding this character. Which leads us to believe that he is either a very small fry or something I shudder to think we allowed to happen under our noses."

Wellington White clicked a handheld device and three faces appeared on a projection screen. "The first one, we believe may be the ring leader, is Andre "Knee" Spencer who has recently changed his name to Cream. He is currently managing a platinum-selling rap artist by the name of Rushie Rush. The next image is Kameek "Kay-Kay" Barnes, whose sensational trial and reputation speaks volumes. We know he's a real badass, but to what extent is still not clear. Lastly, and I believe the most dangerous of the three, is Jamal "JB" Barnes, the older brother of Kameek. Since his release from prison, JB has delved into the political arena in Brooklyn, New York. While he can't run for office himself due to his criminal record, we believe he's a true power player. Sort of like Ozzie over there when it comes to Brooklyn minority politics.

"It could be all of them acting in concert or just one of them. Or a more perplexing enigma: none of them. But whatever the case, we need to find out who or what the BLACK WOLVES are."

No sooner had the director finished his speech, did the avalanche of questioning begin.

A. C. Clayton

A Hidden Truth

"Look closely, son. Look at the damage closely." The Old God began pointing to the hundreds of men in the prison yard. "Study the damage." He then began pointing at individuals and not the collective.

"Take Mel, over there. He can fix any electronic gadget in this place. He's so skilled that the COs actually bring radios and other pieces of electronics from home to get him to fix them."

The Old God shook his head to emphasize the incredulity of it all. "Take Cuba, over there, a man with only two hotpots. He can make any cuisine you want. He can compete on the highest scales of culinary tests. He'll taste a meal and immediately describe the seasoning that went into it. Again, even the CO's secretly purchase his food. That's a hell of a testament. They love his food so much, they're willing to risk food poisoning to satisfy their palates."

He once again shook his head in wonder. The Old God then pointed to the other side of the prison yard. "Zarcal, over there, the Iron God at his usual station: the pull up bar. The one instructing young men on the discipline of exercise and weight-lifting. The guy is like one big muscle, and he's training our young to stay strong."

The Old God pointed his chin in the direction of an intense soccer game. His sights were not on the game itself, but on the sideline. There in the midst of what appeared to be a healthy discussion stood Marshal the Dred, debating theology and history with two Muslims and a Christian. The Old God spoke of Marshal the Dred with great respect. "The man has a degree in theology, but history is where his gift really manifests. Those history classes you attend are because Marshal knows how to teach your story to you. It's not 'HIStory.' It's your story that fortifies the backbone. 'HIStory' is taught in order to break you down. We are surrounded by the gifted, who somehow abandoned or never discovered their gifts or how to make a living off of them.

"These gifts! Imagine if they were all unified for one purpose? Imagine that purpose to be a jailbreak? The trusted electronic turns his master's gadgets into detonators? The trusted cook poisons the warden and his top brass? Zarcal and his warriors overpower the foot soldiers? The historian/theologian gives us a purpose and a meaning? The gifts of our liberation are all around us. So why don't we form Voltron like you youngins like to say? It is because our earliest teachers tested our IQs as babies, in search of the babies whose ways of thinking would conform to theirs, and labeled them geniuses. These babies were plucked from amongst us to ensure that they would never become weapons against them. The rest of us, they stripped of fathers then gave us teachers, who at the very best, would teach mediocrity. The teachers were tasked with the sacred duty of sticking Yacub's needles into our heads to keep us asleep."

"Yacub's needle?"

"Yeah, that's your study for the next week. Tell Merciful I said to give you the Yacub story in the 120. The story is written in allegory and metaphor, but it explains a process, to produce a certain result. Us being in here, the millions of us Black and Brown men and women incarcerated is not due to chance. It's the result of a process. The fact that we are content with it—you know playing cards, sports, watching videos—that's due to a process as well."

Almost as an after thought, the Old God spoke with regret, "It's a lonely place, son, when you're part of the few who understand the design of our destruction, but are still powerless to stop it."

A. C. Clayton

Born and raised in Brooklyn, New York, Clayton grew up in the tumultuous 80's where drugs and gangs were a common lot. Like many of the young men in his generation, he made a series of terrible and grave decisions that resulted in a 15-year prison sentence and the abandonment of his two children. "It was while watching my children grow through pictures and short visits that I knew I had to completely change my thinking."

Since his return to society, Clayton travelled the country speaking extensively on the perils of mass incarceration, as well as, working with troubled teens that precariously flirt with recidivism and marginalization.

Clayton dedicated his time mentoring, counseling and guiding young people who appreciated the sincerity of his efforts. Many youth, to-date, attribute his consistency and caring nature to changing their lives for the better.

For nearly seven years, A.C. Clayton worked tirelessly to complete Center of Gravity, the sequel to his debut novel, Honor Amongst Thieves. He found himself writing on his long train rides to work at his full-time job, as well as, writing into the wee hours of the morning after handling husband and daddy duties for the evening.

Only three weeks after finally completing his second novel, he was taken away from his family and friends at the hands of gun violence. Our husband, father, son, brother, nephew, cousin, teacher, mentor and friend will be missed dearly. We will continue to celebrate his life and carry on the legacy he left for the world to experience.

A. C. Clayton

I dissect the game for you
Break it down into pieces
Show you what lane is true
And hope you take it
To run the race you were molded to run
That's what I'm waiting to see
My young stallion
The reflection of me

When I speak
only the real realizes
that I hypnotize with hidden logic.

Don't mimic what I was son, mimic what I am.
With me your path to victory, its where it began.
I always want you to win.
But the times you loose, you taste defeat with a grin, surrender is a sin to the
God within in.

TO MY SON ROE PORTER
by A.C. Clayton